the Secret Madonna

The Secret Madonna

A NOVEL

J R Lankford

Great Reads Books

Published by Great Reads Books
P. O. Box 2112
Bellaire, TX 77402

ISBN 0-9718694-3-X
LCCN 2008933423

Manufactured in the United States of America

To Devar …

Chapter 1

It was the three hundred sixty thousandth call of the year. As the ambulance turned right on New York's 101st Street and entered Central Park through Boy's Gate, the siren dropped from a ululating shriek to a broken sob. The *Certified First Responder-Defibrillation* unit's orange emergency light strobed in the foggy dark onto a waiting Park Police mini-cruiser. Promptly it led the way to West Drive and turned left into the deserted north quadrant of the park, passing tall lanterns that cast dim globes of yellow light.

The police mini-cruiser stopped and, behind it, the ambulance slammed on its brakes. "They're down there," called the policeman as he jumped out.

The two paramedics grabbed their equipment and a stretcher and pursued the policeman, the younger paramedic scrambling down a footpath to the arch beneath West Drive. He knew the arch separated *The Pool*, which was really a pond, from *The Loch*, which was really a stream. This was only his third time out, but he'd been born in New York.

A flock of startled ducks rose from the water, wings beating, quacking their disgust, as the paramedics arrived at a waterfall. It fed the spring that flowed beneath the great, brooding stones of Glen Span Arch, its gray boulders like a grotto in which lost spirits dwelled. In the daytime, playing children whispered here.

"The last one's under there," the policeman said. He turned on his flashlight and, holding his nose with the other hand, led the way beneath the arch on a walkway that paralleled the stream.

The paramedics followed and then they smelled it too—a peculiar odor, as if newly turned black earth lay wet and steaming in the sun.

"Someone's had a baby," the older paramedic said, "and she needs help. She's lost a lot of blood."

That's when the young paramedic realized it was the smell of afterbirth coming from blankets on the ground.

"Yeah, no sign of her. We're searching the park."

The policeman stopped and pointed his light on a brawny, ashen, once-handsome face. "Here's your patient. There's another one up on West Drive. A unit's already there with my partner."

They kneeled beside the motionless man. He was tall, solidly built and his chest was covered in blood.

"Gunshot. Aw, man. He looks dead," the younger paramedic said.

"ABC's anyway."

The young paramedic bent closely over the man and checked vitals. "Blood in his airway. No breathing. No circulation."

"Get the paddles and hook him up."

He suctioned blood from the man's mouth, did a head tilt, chin lift, and ventilated twice. He checked for a pulse at the carotid artery and felt none.

"Okay, zap him."

"Clear!"

The body arced up and away from the bloody ground.

"Get back! Let 'em work!" the policeman said, moving toward dark figures who had gathered on both sides of the arch—bums who smelled of urine and long unwashed skin.

"Whew! What's that smell?" one bum said.

"Whatchoo think? It's that dead dude."

"Naw, it's something else."

"Zap him again," the older paramedic said.

"Clear!"

The body arced into the air as if seeking release from earth.

The policeman's mobile phone crackled to life. He answered, listened. "Okay, meet you there," he said and disconnected. "Did any of you see what happened?" he said to the bums."

"Just heard a lot of shooting is all," one answered.

The policeman turned to the paramedics. "My partner says the other victim's dead."

"I think this one's dead, too," the young paramedic replied, his voice nervous.

"Yeah, I guess." The other patted the dead man's scarred neck. "Sorry, fella. We tried."

A bum mumbled in a drunken slur, "They give up easy when it's us."

"Shaddup!" the policeman said then grunted, "Serves him right, anyway, running around shooting up the park."

The bum shouted, "You give up easy when it's us!"

Cursing, the young paramedic resumed CPR.

"Come on, he's done for. Leave him," his partner said.

The paramedics sat back on their heels and stared.

In the hush of Glen Span Arch, someone sighed.

"Wow, he's back!" the young paramedic shouted. They scanned the monitor. "We've got a distal pulse. We've got a pulse!"

"Holy effin' Moses! Is he breathing?"

"Yeah a little. Just a little. Intubate?"

"No, use the oxygen mask. Get the stretcher."

"Okay."

"Ready?"

"Yeah."

"One, two, three."

Lifting the nameless man, they hurried from the place that smelled of afterbirth, past the waterfall and gray boulders of Glen Span Arch.

———

The young paramedic stood outside a hospital room door, looking in on the man he'd almost let die three days ago. The man lay in a coma, helpless and alone. No one had asked after him. No one knew his name.

Dr. Lewiston, second in rank in the Trauma Center, entered the hall and saw the paramedic—brand new at the business of saving lives. Sensing the man's despair, Lewiston shook his head and walked up until they stood shoulder-to-shoulder. He folded his arms and gazed in the patient's room.

"You did everything," he said, trying to reassure the paramedic. "You defibbed him twice, packed the wound, gave him Xylocaine, got an IV going. It's not your fault he's like this." He leaned to the paramedic's ear. "Go home."

The paramedic smiled at Dr. Lewiston. "Yeah, I guess. Does he fit in your study like you thought?"

"A cardiopulmonary trauma case involving long-term deprivation of oxygen to the brain? Absolutely!" Lewiston said. It fit so squarely in his target population that, whether the patient survived or not, his research would be one step closer to publication in the *Annals of Emergency Medicine*, adding a little more honor, a little more recognition, to black doctors like him in the field. He couldn't say this out loud. The paramedic was new and might mistake it for callousness.

"Do you think he'll make it?"

Lewiston didn't reply. The patient had been unresponsive when the ambulance arrived and the Xylocaine hadn't stabilized him because he'd almost bled out in the park. In Trauma Room One they'd rushed to control the major bleeders before he went into full arrest. In surgery, they removed a .45 caliber slug and repaired the chest wall it had torn through. The man had suffered a massive stroke from a clot while still on the table. He had survived, but lay in a deep state of shock.

Lewiston had him on a Vitamin C/herbal drip of his own invention, just approved for use in extreme cases like this. He'd learned such seemingly simple things while studying Maasai medicines and found them powerful. Still, in his opinion, the patient wouldn't revive.

Lewiston patted the paramedic's shoulder. "You never know." Gently he turned him toward the door at the end of the hall. "It's not your fault. Go home."

As the paramedic left, Lewiston entered the patient's room. He seemed to have been muscular and rugged. Lewiston stepped behind the curtain where he couldn't be seen, closed his eyes, and clasped his hands.

"Lord," he whispered, "you hold the secrets of eternity. Guide my instruments and instruct my mind, and if you will, take pity on this man."

He heard someone clear his throat outside the door. Lewiston went out and saw a black orderly he knew. They worked well together, but otherwise routinely avoided each other, if politely. The orderly spoke in what was once termed Ebonics. Lewiston spoke with a northern accent that had a slight hint of Rhode Island, as had his parents and their parents before them. He listened to Mozart, Bach, Beethoven in his Chelsea townhouse. Rap music often boomed from the orderly's car as he drove home to Harlem.

Again the orderly cleared his throat. "Phone for you, Dr. Lewiston."

Lewiston nodded and gave a straight-lipped smile, which the orderly returned. Outside these halls they shared nothing, but they understood each other perfectly well.

"Hello," Lewiston said into the phone at the nurse's station.

A pause, then a stranger replied, "Wait a second."

"Hello?"

Another voice came on the line and said, "Dr. Lewiston, I have a request." The tone wasn't an asking one. Lewiston almost lost his bearings, he was so shocked. He hadn't heard this voice in years and had desperately hoped he never would. It belonged to an ultra-wealthy philanthropist who lurked quietly behind the scenes of city and national life, the kind of man found at secret meetings of the world's power elite—the Trilateral Commission, The Bilderberg group, the Council on Foreign Affairs—if he deigned to attend. Few people even knew of his existence. Fewer still realized he was an extremely dangerous man. Lewiston pictured him: a platinum aura of thick hair framing his face, offsetting an aquiline nose and powerful jaw. Prominently jointed thumbs on large chiseled hands, implying a formidable grasp. When he wanted, he knew anything that happened in this town.

"Yes, sir."

"The patient brought in from Central Park three days ago?"

"What patient?"

An angry tone. "The one you're personally taking care of, Chuck. Don't play with me."

"Oh, that one. What about him?"

"Describe him."

Lewiston put his hand to his forehead and tried not to panic. What did the patient look like and why did his caller want to know? "White male. Six-foot-two, kind of brawny. Dark brown hair."

"His neck?"

"What?"

"Are there scars on his neck?"

"Why do you want to know?"

Deadly silence.

"Yeah. Scars. Old ones. Like from brawls."

"How is he?"

"Is he a relative?"

Silence again.

Lewiston's dread increased. Then he remembered the patient was beyond hope. "He's in a coma."

"Prognosis?"

"He'll stay like this or die from complications after a while."

"Bring him."

Lewiston's knees went weak as he stood at the nurse's desk in ICU holding the phone. "What?"

"Bring him to me."

"But—" Lewiston paused, stopped by the coldness he sensed through the phone. Why had he said *but*? He knew of only two people who'd said *No* to this man. One, a senator's wife, died in a sudden accident. Lewiston himself was the second. He'd once refused to falsify a patient's record. The next day, Lewiston's son had disappeared for five frantic hours then been returned in a limo, holding cotton candy from the circus.

"I mean yes, of course. Fine. When?"

"Tonight. I'll have a private ambulance outside. You'll have all you need here at my apartment."

"Me? I can't just—hell, he won't wake up, I tell you!"

His caller hung up and Lewiston slumped against the desk, ignoring the curious stare from the nurse who'd just arrived. In his mind, he was saying goodbye to the *Annals of Emergency Medicine*, and to honor, too. He thought of calling the police— and saying what? The man who singlehandedly financed a policemen's widows fund had asked him to break the law? The same man who helped elect the governor as well as the mayor? Even if he had evidence, Lewiston knew no one would listen. Desperately wishing his patient had been taken to another hospital—putting some other doctor on the line—Lewiston sighed.

"Dr. Lewiston, are you all right?" the nurse said.

He barely heard her. He walked slowly toward the lounge, part of his mind despairing as he thought of his wife, finally back in college, and his twelve-year-old son. The rest of his mind began planning the illegal removal of an unconscious patient in the middle of the night. He stopped at the man's door. He was on life support, his eyes fixed and staring. Most likely he'd never wake— never even know that a man named Brown, who could arrange anything at all, was kidnapping him to the Upper East Side of New York.

Chapter 2

Fifth Avenue

In the ninth floor penthouse of his Fifth Avenue apartment building, Theomund Brown slid his fingers through his platinum hair. His only adornment, a gold ring inscribed in an ancient script, glinted in the afternoon sunlight streaming in from the terrace. He was in his library at a desk made of virtually extinct American chestnut, watching breaking TV news along with half the world.

Brown was trying to grasp how Dr. Felix Rossi would hold a press conference in half an hour at The University Club in New York, instead of being dead.

As photos of Rossi flashed on the TV screen, Brown's private line rang. Without looking at the Caller ID, he knew who it was.

"Hello," Theomund said when he picked up the phone.

The angry voice of His Eminence, Evaristo Cardinal Salati replied, "Greetings, Theomund. What the hell is going on?"

Salati was a member of the Vatican bureaucracy called the Roman Curia—his title, Official of State, his duties unclear. By virtue of his schooling and his birth, he was also Mafia Emiliana, the term unofficially used to denote clergy from towns along the Via Emilia formerly ruled by papal legates. In the Catholic Church, there was no better place to be born, nepotism and cronyism being a fact of life at the Vatican.

"Hello, Your Eminence," Theomund said, his voice controlled and unconcerned, though he felt the same anger Salati did.

"As if the Robert Calvi scandal isn't enough! Have you heard what's being said in open court in London? That millions of both Vatican and Mafia lire flowed through that murdered scoundrel's bank unseen?"

America hadn't reported on the scandal as loudly as Europe

had, but Theomund knew. And it was all true.

"Now this! What is this press conference at The University Club there in New York, Theomund? Isn't the cloned infant dead?"

Yes would be the expedient answer. However, Theomund had no intention of risking his influence with the Catholic Church's favorite son.

Brown said, "I'm not sure."

Cardinal Salati sighed. "God forgive me for hoping it is. May I ask why you're not sure?"

"You want details, Your Eminence?"

Salati humphed. "No, I do not. The Holy See went into chaos when Agence-France Presse published a photo of threads being snipped from the Shroud of Turin. How could such a thing happen in a room full of scientists and priests?"

"Rossi is clever."

"Why is he calling a press conference?"

"We'll know shortly."

"Take care of this, Theomund, if you want our continued help with your business!"

"May I ask if it's the Pope or the Mafia Emiliana who disapproves of the clone?" Brown said.

"If this ridiculous clone survives and seems remotely Jesus-like, all of Christianity will be in crisis."

"I will finish what I started."

"Mille grazie," Salati said and hung up.

Theomund Brown smiled as he put down the phone and gazed at the photo of his father, dressed in Bwana garb, standing on a dusty African road next to Uukwambi King Iipumbu ya Tshilongo, who wore a jacket over his tribal scarf. Behind them rose the scaffolding of Tsumeb mine. It had produced not only billions of dollars of lead, zinc, copper and germanium but also 247 species of other minerals—the finest specimens ever found. The mine's unprecedented ore body descended 1716 meters into the earth. His passion was to find another Tsumeb—a dream, not a necessity. The mineral exploration business begun by his father was already the wealthiest privately owned concern in the world, next to the Catholic Church. In exchange for ridding Salati of the clone he feared, Brown's finances were to be clandestinely allied with Rome's, vastly lowering the tax burdens of Brown's company, Algonquin, Inc., worldwide.

Brown admired the matchless cluster on his desk—lustrous dark-blue azurite, filled with perfect crystals. Too bad celibacy hadn't been as popular among Catholic clergy as Rome suggested it be, but the Church's newly lewd reputation had proved a boon. Theomund had given huge sums to save important parishes. The Vatican already owed him and this clone business would tip the scale.

Theomund turned up the TV volume.

Rossi had just entered the conference room, his black straight hair swept back somberly from his face. There was an air of diffidence in his aristocratic bearing, an ascetic's apology for unseemly physical appeal. As he walked his sister and fiancée to their front row seats, the camera panned to follow them. Until nine months ago, the Rossis had led a quiet existence in Theomund Brown's apartment building one floor below. Suddenly they'd gone into seclusion.

Then, three days ago, Rossi's activities had been revealed. Paparazzi openly scoured the world in search of him, as did, secretly, men who worked for Brown.

Now Rossi was back and about to hold a press conference, of all things.

The TV camera scanned the conference room. Upholstered panels accented high pale walls. Rich taupe curtains draped from enormous windows. At long tables, white-jacketed waiters poured champagne, filled plates with canapés. Beneath golden chandeliers in the center of the room, the cream of New York's press sat on five rows of velvet chairs. Only elite or well-heeled members could hold a press conference at the world's premier private club. Rossi was both.

The press fell silent as Rossi went to the podium and in his library Theomund Brown steepled his fingers and watched the screen.

"Good afternoon," Rossi said, squinting into camera lights. His words went out over every broadcast, satellite, or radio station that hoped for an audience now. The world had talked of virtually no one but him for three days.

"Most of you already know me," he said to the reporters. "I'm Dr. Felix Rossi, a microbiologist and a physician."

"Harvard, wasn't it, Dr. Rossi?" one reporter rudely asked.

Rossi flushed, surely embarrassed that his fine education had come to this, a public scandal. His voice dropped to a near whisper. "Yes, that's right, Harvard. Some years ago, of course. More recently, I organized the third scientific investigation of the Shroud of Turin."

"Louder, please."

At his penthouse, Brown heard someone enter the library, but he kept his eyes on the TV.

"Here you are, sir."

It was the butler. He stopped at Brown's desk, put down a decanter and two glasses on a tray. "And Coral's just arrived, sir."

"Tell her I'm in here," Brown said.

Back at the press conference, Rossi continued his remarks. "You've heard reports that I stole threads from the Shroud of Turin." He paused.

From Brown's left, a decidedly female voice replied to the television set, "What an understatement, honey. We've all heard."

Brown looked up. In the door of his library stood Coral, glorious chestnut hair cascading onto her shoulders and down into cleavage Venus would have envied.

"Let's listen," Brown said and motioned her to a chair.

Coral draped herself onto the seat with an unconscious sensuality that would rivet the attention of any male. Her effect on men when she tried made Coral one of Brown's greatest assets.

"I can't believe Rossi is the one," she said. "Our saintly recluse from downstairs?"

"Ssshh," Brown whispered.

At the press conference, Rossi looked into the cameras. "The reports are true."

"Hooo-ly crap," Coral murmured through pouting lips.

Rossi continued, "Last January I stole two blood-soaked threads from the Shroud. I apologize to the Catholic Church for my breach of their trust and will accept whatever censure they impose, as well as any legal penalties that apply."

"Incredible," Theomund Brown said, deciding to prevent legalities. Rossi would be of no use in jail.

Rossi paused, swallowing, then rushed on. "From the stolen threads I obtained a large cluster of neutrophils—white blood cells found in new wounds. From these neutrophils I extracted the DNA of a human male."

The calm at the press conference ended.

Photographers scrambled to the podium. In a barrage of blinding light, they snapped photos. A network camera zoomed in on Rossi's face.

"Are you saying you have the DNA of Jesus?" someone shouted.

"They're gobbling it up, Theo," Coral said.

Rossi pressed on. "Using Nuclear Transfer, I replaced the DNA in a donor egg with DNA from the Shroud and caused the egg to multiply—"

"That's human cloning!" a reporter interrupted. "Dr. Rossi, are you saying you've done it?"

"I—well, yes."

"Are you an expert in that field?"

"No, I ... actually I've been working in private for several years on various mammals and I've achieved a 50% success rate—"

"Doesn't it take hundreds of attempts to produce even a single viable embryo?"

"Yes, that was once true. I've made innovations. They're documented in personal journals I plan to publish. Half of my attempts yielded viable embryos."

Heads bent as reporters made note of this.

"I implanted an embryo containing Shroud DNA back into the

woman who donated the egg—" Rossi looked down, whispering something as if in prayer, then he gazed into the camera and into Brown's unseen eyes. "At approximately midnight on September 6th, she gave birth to a male child."

"Ohmigod!" Coral said.

Those still seated at the press conference rose to their feet.

"Where are they?"

"What time was the birth?"

"Who is the mother, Dr. Rossi?"

Rossi raised his hands. "Please, please. I can't hear you all at once. Her name is Maggie Johnson."

"Who is she?"

"Was she a virgin?" someone called derisively.

"Yes. Uh … she was …. Maggie Johnson was a thirty-five year old African-American woman. She'd been my housekeeper for five years. Yes, when I implanted the clone, she was as virginal as the day she was born, but—"

The conference room roared with exclamations.

Rossi gripped his hands as if in anguish. "But she died."

Only a few seemed to hear him in the pandemonium. They shouted to their neighbors to be quiet. Eventually, greed for details restored silence.

"The birth was premature."

"You mean Christ may have birth defects?" the same derisive voice called. A chorus of voices shushed him.

Rossi glared into the camera. "I tried to save them, but he was two months premature. His lungs were underdeveloped. Her placenta abrupted. We never made it to the hospital. She bled to death during delivery."

"Wow, I wonder where the bodies are?" Coral said.

"I have a press release," Rossi replied, as if he'd heard her. "The details are there, but I'll be glad to offer proof and answer all of your—"

A reporter with a British accent asked, "Are you saying that after … all this—"

"The Jesus clone is dead," Rossi said.

In the conference room of the world's premier private club, dozens of cell phones snapped open, calling the story in. Some reporters scrambled to outside phones. A handful who'd been standing sat quietly down, or lowered their heads, or sadly leaned on the fabric-covered walls.

Brown said, "Excuse me, won't you, Coral?" He watched her rise and leave the room, femininity in motion.

When he was alone, he picked up the remote to pause a shot of Rossi's face, studying it. Rossi looked sleep-deprived, guilt-ridden, embarrassed, deeply pained. Was he mad? A cunning liar? Would he know how to mask the telltale signs of deceit?

He had the woebegone stare of a man who'd just ruined himself. No respected scientific or religious group would ever welcome him again.

What had he gained from this announcement? If he feared for his life, making his exploits public wouldn't help. Perhaps he foolishly hoped to restore his life to normal. Confess—since everyone suspected him, anyway—take his medicine like a good boy and all would be forgiven? He had to know better than that.

This press conference would put Dr. Felix Rossi in the history books: *mad scientist who tried to clone Jesus Christ*. Perhaps Rossi was only hoping to end the media frenzy. Ludicrous. Paparazzi would keep up with him forever.

No, there could only be one reason for this press conference, assuming Rossi was sane.

The clone was alive.

Theomund Brown turned the monitor off, picked up the phone and pressed a button. "You're still watching?" he asked. "Good. Check out his story, focusing on death certificates. Find out what happened to the bodies. Make sure he's followed."

Brown rose and went out to his terrace.

Like the penthouse itself, it ran the length of the building. Small tables and cushioned wrought-iron chairs, striped lounges, were scattered among the terrace's potted trees, plants and flowers, creating semi-private enclaves.

Coral lay on a chaise, her hair cascading onto pillows. She bent one leg and, unmindful of its perfection, swayed it idly back and forth as she pondered. Theomund intended to find out what. She gazed at him with hazel eyes, knowing their effect—if not on him then on all other males.

Regretting the need to test her, Theomund gauged the tempo of the pulse in the hollow of her throat.

"I hear Sam Duffy died," he said.

He saw a blink, a breath, the skip of a pulse beat, then normalcy. Disinterest or remarkable control?

"That's a shame. How?"

"He was shot in Central Park. That's where the clone was born. Sam was helping Rossi."

"Oh." Her tone was lightly disappointed, but she seemed to be thinking, remembering.

"When did you last see Sam, Coral?"

An *oh come now* glance, then, "When you told me to, Theo."

"You liked him?"

She stretched. "Sam was fun. A good lay. Of course I liked him. Helluva shame he's dead. He was a hunk." She yawned and rose, stretched, then lifted the hem of her dress and pulled it off. Naked, she lay on the chaise and picked up one of her Nora Roberts novels.

As Brown sat beside her, the butler entered. Undressed women had been a part of his landscape for years, but a shrub shielded Brown and Coral. Eyes averted, the butler walked past them to the middle of the terrace. He opened a latch in the brick wall and pulled out a sliding partition, dividing the terrace into two separate halves.

"Thank you," Brown said.

The butler made a slight, conspiratorial bow as he passed their shrub and said, "Certainly."

"Theo, why're you closing it off?"

Brown fixed an unblinking gaze on her.

In response, he saw the slightest shiver as she realized that whatever was or would be beyond the partition was not for her to know.

Brown swept Coral's hair into the hollow of her throat, and then back, pleased at its steadily pulsing beat. Already she'd forgotten Sam Duffy's supposed death. Was he wrong to suspect her of having helped Sam?

He moved his hands over wondrous breasts. She lay back, her mouth open, her eyes shut.

He said, "Do you know what I'd do if you betrayed me?"

Without opening her eyes she replied cutely, "Yes, Theo. You'd put my eyes out with hot pokers, then you'd have me killed."

He stroked her face. "You're wrong about the first part."

Coral opened her eyes and swept them skyward, "Thank goodness," she said and moved his hands back to her breasts.

Theomund smiled. Sex was no weakness for either of them, but Coral indulged fully when she chose.

"Pardon, sir," the butler said. "I think you might want to look over the terrace."

Coral groaned in protest, but Brown stood, went to the side, and looked down as Dr. Felix Rossi, his sister, and fiancée, exited from a taxi onto the building's red carpet. Incredibly, the Rossis were returning to their apartment as if nothing had happened. They didn't know what would happen to them here?

A horde of press jumped from the cars and taxis that had followed them.

Nodding an apology to Coral, Brown returned to his library, passing rows of standing bookshelves fashioned from Honduran mahogany and joined without nails. At his leisure he could browse the art and science, the religion and philosophy of every known society.

He settled into the soft leather of his chair and turned on a monitor. For eleven years, Sam Duffy had been Theomund's faithful head of security while posing as the building's doorman. Happily, Rave, the new doorman, didn't have Sam's inconvenient scruples. Rave would turn on the surveillance cameras and send the output here.

When the monitor came to life, Brown saw Rossi and the women enter their eighth floor apartment, having escaped the press with the help of building guards. Rossi walked down his hallway hung with paintings and kneeled onto an ebony prie dieu below a silver crucifix. He spoke sorrowful words of regret about the deaths of Sam Duffy, Maggie the clone's mother, and the clone.

Brown didn't believe a word. Rossi must be reciting lies because he knew or suspected his home was bugged. The clone was alive, Brown was sure.

He watched the Rossis go to their respective rooms, where Frances, the beloved sister, and Adeline, the treasured fiancée, began to undress. Rossi did, too.

Theomund frowned. If Sam told them about the hidden surveillance would they be doing this?

The ordeal must have shocked some carnality into Rossi because he and the fiancée began to make love. Brown had watched scores of men have illicit sex, unaware of being observed. Tapes of such events were a necessary precaution.

This lovemaking was fascinating, though.

Theomund had seen it before—a desperate, frenzied rite of procreation. It was what people did when someone died—fought death with their own loins.

Rossi caressed the frail woman madly, as if she were kindling and he flint and they fire that couldn't be quenched by her tears. Her face was awash in them. When Rossi entered her body their passion ignited, as if they'd never made love before. Rodin might have sculpted their anguished entanglement, every inch of them straining to touch and be touched. The fiancée didn't seem to orgasm when Rossi did. Only on his last shudder did she writhe, drawing the precious liquid into her womb. If the woman's body was fertile and Rossi wasn't shooting blanks, there'd certainly be a child.

Theomund felt for them, understanding death as he did. It was life's destiny. It happened daily. He imagined the myriad dyings and birthings always occurring—first breaths, first cries, last words, final sighs; eyes opening to the world or closing, never to see again. He didn't fear death. It was too ordinary. He would rule it until it mastered him.

He turned off the monitor, feeling secure. The Rossis obviously knew nothing about their upstairs neighbor, Theomund Brown, which meant Rossi might have told the truth at the press conference. The clone and its mother might really be dead. If so, Salati would be ecstatic.

To make sure, Brown would observe the Rossis.

Brown's Butler entered the library. "The ambulance is here, sir."

"They're coming up on the private elevator from my garage?"

"I saw to it, sir."

As Brown rose to go to the foyer, he heard laughter from the terrace and went to the sliding doors to temporarily lock them and close the drapes. He didn't want Coral to glimpse the new arrival. He saw she'd found something in her book so hilarious that she laughed until tears filled her eyes. He waved at her and entered the foyer just as the elevator doors opened.

There was good ole Chuck, doing just as he was told. He'd become a distinguished physician since Brown found him, a scared broke teenager with no asset but high SAT scores— married too young, a child on the way, but yearning to be a doctor. Brown's largesse had rescued him.

"Good evening, sir," Chuck said, looking equally furious and afraid.

Brown didn't acknowledge him. Instead he walked to the gurney where Sam Duffy lay and looked down on him. His mouth was agape, his eyes rolled up and unfocused. Just as Chuck said, Sam didn't look like he'd awake. If he ever did, Brown would extract the whole truth from him about the clone.

Brown sighed. Almost a year ago, he'd given Sam the task of discovering what scientist was trying to clone Jesus. Sam had done so, but instead of reporting back, he'd secretly aided Rossi.

Why?

Brown had pondered this for the last three days. Working here in the building in the guise of its doorman, Sam must have met the Rossis' maid. If Rossi was telling the truth and she was the mother, perhaps Sam had wanted to protect her. Yet Sam hadn't told Rossi it was Brown trying to destroy the clone.

Loyalty.

Brown nodded to the butler, who led Chuck and the comatose Sam off to the soundproof room Brown had prepared for them.

He returned to his library, absently fingering the pre-Harrapan Indus symbols etched into the band of his father's gold ring. The first known writing, it said, *Iilavartate vara*: a sacred river surrounds Ilavrita, my kingdom. In Brown's case, it was the oceans themselves. He unlocked the balcony doors, pulled back the curtain, nodded to Coral then switched the news back on, running his thumb along the azurite crystal.

In contradiction to Rossi's press conference, a mother had come forth, claiming her child was the rumored Jesus clone. Newly delivered, she was being interviewed for the second time from her North Central Bronx Hospital room. Brown didn't believe her, but he was a man who turned all stones.

He looked at his watch. Within the hour the woman's child would be dead.

Chapter 3

10 years later
Arona, Italy

To the locals it was no secret that an American woman they called *La Mamma Nera*, the black mother, lived with her son outside of town on via Sempione. It ran along Lago Maggiore's vast and beautiful western shore.

They lived in a small villa that had lain empty since the 1940s when a Jewish couple honeymooned there, then fled, warned by the village baker that the Nazis had come. The villa had yellow stucco walls, a garden, a lake house and a porticiollo of its own for a boat.

Behind the yellow walls, Maggie Johnson worried.

Opening her Bible to the gospel of Luke, she turned to Chapter 2, the only one that mentioned Jesus' childhood. She read 46-47: "And it came to pass that, after three days they found him in the temple, sitting in the midst of the doctors, both hearing them, and asking them questions. All that heard him were astonished at his understanding and answers."

At the time, Jesus was only twelve.

Maggie glanced down at the stack of untouched books beside Jess's abandoned lounge chair. Felix Rossi had sent most of them and they were on every imaginable subject. She'd worried they might distract Jess from his synagogue studies. Instead, the volume of *Neviim Rishonim*, Early Prophets, that Rabbi Diena gave Jess had also been discarded after only five minutes this morning.

From her chair on the lake house deck, Maggie watched Jess crouch, bread in his outstretched hand, luring his swan friend, King Silent, from the weeping willow's branches, which dangled in the water.

She'd grown used to having the big birds everywhere—at the villa's door in the mornings when Jess rose, waiting like emissaries to conduct him to the others on the lake; on the banks, waddling behind him as he played. They were royal mutes, native to Europe. Felix thought Jess spent too much time with them. Maggie didn't. How could a boy spend too much time with a swan?

They'd been born days apart, Jess and King Silent. Ten years ago, when she first nursed Jess on this very deck, she saw the poor swan sheltering with its parents, a webbed foot growing on its little back. Unable to come on land and court, or build and guard a nest, the bird's deformity had cost him a mate. Nevertheless, King Silent was the leader of the swans. They all followed where he went.

The bird approached Jess, arched its graceful neck and opened its orange and black bill, while the sun on the lake gleamed off her son's eyes, his hair, the skin on his perfect body. He had the broad facial features and coloring that must have belonged to his people, the first century Jews—brown eyes, bronze skin, thick dark brown curly hair.

"Remember, the rabbi's coming today, Jess," she called.

Jess turned and looked at her, his brown eyes wide, his face such a mask of woe she wanted to immediately relent. "Oh, no!"

"You can't play all the time, sweetheart. You have to study."

He smiled. "I like the way we used to study."

Maggie laughed.

When he was five, Maggie would hold him on her lap and give him a prize for saying letters on the page—a kiss, an olive, a spoonful of gelato—until he learned his alphabet. Bedtime stories became reading lessons. He'd fall asleep in her arms, spelling words. Otherwise, Jess had shown no curiosity about books.

Suddenly Jess froze and stared at a speedboat on the lake. "Mamma! Mamma!" He ran to her, pointing at the water. Maggie saw a flash of red in the boat's white wake. The boat had killed a cygnet, a young swan from the flock.

She held out her arms and he collapsed into her lap, his young body shuddering, his tears wetting the left side of her face. Maggie rocked him on her knees, a lake breeze passing gently over them. Like always, her heart overflowed with love.

"Ti voglio bene," Jess said.

It was how they expressed their devotion to each other. Italian parents didn't say *Ti amo*, "I love you," to their children or the children to them. They expressed their love by saying, "I wish you good things."

Maggie hugged him, aware of what a special child was in her care. "Ti voglio tanto bene, Jess."

He sat up and gazed mournfully at the water where the cygnet died. "May we go on a pilgrimage before the rabbi comes?"

Maggie wanted to say, yes, but she didn't. "Last time Rabbi Diena said you didn't even study your weekly Torah Portion." She stroked his curls. "Have you studied it this time?"

He stood and tossed a stone into the water. "But this week's story is so sad! Why do you want me to learn it? So many of the rabbi's stories are sad." He turned expectantly to her. "I don't think Uncle Felix would mind if I didn't learn it. He wants me to read the books he sent."

It was true. *Uncle* Felix wanted Jess to have a secular rather than a religious education. Only reluctantly had he deferred to Maggie's preference.

"The rabbi explained that this week's story is deep, Jess. First you study it, then you discuss it with him, then the meaning comes."

Jess picked up the book. It was written in Hebrew. He could also read in Italian thanks to Antonella, and English thanks to her. He just wouldn't. He put it down and picked up another book.

"They are only imitating life," he said.

She sighed. "If we do go out a while, do you promise to study when we get back?"

"Signora, mail!" Maggie heard, recognizing the voice of the postman, coming from the villa's grounds above.

"Yes, I promise. I promise!" Jess said.

"Grazie, signor," Maggie called to the postman. She rose to her feet on the wooden deck. "All right. We can go, Jess." She looked at his muddy feet. "Give me a few minutes, then rinse off and put some shoes on. I'll be inside."

Jess jumped up and ran excitedly toward the eight-foot Optimist sailboat, tied up in the porticiollo, originally built for a larger craft. On one of his rare secret visits, Felix had taught Jess how to sail, then left a copy of *The Winner's Guide to Optimist Sailing*—the only reading Jess had done on his own.

She thought of the sudden storms on the big lake. "I'd just as soon you walk to town with me and take the ferry, sweetie pie."

When he nodded, Maggie left the deck and climbed up from the shore on stone steps nearly obscured by pink and lavender hortensia bushes. Reaching the top, she looked back down to the lake and saw King Silent make a puppy-like bark and swim away. She knew the bird would swim to town, visit the other swans for perhaps two hours, and then bring them all back here. The lake's entire swan population had become Jess's pets.

She crossed the villa's short lawn and its driveway then went beneath their bower of roses, planted long ago by Felix's parents before their honeymoon here. It was heavy with late spring blooms. Ten years ago, Felix and his sister gave her the villa so she could raise Jess away from the world's eyes.

The mail was where *il postino* left it, in a bundle against one of the spiral columns of the villa's porch. She retrieved it, went inside, and climbed the blue tile stairs to her bedroom, examining the over-sized letter in her hand. To her surprise, it was from Felix who must have mailed it from Milan before boarding his flight home yesterday.

Maggie entered her room. On the plain salmon-colored wall a painting of Mary's ascension into heaven hung above the fanciful wrought-iron swirls and curly-cues of her typically Italian headboard. A pristine white coverlet was on the double bed and, beside the wooden vanity, an armless flowered chair.

She slipped open the drawer where she kept Felix's letters, each of them chock full of encouragement and well-meaning guilty advice, trying to make up for having to leave them alone here all these years. She usually saved his letters to read at night, but, on impulse, she sat down and opened it. A brochure fell into her lap: *The Queen Mary 2, "the world's largest, longest, tallest, grandest ocean liner ever!"* To Maggie it sounded like the Titanic, about to sink. Why would Felix send such a thing?

She unfolded the brochure and caught her breath. Felix had booked a duplex suite for this summer, using the names on her and Jess's fake passports: Hetta and Jess Price.

Maggie couldn't believe it. Didn't it occur to Felix to start with summer camp? No, Dr. Felix Rossi—accustomed to doing everything first class—booked the QM2 for a Black mother and her plainly Semitic son. He'd booked an adjoining suite for a third unnamed adult.

A cruise? Felix must think the world had forgotten about them, but why risk it? And who was this third unnamed adult? Surely not Felix. Even after all this time, the press would put two and two together if he were suddenly found traveling with a ten-year-old boy. Felix had scrawled on the brochure: *to broaden Jess's horizons.* She looked for a note and found it.

Dearest Maggie –

I'm sorry to tell you this in a letter, but you must admit it hasn't been easy talking with you about Jess on my visits. Whenever I raise a subject you find worrisome, you interrupt and afterward I can't get a word in edgewise.

Maggie rolled her eyes and sat on her white coverlet.

I'm very concerned about you and Jess. He's a bright boy but he never picks up a book, shows no interest in the outside world, has no companions other than you and the housekeeper, Antonella. You're still a fairly young woman, yet there's no one in your life but Jess.

Obviously I feel responsible for this to a large extent and it's time I tried to correct the situation. I think a cruise would do the both of you a world of good. I can't come, of course, but as a surprise, I am sending someone else to accompany the two of you, a dear friend you haven't seen in many years. I hope you'll not only consider the trip, but also agree to go. If you choose not to, I'll cancel your reservation and Jess can go without you. Consider that it might benefit him to be on his own for a summer.

"On his own? With some stranger he's never met?" Maggie said aloud. "Are you crazy?" Angrily, she continued reading.

Also, please use your influence to make sure Jess reads the books I shipped to him, in addition to those Rabbi Diena assigns, which are fairly limited in scope, I feel. I'm sure Jess will do whatever you say, if you persist. If you won't encourage his reading, I'm afraid I'll have to insist upon enrolling him in school.

I am forever grateful for your loving care of Jess and for what you suffered to give him birth, but I feel I must do my best to see that you and he are not unduly warped, especially given the great likelihood that Jess is, in fact, a perfectly normal boy.

In deepest affection and gratitude,
Felix

Maggie slid to her knees beneath the painting of Mary ascending, tears in her eyes. Instead of giving her credit for knowing her own son, Felix was treating her like a rich family's crazy aunt kept locked up in the basement. Before she could pray, Jess appeared, his sausage curls and bright eyes visible as he peeked around the doorjamb. Maggie felt a familiar stab of guilt. Her son had no idea who he really was.

"Oh, sorry, Mamma," he said.

She rose, picturing Jess in the middle of an ocean where he couldn't get back to her. "It's all right, darling."

Reassured, Jess plopped onto her sturdy bed as if it were a trampoline, making her smile in spite of the menacing letter still in her hand. Next he rolled onto his stomach toward the black Madonna statue on her nightstand—a copy of the famous *Notre Dame de Rocamadour* from 12th century France. Father Bartolo — the only priest who knew of Jess's existence—had sent it from

Turin, promising to keep their secret unto death, if need be. Maggie had planned to call on Bartolo for help in introducing her son to Christianity when he was twelve. She'd planned to call on a Baptist minister, too, if she could find one. Until then, she wanted Jess to live a simple life like Jesus had, and learn what Jesus was taught as a child. Felix's letter threatened all her plans.

With his little finger, Jess stroked the edges of the Virgin's and the baby Jesus' crowns, saying, "I think the baby swan is up in heaven by now."

"Yes, Jess," she said.

She watched him bounce to his feet and go over to her dresser and her flowered armless chair, lazily screwing and unscrewing the top to her lavender water, picking up her button earrings and snapping the clips. She always pretended she didn't notice him fiddling with her things and Jess pretended it was nothing, too, though this was a ritual they treasured—his proprietary access to the salmon room.

Parted from her, he wouldn't last a day. Not yet. She wouldn't last a day without him.

Maggie stuffed Felix's letter and brochure in the drawer, careful not to slam it though she wanted to. She retrieved a pair of sturdy walking shoes from her *armadio* and a straw hat to keep the sun off her face.

As she faced her oval mirror stand to pin her hat in place, Jess smiled and said, "Belissima, Mamma!"

She knew her looks were nothing to shout about: short hair, dark sienna skin, nose and lips too thick in her opinion—her only gift medium brown eyes with olive flecks. She was reasonably well preserved for 45. Had she been a looker at the start, she'd probably still be one now, but Maggie had always known she was plain. Nevertheless, she would wear the expensive clothes Felix insisted she have and pretend she was pretty for her son.

"Come along now, darling," she said.

Jess kissed her and was out the door. He waited for her on the porch then pointed across the lake to Angera. Atop a high, chalky cliff rose a stone castle, surrounded by green foliage. "Let's go there, Mamma, to the Angera castle."

Maggie gazed at the white edifice, only two kilometers away. To her, the lake's opposite shore was like a postcard meant for viewing, not visiting. "We've been looking at it so long, I guess it's about time."

Outside the gate, their first challenge was via Sempione, which had no sidewalk so they walked it single file. She always told herself Italians were used to swerving around pedestrians on this 14th century road, which was paved nowadays but still narrow. In spite of Jess's two solo navigations of this street, both of which had stopped her heart, Maggie kept in front when they faced traffic and in back when they had to switch to the other side.

Soon they reached the modern-looking Hotel Concorde, which rose, facing the lake, against a high, rocky cliff.

The townspeople called their cliff *La Rocca* and they referred to the ruined castle on its top as La Rocca, too. A famous bishop named Charles Borromeo was born there in the 1500s. The family owned just about everything around here back then. In 1698 they'd put a huge statue of Borromeo up there. It was the biggest statue in the world until the Statue of Liberty came along. To Maggie the Italians seemed to call all the cliffs and all the castle fortresses on them La Rocca. You just had to know which was which. Borromeo's *La Rocca di Arona* up above their heads or *La Rocca di Angera* across the lake, where they were going.

This was also the most dangerous stretch, the road curving so much around La Rocca that you couldn't see cars coming and they couldn't see you.

"Jess," Maggie called, "keep close to the rock. Stay near me." She kept glancing back at the cars coming fast around the curve, but they circled La Rocca without incident.

Before them Arona spread along the southern tip of the lake, water lapping the white promenade wall, gulls lazily gliding in the sun, red tile roofs making it look like the 14th century village that it was.

They crossed the road to two benches on the grass. Maggie often sat here, transitioning from their cloistered life to making contact with the world. In front of them a green railing overlooked Arona's clay tennis courts and the rocky public beach. All Italian beaches were public, including hers and Jess's, but no one ventured onto those that fronted villas on the lake.

As she settled, Jess went to the railing and gazed down on the beach. As hard as she tried to enjoy the sun and the peaceful water, Maggie couldn't forget Felix's letter. She'd suffered agonies of terror and uncertainty, at first, left alone here with strangers where she couldn't speak the language and still couldn't read it well. She'd pulled bravery from nowhere for the sake of her child. Why did it never cross Felix's mind that she might know best? Closing her eyes, she asked for a sign, hoping the Lord would show her what to do, just as He had for Mary and Joseph in the Bible.

She heard a man's voice singing *O Sole Mio* with carefree joy, as if he were poling a gondola through town, but Maggie knew it was only Adamo.

"Ciao, Hetta," he called, "How are you today?"

There stood Adamo Morelli, the image of Italian manhood, except his thick black hair was mussed and he hadn't trimmed his beautiful moustache and the sexy shirt over his chest was buttoned in the wrong holes. Once again he was full of drink instead of out fishing in his boat. He called her by the name on her fake passport—Hetta Price.

Adamo smiled companionably down at her and stumbled forward. How a sinful man could be so happy, she didn't know.

"Fine, thank you, Adamo," she said as formally as she could. "I hope you're not thinking of taking your boat out right now. Maybe you should go get some coffee?"

He dropped to his knees in the grass beside her. "Jess, Jess," Adamo declared. "Tell your Mamma to marry me, I love her!"

Over his shoulder, Jess called politely, "Ciao, signor Morelli."

Maggie had seen Adamo Morelli declare his love to any female who passed. It was whispered that he really loved his sister-in-law—hopelessly, of course, which was why he often drank, people said. He was as unlike Carlo Morelli as a brother could be. Adamo spoke English and Spanish as well as Italian; Carlo didn't, but Carlo wouldn't be drunk in the middle of the day. He'd be at the municipal center doing something useful for the town or hard at work at the family restaurant. In Maggie's opinion, that was why signora Morelli loved him.

Adamo Morelli spread his arms wide and cried, "Do they not make wooden horses with glue—"

Jess turned and said to Adamo in a deadpan voice, "Wooden horses are made with glue made from horses." It was Adamo's favorite line. Why, she didn't know, but Adamo fell into drunken laughter and Jess laughed, too. He was being kind.

Maggie started to rise.

"No, no. Sit. I will go; I will go," Adamo said. "I must meet my brother's wife and see her safely home." Adamo rose and ambled off, his misbuttoned shirt blowing in the breeze. "Ciao, Hetta, bella mia. Ciao, Jess," he called.

As they watched him leave, Maggie said, "Sweetheart, I know you like Mr. Morelli, but remember the rabbi's teachings."

Jess gave her a teasing smile. "Don't worry, Mamma. I do not plan to drink as much as Adamo Morelli does." He turned to look over the railing at Adamo descending unsteadily to the beach and his sister-in-law.

"Signora Morelli will have her baby soon!" Jess said.

"Now, how would you know that, sweetheart?"

He turned, his eyes merry with conspiracy. "Antonella told me. Antonella tells me everything!"

"Everything? Oh really?" Maggie wondered if Jesus knew such things at Jess's age. Probably so since they kept animals and their homes were usually one big room, she thought. Still she would have a talk with their housekeeper, Antonella. For now, Maggie watched signora Morelli trudge happily across the sand, very pregnant in her gray bathing suit.

Jess asked, "How did it feel when I was in your stomach, Mamma; did you smile all the time, like signora Morelli? Were you happy?"

Maggie felt a sudden desperate woe as the memory of her

pregnancy returned, the happiest days of her life, Sam Duffy beside her every second he could sneak away from Brown, shielding her identity, protecting her. Thanks to Sam, Brown hadn't found her until that very last day. She shuddered at the memory of her last sight of Sam—leaving to confront Brown's assassins as she gave birth. Sam had said what Adamo had, "Marry me, I love you," except Sam wasn't drunk. He'd meant every word.

Now his loss rushed back across the years in all its grief.

She'd asked God for a sign and this was it—a reminder of Sam's death so Jess could live. Felix's interference was nothing compared to that.

Jess must have sensed her pain. He stopped smiling and came to her, sat silently beside her and held her hand, whispering, "Ti voglio bene, Mamma."

Maggie didn't trust herself to reply. Too many tears brimmed behind her eyes as they watched signora Morelli, black hair shining, skin tanned, her belly large—her legs strong and striding toward Adamo across the sand.

Chapter 4

Fifth Avenue

A paper crumpled in his hand, Dr. Lewiston looked through white sheers at the one-way glass doors. He could see Theomund Brown having his breakfast on the terrace. Black linens, silver, oriental porcelain, a black rose in a red crystal vase. On the plate was the same meal delivered earlier to Lewiston: an omelet with green onions and subtly flavorful cheese; thick, meaty bacon and hot French bread; juicy Caribbean fruits, flown in from Brown's island plantation.

Over the years, Lewiston had glimpsed a parade of the powerful out on that terrace. In the middle of an oil crisis, members of the Saudi royal family; when a rich mineral deposit was discovered in Québec, the Québec Premier; during the last big economic downturn, the Vice Chairman of the Federal Reserve; before the last U.S. election, the man who became President.

Lewiston could sometimes see it all from where he stood. He could never hear a word, though, because the room was soundproofed.

Behind him, a female nurse with puppy eyes on a cadaverous face made up his bed. For ten years he'd been sleeping by his patient three and four nights a week, alternating night duty with her. An adjoining walk-in closet had been converted for her use.

Lewiston had never gotten used to it, though even with two beds side-by-side the room was spacious.

He slept in an elegantly draped four-poster with a hand-stuffed twin mattress, a down comforter, pictures of his family on the nightstand, a six-position reading light. The patient had a mechanical bed equipped with every convenient device. Richly designed curtains could be drawn for privacy. In one corner sat a luxurious sofa and easy chairs. Expensive art hung on the walls. The room had a television and radio, but no phone, though Lewiston was free to use his cell. As if by magic, Lewiston had been placed on indefinite leave from the hospital. Records of his patient's treatment there had vanished.

Every other weekend he was here around the clock, his absences from his family explained by a lie.

That first night, after the ambulance entered his private garage, Brown had met them at the elevator and stared down on the man on the stretcher. He'd seemed to be feeling such passionate emotion; Lewiston couldn't tell if he'd embrace the unconscious man or murder him.

"It could take forever," Lewiston had protested before Brown left.

Brown had put a hand on Lewiston's shoulder and quietly said, "Then you will be my guest forever," and disappeared.

Since then, Brown hadn't entered the sick room. Lewiston hadn't been told his patient's name, or why Brown chose to bring him here. Brown just seemed bent on keeping the man here until he woke or until he died. As promised, Lewiston had everything a doctor needed to restore the man to life or care for him until that occurred.

Lewiston stared through the sheers. It was Saturday and supposedly his weekend at home, but Betty, the nurse, had come up with a last minute reason to go out of town. No doubt to suck someone's blood.

He tried not to think about the paper crumpled in his hand.

Off and on over the years he'd felt so desperate about his imprisonment with this still unknown man, that he'd allowed himself to harbor dark thoughts—how, whether, and when to cause his patient's death. Lewiston had never contemplated such a thing before; few doctors did, especially about someone they'd saved. Good thing because their best efforts might not save a life, but all doctors knew precisely how to kill.

In spite of every treatment Lewiston had tried, the diagnosis remained the same: damaged arousal mechanisms of the reticular activating system. The man was still in coma, displaying only primitive avoidance reflexes to pain—a pinprick, a heat source near the skin. Low dosages of anticonvulsants still had to be administered regularly and sometimes via IV. Without them the man would violently seize—a sign of severe intracranial disorder of a brain hopelessly trying to work.

It was ridiculous to expect him to improve.

Lewiston went to his patient's bed. The man lay on his back, his eyes open but unseeing, muscled arms unmoving, once-strong hands useless on the bed. He hadn't budged since they'd found him in the park. Poor guy.

Until recent times, he would have been diagnosed as being in a *persistent vegetative state*. Even with Herculean efforts, most such coma patients would die. But medical science now knew a very few could be aroused from prolonged coma and resume normal function if sensory stimulation of enough intensity, frequency and duration was applied.

It was the families who did it. No one else had the time for a full coma arousal program. A guy like this needed someone to change his diapers all day so they could take out his catheter and avoid urinary infections. He needed someone who cared enough to shine bright light in his eyes—every hour. To run ice down his body—every hour. To make loud noises, call his name and ask him to come back or their hearts would break—every hour of every day for as long as it took. Maybe weeks, months, years.

At first, even loving families went into denial: *this couldn't be happening to them.* That's how Lewiston had felt in the ambulance that night—this couldn't be happening to him. As the families' lives fell apart, anger and frustration came. *Why wouldn't the doctors fix it? Why wouldn't the coma patient wake up and love them, instead of lying there causing all this trouble?* When reality finally set in, depression followed: loss of sleep, loss of appetite, unremitting distress.

This was the long, normal road—the same as when someone died—denial, anger, grief, and then acceptance. The difference was the coma patient wasn't in a grave. The body wasn't in a coffin. It was here, greedy for attention, demanding that someone change its diapers, massage its muscles, feed it, call its name. *Stop your life and give mine back to me.* Every hour of every day.

For ten years, this is what Lewiston and the nurse had done. They'd managed to restore the patient's blink, swallow and gag reflexes; they'd kept his body from wasting away, but that's all.

In the glass doors, Lewiston saw a reflection of the nurse disappearing with the soiled bedclothes. He thought of himself at eighteen, his family assets eaten up by his parents' long illnesses before they died. No way to become the doctor he'd dreamed of and a new wife and baby to care for. He'd never learned what flunky had sent his high SAT scores and pointless Harvard application to Theomund Brown, who at once offered him tuition and support. Now Lewiston was the flunky, his medical career in ruins, indebted to a man who would use intimidation and worse to gain his ends. At least Brown paid him well, allowing his family to live in relative luxury. Until today, all Lewiston had lost was his career.

He'd have to start over—assuming he ever got out of here—because the ten-year long treatment of a single patient wasn't exactly impressive on a resume.

As the butler took a small portable television out on the terrace to Mr. Brown, the memory of the morning's delicious omelet returned to Lewiston like poison.

Bitterly he lifted the paper he'd been holding: a summons to divorce court.

Chapter 5

Arona, Italy

Seeing Sam and herself in her mind, Maggie watched signora Morelli and Adamo until they were out of sight. She rose from the bench above the beach and followed Jess, who rushed ahead to the via Poli, which sloped down into town. He was too young to know the story of her pregnancy, the tragedy and the miracle of the night of his birth.

He was just a boy, slight and long-legged, who never walked straight, but veered off to explore what they passed, climbing on any surface that would hold him, up into every tree they owned, exploring with his hands what could be touched. Just a boy.

Soon the narrow street opened and they were in Arona's heart, in the Piazza del Popolo, the plaza of the people. It was ancient. Maggie loved it.

She loved the huge cobbled pavement, its bricks laid out in ascending arcs which overlapped so intricately, she couldn't tell where one arc ended and one began.

She adored the earthen-colored buildings: pale cantaloupe, thunder cloud gray, riverbank brown, ochre, sunset mauve, the flower boxes, wrought-iron balconies and the brick-red pots filled with bushes to make sidewalk gardens for cafes.

They reached the Hotel Florida, not as big as the Concorde up the hill but comfy and family-like. Across from it, people met daily between lanterns on the stone lake wall: old men walking dogs, shopkeepers on a break, two African workers from Sierra Leone.

Maggie's church, Santa Marta, was right here on the square. She was Baptist and couldn't help that it was Catholic. All the churches in Italy were, or seemed to be. Hers dated back to 1592. She thought of how Sam, who'd gone to church only at Christmas and Easter, had vowed to give up cursing, loose women, and brawls at dockside bars for her. He'd been a sailor in his youth and hadn't got that life out of his system.

Past the church and off to the right was the cobbled Corso Cavour, the walking street where tourists shopped.

On the weekends, the square and all of Arona was packed with them and with locals down for a lakeside stroll from homes and villas in the hills.

Jess hopped across the stone benches beneath the black-trunked linden trees bordering the lake, twirling his arms in the air with the carefree movements she'd come to know as his. He was like the wind, like a bird riding a gust of air, like a fish underwater, he moved with such grace. Jess could be as still as a crane poised on one leg, but when he moved he was as fluid as a breeze.

They left the Piazza del Popolo and made rapid progress down the main lakeside promenade. All day and late into the night, lovers strolled here under the linden trees, kissing and fondling more passionately than most Americans would think suitable in public. Italians didn't seem to mind. Families brought their children here, the old came with their canes, and beautiful Italian girls strolled in form-fitting clothes, their dark eyes bold.

They reached the tour boat marina at the end of the Corso just in time for the 10:30 hydrofoil. Five minutes later they had crossed the lake, got off the boat, and climbed into the tourist bus for the trip up to La Rocca di Angera. A teenaged couple was on the bus.

They reached the cliff summit in no time and the driver let everyone out at the main castle gate, saying he'd be back in two hours. The young couple, arms entwined, disappeared through the gate. Maggie didn't want Jess to come upon them on the grass. They might be doing things he shouldn't see.

She paused at a yellow sign and pretended to contemplate it.

"Jess, honey, what does this say?"

He stood under the arch in the thick stone wall, staring up at the raised double gates. "It says the Borromeo Fortress of Angera is open March 27 to October 31 and visiting hours are 9:30 to 6 pm..."

He was translating the sign without looking at it, having given it only a glance. Odd for a boy who didn't like to read.

She hurried up the cobbled walk and fell in step beside him. Together they reached the castle courtyard and the sheltered promenade atop the boundary wall.

"Once," Jess said as he gazed down on Angera, "lords and ladies walked this promenade, surveying their kingdom."

Maggie followed his gaze to the sea of red medieval roofs, scattered like a child's blocks across Angera's green landscape. White sailboats lay at anchor in the idyllic bay, a tiny tree-covered island at its center. On the opposite shore, Arona nestled against the lake, the spires of its several churches pointing to the azure sky.

Jess turned to her. "This must be the loveliest place on earth, Mamma. Thank you for raising me here, even though it is so far from your home. Whose idea was it? Uncle Felix's? My father's? Or was it yours? Either way, I am grateful."

Maggie averted her gaze. Jess believed his father was Felix's brother, who died before his birth. She hated having to lie to him. "It was Felix's Uncle Simone's idea," Maggie said, spotting the young couple. They'd found their way into a garden beneath the castle wall and were passionately kissing.

Jess saw and seemed transfixed. He whispered. "They are in love! Oh, Mamma, they are in love. And it is exactly like in Shir Hashirim, Solomon's Song of Songs from the Kesuvim that Rabbi Diena says they read at the synagogue on Shabbat Chol Hamoed. To him she is the *lily of the valley*. For them, *flowers appear on the earth and the time of singing is come*. He is kissing her with the *kisses of his mouth*. He will *lie betwixt her breasts*."

Startled, Maggie looked at Jess who was smiling down on the couple. "Jess!" she said. "Didn't Rabbi Diena say the Song of Songs is really a metaphor for love between God and his people?"

"Yes, but I think it is more, don't you mother? She is thinking, *'My beloved is mine and I am his'*." Jess turned to her. "Were you in love with my father like that?"

Why was he asking this?

"Yes, of course you were," he said before she could answer. "All these years you've had no one to call you his beloved. Have you been sad?"

"Well—"

Jess's eyes filled with the tears. "Yes, you have! I didn't think of it until now. You've been so sad, so alone with no beloved to kiss you with the kisses of his mouth. But it's not too late. Mamma, you should have love again! Rabbi Diena is too old. Uncle Felix is married. What about Adamo Morelli?"

Maggie blinked and cleared her throat. "He drinks, Jess, and I think he steals."

"He is honest, Mother, I am sure."

"Once I saw him take an apple and not pay for it."

"Oh." Jess frowned. "Perhaps he would stop stealing for you."

"I don't love Adamo."

"Oh." He frowned again. "Well, I could help you find a beloved, Mamma; I'm sure I could!"

"Jess, Jess, Jess!"

Lost for words, Maggie hugged him. She wasn't really surprised that he should think it all right for a boy to find a man for his mother. Now he was in tears because she was alone. But she wasn't. She had him.

"Let's forget all this and get on with our tour, okay? All right?"

Jess scanned her face as if for confirmation that she was really happy. Maggie wiped away his tears, dislodging useless thoughts of Sam in favor of her duty and her bliss: this gift of a boy, his future service to the world, his new message.

She asked, "What do you want to see first? I think they have a winery and—"

"The Law Court, Mamma. I'll show you."

"How did you know about it?"

"Last week, Antonella gave me her art and history guide to The Borromeo Islands and this fortress."

Surprised, Maggie followed him up an impressive stone

staircase and into a vaulted room, every inch of it adorned with scenes from long ago. The murals were painted in the same nature colors as the buildings in Arona. There were knights upright on horseback, others on foot brandishing shields or waving flags, others in chariots. Some panels held strange creatures: a half-goat, half-fish, a thing with horns, something winged.

"It's just what I thought," Jess said, pointing to a painted arch. "This is Saturn on his throne between Aquarius and Capricorn. Here's the sun and the moon between Leo and Cancer."

Maggie gazed in confusion. "Leo? Cancer?"

He walked closer to the wall. "There was new interest in astrology in the 12th and 13th centuries. That's when they painted this room. I was hoping I could tell if they used it to time their battles or just—"

Anxiously, Maggie took Jess's hand. "Where did you learn all this?"

"From Antonella's guide and one of the books Uncle Felix sent. I've been reading them at night. There's too much to do in the day."

Maggie frowned. "But you don't like reading."

"Uncle Felix wants me to read his books." Jess hung his head and his voice quivered. "If I don't, he might take me away from you!"

"Oh, darling!" Maggie cried. "No he won't. I won't let him!"

For the third time that day, Jess burst into tears. Jess had known Felix's attitude all along and come to the worst conclusion.

"Trust me, darling," she said, "No one will ever take you from me!"

"Really?"

Again, Maggie wiped away his tears. "I promise. No matter what."

Promptly, Jess smiled. He walked beside her, holding her hand.

Maggie wanted to lock Felix in one of the castle dungeons for frightening Jess like this, but she was glad to be leaving La Rocca Angera and wouldn't have come if she'd known what was on its walls. Astrology! How would she explain it to Jess?

They found another tour bus, which took them down to the

boats, and on the short ride back across the deep blue lake, Maggie said, "People used to believe in lots of strange things before they learned any better."

Jess reached into his pocket and threw bread to a lone swan. "Yes, I am beginning to see that. I've already read four of Uncle Felix's books. He will be so surprised."

A seagull flew by, calling.

Jess had finished four books in less than a week? Was that possible?

She chose her words with care, a new feeling of danger settling strongly in her heart, though from what source she didn't know. "In Isaiah 47:13—now they may call it something different in the Torah, if it's there, Rabbi Diena can tell you—but in the Bible, this is what it says about astrologers and astrology.

> Surely they are like stubble;
> the fire will burn them up.
> They cannot even save themselves
> from the power of the flame.
> Here are no coals to warm anyone;
> here is no fire to sit by.

Gleefully Jess laughed. "Oh, Mamma. The only fire I sit by is you!" Loudly he kissed her cheek, then hopped back toward the prow of the empty boat, declaring in a merry singsong, "Ti voglio bene, Mamma. Ti voglio tanto tanto bene."

Maggie said no more.

When the boat docked and they started back, she noticed Jess scrutinized every man they saw. He stopped near one and whispered to her: did she find him handsome enough to let him kiss her with the kisses of his mouth? Maggie shook her head, no, and resisted passing out on the spot.

Without a reminder Jess stopped at the benches beneath La Rocca di Arona so she could sit. Then they walked via Sempione single file and Jess entered the villa by vaulting the gate.

Moments later, Maggie found him on the deck of the lake

house, reading one of Felix's books, *Bhagavad-Gita*, though she didn't know what that meant.

She removed her hat and stretched out on the chair beside him, poring over the strange things he'd said, his sudden reading, and listening for Antonella who would arrive any moment to make their lunch.

She stroked his forehead. "I thought you said you only liked to read at night?"

"Yes, but this book is special, Mamma."

"Remember your promise, darling. You said you'd study your Torah Portion when we got back."

He looked up, his eyes shining, his expression imploring. "I will, but Mamma, listen to this." He pointed at the page, handed the book to Maggie and rose, reciting in great fervor:

> Krishna, Krishna
> Now as I look on
> These my kinsmen
> Arrayed for battle,
> My limbs are weakened,
> My mouth is parching,
> My body trembles,
> My hair stands upright,
> My skin seems burning,
> The bow Gandiva
> Slips from my hand,
> My brain is whirling
> Round and round,
> I can stand no longer:
> Krishna, I see such
> Omens of evil!
> What can we hope from
> This killing of kinsmen?

Maggie listened in numb shock, but Jess laughed in delight.

"Isn't it fine, Mother? Isn't it? Why won't Rabbi Diena teach me something interesting like this? It's all about the prince, Arjuna, and his charioteer, Krishna, who is really God in disguise and—"

Maggie looked down at the book in panic. "Oh Jess, what is this Gita book?"

"Gita means song. Bhagavad means God. It means Song of God. It's the most important Hindu scripture. It—"

"Hindu?"

"Yes, mother. In this story, a great battle is about to start. Arjuna is confused about the right thing to do because he has relatives on both sides. When Lord Krishna answers Arjuna, he explains the Hindu beliefs. He says wonderful things. Like this:"

Jess clasped his hands.

> Who burns with the bliss
> And suffers every sorrow
> Of every creature
> Within his own heart,
> Making his own
> Each bliss and each sorrow:
> Him I hold the highest ...

She stared at Jess, whose genes hadn't come from Buddha or Muhammad or Krishna, but from Christ.

Maybe burning with other people's bliss and sorrow was kind of similar to loving your enemies as well as your friends, but there was certainly nothing in the Sermon on the Mount about astrology or Krishna or finding your mother a man.

It was right for Jess to begin with Judaism, which was mostly the Old Testament and the foundation from which Jesus taught. After all, Jesus was a Jew. But Hinduism was out of the question. If Jess didn't uphold the religion he himself had inspired as Christ, what could it be but a disaster?

How much of the book had he read? Why would Felix give it to him before Jess was solidly grounded in his own traditions?

Maggie rebuked herself for wasting the morning mooning over Sam when God had put his son in her hands. Had she already messed up?

She said, "Come here to me."

Jess looked unsure of whether she was angry with him, but he rushed to her like always and flung his arms around her neck, squeezing beside her into the chair. She rocked him back and forth.

"Didn't you think what Krishna said was beautiful, Mother?"

"In its own way, yes. In its way." For a moment, she let the sun warm them, the breeze cool them, enjoying the bliss of simply being near this boy. More than once she'd tried to contain her feelings. It never worked. All she knew was Jess was hers and she adored him.

"Now, darling," she began, "I want you to look at me."

Jess drew away and knelt before her, his eyes full of trust. He would do, believe, anything she said. Often she agonized over this responsibility.

"There's such a thing as right and there's such a thing as wrong.

He nodded. "Yes I know. You told me, Mother. I won't forget."

She picked up the *Bhagavad-Gita*. "When it comes to religion, this is wrong."

She saw hurt come into his eyes.

Maggie felt the agony again, but this time there could be no doubt. God would never forgive her for making an infidel of his son. "Jess, the true religion comes to us first through the Jewish tradition in the Old Testament Rabbi Diena is teaching you. But it's through the New Testament that God really speaks to humankind. I was going to wait a couple more years to introduce you to it. Christianity is the true religion, Jess."

Jess looked surprised. "You don't think the *Bhagavad-Gita* is beautiful?

"Just because something's beautiful, doesn't mean it's true or good for you."

He looked at the book and in a quiet voice asked, "Give me an example?"

Maggie closed her eyes for a moment, wishing God hadn't allowed so many religions. What was beautiful but not good? She gazed across the green-blue watery expanse.

"The lake is beautiful. But if you end up in the deep part without a boat, it could kill you, so in that sense it's bad."

She felt proud of her example until Jess said, "Mother, what should I do?"

His question troubled her, but she said, "I don't want you to read it, Jess."

Immediately he rose, took the book and tossed it into the lake.

"And I don't want you to study astrology."

Solemnly he said, "I won't. Ti voglio bene."

His vow of affection at such a time took her breath away. It was clear he had wanted the book. With no sign of resistance or complaint, he stripped down to his swimming trunks, saying, "Ti voglio tanto bene, Mamma," even as his Krishna book sank into the depths.

Who else could love like this? Who else but Jesus?

He hopped from the deck onto the ground, calling, "Ti voglio tanto tanto bene!"

Maggie thought she would weep if he kept this up.

"Ti voglio tanto bene, Jess."

Naked now except for trunks, he reached the shore, slipped on his life vest, pushed his boat into the water and hopped in. He lifted the little sail, shouting, "Mamma, ti voglio proprio bene!" in the raucous joy of an Italian boy. He'd heard the village boys beyond the walls and imitated them—their words and how they spoke—*Non rompere*, "don't break my bones," was a favorite until Antonella told him it meant, "mind your business" and wasn't polite. Jess had never asked to go outside the walls and play, as if he knew his destiny was different from the other boys'.

"Ti voglio proprio bene," Maggie whispered, her self-doubt complete.

It was hard enough being a Baptist forced to attend a Catholic Church and raise a Jewish child, now she had to deal with Krishna, too? You'd think God would know better than to permit so many books, when any fool could see a person only needed one—the right one. Others might wonder which that was, but

Maggie didn't. She had proof in the form of her son. Who could doubt he was the Lamb of God? A compassionate spirit. An uncomplicated mind. Dutiful. Unearthly in his love.

Watching him, Maggie rose. She went inside the lake house and picked up the phone. She dialed Antonella's number and tapped her feet, waiting for an answer.

"Pronto?" Antonella said.

"It's me, Antonella."

"Mi dispiace, signora. Vengo subito."

"It's all right. You're not late. I need you to call Simone for me."

"Sì, C'è un messaggio?"

"Tell him he's got to phone Felix. Today, Antonella. He's got to tell Felix to call me back right away."

Chapter 6

Fifth Avenue

The TV set on the terrace was tuned to CNN—another of the periodic stories about the rumored Christ clone. Lewiston could tell by the logo that flashed across the screen: a sun rising among clouds and a longhaired, long-robed man in shadows, his sandaled feet on the words *The Cloning of Jesus*.

What nonsense.

The camera focused on a reporter standing in Central Park before one of the ever-present long lines of people. He approached a woman who held a sign that read OLIVE. She was with that crackpot group, Our Lord In Vitro Emerging.

Lewiston flicked on the room's TV to hear the reporter interview the woman.

Ten years ago, OLIVE held prayer vigils, marches, sit-ins, took signed petitions to Congress to protest legislation meant to stop the Christ-cloning stunt. No need. The scientist involved held a press conference revealing the supposed clone and its mother died in childbirth.

Nevertheless, on most days, at least one OLIVE fanatic was in the line that usually wound far along East Drive to a waterfall in front of one of the big arches. OLIVE claimed to have helped the clone and its mother escape to parts unknown after the birth in Central Park. That same day, their website was hacked and the homes of key OLIVE participants broken into—or so OLIVE said.

Of course it was just a publicity stunt.

The camera zeroed in on an alcove under the arch. It could only be reached by leaving the sidewalk and fording the small stream. On a ledge in the alcove was a statue of a virgin and child, decked with flowers. The police were rumored to have found a bloody blanket and afterbirth there ten years ago. The mayor held a press conference saying it wasn't true. This fact hadn't prevented streams of people from filing by each day, hands clasped in prayer, or holding crosses, fingering rosaries.

The supposed site of Jesus' rebirth in Central Park—according to OLIVE, anyway—was a cash-paying tourist draw. Never mind that none of them had seen a hair of the clone's head. New York had learned to accept them like Roswell, New Mexico accepted UFO fanatics.

Lewiston noticed Brown sometimes studied them from the terrace. He'd scan the line with binoculars as if to trace soldier ants back to their hill. Why was he interested in them?

Lewiston heard the nursemaid return and say goodbye. Brown had made it clear she was his equal in this room, her unspoken role to report anything medically suspicious.

"Goodbye, madam," he replied, angered by her having stolen his weekend off, though she had no husband who might divorce her.

He looked at his watch, picked up a flashlight and mechanically swept it across his patient's open eyes, picked up his right hand and massaged the strong limp fingers, monitoring the drip-drip-drip of anticonvulsant medication into the man's IV, made necessary by recent seizures.

Drip-drip-drip.

Lewiston hadn't called home, yet, to say he wasn't coming. His son wouldn't wait at the house for long, anyway, like he did when he was little, listening for Daddy's footsteps, his eyes mournful and confused. *Dad, why aren't you ever home anymore?* Once his wife would have tried to keep breakfast warm, looking at the clock. She'd give up, go in the backyard and do some gardening, madly pulling up healthy plants and spreading new seed. *Darling, is it me? Is it another woman? Why aren't you ever home?* He knew she didn't believe his half-lies: *the foundation that gave me scholarships has collected on my promise to work for them if called. It's proprietary, I can't discuss it; but on three or four nights a week and every other weekend, I'll have to be away from home. She could reach him on his cell phone any time. "Could she visit him on the job?" No.*

Why she hadn't left him before, he didn't know. He knew why he'd done nothing—fear of Brown. At first Lewiston tried to extricate himself by simply not showing up. Two goons came to his house and scared his wife out of her wits. He didn't try that again. Then he thought of moving his family to another country and applied for a passport for his son. On the day it arrived, their mail was delivered by one of the goons. His wife asked fewer questions after that.

He put the divorce summons in his pocket, wanting to take his life back in the one way he knew how. Could he do it?

Eyes clouding, Dr. Lewiston gazed at his patient. There was no hope, yet he lingered.

"Who are you?" he asked aloud in frustration. He began a deep pressure massage of the man's arms. It was part of the coma arousal therapy he and the nurse had carried out on the punishing hourly schedule, Mozart or Chopin—which she hated—playing in the background as they tried to get a response: a facial grimace, pupil constriction, startling in reaction to loud noise.

"Who in the world are you?"

His massage reached the man's once-solid shoulders as the only non-classical selection played: the cooing of cape turtledoves. He'd recorded it on his last African trip and loved the sound. "Not a ballet dancer, anyway, that's for sure. More like a …Let's see. What did we decide last time? A wrestler?"

He massaged the neck with its faded scars.

"What about a boxer?" Lewiston looked at the unruined hands. Not a boxer.

Out of habit he followed his usual routine, applying alternately light and heavy chops along the still thighs. It hadn't helped the man wake, but Lewiston's own strength had increased substantially.

"Okay, you were a weight lifter. Used to be. Lost definition but the muscle was still there. You were once a weight lifter."

He paused.

"We've agreed you weren't married. No ring and you just don't have that married look. We've agreed you were a success with the ladies. You've got enough equipment for it, no need to brag. I'm not bad myself. What did they call you when you were a body builder? Handsome Jones?" It was Lewiston's favorite nickname for the man. "No, Rock. Rock Handsome Jones the weight lifter, the body builder. Toured the world. We've decided it was the ladies, not the guys." Lewiston remembered his initial physical exam, which tended to support this conclusion. "Rock Handsome Jones the body builder. Adored by ladies the world over."

He finished his chopping and stood upright.

"That's who you were. That's why no one's ever looked for you, friend. Too many women. Never settled down. Parents dead or too old to keep up with you. That's it. Mother in a home. Alzheimer's patient. She can't even remember your name."

Lewiston stopped and read the divorce summons again. "What am I doing?" Sighing, he put his hand in the man's unmoving hand, patted his shoulder, asked God to forgive him, turned the flow regulator and stopped the IV's drip.

It surprised him that he shook with fear, given the man was dead, for all intents. Lewiston's action was only a technicality.

He hoped for cardiac arrest, quick and painless. It could be postictal respiratory arrest or pulmonary edema if the seizure lasted long enough. Any of these would kill him.

Lewiston didn't turn away, though it would take a while for the medication to leave the man's bloodstream. He held his patient's hand and kept praying, "God the Father, God the Son, God the Holy Ghost," then he stopped, remembering that a district attorney would consider him a murderer. That's what a doctor's failure to sustain life was called.

His gaze fell on the IV with no drip.

"All you've had in this world is Mr. Brown. Not exactly warm and fuzzy. He's not a relative, that's for sure. He's never set foot in here to see about you, never even asked if you're comfortable. You have something he wants. Must be. You have something he wants and that's the only reason he's kept you alive. You have something or know something. What is it, Jones? What in the world is it?"

Lewiston didn't know if there really was a hidden power behind world affairs, but if so, Brown either belonged to it, influenced it, or was it. In the middle of all this power lay Handsome Jones. Why?

Lewiston glanced at the wall clock. Only moments had gone by. If he started a saline solution, the anticonvulsants would be flushed away much more quickly. A cold thought, yes, but for Lewiston it wasn't murder. He was only letting nature take the course it would have taken long ago if Brown hadn't intervened.

Lewiston changed the bags and started a fast drip, not worried that anyone would come in. No one ever had.

Now and then he paced. He didn't eat. He didn't read. Time passed slowly.

Strangely he thought of the black orderly who played rap music and spoke Ebonics. They'd had little in common, but Lewiston knew he'd missed exchanging their straight-lipped smiles, which said nothing and everything. He thought of his wife and son and wondered if one or both of them was crying. He looked and listened for any sign of change.

It came suddenly.

A low gurgle in the throat.

Lewiston was at the window, staring out at Brown's TV, then down at the line of people always in Central Park. They carried bibles, pushed babies in strollers, carried toddlers on their shoulders.

He heard the sound.

In fear and hope he turned. There was no expression on Handsome Jones' face but the lips had parted, the limbs were stiffening. He saw a slight, slow jerk of the foot. He watched the color begin to darken from sick room pale. Like someone who was starting to need air.

The monitors blinked and beeped. Lewiston wanted to shout a code blue, but reminded himself this wasn't really a man in distress; it was a permanently unconscious body.

Still, he had to restrain himself from rushing to the bed as the man's color deepened. He watched the stiffening increase until it affected all the limbs, watched the jerking increase, become spasmodic. His patient was having a global seizure as his brain misfired and sent erratic pulses jolting down his spine like lightening bolts. His midriff arched into the air and the man became engulfed in his body's storm. He was either having atrial fibrillations, which he could survive, or ventricular fibrillations, which he could not. Hating himself, Lewiston hoped for the latter.

He didn't check the monitors but he didn't look away. He must witness this death of Handsome Jones, neck spasming, stiffly turning, eyes open now, allowing Lewiston to see what he'd never seen in them before.

A man!

Impossible.

Not dull, vacant eyes, but the light of comprehension pleading *I am here!*

Chuck Lewiston, M.D. screamed, "Oh God!"

He shot across the room, the patient monitor he'd ignored emitting a high, steady wail that signaled a flat line.

Suddenly Mr. Brown was at the door in a tuxedo, his tie dangling as if he'd been getting dressed, but Lewiston ignored him and shouted, "God! Oh God!""

With the instant responses of an emergency room physician, he stripped his patient's chest and used defibrillator paddles to shock the man who'd come to life against all odds. The wailing stopped. The monitor blips returned. Lewiston injected a full dose of anticonvulsant into Handsome Jones who, by some miracle, had risen from the grave.

Chapter 7

When the phone rang, Felix Rossi resented the intrusion, having just returned from visiting Maggie and Jess in Italy. He and his eight-year old daughter, Ariel, were playing horsie on the Persian rug in their long hallway. Felix, the horse, was on his knees and Ariel was gently beating his hip with her riding crop.

"Go, Daddy, giddy up! You're such a slow horse!"

Felix stretched out, lowering her to the floor. "Ari, dearest," he said. He grabbed her by her underarms and tickled her. "You're a tyrant!"

Ariel laughed, and begged, "Daddy, please?"

He kissed her forehead and rose. "That's enough. Daddy's tired. He still has jet lag from his trip." When she lay limp in mock disappointment, Felix picked her up. "And you're getting too big for this, my love!"

"But when will we go riding in the country again?"

Felix kissed her. "We'll go this weekend. I promise. We'll take the horses and stay the weekend in Vermont. Happy?"

She hugged his neck. "Yes! Oh, but Daddy, I lost my riding gloves!"

"Well, we'll just have to get you a new pair."

It was when he had her in his arms that the phone rang.

He resolved not to take the call, whoever it was, but seconds later Sharmina appeared in the hall. Sharmina had been a comfort in the past ten years. She wasn't as conscientious as Maggie had been, but she was just as warm. Ariel adored her.

"Sharmina!" Ariel called. "Daddy's taking us to Vermont this weekend, with the horses! Will you come with us? Please?"

Sharmina laughed. "Me on a horse? Come here, Dumplin'.

Your new dress came this morning and your Momma's bringing it to your room in a minute." Sharmina said to Felix, "Dr. Rossi, your uncle from Italy is on the phone."

Felix was expecting Uncle Simone's call, but at a later hour. "Tell him I'll be right there."

Ariel tucked her head in Felix's neck and mumbled, "Daddy, thank you for taking us to Vermont. Twinkle will be so happy."

Twinkle was her Shetland pony. They all had horses boarded at a stable across Central Park: Adeline's Andalusian, *Moonless*, Frances's Arabian, *King*. Felix didn't ride. Often he'd follow them on a bike, though lately it had gotten a little hard on his knees. But he liked to see the women he adored riding the horses they loved.

As Sharmina followed them down the hall, he carried Ariel to her bedroom to see her new dress. The room had been the guest room where her mother had often stayed before they wed. Now it was transformed and not only to install a child's decor.

Before he died, Sam had told them everything about Brown in the penthouse upstairs. Felix shuddered at the thought of what they'd endured to protect Maggie and her child—months under surveillance via secret monitors to convince Brown the clone was dead.

One day, in desperation, Felix had thought of what to do: redecorate. Adeline had been pregnant by then. The need to install a nursery was a perfect excuse to redo other rooms as well. When contractors tore out walls and fixtures, out came the mikes and bugs, so small and innocuous-looking that, if seen, they weren't recognized. He had hired an expert debugger who pretended to be an electrician. Bugs had been removed from all the bathrooms except the powder room in the hall. They were removed from all the bedrooms except Frances's who'd volunteered to soldier on so Brown's people wouldn't become suspicious. They'd just think the demolition destroyed or disabled the bugs.

Felix sat his precious Ariel on her Laura Ashley bed—the Cumbrian divan with drawers, or so she'd proudly informed him when it arrived. At night, when she lay beneath lime green sheets printed with moons and stars from a crayon drawing she'd made, when she showered behind a curtain of those same moons and stars, prying eyes couldn't see her. When he made love to Adeline, no one watched. The kitchen, living room, dining room, library, hall remained bugged, but without privacy in their most intimate moments, Felix couldn't have endured the years of being observed.

They'd talked about moving but given up the idea. Brown would find a way to follow them, put in bugs they didn't know about next time. Better the hell they knew right here.

He heard his sister, Frances, at the door behind him. She had the Rossi nose and the auburn hair shared by some of their mother's relatives in Turin, Italy. Felix had the dark looks of their father's people. For his sake, for Adeline's and Ariel's, Frances had refused marriage proposals from the men who took her out on dates. Frances knew they were still at risk, however calm things seemed. She wouldn't leave them. She had hardened herself to being watched

Now and then he saw her slip into the long line in Central Park to visit Glen Span Arch where Jess was born. Now and then Felix did, too. He'd kneel before the statue of the virgin and child and ask forgiveness for having tried to clone Jesus, of all people. He knew it had been part ego, part impulsive reaction to the startling discovery that he and Frances, raised as Catholics, had Jewish parents. Tormented by the Nazis, his father had hid that fact. Felix learned it just before examining the Shroud of Turin.

Unfolding the Shroud that day, he'd had the wild idea that if a Jew brought Christ back it might end the misguided persecution of Jewish people once and for all. Now Maggie had a boy Felix could never abandon, though Felix had long since figured out the truth. Jess didn't have the genes of Christ.

"Ariel, darling, do I hear you have another dress?" Frances said. "You are such a lucky girl! I don't suppose you really need what's behind my back."

Ariel ran toward the door, trying to reach behind Frances' back. "You have a present for me, Aunt Fran! I know it!"

Frances kept avoiding her until Ariel gave up; then she

produced a box with red and white hearts and the word *Moschino* on it. "I thought you'd need shoes to go with your Paris dress!"

As Ariel squealed in delight, Adeline came in and swooped her daughter up, her pale hair contrasting with Ariel's dark hair when they put their faces together and kissed. Felix wanted to stay and watch the unveiling of the dress, but he remembered Uncle Simone was waiting on the phone. "I'll be back," he said and went to take the call in the kitchen.

It had become a habit to alternate his phone conversations between rooms that were private and those that were bugged. Felix looked forward to these weekly calls because he regarded his uncle with more than familial affection.

It was Simone who'd saved Maggie and Jess by offering the villa on Lake Maggiore. It had belonged to Felix and Frances' parents before they fled the Nazis. Now it belonged to Simone.

Because of him, Maggie had local support: the housekeeper, Antonella; Rabbi Diena who taught Jess; a banker who quietly handled money transfers from New York to Arona. Surely there were others helping at Simone's request. When Felix first left Maggie and her baby on the lake, Simone vowed that if Catholic Italians could hide Jews in WWII, in return he, a Jew, could hide a woman who thought her child was Christ. *Ninety percent of Italy's Jews survived the Nazis,* he had said. *In this country, we know how to save a life.*

Felix picked up the receiver. "Ciao, Uncle Simone. Sorry to keep you waiting."

"Ciao, Felix. I am calling on behalf of my wife who misses you already."

Felix straightened. *I am calling on behalf of my wife* was code that he was calling for Maggie. Felix made himself laugh. "Simone, you must tell Silvia I have a wife and child now myself. I can't always be in Italy letting her feed me."

"Hah! She says the house is big enough for you all. However, if she can say hello to everyone, especially her grand niece, perhaps she will be satisfied for a time."

Satisfied for a time meant he was to phone Maggie as soon as he could.

"Of course, Uncle," Felix said and called for Ariel to come. Wearing her new shoes, she ran down the hall, said ciao to her *zio* and *zia* in Italy and told them about her trip to Vermont. Then Frances and Adeline picked up extensions and talked.

"Ciao, Simone," Felix said when they were done. "Please call anytime."

Felix hung up. Simone would tell Maggie to expect his call. Now he must only devise a pretext for leaving the house—one that would satisfy watching eyes. He remembered the lost riding gloves and phoned down for a limousine from the pool shared by all the tenants except Theomund Brown.

Down in the lobby moments later Rave, the doorman, escorted Felix to the limo's open door. Felix gave his destination to the driver so Rave could hear, "Miller Harness Company on East 24th, please." Rave's insolent puppy eyes indicated he'd heard. He had a sister with the same odd eyes—a nurse. Felix had seen her once or twice in the building.

They pulled from the curb, turned right and drove south for fifty blocks down majestic Park Avenue to Grand Central Station and around it to the Pierpont Morgan Library that held the world's finest collection of rare manuscripts. Felix no longer had the privilege to research them. More than all the other snubs, this one had stung, as if the cloning had branded him incapable of serious thought.

The limo continued south and turned left onto 24th, only blocks from the historic Gramercy Park neighborhood. Felix told the limo not to wait, he'd phone or catch a taxi back. He bought Ariel's riding gloves at Miller Harness, then walked south until he reached the high iron fence surrounding Gramercy Park. The gates were locked and only neighborhood residents had keys, but strolling around it was as pleasant as being inside. Felix took out the 2.4 Ghz digital spread spectrum phone he'd bought to prevent eavesdropping on his calls to Maggie. It wasn't listed in his name in case Brown decided to search his phone records. It was registered to a church friend of Sharmina's. He dialed Maggie's number in Arona, wondering what could have gone wrong since yesterday.

Jess answered the phone, saying, "Pronto?"

"It's Uncle Felix, Jess, how are you doing?"

"Fine, Uncle. Did you get back okay?"

"Yes, I did. May I speak to your Mother?"

"I have a surprise for you, Uncle," Jess said.

"You do? What is it?"

"I read four of the books you left, almost five. I am doing much better with my reading, now."

"Four? Is that right?"

"Yes."

"Well, that's good, Jess. We'll talk about them soon. May I speak to your Mother?"

He heard a clatter then, "Mamma! Uncle Felix is on the phone!"

In a moment she was there. "Felix, I'm glad you called. Listen, we have to have a serious talk about—" she paused. "I had to make sure Jess went outside. Felix, I know you have your doubts—"

"You mean about Jess?"

"Yes."

Felix sighed. "Actually, they are more than doubts."

"How can you *say* that?" she said in a pleading voice. "You were the one who made him from that Shroud DNA. You were the one who put him in my womb. You were there when Jess was born!"

Felix looked through the iron fence at a mother and her toddler, feeling bottomless regret for what he'd done to Maggie and her son. He should have told her the truth on his last visit instead of being such a coward.

"Maggie, listen. I should have told you what I learned—"

"No! No, I don't want to hear it. You need to listen to me."

"All right."

"First of all, we are not going on any cruise! Suppose somebody gets curious about an African-American woman and her Semitic son? And who is this *other* person?"

Felix had hoped she'd at least consider the cruise. "Sharmina. Your friend. It was going to be a surprise."

"Well, that's very nice of you, Felix, and yes I'd love to see Sharmina, but not yet. Jess isn't ready for this. I'm not going on any cruises now and neither is he, so you can just turn those tickets in and get your money back."

Again he sighed. "All right. I'll give in on the cruise, but —"

"Thank you. Next, do you know all those books you left here?"

"Jess said he read four. Did you ask him to tell me that?"

"No, I didn't."

"Well, perhaps you should talk to him about not making things up. I had a fine bookstore select the best sources in several fields, the best novelists, the finest biographers and historians. I've questioned Rabbi Diena. Yes, he's a fine teacher as far as he goes but he is not keeping abreast of the world. Jess has too active a mind to restrict, but he certainly couldn't have finished four already."

"Are you saying Jess lies? For your information, he doesn't, Felix. Never! But did you ever actually look in that box of books?"

"Well, not at every one of them, no."

"Did you know one of those books was about astrology?"

"Oh. No, I didn't. I guess I wasn't clear enough in my instructions to the bookstore. They were supposed to include religion, not all beliefs. I'll have to speak to them."

"Well," she said as if she'd triumphed over him, "it may be just a little too late for that. Just a little too late. Did you know one of them was the Gita book?"

"Gita book?"

"Baga something."

"*Bhagavad-Gita?*"

"Yes, that's the one."

"So what? He needs to know—"

"Well, he's not interested in Judaism anymore, Felix. He's not interested in Christianity, Felix. My son is interested in Krishna though he has Jesus Christ's genes!"

"He doesn't."

They both paused. Felix had reached the Southeast corner of Gramercy Park where, on Greg Wyatt's fountain, giraffes danced around a smiling sun and moon. He could hear Maggie's breathing. He could hear the toddler laughing in the park. The time had come.

"I know who Jess is, Maggie."

Immediately she replied, "So do I."

"Jess is a clone of Max Segre."

"Who?"

"Max is the Jewish scientist I picked for the team. He touched the Shroud barehanded shortly before I snipped the threads. He'd cut his finger the night before. Jess looks Semitic because he's a clone of Max."

"That's ridiculous!" Maggie said. "Why would they let somebody touch the Shroud barehanded?"

'Hundreds have touched it. It's never been in a sterile environment."

"But you said —"

"Maggie, a cluster of neutrophils from Jesus' wounds couldn't have survived this long."

"That's not what you said back then. You said the energy from the Resurrection preserved the blood!"

"Wishful thinking. I made a mistake. A terrible mistake. I asked Father Bartolo to search the photos and there it was. Max touched the threads with his cut finger."

"Back then, Felix, you were sure enough of the DNA to risk my life, your sister's life! Sam *died* because you were sure of the DNA, Felix. Sam died!"

"Don't we owe it to Sam to find the truth? Don't we, Maggie?"

"No, Felix," she sounded on the verge of tears. "No, don't make up these excuses; Jess needs you! He needs you to believe in him and help him fulfill his destiny."

Felix leaned against the fence and stared at the Corinthian columns framing the entrance to the high rise called The Gramercy. It was built in 1883 and James Cagney had been a tenant.

"All right, let's settle it once and for all then," Maggie said. "Come and take a sample. Do a DNA test!"

Felix couldn't. Since the day of the press conference and Felix's public disgrace, Max wouldn't even take his calls. He'd surely never submit to a DNA test Felix requested.

"I wish I could," he said.

"Wait! What are we talking about? We don't need to do any test, Felix. We already know. I know and so do you. The proof is right here in my body. You know I'm a virgin again, Felix, though I gave birth! You know it! You examined me yourself the same night when we were flying over here."

Felix remembered the night of Jess's birth in Central Park. In the darkness, in a delirium of sorrow that Maggie had almost died, he thought her virginity had been restored. Absurdly, he'd believed that a long while.

"I don't know any such thing. You had blood all over you; I didn't have my instruments; and a Gulfstream V Jet isn't quite the same as a hospital examination room, Maggie. If it exists, this is just a physiological condition. After birth trauma, the vulva and vaginal canal can heal in any number of ways. If you'd let me examine you again—"

"No, thank you! I already used a mirror and looked for myself. Anyway," she started crying. "You'll just explain it away with some stupid medical term!"

"Please don't cry, Maggie, I—"

" It's Jess you're betraying, not me. But that's all right. I'm his mother. I'll do it alone. I'm calling Father Bartolo as soon as we hang up. You might not help, but I know he will. He really hopes Jess is Jesus. I'm going to tell Jess who he is before he gets lost and starts to believe in Krishna."

"You will not!"

"Don't talk to me like I'm still your employee, Felix. Whoever Jess's father is, I'm his mother and I'll decide—"

"Maggie, that's enough! You forget there's a man who might kill Jess if he ever learns he's alive. Do you want to ruin all the precautions we've put in place?"

She sobbed, "You think I've forgotten? How could I forget? That's why we have to be careful. We have to take our time and explain things to him so he doesn't overreact or tell anyone and put himself in danger. We—"

"Maggie, stop this!"

Felix closed his eyes, overcome with shame for having destroyed not only his own life, but his sister's and Maggie's all those years ago. He should have been their protector. Now Frances couldn't have a life of her own and Maggie was close to going over the edge.

He felt despicable for what he was about to say, but he had no choice. "I think you're under too much stress, caring for Jess alone. He's a bright boy who needs mental stimulation and the company of other children. Given his language talents, he should have read a great deal more by now than he has. I … I have some other brochures I'm sending you. We can discuss them when I'm next there."

"More brochures? What kind?" Maggie sniffed.

"I've thought of a safe way to do this. Please just listen for a minute. They're … they're brochures for good—I mean truly excellent, Maggie—boarding schools."

He flinched.

Maggie had slammed the phone down in his ear.

———

… Maggie, my girl … Maggie, my girl. It's so dark where I am I can't find you.

… Wake up, you goddamn fucker! Wake the hell up! They're trying to kill you. Somebody's fucking trying to kill you.… Wake up, grab him by the throat and choke his ass to death! Shit, it's dark in here. Where the hell am I?… I need something to eat. I'm hungry. Hell, I need some goddamn food … I need light, I need touch, touch, touch. I need heat, warmth, fire. Where did the world go?

Maggie, are you all right? They didn't hurt you, did they? I swear I'll kill Brown myself if he hurt you. Please be alright!

… Maggie? Fuck that shit, you idiot! It's you they're trying to kill.

Chapter 8

Brown's Penthouse
Fifth Avenue

"You should have tried murder earlier, Chuck."

A man's voice.

Lewiston scrambled to a sitting position, white shafts of morning sun streaming into the room. Exhausted, he'd fallen asleep in his clothes and forgotten to draw the drapes. His arms and neck and back ached from the effort he'd expended yesterday, stabilizing the man he'd nearly killed.

At the foot of Handsome Jones's bed stood Theomund Brown. He wore a dark linen jacket and summer fedora. He hadn't said a word last night, just watched. When Jones's vitals were back in the normal range, Brown had left. Now he stared at the patient whose eyes were open and gazing back.

"What do you mean?" Lewiston asked fearfully.

Brown didn't reply. He just stared at Handsome Jones. Twice in the night Jones had awakened and looked around, impassively. Now he slept.

He was still in a light coma but, given the case history, this was amazing progress, though science had found no pattern to restoration of cognitive function. It could be fast or slow and everything in between. Some functions could return quickly, others slowly or not at all. Both the family and the doctor simply had to wait and see.

His patient had diffuse brain injury from oxygen deprivation. Anti-seizure medication had suppressed abnormal brain activity. Had it also suppressed the brain's efforts to heal? Lewiston wanted to research this problem. He'd like to write a paper about the case of Handsome Jones, but knew he couldn't.

As Brown stood there, Lewiston glanced around the soundproof room, realizing it must have been under visual surveillance all along.

"Who is he?" Lewiston asked, rising.

Brown raised his eyes and Lewiston marveled that a human being could have such a gaze—fearless, shrewd, magnetic, unbending. It cowed the guests who periodically stepped out on the terrace. When they first met, Lewiston found it frightening, too. He still did. If there'd been another recourse after his parents died when he was a teenager, he wouldn't have accepted money from Brown. By the time Lewiston learned how dangerous Brown could be, it was too late to extricate himself.

"Do it again."

"Do what?" Lewiston asked.

"Stop the drip again."

"It could kill him this time!"

Brown's gaze hardened. "No, Chuck, you won't let that happen." Brown slipped his hat and charcoal jacket off, sat on the corner sofa, and propped an ankle on the other knee as if he were settling in.

It was pointless to argue. Just the chance of Handsome Jones awakening brought Brown here for the first time.

The door opened and Betty the nurse entered, saying, "You can take today off I—" Her puppy eyes widened in surprise when she saw Brown. "Oh! Good morning, sir."

Brown pointed to the door. "I don't need you any longer. See the butler as you go."

She glared at Lewiston as if he'd betrayed her. "But, sir, if you'll—"

"Your work was fine. Leave," Brown said.

His gaze went to the door and Betty hesitated only a moment before walking through and closing it.

Lewiston felt satisfaction at her dismissal. She'd acted like a warden, watching him and questioning his instructions.

"I do need help, though, you know," he said to Brown.

Brown took out a small leather pouch and withdrew a cigar. "Someone else is coming." He nodded at the IV. "Go ahead."

Lewiston stalled, worrying. He'd saved his patient before, but only barely. "You probably shouldn't smoke in here."

"It will irritate the patient?" Brown produced a gold lighter. "That's the idea, isn't it?"

"He's not a lost cause anymore, so I can't endanger him."

"Really? That's why you did it? Because he was a lost cause? Not because your wife has asked for a divorce?"

The mention of his wife gave Lewiston a chill.

Smiling, Brown lit the cigar. It looked expensive, surely rolled for him from choice tobacco. To Lewiston's eye, he puffed it in a vulgar way—not pornographically but in an indecent display of appetite, as if inhaling not just the smoke but the plant from which the leaf came, the hands that rolled it, the backs that bent to sow and harvest it, the soil in which it grew. Yes, Brown would know about his divorce summons.

"I'm a doctor. I don't kill people." Remembering that this was exactly what he'd tried to do to Handsome Jones, he added, "I mean—"

Brown snorted. "Every doctor kills."

The swift memory of three dead faces from his early emergency room days kept Lewiston from replying. Indigestion diagnosed instead of a heart attack for one—an overweight man who'd eaten an outrageously heavy meal. Penicillin injected into a teenager who was allergic. Internal bleeding missed in a child who'd fallen down the stairs. Early in his career, he'd killed them, all right. Most doctors had fatal cases involving their own human error but they tried to be consoled by the hundreds more they saved. Somehow these faces faded, but the dead ones never went away.

"I've never intentionally killed a viable—"

Eyes closed, Brown let the smoke float out of his mouth. "Chuck, what are your plans after this?"

"Plans?"

"When you're done here."

"I ... I don't know. I've been here for ten years."

"What if your work here could be published? I'm certain a way could be found. You've done some innovative things. What if your old cardio-pulmonary arrest research could continue with full funding? If you'd like to leave with your career restored, that can be arranged."

The door opened.

It was the butler, wheeling in a silver cart. On it were two baskets of baguettes, fresh Caribbean fruit flown in, eggs poached and fried the way he and Brown liked them, ham for Lewiston, genuine Peameal bacon from Canada for Brown, coffee, tea, a glass pitcher of newly-squeezed juice.

The cart passed Lewiston's four-poster, the patient's hospital bed, and then the luxurious corner sofa where Brown sat. The butler unlocked the terrace, extended the leaves of the cart and set it up for breakfast outside.

"I don't feel up to food," Lewiston said, surprised to find himself beguiled by Brown's offer: lost career restored; his research published in the *Annals of Emergency Medicine*, just as he'd always dreamed.

"All right, then." Brown nodded toward the IV. "Stop the drip."

There was a knock at the door. The butler, about to leave, opened it. Lewiston did a double take. There stood the exquisite woman he'd now and then seen out on the porch, long chestnut hair obscuring half of her lovely face. He'd never been in the same room with her.

She pushed the hair aside and he could tell she'd had very expensive plastic surgery done by one of the best—a nip here, a tuck there—no doubt to keep her face in the same condition as her flawless body. She looked twenty-five, thirty at the most. In reality, she could be forty. It was impossible to tell. But she was gorgeous—femininity in the extreme—the kind of woman men dreamed of, and that faithful married men hoped never to meet.

She looked at him and said, "Hi, there," and in spite of himself Lewiston grew a little weak.

"Come in Coral," Brown said to her, and then to Lewiston, "This is your nurse replacement. She knew your patient." Brown smiled at her. "Didn't you, Coral?"

Coral sashayed into the room past Lewiston, seeming to know their eyes were all over her, but when she reached the patient's bed she froze and looked shocked.

"God, it's Sam Duffy!"

So that's your name, fella, Lewiston thought.

When no one responded, she swayed over to Brown and lowered herself onto the couch beside him. Brown took her palm and kissed it, and then rested his hand in her crotch as if it were an armrest he owned.

Brown said, "He's been in a coma, but Doctor Lewiston has found a way to bring him back."

Lewiston cleared this throat. "If I do, you should be prepared for anything from altered personality to a waking vegetative state."

Coral looked up when he spoke.

Brown let the back of his hand travel up and over one of Coral's half-covered, amazing breasts. "We'll try to give your patient a good reason to wake up."

Lewiston concluded she was just a whore, but if so, what a whore. Plenty of guys would offer huge sums for a night with her.

"Coral, would you visit with Sam? There's breakfast outside if anyone gets hungry."

Brown parted the window sheers, turned to Lewiston and repeated, "Stop the drip." Then he stepped onto the terrace and closed the glass doors.

Lewiston went to the IV and stopped the drip, determined to get out of here while making sure his patient didn't die.

Coral came to the bedside of the man she'd called Sam. She stared at the one-way glass doors as if to verify they were closed then spun around to Lewiston, put her mouth to his ear and whispered, "How long has he been here?"

Lewiston put his lips to her ear, whispering, "Ten years."

She drew in her breath then put her hands on Sam's face.

Lewiston half expected a lewd display, but to his surprise she nuzzled the man nose to nose as if it were something she'd done before. She hovered over him, acting not at all like a whore. Instead he saw her shiver, saw bright tears fall. She whispered, "Sam, Sam, it's Coral," and kissed him over and over, like someone out of her mind with joy.

Chapter 9

Brown's Penthouse

Sam Duffy lay with his eyes open, Coral holding his hand. It had been two hours since the IV stopped. As instructed, Dr. Lewiston had flushed the medicine from Sam's bloodstream with a saline drip. So far there had been no seizure.

"He's so thin," Coral said and ran her hand across his shoulder. He thought she'd pitched her voice low so as not to be heard by Brown beyond the curtains. Lewiston felt she shared his discomfort at Brown's renewed presence in the room.

"Thin?" Dr. Lewiston laughed and removed the tip of the infrared thermometer from Sam's ear. It registered 98.6, like it should. "Can you guess where I got these muscles?" He pointed to his biceps. "That's from one hundred fifty range-of-motion exercises to each of this guy's joints every day for ten years. It's from alternate movements to his arms and legs, from deep muscle massage several times a day. You haven't seen what happens to patients who're really allowed to waste away in bed." Lewiston shook his head. "Your Sam Duffy isn't thin."

Coral blinked at him, then raised her voice, glancing at the curtain as if to see Brown on the other side. "Sugar, I knew what he was like before. Every muscle. Know what I mean?"

Lewiston felt himself flush. He left the bedside and returned with a cart, passing Brown who'd settled into the corner sofa with his newspaper.

"Why isn't he acting like he recognizes us?" she said. "He looks at me, but he doesn't seem to see me."

"Give him time; he's doing well. You just don't know how great. I'm going to run tests now."

Lewiston began the same battery of sensory stimulations he'd conducted on Sam for ten years.

Now Sam blinked when bright lights were shone into his eyes. He jerked when Lewiston moved out of eyesight and clapped two blocks of wood together near his ears. Sam flushed when ammonia was held under his nose. He jerked his foot back when Lewiston ran a tongue depressor along his sole.

At each reaction, Lewiston grew more hopeful and, at each one, Coral murmured in excitement. He hoped she really did love Sam Duffy because it would be a modicum of compensation for this long doctoring—to know someone's happiness might be restored. He thought of his wife, his son now in college working on a masters in engineering, and of how he'd missed so much of their lives. His son had bitterly refused to consider medical school. *I don't want to be like you, Dad*, he'd said. If Sam Duffy awoke and Lewiston could resume his life, perhaps his own family's happiness might have a chance of being regained.

"This is really wonderful," Lewiston said. "He's responding. We won't know for a while what's happened to his brain but his autonomic nervous system seems intact."

"Then use it," he heard from the corner sofa.

Lewiston pulled back the curtain he'd drawn and looked at Brown whose eyes were raised from his newspaper. "Beg pardon?"

"His nervous system's working. You're trying to stimulate it. Stop fooling around and stimulate it. Go ahead, Coral."

For a moment there was silence as Brown's meaning registered. "Listen," Lewiston said, disgusted at the idea. "You can't mean—"

"Is there any real danger, Chuck?" Brown asked impatiently.

Lewiston tried to think instead of being angry. Ordinarily they'd have to worry about brittle bones but Lewiston had taken pains to prevent skeletal problems in his patient. He'd supplied calcium supplements, used the bed as a tilt table so gravity could help maintain bone strength.

"No danger to his body, I don't think, but his brain might seize from too much stimulation too fast."

Brown stood, walked to the door, then turned as he grasped the handle. "Then, Dr. Lewiston, it's best you stay, in case that occurs." Brown walked out and closed the door.

Panicking, Lewiston turned to Coral whose eyes rolled to the ceiling in implied sympathy as if she agreed Brown's suggestion was awful. It encouraged him to ask the questions that had plagued him for ten years. He moved closer to her and whispered, "Who is this guy to Brown? Why is he so desperate to wake him up?"

Coral whispered back, "It's a real bad idea to quiz anybody around here, Doc."

She obviously knew the room was bugged because she looked sorry for him and pressed her lips together as if to say, *hang in there*. She raised Sam's hand, kissed it and put it down, lifted his gown, and began paying expert attention to Sam's anatomy.

Lewiston stepped away, deeply embarrassed. In one glance he'd noticed the ample cleavage of her breasts and that her skin shimmered like moon dust and her chestnut hair was glorious and that her bare toes were painted rosy gold in her high heeled gold sandals.

Instead of becoming aroused himself, as he'd feared, his mind reverted to doctor mode, realizing Brown's scheme could actually work.

At first there was nothing, but Coral persisted, whispering to the man she'd seemed to love. Minutes later he still saw no reaction, which, in his newly considered professional opinion, was an extremely bad sign. There were corpses who'd rise from their graves to experience this. Coral seemed to be willing Sam to life with her touch, with her mouth, yet nothing happened.

Lewiston was about to suggest she stop, when Coral suddenly said, "There's my baby; there we go!" She lifted her face and motioned to Lewiston, "Look, look!" and he saw that Sam was nearly erect.

Lewiston rushed to the bed, saying, "Call him, shake him, say his name," as he prepared an injection.

"Sam! Sam! Wake up baby; it's Coral. Sam! If you wake up, I'll give you a cowgirl you wouldn't believe."

Lewiston stared at the mesmerizing woman who was

proposing to screw his patient's lights out as he lay in bed.

"Ohhh, fuck!"

Startled, they both turned and stared at Sam's face, which was now broadly grinning at Coral. "Hey, babe," he whispered in a voice gravelly with disuse, "Hey babe—"

"Don't try to talk," Lewiston said. "Take it slow."

Sam coughed. His eyes rolled in their sockets as if they weren't under his control, then they refocused on Coral. "Baby, who ... whoever you are," he whispered. "Drag that cu ... that cunt over here, w ... would you?"

Coral looked surprised, but she quickly laughed in delight, rose and threw her arms around his neck. "Hi, Sam. It's good to have your horny ass back!"

She kissed him, but he turned his head, gasping. Quickly, Lewiston put an oxygen mask on Sam, checked his pulse and listened to his heart, growing jubilant at the signs his patient would be all right and that he himself would soon be going home.

"That's enough excitement for now," Lewiston said. "You need to take it easy."

Sam reached up to remove the oxygen mask, but Coral patted his hand. "Take it slow, Sam. Take all the time in the world." She gestured with a sweep of her arm. "Mr. Brown's given you all this out of the kindness of his heart. He'll give you a few more days."

Sam was staring at her cleavage as she talked.

He pulled the mask down and spoke in a raspy voice. "Where am ... where am I?"

Coral and Lewiston looked at each other. "You're at Brown's," she said.

"Who's Brown?"

She frowned. "You don't remember?"

"No." Sam groaned and tried to stretch. "God," he coughed, "I feel so weak!"

Lewiston was more deeply touched than he'd expected by the sight of movement in the body he'd kept healthy and alive. Now Handsome Jones had risen, he was going to be fine. He said, "You've been in a coma a long time. You were shot. The paramedics found you in Central Park."

"When?" Sam asked.

Lewiston looked away.

Coral said. "It's been ten years, Sam."

Sam seemed unable to comprehend that. He looked around the room, his gaze returning to Lewiston. "What ... what are you, my nurse?" he asked with disdain.

Lewiston felt stung.

"Sam!" Coral said. "That's Dr. Lewiston. "He's been caring for you here the whole time."

"Oh yeah?" Gasping, clearing his throat, he looked at Coral. "And ... and ... who are you, angel?"

Slowly Coral slid down onto a stool, the joy on her face disappearing. "I'm Coral. We used to know each other, honey."

When Sam tried sitting up, Coral and Lewiston helped him, propping pillows behind his head. Then Lewiston brought a glass of water and a straw, knowing he had to take his time, let his patient take his time, and that gratitude was unimportant because this was nearly over at last.

"So where am I?" Sam said in a stronger voice when he finished drinking.

Lewiston said, "You're in a penthouse on Fifth Avenue. It belongs to Theomund Brown. Apparently you used to work for him. That's all I know. Coral?" He turned to her.

She shook her head. "Sugar, like I said, I'm not an information source around here."

Sam whistled low as he looked around. "Fan ... fancy digs."

"The best," Coral said.

Lewiston couldn't read her. Was she on this guy's side or Brown's? He sensed their interests were different.

"One more ... more question," Sam said, seeming to gain control of his voice.

"Yes?"

"Who am I?"

In the silence that followed, Lewiston walked to the bedside table and opened the drawer. He withdrew something and handed it to Sam.

"This is yours. It's the only personal thing we found, other than your clothes. I've been saving it for you."

Sam gazed at the penknife, its handle grip made of whale ivory.

"It has scrimshaw on it from the Inuit," Lewiston said.

Sam looked up at Lewiston. "An Eskimo knife? Is that supposed to tell me something?"

They heard the doorknob turn. Brown reentered the room, followed by a guard from the building, who closed the door and stood with his back to it. Lewiston knew the building guards were armed. He wasn't surprised to find they were also under Brown's control.

"Whoa!" Sam whispered. "Is he going to keep people out or me in?"

Brown said, "Both." He came and patted Coral's behind. "Good work. Wait outside, but don't leave."

"Yeah, angel." Sam turned his gaze from the armed guard as he spoke. "Don't even think of leaving."

Coral touched Sam's hand, a blank expression on her face, and walked out.

"I'll give you some privacy," Lewiston said to Brown and started to follow her.

"No, have a seat," Brown said.

Lewiston didn't want to become further involved. He hadn't run tests yet, but he was reasonably certain it wouldn't take long for Sam Duffy to be on his feet. His job should be ending. Why did Brown want him to hear anything? He sat on the stool Coral had vacated.

Brown leaned on the railing at the foot of the bed, looking intent as if he meant to penetrate Sam Duffy's mind. "It's a little too convenient that you don't remember."

So this was why Brown had wanted him to remain.

"I take it that you're Mr. Brown," Sam said, looking less afraid of him than others did—out of ignorance, no doubt.

"Yes."

"I work for you?"

"Yes."

"Do you pay me well?"

"Very well."

Brown had done nothing to reveal himself, but Lewiston still felt Brown's anticipation. What Sam would say seemed of utmost importance to him.

Sam again looked around at the expensively furnished room. "Yeah, I guess you could afford to pay me. Mind telling me for what?"

Brown gazed at Sam, his eyes calculating something. "You were a private detective when I met you twenty-one years ago. Before that you'd been a merchant seaman. It was your idea to come here as a doorman to supervise the building staff and provide me greater security. You don't remember?"

Sam stared at him. "Well, everything's fuzzy."

"What does that mean?"

"I don't know who you are or any of the stuff you're telling me. I don't remember this place. I don't remember the doctor."

"That's not a memory failure," Lewiston interjected. "We'd never met before your injury."

"Anyway, I don't even remember that fantastic piece of ass who just left. Was she my girl, or what?"

"She's a whore," Brown said.

"She's a fucking gorgeous one."

"You remember nothing?" Brown waved the guard over. He jerked the guard's gun from its holster and began tossing it menacingly back and forth in his hands. "Nothing?"

Sam, seeming frightened, looked at the ceiling as if trying to recall. "Nada. Zip. Nothing's there. All I remember is waking up and feeling that angel's hand or mouth or cunt." He gave a hollow laugh as Brown tossed the gun. "Shit, man! I hope that's how I die."

"You weren't this vulgar before," Brown said, and returning the guard's gun looked at Lewiston. "What's your medical opinion?"

Lewiston snorted. "Post-traumatic amnesia, obviously. You ought to say a prayer of thanks that he's sitting up saying anything at all."

"I don't pray," Brown replied. "Can you medically verify his memory loss?"

"Listen, buster," Sam said. "You think this is a con? That I'm some liar?"

Brown looked unimpressed. He said to Lewiston. "What about personality change? He was different before."

As they talked, Sam yawned and his eyelids drooped.

"Likely," Lewiston said. "It could be a mild anti-social personality disorder from the initial oxygen deprivation or the fact that this guy's brain's been scrambled for ten years."

Brown jiggled Sam's foot. "You've been asleep long enough."

Sam peered back through one open eye. "Would you mind telling me my last name if that's not too much trouble?"

"Duffy," Brown said.

"Sam Duffy. That's me?"

Brown turned a suspicious, searching glance on Lewiston and took him aside. "This is real?"

"Amnesia is obviously internal to the mind and impossible to medically verify, but, yes, I think this is real. It's retrograde amnesia, inability to remember events before a trauma."

"What will it take to get his memory back?"

"If he can get it back, you mean. This isn't my field. You'll want to bring in someone else, but I'd say intense exposure to things and people from his old life, especially if there was a strong emotional tie."

"Hmm," Brown said. "Maybe I don't want him to remember so fast."

Brown walked close to Sam on the other side of the bed. He patted his shoulder as if he were a son. "I saved your life, Sam Duffy. Without me, you'd be dead."

Sam turned to Lewiston for confirmation and Lewiston nodded.

"When you're stronger, I'll want a favor."

Sam looked tired, now, but he returned Brown's intrusive gaze. "Sure, one. Maybe two. More would depend on the price."

Brown laughed. "Name it."

Sam humphed. "What order of magnitude are we talking?

Hundreds, thousands, hundreds of thousands?"

"Try more."

"A million?"

"Yes."

Now Sam's head sank weakly onto the pillow, making Lewiston move toward the bed but Brown motioned him to stop.

"You serious?" Sam whispered, his face wreathed in happiness as if he'd awakened in heaven.

"Always."

Sam's head turned toward the guard at the door. "If I say no, is he going to shoot?"

Brown said matter-of-factly, "He has permission to halt your unapproved departure by force, but not to kill you."

His eyelids closing, Sam slid lower in the bed. He yawned again and smiled. "Hell, I'd take out Jesus fucking Christ for a million dollars."

"Well put," Brown said, "very well put. I'm growing fond of the new you, Sam." He left the bedside, nodding for Lewiston to resume care of his patient.

Chapter 10

Arona, Italy

Maggie spread the new brochures from Felix across the polished wood surface of the villa's kitchen table. The brochures had been here for only a month, but their edges were frayed, she'd pored over them so much. Now Felix was calling practically every other day. Which boarding school did she like for Jess?

None.

Felix had threatened to make the decision himself since their contract gave him the right to determine educational matters for Jess. Consulting her was a courtesy. Maggie didn't have a copy of the contract anymore and she'd never actually read it through, but she was sure he was right. To gain time, she had to pretend to be considering.

Again she opened each brochure, glancing at the photos: Eton, Gordonstoun, Harrow, Winchester. Apparently, boys at prep schools in Britain wore long socks, short pants, long-sleeved shirts, a tie, and a matching cap and jacket. At one school they wore capes and funny hats. At another, just jackets or white sweaters trimmed in black. Some boys went to class in tails. They seemed to always have on ties, in any case. American schools were different: Thomas Jefferson, St. Andrews, Philips Exeter, Groton. There, boys could wear more of what they liked, which at one school seemed to consist of giant pants that billowed around their little legs, and shirts down to their knees. She saw no swans anywhere, except in Eton's brochure, and no great emphasis on religion.

She couldn't relinquish her duty to Jess when he was her whole life's purpose. Why else had God kept her a virgin until Felix implanted the clone of Jesus? Why else was her virginity restored after she gave birth? Why else hadn't she fallen in love until she met Sam, the man who would give his life to save Jess?

She gathered the brochures and went out to the back steps, which wound down through the kitchen garden to the front yard. She saw Jess in the study with Rabbi Diena, being tutored. Antonella was busy with the laundry.

Maggie plucked a rose from the bower overhead as she passed it, crossed the lawn and descended to the lakeshore.

A red wooden motorboat with a little cabin and green trim bobbed cheerfully on the lake, just outside their porticiollo, a private harbor. It was fully enclosed by medium-low concrete walls except for an opening between its two lantern-encaging crows' nests through which Jess took his sailboat in and out. A white handrail ran along the top of the walls providing something to hold onto when a person walked along them.

Maggie stepped onto the wall and walked to the crow's nest where the motorboat was tied. She looked down into the boat and her heart sank. Adamo Morelli was fast asleep.

She should have known.

"Ciao, Hetta!" he said, suddenly laughing.

Adamo was always making jokes. He sat upright, his long frame rail thin from taking in so little food as opposed to drink, and stretched out his arms. "Never will I disappoint you," he said.

Maggie had her doubts about that.

He pulled the boat closer so she could climb down. When she settled in, he maneuvered the boat to the far side of the porticiollo, where they couldn't be seen from the villa's windows.

Just weeks ago, Maggie couldn't have guessed she'd be meeting the town drunk like this. She said, "Thank you for coming, Adamo," and looked down at the brochures, embarrassed to be here.

"You are sure Jess's uncle will send him to one of these places?"

"Yes, I'm sure."

"But how can this be; you are his mother?"

Sudden tears streamed down Maggie's face, like they had three weeks ago when Adamo first passed by in his boat.

Maggie had been on the lake house deck, reading the long

letter Felix sent because she kept hanging up the phone. It said he'd much prefer to talk with her than write, but she'd left him no choice. The letter contained Felix's recollection of his colleague, Max Segre, cutting his finger during his daughter's naming ceremony the night before they examined the Shroud. The next day, Max had touched the area from which Felix stole the threads. To be sure, Felix had contacted Father Bartolo who had been involved with the Shroud research. He asked Bartolo to search the photographic record of the Shroud team's work. A picture of Max touching the Shroud arrived in response. Maggie had examined it, and the portrait of Max Segre that was enclosed.

Yes there were one or two resemblances. Max and Jess had the same thick hair and similar eyebrows, but the eyes, mouth and facial lines were different.

Felix saw only similarities and concluded Jess was a clone of Max Segre, not Jesus Christ. He reasoned that Jess, as a normal boy, needed to lead a normal life. He said boarding school posed virtually no danger since Jess had always used his assumed name and they'd convinced Theomund Brown of the clone's death. If princes could safely attend boarding schools, the letter said, so could Jess. Children away at school sometimes had personal guards and, if she insisted, he'd get one for Jess.

Alone on the deck, Maggie had burst into tears. That's when Adamo came by in his boat. He moored it, came ashore, weaved his inebriated way to her and, when he found her inconsolable, sat down and patted her shoulder. Adamo had also come by the next day on his boat and the next, but he wasn't as drunk as before. At length he'd persuaded Maggie to tell him what was wrong and, in desperation, she had—leaving out the details of who Jess really was.

Now as she sat in Adamo's boat once again Maggie trembled, sure of what the brochures really foretold. Even if no one found him and hurt him, Jess would be in danger because he wouldn't stay at the school. He'd do the same as he did when she tried enrolling him in a local school. He'd come home. He'd cross dangerous roads, cross oceans if need be. If he was forced to stay, he wouldn't eat or sleep. He wouldn't survive apart from her and the swans. Not yet. Neither would she survive apart from Jess.

"If you keep crying, *Cara Mia*, we will have to dig another lake."

In spite of her sadness, Maggie laughed.

Gently, Adamo took the brochures Maggie gripped in her hands and examined them, saying, "O, Madonna!" which was what Italians said when Americans said "Oh, God!" It was one of the things that made Maggie like the country.

"To be truthful," Adamo said and shook his head, "I have never understood the Americans and the British. They rip bambinos from the bosoms of their mothers and send them off to strangers. It is not the Italian way."

"No?"

"Look at me," he said. "Every day my mamma still cooks pasta for me."

"Yes, but do you always eat it?" Maggie pointed to his thin chest.

"That is beyond the point, though you sound just like her. My point is this. Nobody leaves home in Italy until they marry. Even if we go to college, we come back home. *Cazzata!*"

"Don't curse."

"Si, forgive me, Hetta. I only want to help you. I know what it is to lose the one you love." Adamo looked off toward the *gola* where Lake Maggiore narrowed and Maggie wondered if he was thinking of his brother's wife. "But I cannot imagine losing a child so young."

Maggie's voice shook. "Neither can I."

"Do you know what we say in Arona about your villa?"

"No, what?"

"We say it stayed empty all those years after the Jewish newlyweds fled because it was waiting for a very special love to return."

"Oh, isn't that nice."

"Sometimes I pass by in my boat just to hear your happy voices —you and Jess—and I am not the only one."

Maggie gazed at Adamo. She took a deep breath. "Maybe the time has come for the villa to be silent again. I have enough money to buy another one, if it's small. It should be in a town far away from here. I would need someone to help me move away in the middle of the night."

Maggie actually had a great deal of money. For ten years, Felix had not only paid all their household expenses, but also the sum stipulated in the contract. She hadn't spent a dime of the latter.

Adamo smiled. "This someone, he should be a little sneaky, yes?"

Maggie nodded.

"And no one should suspect him because he is drinking all the time?"

Maggie nodded yes.

Adamo started maneuvering the boat back to the crow's nest. As Maggie climbed out he said, "I will see if I can find such a person for our dear Hetta and perhaps he can find such a place. Naturally, we must not mention this to my brother, Carlo, who is always on the side of *la autorità* and the man. Me, I am always on the side of the woman and love."

Maggie kissed both his cheeks and squeezed his hands in gratitude.

"Do not worry, Hetta. I will not let them melt our Mamma Nera into glue from which to make a wooden mamma—like they melt real horses to make glue for wooden horses."

Maggie didn't know what to say, except, "Thank you." Adamo was always saying something odd.

Looking about to see if she'd been observed, she returned to her room in the villa and knelt at her pristine bed, terrified at what she'd decided to do, but determined.

She repeated what had become a daily prayer. "Father, if Adamo is meant to help us, if that's why you sent him by on his boat, please give him the strength to fight the evils of drink long enough to do your will."

Chapter 11

Sam Duffy focused on the bedside drapes, determined to walk toward them without Dr. Lewiston's support today. For the past month he'd been practicing the individual components of walking: step, shift weight, lunge forward, foot up, shift weight, foot down. The hard part was putting it together every time.

Something crossed his mind: *become the drapes*. Where he'd heard such squirrelly crap he didn't know, but he decided to try it. He analyzed the sumptuous curtains, threaded in gold as if for a prince. *I'm the prince and those are my fucking drapes.* He pictured yanking them down and wrapping them around him, the gold threads strands of sunlight in which he'd never know darkness again.

He let go of Lewiston. "Let me try it."

"You're tired."

"I said let me try it!"

"All right, just be careful," Lewiston said in the almighty-doctor-ministering-to-uncouth-sod voice that irritated Sam.

Ignoring it, Sam moved. Step, shift weight, lunge forward. *Become the drapes.*

He started to keel over. *Become the drapes.*

Foot up. He wobbled. Shift weight. He started to fall. *Become the fucking drapes!*

Foot down, foot down, foot down, he commanded. Step. Shift weight, lunge.

Sam was walking.

Foot up, shift weight, don't fall, Duffy, stay on your goddamned feet! Foot down, down, down.

Become the drapes. Become the drapes.

He was walking.

The gold threads in the curtains gleamed like dawns on his horizons. No more years of darkness. No entombment in a body that wasn't dead or alive.

In triumph, Sam grabbed for the drapes and fell onto his bed, bringing them with him.

Lewiston was there. "Are you all right?"

"Sure," Sam said, wrapping the curtains around him like a toga. "I'm the fucking prince."

He rose and repeated his victory, crossing the room again and again until he was steady on his feet and felt he could walk, run, sprint, jog, saunter the earth forever, just him and these great feet. He reached the terrace's glass doors in a sure stride and stopped, wriggling his toes. He was tired, but he didn't care. He could walk.

Behind him, he heard Lewiston applaud his progress and say Brown would be proud. That was a no-brainer. Practically every afternoon Brown had come in to fill Sam's head with mysterious facts, then grill him on them. Of course Brown would be proud he could walk. Sam had almost learned to like Brown. If you cooperated he was generous, tolerant. If you turned on him, no question he'd break your balls.

Sam didn't like Lewiston. He was too sure of himself. Nothing was sure to Sam but the now. This breath, this heartbeat.

Worse still, Lewiston was too damned good looking. Except for his glasses and boring preppie clothes, Lewiston looked able—if he wanted—to give Sam a run for any available woman around. Not good because Sam wanted women most of all. He knew that's what he needed to fill the awful yearning inside him, the hollow feeling always there. He had ten years of lost living to make up for. The quicker he got rid of his doctor, the sooner it could start.

Lewiston's presence was doubly irritating now that Sam's attention was on the woman on the terrace—the one who'd apparently sucked him back to life. It was rare to see her out there with Brown, because usually if someone was there that side of the terrace was closed off. One time the partition slid back as if something bumped it and Sam had glimpsed a Japanese guy in an expensive suit behind the greenery, his eyes bulging and staring down, like he was getting the best blow job of his life. Sam hadn't seen the woman. Was it Coral? God, he wanted her.

A month ago, Sam had gray in his hair. Now, thanks to the ass-pain Lewiston, and Grecian formula, it was gone. Sam had less flesh on his bones than he'd prefer, less muscle, but his body was unmistakably a man's. From the first they'd brought in weights and told him to take it slow. He'd wanted to pump them night and day but he forced himself to train right, dying to look good for this broad.

Now there she was, right next to Brown, eating breakfast and wearing nothing but a short, sheer gold robe over a short, sheer gold nightgown. He wanted to open the glass door to get a better view of her nipples through the thin fabric. They were driving him crazy. It didn't help to see Brown reach out from behind his paper and rub her thigh. Sam wondered what it would take to be with her. Would Brown have to order it, would she come on her own, or would he have to pay?

He grew so aroused watching her that he called to Lewiston, "Do you have to be in here every damn minute?"

"No," Lewiston said, sounding angry. "If you can make it back to bed on your own, I'll join the others for breakfast."

"Yeah, I can," Sam said, watching Lewiston's reflection in the glass. "Do that."

When he heard the door close, Sam looked down at the erection swelling in his pajamas, thankful that they'd finally put the guard outside the door. God, he wanted that woman. She was hot. She'd made him hot. How the hell would he get her? He didn't want to jerk off when she was right there—right there!

She turned and looked in his direction as if she'd heard him. Had she seen his stiff pecker through the sheers? He watched her say something to Brown that he couldn't hear because, as he'd finally realized, this was a soundproof room. She stood. Was she coming to him at last? The passion he'd poorly controlled turned to a frenzy of desire.

Sam went to the door, dizzy with anticipation. He imagined

her approaching footsteps and grew rock hard with desire. She would give him what he'd missed for ten long years.

She smiled when she opened the door then came in, saying, "Would you like some company?"

Sam didn't answer. He was staring at her fantastic boobs. He couldn't recall if he'd ever seen better ones and he didn't care. Love the boobs you're with. They were double neon blinkers flashing his name. The right one said *Sam* and the left *Duffy*. The V-shaped shadow he could see between her thighs said *cum*.

She approached him and put her mouth to his ear, urgently whispering something. He couldn't tell what. Something about Brown, as if Sam cared a fuck about him right now.

Sam reached up and gripped her breasts that were so near, dragging his thumbs over the fantastic nipples.

"Ow!" she said. "Not so hard, baby. They're real."

Shaking, he opened her robe then dropped it to the floor. He reached for the hem of her gown and pulled it over her head, shaking more.

"Not talking today?" she said. "Okay, Sam. Go ahead. I guess it's been a long time."

He took as much of her breast as he could manage into his mouth and sucked, groaning at the taste of it, the woman smell, the feel of it, yet somehow needing more, more. He didn't know why she cried out because he was on fire, feeling good though he was a lot dizzier now and couldn't make out her words. Something about hopping or shopping or stopping. Then they were on the floor and he didn't remember how they'd got there. He was gripping those breasts and holding on for dear life so they wouldn't get away and leave him in darkness. He squeezed the nipples, trying to make them sit up more so he could suck them better.

For a moment his vision cleared and he saw her face was wet. She was crying. She'd gone quiet and gritted her teeth, so it must be feeling good. When had his hands gone down between her thighs and gotten wet? All his fingers were wet. Had she lost it and pissed on him? It didn't matter because now he was finally in her hot vagina and his frenzy was complete. He was slamming it, slamming it, gripping her, holding her down with all his strength. It felt like it would go on forever, gripping those neon blinkers flashing his name, gripping her ass, knotting his hands in her hair, putting his hand in her mouth and finger-fucking her throat and then slamming it, slamming it until he was dangling off a cliff of white hot blazing heat and not going over just hovering there in the burning light ... no darkness anywhere. Still he needed more.

He heard something like *peas. Peas post. Pease pot. Please stop.* He didn't know where it came from. He didn't care. He was on that cliff edge, hovering like a bird, staring in the face of beautiful devils who urged him on. *Come,* they whispered. *Ride the woman to us,* they said.

His breath came and went in shuddering grunts and the devils were singing, no screaming. He couldn't stop to see why. He had to slam it, slam it, penetrate it, nibble the moist nipples, knead the supple skin, shove his pecker anywhere, everywhere, ram it up her, hold her still so she would bite it, fuck it, suck it, to help him plunge over the white hot burning cliff.

Instead someone was screaming and he couldn't get his breath and the cliff disappeared and his world was suddenly trembling in waves of pain.

When Sam awoke, he wasn't dizzy anymore but his head ached. People were standing at the foot of his bed. Mr. Brown. Dr. Lewiston.

"Hi, there," Sam said, hiding his fear. The pain was worse when he talked. How long had he been out? "Did I fall asleep again? How long this time? Not ten years, I hope." He managed a laugh. "Anybody got an aspirin?"

They both stared.

"Okay, can I *buy* an aspirin off you?

Without speaking, Lewiston brought two and some water.

When he'd swallowed them, Sam said, "So what's up?"

"I think he's all right again," Lewiston said to Brown. "I might have to put him on medica—"

Brown raised his voice. "Would you come now?" He spoke to someone out of sight.

Sam grew concerned, then terrified, as the guard appeared and took out his gun, cocked it, and held it to the temple of Sam's head.

"As long as you work for me," Brown said in a hard voice, looking at Sam with contempt, "don't do that again. Understand?"

Sam had no idea what he was talking about, but the correct response was plain. "Definitely. You got it. Hey, I'm sorry, man."

Brown's eyes grew colder. "Unless I order you to."

Dr. Lewiston held his stomach like he might get sick.

"Sure, unless you order it."

Brown nodded.

To Sam's relief, the guard uncocked the gun and left the room. So did Lewiston. Sam didn't dare ask Brown what he'd been ordered not to do, but he ventured, "Are you going to tell me how long I was out?"

"Not long." Suddenly, Brown's icy glare turned to a smile. "To show there are no hard feelings ..." He turned his head and called, "Coral?"

She appeared from around the rehung bed curtains wearing her gold sheer robe and gold gown. Her neck was bruised; there was a long scratch on her arm. Who had hurt her? Not him. Or had he?

Desperately, he hoped he hadn't messed up because he wanted more from her. Much more.

"Hey, if that was me, I'm sorry, angel."

Brown said, "Coral, give Sam what he should have asked you for."

She stared at Brown as if she didn't believe her ears and Brown looked back, his gaze unfaltering. Still he went and ran his hand down Coral's back and said to Sam, "You do anything else without her permission and you'll regret it until you die."

"He means it," Coral said in a tight voice.

Sam thought so, too. "I got it; I understand."

But when Brown left the room Coral lingered, seeming nervous, red bruises prominent against her moon dust flesh. She was phenomenal, even now. He must have really lost it.

"I don't know what happened," he insisted. "I don't remember. I really don't."

She sighed and unset her jaw then came and lay hesitantly beside him. When he didn't move toward her, she spoke tonelessly. "I could tell you didn't know what you were doing."

"Whew! That's a relief." He was transfixed by the swell of her hips and what he remembered was between them. "Can I touch you?"

She looked wary.

"Please. I need to."

Her lip trembled, but she closed her eyes in what he took for assent.

He ran his hand down her silken arm and was relieved to see she let him. "Hey, I'm sorry. Really sorry."

"You're different, Sam," she said and, touching a finger to his chin, opened her big hazel eyes which were full of rebuke. "You used to be a great guy, you know. You never hurt anybody, Sam. Never."

She'd spoken in a barely audible whisper. He didn't know what to say but his pecker did. It had risen and was begging for attention. Coral saw and said, "All right, I'll give you some company. This is for old time's sake, okay. After this, no more, until you remember me."

He was watching her cleavage. "I understand."

Afraid to make a mistake, he let her do all the work and Coral kept her promise in spite of being hurt. She screwed him grudgingly, though, like it would really be the last time ever. Still he returned to the burning cliff and stayed a long time and finally she was there, too, looking blissful but sad. Then he plunged over and down, down, down, screaming his orgasm like a kid who'd lucked up. She put her hand over his mouth so the others wouldn't hear because she didn't know, or had forgotten, about the soundproof room. He fell onto her body and into a deep, deep sleep and awoke alone in a panic, remembering a recurring dream.

A waterfall. Lazy summer days.
Some guy. Weird guy.
Stupid type, a real do-gooder ... another waterfall. Danger everywhere. This guy dying like a dog late at night in a park to help somebody out. Who WAS this guy? What an asshole.

Sam rose, shaking off the dream. To his surprise Coral was gone and he saw a breakfast tray in the room. He went to it, lifting a silver cover from an almost eggshell-thin black porcelain plate—nothing but the best here at Brown's. The smell of bacon rose, so intoxicating he ecstatically closed his eyes and inhaled, then put a whole slice in his mouth and chewed slowly, letting his taste buds celebrate. Logically, he must have had bacon all his life, must have had eggs, butter, sugar, salt, yet to Sam's senses they still felt intensely new, like Coral had.

He swallowed and reached for a second slice then noticed a wallet beside the flower vase. He saw a suitcase on the floor beside the tray. He opened it and, on top of the clothes, saw the whale ivory scrimshaw knife they said was his, though when and where he got it he couldn't recall. It lay next to a big damned gun.

Sam picked it up and checked it, realizing he knew just how to use it. It was loaded. The safety was engaged. He opened the wallet and found it full of money, but no ID. He counted ten thousand dollars and saw a paste-on note that said, *expense money.* Some expense money. They'd stopped making bills this large in the 60s. Sam wondered how he could remember that and not his own name.

Did it matter when his present looked so bright? He was alive again. He'd just had his brains screwed out. He had funds. He planned to use them to rediscover the pleasures of the world.

He saw clothes laid on the sofa and shoes below and he inspected them. He snorted when he saw the shoes looked like K-Mart specials; the suit was off some bargain basement rack; and the watch said Timex. The set of cotton underwear said: Fruit of the Loom. He saw a note attached to the briefs:

It's time to begin. In celebration, you'll be having lunch with a friend. Memorize the contents of the next page.
  Eat, shower, shave, dress. Leave at noon and take a taxi there. Listen. Look. Don't try to screw the women you meet. Use your head. Remember everything I've told you. Memorize this number and call me in private when there's something to report. A failure of allegiance will have consequences.
  888 672 7696
  P.S. Leave the note. Take the suitcase and don't return until I say you can.

Was this the start of his secret mission? Sam chuckled, realizing as he studied the phone number that he must have been a damned good private detective in his day. On a telephone keypad, the numbers after the area code would spell out *Mr. Brown.* Easy to remember. Hard to figure out. Just like the owner of the phone.

He studied the second page of instructions as he'd been told, deciding amnesia might not be so bad if things were going to be this simple. After lunch he could buy himself some decent clothes, check into the best hotel in town, and proceed in total comfort with whatever Brown meant for him to do.

Sam tried the knob and found the door opened for him. He made his way to a foyer lined in glass cases filled with crystals and gems. He took the waiting elevator and arrived in what he assumed was Brown's private garage, suitcase in hand and eager to start. Someone had hailed him a taxi, which pulled up. It looked nothing like any car Sam recognized—no angles; sort of aerodynamically rounded. Apparently, styles had changed a lot in ten years.

Sam got in and they were stuck for a while, unable to back out into the street because traffic was slow.

As he waited, he saw a woman emerge from Brown's elevator

and head for what, even now, he recognized as a Rolls. She seemed about to be chauffeured somewhere. He was taken aback when he realized who it was. Coral, but somehow not her at all. The sway in her walk was gone. The sparkle was turned off in her eyes. Had he done that?

She saw him and her gaze was like stones weighing him down.

He lowered the window, intending to apologize again on the chance it might one day get him back in her pants.

"If you hadn't passed out, you would have killed me," she said.

"Me?"

"Yes."

She was crazy. Hot as a volcano and out of her mind. Sam leaned back in the taxi seat and closed his eyes, thinking of how the bacon smelled.

Chapter 12

Brown's Penthouse

In the lobby of his penthouse, Theomund Brown smiled at Dr. Chuck Lewiston who was waiting for the private elevator to arrive and trying to hide his impatience.

"I can't say that I've actually enjoyed the past ten years, Theomund," Lewiston said, "but I'm grateful that my family was taken care of."

Chuck had long ago decided to use Brown's first name on the last day of his servitude here.

"My pleasure," Brown said, "for a job well done. You did what I asked. You're free now, Chuck. Expect a call from your hospital. I intend to restore your career."

"Thanks. I'd prefer to do it on my own. No strings pulled, if you don't mind. I'm grateful for the offer, though."

Brown patted his shoulder. "I'm not surprised. All right, then."

Lewiston nodded, uneasy in Brown's presence though he tried to tell himself that Brown was just a man.

The elevator came. Lewiston stepped inside, gave a friendly half salute, and entered the code for the downstairs lobby. He knew Brown, in his paranoia about security, would change the elevator codes as soon as he left.

The doors closed at last and Dr. Chuck Lewiston slumped against the posh elevator's wall, weakened by the sudden lift of his ten-year burden. He wanted to shout in joy but he held back.

Instead of leaving from Brown's private garage, as he'd done for ten years, Lewiston stepped out into the lobby. Rave the doorman offered a snarl of a smile and asked if he'd like a limo.

"No thank you, Rave," Lewiston said and swiftly walked ahead of him. "I can manage on my own."

Outside on Fifth Avenue, Lewiston breathed the early morning air. He walked to 96th Street and, as soon as he turned the corner, leapt off the ground and pumped his fist. He was free.

Fists clenched, he jogged to Madison and across it, to Park Avenue and across it, speeding up with each step until he was racing, eating up the pavement in long strides like a lion. At Lexington he entered the subway, descended the stairs two at a time. On the moving subway train, the rhythm of the wheels echoed his thoughts: *It's over! No more of Theomund Brown! No more!*

He exited the subway in his Chelsea neighborhood at 23rd and 8th and almost skipped the few blocks to his own street, taking in the red brick town homes, the iron grillwork fences and railings, the brick and brownstone steps. Outside his door, a jade Porsche and a silver Aston Martin were parked where his wife's Volvo usually was. No doubt they belonged to prospective buyers of one of these historic homes.

Chuck Lewiston leapt up the stairs to his door and used his key. The door opened. He stopped. There in the vestibule stood his wife and his son, peering quizzically at him. Had they seen him coming?

For a moment he just took them in: she beautiful with her graying hair cut short in a stylish Afro, in her ears the golden hoops he'd brought back from Namibia. His son was tall and elegant, dressed for work in a well-cut suit.

"It's over!" he shouted. "I'm free! We have our lives back! I'm free!"

Then he saw the keys in their hands.

"Chuck," his wife said, "If you think you can make up for all these years just like that with an expensive car—"

"What?"

"I'll take the car, Dad," his son said, "but it doesn't change things for me."

"What cars? What are you talking about?"

"The dealer called this morning, like you instructed. They told us when the cars would be delivered."

"What dealer?"

"Oh Chuck!" His wife turned and went into their living room, which was decorated with souvenirs from his African travels. An ebony mask. A chair in which chieftains had sat.

She picked up two note cards from a small leather-covered table and handed them to him. "And I don't think these were very cute."

He took them from her hand and read. *Don't drive off a cliff. Love, Chuck. Love, Dad.*

He hadn't sent them. He hadn't bought the cars.

Don't drive off a cliff. Like the senator's wife had? Lewiston had been in the emergency room when she arrived. She'd talked to him before she died. Brown had known he'd be on duty and, Lewiston was sure, Brown had controlled where her car would crash.

Chuck Lewiston dropped into his tribal chieftain's chair and sobbed until his wife and son began apologizing for not appreciating the cars. His wife kissed him. His son patted his shoulder. They said they were grateful; it's just that he'd been gone so long.

Lewiston had studied the history of slavery in America. He'd seen the African dungeons from which the slaves were shipped. The feeling he'd had while standing in them came over him now.

Blindly Lewiston rose without looking at his wife and son. He left his home, berating himself for acting like tourists do on safari—wandering up to wild animals as if they were in a zoo. He should have realized he was actually still walking in the bush, part of the food chain dominated by Brown. He'd let down his guard when his senses should have been strained for danger.

Back at Brown's building, Rave opened the door with a smiling snarl. Inside, Chuck found the elevator codes unchanged. He went up to the penthouse and the butler showed him into the library where Theomund Brown was patiently waiting.

Lewiston sat before Brown's desk. He wanted to shout: *what do you mean by telling my son, and the woman I love, don't drive off a cliff?*

Instead he looked Brown in the eye, holding his gaze like a

lion. "What's it going to take to get my life back?" he said.

As Theomund Brown replied, Chuck Lewiston returned his placid gaze, not looking away or flinching, even when he heard the chilling instructions.

———

Theomund answered his private line and heard Evaristo Cardinal Salati's agitated voice say, "Theomund!"

"Yes, Your Eminence."

"A month ago, one of our priests took a sudden interest in the photographs of Rossi and his team examining the Shroud. His name is Bartolo. I learned of it yesterday. I have had his telephone records searched. Before examining those photographs, Bartolo received a call."

"Who from?"

"A U.S. cell phone number. We're searching for the registration."

"I have news as well," Brown said. "Sam Duffy has revived. I'm making use of him to learn the truth. If the clone lived and is now a ten-year-old boy—"

"My previous instructions remain, as does your reward," Salati said, sighed and hung up.

Brown allowed himself a smile of satisfaction. Ten years ago, he'd been disappointed only for financial reasons to conclude the clone had died. It meant he hadn't gained access to the Vatican bank, and its many hidden ways of disguising and rechanneling funds. Theomund still desperately wanted that access, which is why, as a precaution, he'd kept Sam alive.

It didn't matter that in all these years he hadn't found the equal of Namibia's Tsumeb mine, its unique pipe-like cavity exposing basement rock formed 2.1 billion years ago at the end of the earth's Quaternary. Brown had made new fortunes in the Kalahari manganese field and lesser sites in Africa and in both Americas. His need for creative banking was even greater than before.

For personal reasons, though, Theomund had been glad to believe the clone was dead.

He put the receiver down and slowly opened a drawer, withdrawing a leather folder inscribed in gold, *DeathScopes*, the name invented by the astrologer who cast them long ago at his father's bidding. Brown opened the folder to the first sheet, stained with what had dropped unbidden from his eyes—the only tears he'd shed in life—on the day his father died.

Out on the terrace, the leather folder in his hands, he gazed at Coral, asleep on a chaise. Sam had hurt her in a way no one had. Coral was used to rough sex — not from him, of course, but from men who sought power they didn't have inside, cowards who needed to hurt a woman to feel like a man. Brown despised them as he used them. Coral knew how to handle them. They hadn't hurt her. Sam had.

It might have ruined Coral — for herself and for Brown. That's why he'd sent her back to Sam, who'd almost killed her. If she'd nursed the pain and shock, it could have ruined her.

He went to the chaise, gazed gently on the violent bruises at her throat, stroked her hair until she awoke.

She rose and looked at him, obedience in her eyes, but no warmth, no fire. Brown handed her the leather folder and sat at her feet on the chaise. "Would you read it?"

"All right, Theo." In her sexy mezzo voice she dutifully read aloud. "*With your Sun and Mars in Leo in the 4th house of home: you are a king who will boldly reign from the privacy of your own castle. Since all planets but two are below the horizon: your activities will be unknown to the world.*"

She looked up. "Theo, is this about you?"

"It is. Skip the astrology parts."

"*You will take a comfort close to fondness in those who work for you, and feel the need to be fair to them. A threat to national security will be felt as personal. You will assist the country more than once.*"

"More than all the Joint Chiefs, I'd say," she offered loyally. "*But forming genuine bonds with others does not come naturally.*"

She paused as if she'd offended him.

"That's correct, as we both know."

Coral's gaze returned to the sheet. "Theo, this part I gotta read.

The Star of Bethlehem had just risen above the horizon when you were born. It is the Jupiter/Saturn conjunction. Wise men from the east saw the one of their time as a symbol of the birth of a king. For you it is in the earthy sign of Taurus. In some sense, on this earth, I daresay you want to be the only God. In this you will succeed, to some extent."

She looked up, frowning.

"Just keep reading."

"However, the conjunction also rules your 8th house of death from the 12th house of hidden things, including assassins. It is likely you will die outdoors on dry land. Beware the one worthy of respect who is motivated by the birth of a king. Since the 12th house is the natural home of Pisces, the sign of the Jews, the assassin may— literally or figuratively—be acting on behalf of the same king the wise men sought.

"What a bunch of crap." She tossed the folder aside.

"There's a second sheet." He handed it to her. "It was my father's. Read the last paragraph."

"Uranus, bringer of sudden electrifying events, occupies a water sign and rules your 8th house of death from the 9th house of foreigners and foreign countries. You will likely drown in a foreign country during a storm." Coral paused.

"My father's yacht was engulfed in a sudden Mediterranean storm off the coast of Malta, drowning him."

Brown didn't add that it happened as his father was helping rid the Catholic Church of the blackmailing banker, Roberto Calvi.

"Ohhh God," she breathed, "But that doesn't mean—"

Brown rose.

She followed.

He stood at the edge of the terrace, taking in his commanding view of Central Park. He felt her arms come around him.

"When I was a boy, I had dreams."

"Tell me about them," she said, turning him around.

"I dreamed of a child. Stars were shooting from its mouth. The heavens rejoiced at its birth but I was left in darkness."

"Oh, Theo. Do you still have that dream?"

"Only sometimes," he said.

"What do you think it means?"

"Perhaps the clone is still alive."

She frowned. "What clone? You don't mean Felix Rossi's—"

"Yes. At first I searched for the Jesus clone. I watched Rossi's every move. All of them. His sister, his wife, even his child."

If Rossi hid them, Brown thought, he'd done a first-rate job. Every vestibule, every room Rossi visited had been searched, except his Italian family's home in Turin. The uncle was alert and well connected. It was impossible to bug his home. So Brown's men had painstakingly listened from outside through directional mikes. When Felix was there, they'd watched every window and door. Nothing.

"Oh, wow," Coral replied. "Well, maybe that means there isn't—"

"I have a feeling the clone may still be alive."

"If you say so, I know it's true." She squinted in thought. "Theo, so that's why you kept Sam here all this time? You think he—"

"I told you Sam was helping Rossi."

"And you think now Sam can help you find the clone?"

Theomund didn't answer. He'd shared enough to be vulnerable to her for a moment, if far less than she'd been with Sam.

She hooked an arm around his neck—the arm with the long scar. Together they stood, not talking, the sun above, New York traffic a faint roar below, her body pressed to his.

Chapter 13

Broadway

From Sam's vantage in the taxi, the building wrapped itself around the corner of 80th and Broadway and took up half the block. It had big display windows and a red brick facade, topped by a long white sign with the words *Zabar's* and *Wares Fair* alternating in big slanting letters. At least it was something he remembered.

Everyone in New York knew this gourmet grocery.

He paid the astronomical $4.40 that the taximeter read and added a tip. Since he was early for his appointment, he bypassed Zabar's restaurant on the corner where he'd been told to go. Instead he walked farther down Broadway to the market entrance, marveling at the strangely shaped cars passing in the streets and at the odd way people looked.

No curls, big hair, or padded shoulders on the women. No tight waists. Their clothes and hair were flat and straight and the hair was blunt or jagged at the ends. Thin ties for men were gone. Guys walked around in near-bibs with colorful designs. Collars were bigger—much bigger. Some could have gone on pirates' shirts.

Shaking his head, he entered the grocery aisles and strolled about, his suitcase in one hand, whistling at the cheeses, the hanging sausages, the olives, the wines. No need to search for a clerk. The staff was everywhere, eager to help and conspicuous in clean chef whites with little caps.

Whatever Brown had in mind must involve a person who didn't shop on a budget.

He paused before one of the small black chalkboards all over the store. Hand lettered in multiple colors were the day's offerings of smoked fish and caviar.

Two ounces of Russian Osetra Caviar came to more than seventy dollars now? Incredible.

Sam decided to head for the corner deli and get some food because he was starting to feel weak. He heard a commotion and turned to see a woman rush in his direction, screeching as if she'd seen the goose that laid the golden egg, bumping into people, her arms flung out, her eyes on something behind him.

He stepped aside.

She veered and collided into him, almost knocking him over. Her arms came around him. She cried, "Sam! Sam! Sam!" and kissed him on the cheek.

He felt her body against him, smelled the scent of orchids in her auburn hair, saw tears in her eyes and, overcome, Sam laid one on her lips, right there in front of Zabar's caviar and salmon display.

Instead of seeming surprised, she returned his kiss, but quickly broke it off, stepped back and held him at arm's length.

"Sam, you're still a dog, God bless your rotten soul! Oh my God, I can't believe it's you! You're not dead! You're alive? You're so thin! Are you all right? Where in the world have you been?"

Sam stared at her, not knowing what to say. Her clothes, her makeup, the diamonds in her ears said she was rich. Yet he obviously must have known her and known her well. Was this his unknown lunch companion?

She shook him. "Sam, it's me, Frances!"

So this was Frances, Felix's sister. Nothing about her was familiar, not her *every-hair-in-place* hairdo, manicured nails, chic leather skirt and matching blouse. He knew it hadn't come off a department store rack. She wasn't as gorgeous as Coral but she was definitely a woman—the kind Sam hadn't expected would give him the time of day.

"Oh, hi, Frances," Sam said, trying to sound equally enthused.

Frances let go of him and stood back while well-dressed shoppers gaped.

"You have no idea who I am, do you?" she said, her eyes now wide in dawning confusion.

"Uh, I wouldn't say that."

"You don't remember me at all," she insisted, "but aren't you Sam Duffy?"

He remembered the part of Brown's instructions that said, *Use your head.*

"If you say so, maybe I am."

She frowned in apparent distress "You're not sure?"

"I have amnesia, babe. Until a month ago, I'd been in a coma for ten years." He hadn't caught himself and now had to wonder if he should have called her babe.

Frances put her hand to her mouth. Looking distressed, she grabbed him by the arm. "You're coming with me! You're not getting out of my sight. Come on. There's somebody else here that you know."

He found himself outside, being dragged down the street to the very restaurant where he'd been told to go. He tried to dig for more information.

"Big coincidence that we ran into each other," he said.

"An amazing coincidence. I almost never come here. This morning, Adeline and I decided to meet here for lunch."

Now Sam was confused. Had Brown known about the women's lunch plans? If so, how?

"Who's Adeline?" he said, though he'd already been told.

Frances opened the glass door to the corner restaurant. It was a small, crowded room with two long rows of slim counters and stools, nearly all full of people eating Zabar's ultra spiffy soups and sandwiches and desserts, drinking its coffees and teas, eating its sorbets. Sam couldn't believe who was sitting on one stool, looking impatiently toward the door—Dr. Lewiston. Why had Brown sent him? But Frances approached someone else, a blond so fragile she looked like she'd break if a man tried to hold her in his arms.

These were two of the women Brown specifically didn't want him to fuck. The note hadn't been clear about whether Sam should leave other females in New York alone except the working girls. Not that Sam found the latter option repulsive. The idea excited him, in fact, and made him wonder if he had preferred whores before.

"Sam!" the blond said. She got off her stool and came to him, tears suddenly in her gray eyes, just like the first broad. "Sam Duffy!" She took both his hands, squeezed them, then kissed him on the cheek, saying, "Thank God, oh thank God!" while Frances resumed kissing him on the other, saying, "Sam! I can't believe it's you!"

Lewiston approached, looking annoyed, nervous and determined all at once, while all of Zabar's deli gaped.

"Bob! There you are. I've been waiting for you."

The women turned and looked at Lewiston. Sam noticed a slight gleam come into Frances' eyes. Nothing conspicuous, but Sam—wired for sex—noticed. He thought, *Fuck you, Lewiston.*

Sam said, "Frances, Adeline, this is—"

Lewiston interrupted. "Hi! I'm Dr. Chuck Lewiston. Bob is my patient."

Frances turned. "His name is Sam Duffy, not Bob. Is Sam ill?"

Lewiston gave a good imitation of being surprised. "Just memory loss. He's been in a coma. A month ago he woke and this is his first time out. We're celebrating," Lewiston turned to him, "and now we know your name: Sam Duffy."

Sam glared at Lewiston. He'd looked forward to not having him around. Now this. Still, Brown had said to do the logical thing.

"Yeah, guess I owe Lewiston here my life."

"Oh my! Are you all right? How do you feel? You look thinner," Adeline said.

"Fine. A little weak, but fine."

Sam saw a guarded look cross Frances' face as she turned to Lewiston. "You took care of him for ten years? Why?"

Lewiston said, "Sam was found in Central Park and practically given up for dead but we stabilized him in the emergency room, then operated. We had no idea who he was. When it was clear he'd need extended hospitalization, I brought him to EverCare, a long-term treatment facility, as a charity case." Lewiston gave a pleasant, lying smile.

Sam remembered his instructions: get on the good side of these two broads and don't let them know he was in contact with Brown.

"How wonderful of you! We thank you," Adeline said. "Let's sit together, all right?"

He noticed Frances' guarded look had gone. Now she had a sappy look that to Sam meant she was being gracious to a man she might want to bed. In Sam's mind, getting rid of Lewiston switched to a high priority.

On the way to their seats, they squeezed by the people in Zabar's deli, Sam automatically assessing them: two Asian women who sat back on their stools as they ate, sneaking peeks at everyone, their long hair falling in their laps; a chubby sandy-haired boy and his flabby father, both of them dressed in Armani or Prada which told everyone to treat them well so they wouldn't have to fight; a woman in a sari, oblivious to others as she read; a black man with his hair in a ponytail, a camera on his arm and a black T-shirt that said *The World is Ours*—an intellectual sort; an older man with a trimmed white beard, a red windbreaker, rumpled khakis and clean Dockers, trying to look inconspicuous and poor—in case Lewiston or the black photographer wanted to mug someone. Sam would have taken bets the bearded guy was the richest person here.

As the four settled onto stools, Sam wanted to chuckle. No doubt Adeline and Frances considered it slumming to eat here. Sam remembered seeing real slums, here and in other countries, that would shock the designer gloss off their cheeks. Why he'd seen them and when, he couldn't recall.

Sam noticed Frances sat across from Lewiston and began, "So you saved Sam ..." while Adeline sat across from Sam and started explaining who he was. He already knew he'd been their doorman, just not when.

Listening, he realized they lived in Brown's building. Was that how Brown knew the women would be here for lunch? Had he bugged their apartment? As Adeline talked, Sam's gaze drifted now and then to her small, pointed breasts, over to Frances' medium round ones. He wondered if Brown also had cameras in the women's apartment and envisioned what he would see, if so.

"So that's who you were," Adeline was saying when Sam looked up again. He tried to gauge from her expression if what she'd said was really true. He'd been their friend. He'd helped them.

"What did I help you do?" he asked, looking at her with open curiosity. Brown had been cagey about that part.

Adeline flushed and didn't answer. Frances took out a cell phone and pushed a memory button, saying, "I'll call Felix," then she rose, walked outside, and leaned against the glass display window as she talked.

Sam excused himself, saying he'd be right back.

In the cramped rest room he took out the cell phone he'd found in the suitcase and dialed 1 888 Mr Brown.

Chapter 14

Arona

Instead of being in the garden or at the shore, all afternoon Maggie was at her bedroom window, disturbed as she looked out at Jess. Antonella traipsed up and down the stairs bringing the laundry one piece at a time, it seemed. It gave her an excuse to peep in on Maggie each time she passed by her open door.

"Scusi, signora, va tutto bene?" Maggie heard. She turned to see Antonella standing in the doorway. She was a small woman, her hair short and naturally waved. She wore no jewelry, only dark dresses and over them her souvenir aprons. Antonella had collected one from each place she'd ever been. Today Rome's Coliseum was on the front of her torso. She held a single washcloth. Maggie was sure she'd washed a good dozen. They'd been special ordered, because Italians didn't use terry cloth squares to bathe.

"Si, Antonella. I'm bene."

Maggie was not.

Since the day she'd met with Adamo, Jess had grown progressively strange. Daily he studied his Torah Portion because she asked him to, but as soon as he learned it, he closed the book and picked up another. No longer reluctant to read, he seemed to be consuming books like peanuts. *The Aenead* by Virgil. Four hundred forty-two pages. When Jess finished it, Maggie resolved to read it, too. Devoting two hours a night, her progress in two days? Page 240. Jess's completion time had been two hours. Antonella said she'd seen deaf children at the local convent read that fast because they didn't have to sound out their words.

At least Maggie understood when Jess talked about the sack of Troy and hopped about the deck declaring, "I do not trust Greeks bearing gifts!" This past week she'd understood little else he said.

Quarks. Charms or some such thing. What were they? Physics, he'd explained, as if she'd know what that meant. He read Stephen Wolfram's *A New Kind of Science* in a day. Over a thousand pages about cellular automata, whatever they were. Jess announced the book would change the world.

Facing the now-obvious truth, Maggie had retreated from their long hours in the garden and on the deck. Felix had picked the wrong woman to mother Jess. Far from being slow in academics, like she'd feared, her son was a genius. Every gift he had was something Maggie lacked.

Physical dexterity. She watched him hang over the railing around the porticiollo, dropping bread to King Silent and the other swans. Though both feet left the ground as he balanced on his midsection, Jess was in no danger of falling.

Compassion. Nothing Jess heard or encountered altered his single-minded view of other human beings. He loved them. Adamo when he was drunk. The neighbor boy who one day threw stones over the wall. A man the newspaper said had embezzled from widows' pensions. A murderer due to be executed in the U.S.A. In their anger, their deceit, with blood dripping from their hands, Jess loved them.

Intelligence. His vast superiority to her was now plain. But in recent days Jess had begun to outdistance Rabbi Diena, asking questions the old man couldn't answer.

Was Felix right? Did Jess need instruction from minds far superior to any here? What frightened Maggie was that it had happened so fast. He'd always been agile, but today if he'd walked on water she wouldn't have been surprised—and shouldn't have been, she reminded herself. After all, he was Christ. But seeing him change before her eyes was unnerving.

She worried it was happening too fast and it made Maggie remember something Felix had warned her of. Accelerated growth, accelerated aging. All day she'd tried to remember exactly what he'd said. Something about his mitochondrial DNA being thirty-five years old at the start instead of new. It was the only part of him that came from her.

"Signora, go to him," she heard, and realized Antonella was still standing there with the washcloth. She sneezed and, unthinkingly, used it to blow her nose, then looked apologetic.

"Non importa," Maggie said.

"Go to him. Adesso."

Maggie sighed. "What will I say when he asks questions I can't answer, Antonella? Soon he's going to realize I'm ... I'm just a fool." Maggie engaged in the expressive hand waving she'd learned from the Italians. "Stupida! Non interessante! Brutta!"

"Non brutta, signora; non stupida."

"Ignorante, then!" Maggie insisted.

"No, no,"

Maggie stopped waving her hands, covered her face and said, "I'm dumb as dirt, Antonella, and that's the truth. What am I going to do?"

Antonella came to her.

Together they stared out of the window at him, their arms around each other, until Maggie realized Jess had been bent over the railing all this time. He wasn't just holding out bread to the swans, he was talking to them in some kind of despair.

She didn't remember how she got downstairs, but Maggie found herself outside, running for the porticiollo. She stepped onto it, raced across the walls to Jess and heard him say as she drew near, "Please go to her, King Silent. See if signora Morelli is well and if her baby comes."

Maggie slowed as she reached Jess. "Darling, what's the matter?"

He slid down and watched King Silent drift away. "I am worried about signora Morelli."

"Signora Morelli? But why?"

Jess lifted his face to her, his brown eyes wide with sadness, his cheeks flushed. He held out his arms and Maggie bent to him, hugged him, stroked his forehead. He had a fever. She could feel his heart beating too fast.

"Antonella!" Maggie screamed. She picked Jess up and struggled with him along the narrow wall.

"Antonella! Antonella!"

Then Antonella was there, wading into the water in the porticiollo's open end and reaching up for Jess. Maggie handed him to her and jumped down into the water, too. Together they carried him ashore, to the house and up to his room. Maggie stripped his wet clothes off and put him in his bed, while Antonella found blankets and wrapped them both.

Jess didn't protest, but he kept saying, "Mamma, Antonella, I am all right," his eyes too bright, his cheeks too warm.

He didn't look all right. Jess shivered, scanning the air. Antonella brought children's aspirin, a thermometer, an ice bag, phoned the doctor and yelled that she was making American chicken soup.

Maggie sat on the bed with Jess cradled in her lap, like always when he was sick. Only when she saw his temperature wasn't so very high and only when he'd gotten the pill down, did she pause to think. Was he sick or was it something else?

As she held him, not talking because she was too afraid to speak, too frightened to even pray, she looked around his room— a typical boy's, full of things Felix had bought him. A baseball club and catcher's mitt. Train sets. Building sets. With one he'd made a model of a chromosome. Science kits. Model airplanes and boats, remote-controlled. A variety of action figures, all weaponless. Jess's computer sat on his desk, along with his keyboard and a joystick for computer games. The scooter with which he raced along the driveway was downstairs. Books were now everywhere. Felix had given him an account to order them off the Internet.

A typical boy's room for a boy who wasn't typical at all.

"When will the doctor get here?" Maggie asked as Antonella entered with the chicken soup.

"Presto," she said. "Sua moglie said he is gone to see signora Morelli and she will call him there."

When she heard this, Maggie gazed down on Jess, who by now had fallen asleep, her cherub from heaven.

"Don't tell me something is really wrong with signora Morelli?"

They heard the high clanking of the bell downstairs. When Antonella left to answer it, Maggie hugged Jess tighter humming, *I want my Jesus to walk with me.*

Then the doctor was standing in the bedroom door. Dr. Cecagallina who Jess said had noble hair because it framed his face like a Roman helmet. He was out of breath, staring down at Jess as if something were terribly wrong.

"Signora Price, may I ask you," he said. "But has Jess been here all the time?"

Maggie trembled and held Jess closer. "Why, what's the matter?"

"Signora Morelli—"

"What about her?"

"We thought …they thought. My English is not so good. It is difficult to find the English words to say to you. She was very ill, very ill and then …"

Suddenly Adamo Morelli was in the room, weaving only slightly on his feet, and Maggie felt Jess stir in her arms.

He sat up, smiling, no sign of fever, his face no longer flushed. "Mamma! Krishna took me in his chariot to see signora Morelli! She is well!"

"Jess, Jess, sweetheart!" Maggie kissed him in wild despair. "No! What are you saying?"

Slowly, the doctor sat down on the edge of Jess's desk.

"Mamma! You should have been there! It was so fine. Krishna swept his jeweled sleeve above signora Morelli's brow and said to me:

There never was a time when I did not exist, nor you, nor signora Morelli, Jess. Nor is there any future in which we shall cease to be.

Do not cry. What is this weakness? It is beneath you.

"A serene spirit accepts pleasure and pain with an even mind, and is unmoved by either."

Maggie swallowed, terror nearly keeping her from opening her mouth. "What happened?" she asked the doctor. "What exactly?"

"She is very ill, signora Morelli. Then all at once she is not. She is fall-ed … No, she had fall-ed on the beach. Signor Morelli and his brother bring her home, sure she will be all right. But she is not all right. I come. I am there. I see her holding her—" He turned to Antonella. "Come dite lo stomaco?"

"Stomach!" Antonella replied impatiently.

"Oh! Si, si."

"Let me translate," Adamo said, looking down on Jess.

Dr. Cecagallina spoke.

Adamo said, "She held her stomach and screamed in pain. Then, presto!" He snapped his fingers. "She screamed no more. Her pain was over. She was well. She had recovered. She and the baby were fine. Signora Morelli told me—" He paused and looked uncertain, questioning Dr. Cecagallina about what he'd just said.

"What, what?" Maggie pleaded.

Adamo continued, "Of course, you must remember she was not herself, but signora Morelli said that she was certainly never ill. She declared she was well all the time. She declared she was not in her bed where Dr. Cecagallina found her. Her husband says yes, but she says no.

"And I also say no," Adamo added, "because I was at the beach. I tried to catch her before she fell." His eyes were black with despair.

Adamo continued the translation, "She tells the doctor she didn't fall and she made no screams of pain, however—signora Price, believe me—I heard them with my own good ears. I heard her cry aloud; I saw her gripped in very great pains. But signora Morelli told me she was not there in her bed when I came."

Dr. Cecagallina stood and went to Jess. He spoke in Italian. Adamo and Antonella gathered round to discuss the correct translation of his words.

Adamo frowned, but said with certainty, "Signora Morelli declares that she was on the water with the swans and the swans were with your son."

Chapter 15

Felix finished packing for his trip to Italy. Maggie had refused to speak to him for a month and it was time to get matters in hand.

He sat at his bedroom desk to write a long letter full of stories, jokes and puzzles to entertain Ariel while he was gone. He wrote such a letter and hid it in her room where she would find it whenever he had to travel without her. It only happened when he went to Arona. Felix no longer received invitations to address or even attend prestigious conferences around the world. Hospitals and private clinics no longer phoned him to consult. If it weren't for his wealth, the Rossis would have vanished from the respected side of the New York social scene. Few of them wanted to be photographed with a mad scientist.

Adeline and Frances were still accepted at major charity and social events—if with unmasked sympathy. New York had decided it wasn't their fault that Felix was insane.

Except for puttering in his lab now and then, Felix had immersed himself in full-time fatherhood and treasured it. He often felt a divine plan had emptied his life so Ariel could fill it.

When the phone rang, he was drawing a cartoon of a little girl on a horse above the words: *Ariel in Vermont*. Their trip had been glorious, a living idyll to be treasured for a lifetime. Instead of staying a weekend, they'd kept Ariel out of school an entire week. The only blot on their ten days of uninterrupted joy was the knowledge that he'd have to separate Maggie and Jess.

He couldn't avoid it anymore. Maggie had become fanatic in her obsession with the idea that Jess was a clone of Jesus. She was warping the boy and would ruin him if Felix didn't intervene.

Felix answered the ringing phone. He listened to Frances's excited voice, said, "I'll be there," then hung up and stumbled to the ebony prie dieu in the hall, absolved of his greatest sin.

Sam Duffy was alive.

Felix dropped to his knees beneath the silver crucifix, murmuring snatches of prayers, "Our Father, which art in heaven, hallowed be thy name! Spirit of wisdom and understanding, enlighten our minds to perceive the mysteries of the universe in relation to eternity."

Felix crossed himself and bowed his head, fighting for self-control in case Rave was watching on the hidden cameras. Sam was alive, not murdered, his blood spilled in Central Park by those who would have killed Jess in Maggie's womb. Sam hadn't died as a result of Felix's single-minded pursuit of a Jesus clone.

Many times since that night Felix had tried to understand why Brown, a wealthy and powerful man, would fear a child—even one who might have the genes of Christ.

The night Jess was born had seemed biblical in its horror and its overwhelming joy. Maggie was Mary, giving birth under Glen Span Arch, where they'd sheltered from pursuers. Brown was Herod, trying to slaughter her child.

In this frenzied self-delusion, Felix had brought a clone of Max Segre into the world. Felix rose to call downstairs for a limo, then stopped. The cars and drivers belonged to the building's limo pool and Brown was in control of everyone who worked here. He couldn't let a limo take him to Sam. Jess didn't have the genes of Jesus, but Brown didn't know that. If he knew Sam was alive, Brown would certainly want to question him to verify the death of the clone.

Felix grabbed a light jacket, his keys, and took the elevator down to the lobby.

Rave opened the door, his expression betraying only the slightest mocking line around his mouth that to Felix always said, "I've seen your sister naked, chump."

"Shall I call a limo for you, sir?" Rave asked as Felix stepped outside the glass door and onto the carpet beneath the building's awning.

"No thanks, Rave." Felix looked up and down the street and

sighed. "It's a nice day. I think I'll walk a while then catch a cab."

Rave tipped his hat. "Of course, sir. Enjoy your walk."

Felix forced his feet to stroll down Fifth Avenue. On 90th Street he turned left, ran one block to Madison and flagged a cab. In no time it was pulling up to Zabar's glass and red brick facade.

Felix got out and as he paid the driver, he heard his nickname, "Flix! It's him. It's really him!" Frances and Adeline rushed to him, one excitedly rubbing his back and the other pulling his arm.

He told the driver to keep the change, turned to them and as they exchanged nervous hugs, he asked, "You're absolutely sure?"

"Absolutely! Flix, it's Sam!" Frances insisted.

"And he doesn't remember?"

"Nothing!" Adeline said and he could tell by her amazed expression she was convinced it was true.

As Felix opened Zabar's restaurant door and walked in, a man rose from one of the stools. No doubt about it. It was Sam. Thinner, yes. Older. Still it was the man who'd done the impossible for them—months of guarding Maggie, months of making them all safe in Felix's and Frances' cottage on Cliffs Landing, months of keeping Brown off their trail. When Sam first barged into Felix's Cliffs Landing home, he and Felix had fought.

Now Felix ignored the crowd of Zabar's lunchtime customers, walked up and put his arms around Sam, patted his back, held him, unable to do anything but hug the man who all these years they thought was dead.

When Felix stepped back, Sam seemed vastly amused. Grinning, he held out his hand and said, "Guess I don't have to ask whether you and I were friends. Hi, Felix. I sure wish I could remember you, pal."

Felix sat down. "Isn't there anything, Sam? You don't remember—" Felix stopped, realizing he'd almost said, *Maggie*, It was too soon for that. For their safety, Maggie and Jess must stay dead to the world. He couldn't talk about them until he learned where Sam had been all this time.

Sam was grinning strangely. "What were you about to say?" he asked.

"Nothing, it wasn't important. Tell me everything. What happened to you?"

Felix was introduced to Dr. Lewiston and instantly liked him. They exchanged information about their medical schooling. Felix had a dual MD-PhD, Harvard 1976. Lewiston had an MD, Harvard 1980. He learned the story of the paramedics and the emergency room, then about EverCare and felt grateful to Lewiston.

"But why was there an obituary in the paper?" Felix asked.

Lewiston said, "Another man was found dead in the park that night. He must have had Sam's wallet. Maybe he shot you, Sam, then stole from you. There was plenty of money in that wallet, I heard."

Felix made no comment. Sam certainly had money on him that night. Felix had withdrawn a large sum so they could resettle before Brown found them, and then later disappear. Felix had given some to Sam for fake IDs, a moving van, and such.

"Sounds like maybe there were two thieves and one turned on the other," Sam added. "I wonder what happened to my wallet? I could use some money."

Lewiston shrugged.

Felix said, "You won't have to worry about money, Sam."

Though they huddled around the counter like a group of old friends—Frances and Lewiston on one side, Adeline, Felix and Sam on the other—the conversation deteriorated in awkward pauses. What would they do now? What would Sam do now? He didn't know, he said. Since he'd just awakened and this was his first day out, he had no plans to speak of.

Felix should have been the one to fill the awkward pauses but he couldn't. They couldn't take Sam to the building and let Brown see him because Sam had betrayed Brown, who didn't seem the sort to forget a grudge. They couldn't put Sam up at their place across the Hudson on Cliffs Landing because Brown knew about it, too. Felix thought it better for all of them if Brown continued thinking Sam was dead, at least for now.

Then Felix remembered Maggie. She, most of all, should know Sam was alive. It was for her sake, not theirs, that Sam had risked his life. Also, Sam's reappearance might lessen her obsessions about Jess.

During one of the awkward pauses, Felix stood and held up his cell phone, saying, "I'll—I'll just be a minute. I need to make a call," and they all nodded saying "certainly" and "sure" as if grateful for something to say. Outside on the corner of 80th and Broadway he dialed Maggie in Arona on his cell that scrambled calls, thinking of how to make sure she didn't hang up this time.

"Pronto."

"Come sta, Antonella. "

"Molto bene, signor Rossi! Grazie."

"Posso parlare a Maggie? È importante."

"Si, Signore. Un attimo."

"Grazie."

He paced the sidewalk.

"Felix? Oh, my lord. Am I ever glad you called."

"What is it, Maggie?"

"It's Jess!"

Felix stopped pacing.

"Felix, I was right all along! We can't wait anymore. He's upped and made his first miracle."

"What?"

"He saved signora Morelli from horrible, horrible pain."

"What? How?"

"Same way Jesus did, Felix. How else?" She sounded frantic.

"Calm down, Maggie. Just calm down. Now tell me what happened."

He listened, frowning, not seeing passersby or hearing yellow New York taxis honking as they passed.

"Maggie, now think carefully," he said. "Had signora Morelli seen Jess feed the swans before?"

"Well, yes, I guess. Yes, she did. You mean she could have just dreamed him doing it or imagined it? But how do you explain Jess knowing she was sick?"

"Did Jess swim at any point or go out in his boat? If he went out far enough he could see the public beach and any commotion,

I think. Did he know signora Morelli enough to recognize her?"

"Yes."

"He could have seen her fall and been upset by it."

Maggie grew silent, then, "I guess that's logical. Yes, you're right, Felix. I guess it could have happened like that. Just in case, I sent Antonella to talk to signora Morelli and I talked to the doctor and begged them both not to say anything about this to anybody, especially strangers. It could endanger Jess really bad. And they agreed."

"You mean they both believe Jess worked a miracle?"

"What else could they think?"

"That's dangerous for Jess."

"I know. Which is why I made them promise—"

"We can't count on two people in a small—"

"Four people. Carlo Morelli the husband; his wife; his brother Adamo; and the doctor. I can count on them, Felix. They won't spread a story like this to anybody who might hurt us. I've come to know these people. What worries me is the Krishna part. That's what I warned you about."

Felix sighed. "We'll discuss it when I come."

"And what was it you said about accelerated ag—"

"Maggie, there's something I need to tell you. Are you sitting down?"

"Do I need to be?"

"Yes."

There was a pause, during which he crossed the street.

"Okay, Felix, go ahead."

"All right." Felix swallowed. He saw a traffic light turn yellow, jiggled the latch on the pinkish-beige *New York Observer* newspaper dispenser, trying to find words.

"Maggie brace yourself."

"I'm braced, Felix, go ahead."

"Sam's not dead."

He heard the phone drop.

"Maggie? Maggie?"

"I'm here. What did you say?"

"I've just seen him. Sam's alive."

He told her everything and she listened without interrupting. When he finished, she murmured, "Bring him."

"Oh, Maggie. No! He doesn't remember. Don't get your hopes up. He doesn't know us."

"Bring him, Felix."

"I'm sorry, Maggie. No, I won't. I'll do no such thing. It's too soon."

"Bring him, bring him, bring him!" Maggie said, her voice rising in an urgent plea.

"No! I'm not going to do it so there's no point in asking."

Her tone became angry. "Bring him here to me, Felix Rossi or I'll never speak to you again as long there's breath in my body. Bring Sam to me! Bring him, bring him. Do you hear me? I don't want no *ifs, ands or buts*. Don't give me none of your scientific logic, do you hear? As if logic could have a single thing to do with this. It's a miracle. Sam belongs here now. Jess made a miracle and now here's Sam and that's another one, I tell you. God is talking to us, Felix, and you can stop up your ears all you want. Me, I'm listening with the ears my spirit has. I'm seeing with the eyes of my soul. You bring Sam Duffy here to us, Felix Rossi. God in heaven, bring him. Don't darken this door if he's not by your side. Just bring him. Merciful heaven, if—"

As he listened, Felix realized the only prudent thing was to get Jess off to boarding school immediately if people in the village were starting to focus on him. In the meanwhile, Maggie and Jess should have someone other than Antonella there, someone who might get Maggie's thoughts back into the real world.

Felix raised his eyes and looked across the street. He saw Sam wave from the window of Zabar's.

Chapter 16

As soon as Sam's taxi pulled into Brown's private garage, he got out and went to the elevator, telling the driver to wait. In his call to Brown from Zabar's small restroom, Sam had been told to return to the penthouse immediately.

The butler led him to the library and the room was somehow familiar to Sam. Mahogany bookshelves; a carved desk made of old, rare wood, a big crystal on it; computers with access to information Sam suspected not too many others had.

He saw a large black book on the desk. It looked like a photo album. Instead of sitting on the leather couch, Sam went to the desk and opened the album. He was pretty surprised by what he saw. Newspapers articles. Ten years old. About cloning in America. From the London Times. He flipped the page, then the next. American newspapers now. Australian, Canadian, Italian, French. All of them talking about a Jesus clone. What in hell was that?

Sam took the album and sat on the couch, reading. The story was incredible. Felix Rossi, whom he'd just left, had tried to clone Jesus Christ. The news had set the world on fire. Then, just like that, no more clone. It was dead.

"You're more inquisitive than you once were."

Sam looked up.

Brown stepped from behind one of his bookshelves. He'd been there all along.

"Is that right?" Sam pointed to the album. "This is some helluva story."

"Yes." Brown came to his desk and sat down. He wore a white shirt. Gray slacks. Hell of a weird looking gold ring on his hand. "What's happened since we spoke?"

"Like I said, Felix wants to take me on a trip; I don't know where."

"What did he say, exactly?"

"Uh, let's see. 'I'd like you to come with me on a trip. I still have an old passport of yours under the name Chuck O'Malley.'"

Brown's eyebrows went up. "What did you say?"

"I said something like, 'A fake passport? What were we up to, Felix'?"

"What else?"

"He said he'd tell me later, but he thought the man who did it would update the passport for us today. He said he'd get it taken care of, but I had to agree not to discuss this with anyone. I said, 'Scout's honor. Not a soul.' Did I do right?"

"Utterly. Tell me the plan."

Sam looked at his watch. "Three hours from now, I'm supposed to be at New Jersey's Teterboro Airport where Felix and I are going to board a private jet for parts unknown. Do you want me to go?"

"Yes. Try to find out if Rossi's also traveling under an assumed name."

Sam closed the album. He slid it back onto Brown's desk. "You don't think the clone is dead, do you?"

"I don't know," Brown said. He seemed to want Sam to figure this.

"That's where I come in. I'm your only ticket to Rossi, and Rossi knows the truth about the clone. If it's alive, it's a ten-year-old kid, by now, assumedly a boy. Let me guess. You want me to kidnap him and bring him here so you can benefit from his miraculous powers."

Brown gave a half smile that to Sam looked creepy. "If the boy's alive, I want you to kill him."

"Whoa!" Sam said. "Well, well, well, you get right to the point." He rubbed the expensive leather on the couch, thinking. "I see you're not scared of selling your soul to the devil."

"There is no devil."

Sam looked up, remembering the ones who sang to him. "You seem to be pretty sure."

Brown sat back in his leather chair, eyeing Sam. "Charles Manson."

"Who? Oh yeah, him. The Helter-Skelter guy. What about him?"

"He's the proof there is no devil. His father abandoned Manson before his birth to a teenaged prostitute. His mother abused him when she wasn't trying to give him away. He spent his childhood in foster homes, juvenile detention homes and prisons. Yet Manson had the intelligence and charisma of a Gandhi, a Churchill. A devil wasn't required to warp Manson's gifts. Human frailty was enough."

"So I guess you don't believe in God, either, if you're ready to kill a clone of his son."

Brown stared at Sam with unreadable eyes. "I do believe in God."

Sam's mouth dropped open. "You gotta be kidding."

"Anyone of true intelligence knows there is a God, though certainly not of the kind worshiped in mosques, synagogues and churches. The one who made this world is a creator of patterns and possibilities. He or she or it created phenomena: opposites, consciousness, personality, a cause and effect system that churns reality out in cooperation with and response to human minds. We ourselves are the ghosts in God's machine."

"Oh yeah? Well, suppose he gets mad at you for killing his kid's clone?"

"That's a possible, if unlikely, result of what I will do. Are you saying you have religious reservations?"

Sam snorted. "Hell, no! All I have is money reservations, friend. If I'm going to the devil, I'm going rich. I'll need another million bucks."

Brown stood. "There's a bank account in your name at Chase Manhattan. It has a million in it now. Don't run off with the funds. I'd find you. It wouldn't be pleasant. Another million will be deposited when I know the boy is dead."

Sam stood and held out his hand. "You've got a fucking deal."

Brown said, "I'll take the gun. You can't get it through customs."

"What if I run into trouble?"

"When your flight lands, phone and tell me where you are. I'll see you have a gun. Report back every 48 hours. I'll be nearby in case you require support." Brown opened a drawer and handed Sam a sheet. "Here are the rest of your instructions. Read the page and leave it here. How do you feel?"

Sam looked up. It was a serious question. Brown wanted to make sure his errand boy was fit for the task. The fact was, Sam felt tired, but there was too much money at stake to admit that. "Compared to the past ten years, I guess I feel great."

"Good."

Brown rose. "I've discovered a new mineral deposit in Siberia, Sam."

"Oh yeah?"

"Early specimens outshine Columbian emeralds, the world's best. What you discover may be more important, though."

Brown left.

Sam read the page of instructions, shook his head at Brown's cold-bloodedness, but decided he didn't give a damn. He returned to his waiting taxi and asked it to take him to Central Park West. He got out at west 101st, entered Central Park through Boys' Gate and got in line with the Jesus freaks heading for Glen Span Arch. That's where rumor said the clone was born ten years ago, according to the papers. That's where Sam had been shot ten years ago.

The line wound past the end of *The Pool*, which was full of mallards. Beneath a footbridge, the water cascaded down massive rocks into a stream that ran beneath Glen Span Arch. Its great, moody boulders formed a natural cathedral for this second supposed birthplace of Jesus Christ.

It was baloney, of course, yet Sam felt curious when the line reached the arch. He went beneath it and saw a cheap statue of The Virgin Mary with a blue-eyed child. It was roped off in a rocky cave. If a kid had been born there, the mother would have had to wade across the stream and perch on a rocky ledge. He looked down on the sidewalk where he stood and decided if he'd had a vote he would have laid her on the ground right here, against the slight recess in the wall.

Had he really been involved and, if so, whose side had he been on? Felix's or Brown's. Felix claimed Sam had been his friend. Was that true? If so, had a mugger really shot him or had someone else? Obviously he was in no danger from Brown now, but what about ten years ago?

It didn't matter because Sam knew whose side he was on today. Brown had offered him two million dollars. Rossi? Not a definite dime.

Still he wondered who had shot him.

All around him people knelt, saying their rosaries and their prayers as if this were a sacred grotto. Though the logistics of the birth were flatly impossible, they still believed. Brown believed, too, if in a weird way. What was the reason for this God machine Brown thought we were all ghosts in? Brown had seemed a smart man. Yet, in the end, he thought pretty much like this crackpot crowd.

Sam backed away and leaned against the wall opposite the roped-off virgin and child. There was nothing familiar here. Not a shred, not an ounce of memory had returned. He looked at the waterfall to his left, the boulders, the woods to the right, just to be sure, quietly whistling *Too-ra loo-ra-loo-ral* to himself. He granted that it was peaceful under here and he especially liked the sound of the waterfall. He could almost pretend there were no crowds. No one paid attention to him standing there except a pair of pigeons. They ambled over, pecked at the sidewalk where he stood, and settled at his feet.

"Dumb birds," he whispered.

Sam looked at his watch, left the park, and flagged another cab for the trip to Teterboro. As it crossed the Hudson River, he looked back and realized something was missing from the New York skyline.

"What happened to the damn Trade Center?" he said.

The driver said, "You kidding me, right? Where ya been? On Mars?"

"Kinda. I've got amnesia."

"Terrorists. They hijacked two airplanes, flew them into the towers and killed a few thousand people."

"Shit!" Sam sat back. "What a world."

He saw the cliffs of the upper Jersey shore, heard the tires thumping across the joinings of the bridge and forgot about the Trade Center because he was enjoying being over the water. He began to feel intensely nostalgic, for what he didn't know, and looked toward the Jersey docks, wishing he had a cold beer in his hand. Brown told Sam he'd been a merchant seaman. Maybe that was why.

"Hey, driver," he said. "There any bars down by those docks?"

"Jersey docks?"

"There ought to be some place where the sailors go."

"Yeah, yeah. I know one or two. You want I should take you?"

"No time to visit, but if you could show me …"

The driver patted the dashboard. "As long as we're on the meter, pal, I'll take you anywhere."

"Thanks." Sam sat back, anticipating. Exactly what, he wasn't sure.

Soon they were driving along the Jersey shore, warehouses all around, big container ships being unloaded at piers. The driver turned down a small street and there was a bar. A working girl tottered toward it on sharp-toed high heels and tugged at her short skirt.

"Oh, hurt me, baby," Sam whispered.

"You want I should stop?"

"Definitely," Sam said.

The cab pulled up beside her at an alley and she smiled and leaned into the window he'd rolled down. Like twin water-filled balloons, her breasts rolled pendulously in.

"Wanna party?" she said in a *Joisey* accent.

Any boobs were better than none. Sam's hands answered by squeezing them.

"Hey, not in here for Chrissake!" the driver said. "Get out. I'll park and wait."

"Nah, I got no time," Sam repeated as the girl withdrew. "Listen, baby, how much just to show me what you've got?"

She smacked her gum, sizing him up, then set her jaw and said, "Ace-deuce, honey."

Sam handed thirty dollars out the window.

The working girl yanked up her halter, then hiked up her skirt. She was naked underneath.

"Hey, not on the damn street!" the driver yelled. "Use the freakin alley."

Sam reached out and put his fingers where the rest of him couldn't go.

"That's it, I'm outa here!" the driver yelled at them.

"All right, let's go." As the cab pulled away, Sam memorized the explicit view.

———

Maggie was well aware how silly it would seem if anyone knew she was acting like a character from an opera. Cio Cio San, in this case. *Madama Butterfly*, her favorite.

All Italians seemed to know all Italian operas and thanks to Antonella, Maggie knew this one best, particularly the aria *Un Bel Di*, "One Fine Day," and the famous humming song. The story went like this. Cio Cio San, a Japanese girl from a respectable family, marries an American naval officer in a Japanese ceremony and when he is called back to duty, has his child. She faithfully awaits his return for years. Then one fine day, *un bel di*, she sees his ship on the horizon. It's called the Abraham Lincoln. She dresses up and waits all night. That's when the humming comes. Late next morning he arrives, bringing an American woman. He wants to take his son to America to be raised by her, his real wife. Imagine that. Naturally, Cio Cio San kills herself, which, for the Japanese back then, was an honorable thing to do in such circumstances.

Maggie loved the part where Cio Cio San and her maid stripped the garden bare of blossoms and sprinkled them in the house so when he came his feet would walk on flowers. It was so tender and so sad. Poor girl took every bloom off her cherry trees for him.

Thank goodness Maggie had sense enough not to do that. The hortensia were still on the bushes by the stone steps and the roses were still on the bower above the garden wall.

But Maggie had done everything else Cio Cio San did. It must be how women were. She'd sent Antonella shopping for the freshest fruits, vegetables and fish, the most aromatic cheeses, the finest sausages. Trays of delicious things sat in the refrigerator, ready to be baked, run under a flame or eaten chilled. Sparkling glass pitchers awaited the fresh juice they would make. The pasta maker awaited eggs and flour. She and Antonella had scrubbed the house until their knuckles were raw, changed all the linens on all beds, all towels, beat rugs, cleaned windows.

Meanwhile Jess, fully recovered and back to acting like a normal ten-year-old, had pestered them with questions, "Who is coming, Mamma? Is it just Uncle Felix? Who is coming, Antonella?" He knew they never prepared for Felix's arrival like this.

At first, Maggie had avoided answering as Jess followed them around, trying to help but only getting in the way. Finally, right before his bedtime, she told him Felix was bringing a friend in the morning. That only brought on more questions because Jess knew they never had strangers as guests. It took forever to get him to lie down and turn the lights out.

As soon as he did, Maggie soaked in a tub full of perfumed bath salts, gave her face an apricot scrub, patted on a mud mask. She washed her hair, curled it with a hot iron and then put the curls in curlers to make sure her hairdo stayed in place more than a minute. Before turning in, Antonella, who was no fool, slathered Maggie's hands with *vaselina* and slid cotton gloves on. It would soften her hands overnight. Their visitor, signor Duffy, probably liked soft hands, Antonella said and smiled. Maggie was too shy to confirm what Antonella plainly knew.

Under her pillow Maggie had tucked the beautiful silken nightgown Frances bought for her birthday one year. Not that she would put it on anytime soon for a man she hadn't seen in ten years. When the time came, she would act like a lady as she'd done all her life. Her mind and her principles would stay in control.

It was her heart acting the fool like this. Curls. Perfumed bath salts. Silken nightgowns. Listening to the opera about Cio Cio San. It was the arrival of the only man who'd ever loved her—just in the nick of time to save her from losing Jess. Sam would stand up to Felix just as he'd done before.

Like Cio Cio San, Maggie couldn't sleep. At midnight she left the house and crept down to the lake with a tape player and a tape.

Instead of sitting on the deck of the lake house, Maggie dragged a deck chair down to the shore and placed it where the Weeping Willow's branches dropped like a curtain into the water. When she wasn't pacing along the shore, that's where she listened to Cio Cio San sing, though it was hard pushing the tape buttons with the gloves on.

Un bel dì, vedremo	One fine day, we shall see
Levarsi un fil di fumo	A thread of smoke rising
Sull'estremo confin del mare	Over the horizon
E poi la nave appare	And then the ship will appear

Maggie had been surprised when Antonella told her it was a black woman named Leontyne Price singing. Antonella must have picked it out just for her. It made Maggie feel closer to the music, knowing a woman like herself had sung Cio Cio San.

Leontyne's voice was so full of yearning, even if you didn't know what *Un Bel Di* meant, you could make a direct translation from the music and guess a woman was dreaming of a future day.

Waiting, waiting, waiting.

Maggie was waiting, too. Behind the Weeping Willow, walking along the shore, out under the lanterns in the porticiollo's crows' nests, looking at the lights blink off on the hills, looking beyond the Gola to the north where Sam and Felix would come from, and listening to the humming song. That part was only violins, a harp and voices humming.

That was all. No singing. Just humming. If you didn't know

Cio Cio San was waiting up all night, the music told you. It was haunting, the sweetest sound Maggie had ever heard—other than Jess's voice, his laughter—this music Puccini wrote to tell how Cio Cio San stayed awake for love.

It reminded Maggie of the beautiful *Song of Songs* and how right Jess had been in his interpretation of it:

> By night on my bed I sought
> him whom my soul loveth:
> I sought him, but I found him not.
> I will rise now, and go about
> the city in the streets, and in the
> broad way will seek him whom
> my soul loveth:

All night Maggie stayed away from her pristine bed and played the humming song by the lakeshore, thanking the air for being air, the night for being night. He whom her soul loved was almost here. She watched the crescent moon drag stars across the sky, sweeping it empty for the sun.

Chapter 17

Sam sat straight in the plush leather seat, smiling at Felix, or trying to, until the Gulfstream Jet took off. He wasn't tired, he was exhausted. He couldn't reveal it and cause Felix to do something stupid like delay the flight and take him, a recent coma patient, back to Lewiston and EverCare, where Brown had documented Sam's phony stay.

Felix had only reluctantly accepted Lewiston's medical okay for the trip.

Now that they were in this jet, no one but the two of them, it crossed Sam's mind that Felix had to be filthy rich, too. He swept down streets and through rooms like Lord Byron, and he wasn't pretending. It was if he'd always owned the world. He looked the part, his black hair a bit long but well bred, his shirts and suits slightly loose in that *I'm-a-lord* carelessly rich-as-hell style.

Even this plane fit the image. Sam was six foot two but he hadn't had to crouch when he came aboard. He thought he'd get to drop right into his seat but he'd first had to follow Felix past a long credenza and a table that had four plush upholstered seats before they arrived here in the section with the full-length designer sofa.

Sam was dying to go over and lie on it. Instead, he sat across from Felix in a blue leather seat that was as big as an easy chair and sipped his drink like Felix did. He thought if he gulped it, he'd pass out.

He nodded at Felix and looked up and down this long damned plane. It seated twelve in abject comfort—fourteen if they squeezed in on the sofa.

He waited until the plane rose above the clouds, the weather, and commercial traffic routes and he saw the curvature of the earth. Then Sam let himself yawn like hell and slapped his cheeks to keep from feeling dizzy.

"You're that tired?" Felix said, dropping his paper and staring at Sam.

"Yeah, I guess."

Felix was on his feet. "You'd better lie down and let me take a look."

"You're an MD?"

"Yes. Now let me examine you."

Thank God! Sam thought and gratefully rose and eased himself down on the gray sofa.

Felix helped him out of his K-Mart looking jacket and shirt and then retrieved and opened a huge medical bag.

"Damn, what's in that?" Sam said, looking down.

It was a black leather case, which opened to give access to two upper compartments and a lower main one.

Felix smiled. "Yes, only paramedics use such bags, nowadays, or doctors with rural practices. I bought and equipped it for—"

Sam pretended he didn't notice Felix had stopped in mid-sentence and flushed. *For the clone, Felix,* Sam thought. *Your big-assed medical bag is for the clone. On every visit, you're prepared for the worst.* Sam wondered if clone illnesses were like everybody else's, not that he gave a damn.

Felix cleared his throat and started examining Sam who coughed when asked to, Felix's stethoscope on his chest or back.

Sam felt relieved when Felix sat down again and said he seemed all right. Sam didn't want to slip back into a coma again. The years of emptiness frightened him. The amnesia did, too, though he hid this from everyone. He couldn't say he liked Felix; he was too fucking weird, trying to clone Jesus and all, but he didn't get under his skin like Lewiston had.

Sam lay on the sofa, sipping scotch, looking at space above, earth below, and fighting to stay awake so he could figure this all out.

If Brown was right, there was some kid running around thinking he was the Son of God. There was some broad who thought she was Mary. If Brown was right, Felix was dumb as shit to have let him on this plane. Sam almost hoped Felix had something up his sleeve because it didn't feel right for things to be this easy. It felt like he was about to be sucker-punched.

Maybe they'd trusted him. Maybe they still did.

Sam let the concept roll around in his mind. It felt alien. Trust. What the hell was that? A euphemism for incomplete information. You either knew or you didn't know. Trust was the first step in being sucker-punched.

A fruit and cheese spread appeared on the bar at the front of the plane, put there by the co-pilot slash steward. What a job description. Wanted: supersonic jet pilot, good with canapés. Felix filled a saucer and brought some to Sam and, when he popped the cheese into his mouth, the musky aroma filled his nostrils and he was wide awake. For a moment the taste was as good as sex.

Sam remembered the last view he'd had of the working girl. He excused himself and went to the john to jerk off. He resented having to do it. He had a hunch that in his other life, he'd always had a ready supply of pulsating twats.

Still Sam felt reasonably satisfied when they came down out of space and he found himself in Turin, Italy. His respect for Felix rose when he caught a cab and deposited Sam at the small Hotel Victoria in the heart of town, not at the Rossi family home, which, Brown had told him, was on the hill behind the River Po.

After phoning Brown to give his location, Sam unpacked his suitcase in the pleasant room and waited. In less than an hour, there was a knock at the door. Hotel staff bringing a package delivered for him. Sam tipped the boy and opened the package. Two boxes wrapped in paper lay inside. The first held vials of medicine, one for Sam to take—Plan A. Another to give to the kid if Plan A failed. The second box contained a gun, as Brown promised.

On the flight over, Sam had put two and two together and realized why Brown sent Lewiston to Zabar's—so he'd be a known quantity to Felix. Still, Sam disliked the prospect of seeing Lewiston again and hoped to think of a way around it.

He also hoped to find a way to turn the tables just enough to get money out of Felix, while he was getting it out of Brown.

Sam lay drowsily on the plump mattress in his cozy room at the family-run Hotel Victoria, the lights on and the curtains open, remembering Coral and the working girl.

———

When Felix's taxi entered the arcaded Piazza Vittorio, the dome of the church of Gran Madre di Dio loomed on the green hill beyond. The cab crossed the River Po and ascended behind the church to the Strada Sei Ville, a gated private road of homes perched on the emerald hillside.

It stopped in front of a black iron gate that had been turned into a work of art. Its thin bars leaned and staggered in irregular groups, joined by large graceful designs, as if a flock of captive birds had broken through and left their wings behind.

Felix reached out the window, inserted a card and the gates opened. Down a short driveway, the taxi stopped in front of the Fubini family home—his long-dead parents' original home. Had it not been for the Nazis and World War II, he and Frances would have been born in this grand villa, been raised as Italian Jews instead of Catholic New Yorkers.

The night the Nazis came, his aunt and his parents weren't here. They were out at the little villa in Arona where Maggie and Jess now lived. Warned by the village baker, they fled on foot into the woods on a cold, bitter night. His mother, seven months' pregnant, lost the child. His father, traumatized, resolved never again to expose his family to a danger so easily avoided. On that night he abandoned their Jewish identity and they emigrated to America as Italian Catholics.

They had escaped, but left their wings behind.

Simone and Silvia were among the lucky ones who lived out the war in hiding and regained their property afterward. In back of this wonderful iron gate, the Fubini family's Jewishness had survived. Felix got out of the taxi and looked up to the imposing villa where, all these years, Uncle Simone had awaited his brother's return. It never came. His parents had died in an auto accident. Simone had embraced Felix and Frances in their father's stead.

The doors opened and Aunt Silvia came out, arms wide, calling, "Ah, Felix, mio caro nipote! You are here!" They met halfway up the double staircase. She smelled of rose and olive when she kissed both his cheeks.

"It's wonderful to see you, Silvia. Is Simone here?"

A man with a neatly trimmed salt-and-pepper beard and round, smiling eyes appeared between the great double doors. He looked so much like Felix's father.

"Where else would I be but here in my own home, nephew?" He held out his arms and Felix embraced him.

Ignoring Felix's protest, Silvia picked up his suitcase and carried it inside. Simone and Felix entered behind her and the great double doors closed.

As soon as they did, Felix whispered, "How quickly can we leave, Uncle?"

"Leave?" Silvia whispered back. "Won't you at least have a little pasta? *Devi mangiare!*"

Grinning, Simone gestured broadly as if preparing to state the flatly obvious. "My good wife. Why do you worry? Our Maggie will feed him until he cannot move!"

Silvia laughed. She handed Felix's suitcase to him and kissed him goodbye.

In the cellar of the house, Uncle Simone opened a hidden door and led Felix down a now-familiar corridor that—until Felix came with Maggie—hadn't been used since the Nazi occupation.

They paused at a small table that held a recorder. Felix took the sheet Simone handed him then sat and recorded his part of conversations written there. In Felix's absence, Simone and Silvia would play this tape for Brown's spies, assuming there were still any here. If they were and they wanted to listen, they'd have to point laser-based directional microphones at the windowpanes to eavesdrop from outside because Simone had made sure not a single bug was installed in his home. By this ruse, Felix's visits to

Maggie had eluded Theomund Brown's detection all these years.

When Felix finished, they proceeded to the end of the corridor where Simone knocked on a wooden wall. It opened and he shook hands with a man who lived in another house on the hillside. He was about Felix's height and had the same dark hair. He handed Simone a set of keys, exchanged clothes with Felix then entered the corridor going toward Simone's house. A few moments later Felix and Simone were in the neighbor's van, driving down Strada Sei Ville. As they passed the Fubini villa, Felix glimpsed Silvia through a window, talking to a man. To all appearances, Felix was still in his uncle's home.

They reached Arona in just under an hour. Felix got out and opened the gate to the yellow villa and his uncle drove the car in. He closed the gate and followed the car along the driveway to the front of the villa, which faced the lake.

Maggie was there when the car stopped.

She glared at Felix then her eyes sparkled as she searched the car. If Felix wasn't mistaken, she had polish on her nails, lipstick on her lips, and she'd done something to her hair. As he drew closer, he could smell the lavender water she used.

She ran to the car, looked in, and when she saw it was only Simone, the disappointment on her face almost broke Felix's heart. He would have to talk to her, prepare her, get her to be sensible.

"Hi, Simone," she said. "Welcome." She looked at Felix. "Hello, Felix. You and I need to have a talk. First, where's Sam?"

Simone gazed at Felix in surprise. "Who is this Sam?"

Felix replied, "He's the one who saved Maggie that night—"

"But I thought—" Simone began.

"No, it turns out he's not dead. We ran into him. He's lost his memory. He doesn't know us."

"Ah, too bad," Simone said.

Maggie stood there, her arms crossed. "Where is he, Felix?"

"I left him at a hotel in Turin."

She reached for the door. "All right, then. Drive me there."

"Uncle Felix, Uncle Simone!" It was Jess. He appeared at the top of the steps that led to the lake. "Uncle Felix!" Jess ran to him. Felix lifted him off the ground. "Oh my! How you've grown, Jess, in these few weeks. How you've grown."

Simone chuckled and inclined his head toward them. "You see how I am ignored?"

"I should think so," Felix said, "You get to see him all the time. I don't."

"True, true," Simone said.

"Ciao, Uncle Simone," Jess called.

"Ciao, Jess." Simone turned to Maggie. "Shall we go in and leave these two lovers alone for awhile? Perhaps you have some limonata to slake an old man's thirst?"

"Jess," Felix said. "I have a feeling that right about now a brand new sailboat, perhaps a Mirror Dinghy, is heading toward your porticiollo."

"Oh, Uncle Felix!" Jess shrieked and kissed him enthusiastically on the cheek.

Maggie glared from Felix to Simone as if guessing their plot. She pressed her lips together, said nothing, and then led Simone under the bower of roses and into the house.

Hand in hand, Felix returned with Jess to the lake. A boat was indeed heading toward them, its two red sails and blue spinnaker billowed out by the wind. It was eleven feet long compared with Jess's eight-foot Optimist. Strong and buoyant, it could be sailed, rowed, or could support an outboard motor on its transom. It was an ideal first Dinghy for beginners, a single-hander.

When it reached the porticiollo, a smiling man handed it over to Jess, who got in, Felix following. Needing no instruction, Jess promptly got the Mirror Dinghy out into the middle of Lake Maggiore and with swans swimming and gulls diving, Felix learned first hand about how Krishna, the Hindu God, had saved signora Morelli's life.

This would have disturbed Felix, if he didn't know the truth of Jess's identity. Instead, he gazed with affection into the honest face of Jess—the twin of Max Segre he'd created.

As a result of that one act, Maggie had nearly died in

childbirth; Sam—mortally wounded—had lost his memory and ten years of his life; his sister, Frances, had barely escaped death at the hands of Brown's thugs, and Felix had nearly lost the love of Adeline, the woman he adored.

Now, Gods were of no importance to Felix compared to the people he loved. Whatever happened, he wouldn't let this child down.

He took control of the Dinghy and pulled Jess against his chest, ruffled his hair. Together they drifted with the waves on the cool, beautiful lake, green hills surrounding them, white swans gliding near like feathered courtiers to this boy.

"What do you think about Krishna, Jess?" he said.

"It is hard to discuss him, Uncle Felix. He is a very great mystery."

"All gods are, I suppose."

"Yes, but Krishna seems particularly so. It is part of why I like him. He warns us that his glory shines through our tears as well as our laughter and that one is the author of the other, in fact. He explains he is death as well as life. He is our hatred and our darkness, not just our tenderness and light."

Had the books he sent already fortified Jess against Maggie's beliefs? "What about Jesus Christ? What do you think of him?"

Jess sat up. "I don't know him very well. I think he must have been very nice, though, for the most part. However, I'm sure the moneylenders didn't like him smashing their things and I don't think it set a very good example. Do you?"

When Felix laughed, Jess flushed.

"I am not certain, I suppose. I must study Jesus one day. Meanwhile—" Jess paused.

"Yes?"

"When I am old enough, Uncle, may Mamma and I go to India so I can study yoga? I want to learn the early Vedas and all the Upanishads. I want to follow in the footsteps of the great Hindu sages."

Jess raised his arms to the sky, the sun on his face, and quoted Ramakrishna, "The winds of God's grace are always blowing; it is for us to raise our sails."

Felix was quiet, then he asked, "Does your mother know about this, Jess?" and Jess rose to his knees, looking worried. "Oh no, Uncle Felix. I cannot tell her yet. She and Krishna do not get along! I was hoping you would talk to her for me. I will not go to India unless she approves."

Felix wondered if Jess would refuse boarding school if she disapproved. "The thing is, Jess, parents always have a hard time when their children first go away to school, especially mothers."

Jess settled back, looking puzzled. "The parents let them go away alone?"

To sound light-hearted, Felix laughed. "Well, of course, Jess. Yes, they do."

"They aren't sad? They don't cry at night?"

"Well, some of them, I suppose, but not for long."

"Uncle Felix," Jess said sadly. "I would cry forever and ever and ever."

"No, you wouldn't." Felix ruffled Jess's hair and changed the subject.

When they returned to the villa, Simone had gone, promising to return when called.

Felix and Maggie closed themselves in the living room and on the floral sofa had an urgent talk, though not about Jess's schooling. Felix thought it wise to save that for tomorrow.

Maggie stood by as he dialed a number in Turin and asked to speak to Father Bartolo. He'd been the priest assigned to watch almost eleven years ago as Felix's team examined The Shroud of Turin that fateful day. Bartolo had guessed their secret and visited Maggie before Jess's birth. If the priest came now, he could help convince Maggie of who Jess really was.

Felix didn't tell Maggie this. She thought they were calling Bartolo because he'd met Sam and might help with his amnesia.

Leaving Jess with Antonella, Maggie and Felix took a taxi down via Sempione, around the cliff called La Rocca, past the public beach and the tennis courts and into town. There they caught the train to Turin and took a second taxi, planning to pick up Father Bartolo after a visit to the Hotel Victoria.

Chapter 18

The sun was in Sam's face when he walked into the lounge and at first he couldn't see them. He could only make out the white ceiling and white posts, the green walls, the white curtains open at the big plate glass window behind them, letting sunlight in. He walked across pale fleur de lis swirling on the dark green carpet and stood beside a chair upholstered in pink and yellow stripes. He assumed they were studying him, but no one spoke.

A woman rose and stepped forward out of the light where he could see her. She was black. Felix hadn't mentioned that. On sight, he couldn't peg her. She wasn't voluptuous like Coral, didn't have the pampered beauty of Frances and Adeline, wasn't titillatingly corrupt like the working girl.

While Felix was gone, Sam had taken a short walk and in the course of it learned he spoke Italian. Sam learned Turin was full of prostitutes from somewhere in Africa. Why, he didn't know. Maggie was nothing like them.

To Sam she was a blank slate. He couldn't ascribe adjectives to her.

Except this was the woman Brown's second page had told him definitely not to fuck. Too bad, because as soon as he saw her face, he wanted to take her upstairs. She had beautiful, beautiful eyes, but otherwise she was plain. Even the working girl in Jersey had more sex appeal.

Nevertheless, Sam wanted her.

She came and touched his face as if he were a mirage and for a moment it felt like he'd been homesick but now it was over—a squirrelly thought, he knew.

She said, "Sam?"

"Hi," he said.

Next thing he knew she was kissing him like she was dying and nothing else could save her.

If they hadn't been in public, if Felix hadn't been there, he would have been all over her. Instead, Sam remembered Brown's note and reluctantly stepped back, putting his hands in his pocket to hide himself. No point in blowing a million bucks.

He had trouble concentrating when Felix began to talk. In fact Sam had no idea what Felix said. Sam just nodded, his eyes glued on the woman, dying to have her.

She didn't move back. She stood there, saying, "Don't you remember me, Sam?"

On the flight, Felix said they were visiting the woman he'd been engaged to, and her son, but when Sam asked, Felix assured him that her kid wasn't Sam's. He was so emphatic about it, Sam knew her kid had to be the clone. It had been there in the newspapers.

If she was supposed to be the new mother of Jesus then Sam wondered if they'd had sex. Maybe it didn't matter. She seemed to want him, now, as much as he wanted her.

He didn't show it.

He just stood there with his hand in his pocket, trying to cover his pecker.

She stepped forward and laid her head on his chest and he could smell her lavender perfume. She put her hands up around his neck and they were soft against his skin. How the hell was he going to keep his paws off her?

"Maggie," Felix said and it startled Sam because he'd forgotten Felix was there. "Maggie, he needs time. Sam doesn't remember you."

Who the hell gave a shit about that?

Felix took her by the shoulders and she stepped away, her eyes tearful. He had to make this good. Brown's number one instruction was to gain her trust.

"Maggie, is it?" he said. "I wish I remembered you. I swear I wish I did."

She was shaking. Sam didn't recall ever seeing a woman faint, but her eyes rolled up and if he and Felix hadn't caught her, she would have hit the floor.

As he lifted Maggie and laid her on the couch, Sam knew exactly what he wanted to do, except they were in public and Felix was there and Brown had given indisputable instructions. He planned to call Brown right away, as soon as he was alone. He'd call Brown to see if maybe there'd been a mistake. He planned to ask if there was any way he could be allowed to ball this broad.

He sat by her, holding her hand, and even though she was out like a light, her touch was like St. Elmo's fire jumping all around his hand.

When she opened her eyes, she whispered to him in a voice Felix couldn't hear, "Sam, we were in love, don't you remember?"

He bent and whispered, "I don't remember, but I can feel it, Maggie. I can feel that I loved you before."

Apparently that did it.

She and Felix excused themselves and went outside. They sat on benches in front of the hotel. Through the window he could see them arguing, see her crying, see Felix turn red, look helpless, then fume. Then she cried again. It crossed his mind that Felix might be screwing her. If so, that could complicate things. Felix might want him to stay out of her pants so he could keep getting in them himself.

They called a cab and drove off, saying they wouldn't be gone long. Sam missed her, wanted her back, paced the lobby waiting for their return. To his relief, they came back a few minutes later, this time with a priest. Sam didn't know why they'd brought the priest and he didn't care. He'd gladly marry her on the spot if that's what it took. She felt more important than anything. He didn't know exactly why.

At first they all sat in the lobby, then for greater privacy they went up to Sam's room.

Sam didn't like the priest. His name was Father Bartolo and he seemed to know good as well as bad things from Sam's past. He asked questions. *Do you remember me? Where have you been? Do you recall your faith in God?* to which Sam gave common sense answers *No. I don't remember. Of course.*

Then the priest blessed Sam and they all knelt and asked for guidance. Bartolo asked God to forgive him for hiding something, he didn't say what. Everyone seemed confused except Maggie.

At some point she got off her knees, her expression determined, her gaze straight, and told him the story he already knew. Felix had made a clone of Jesus. She'd been the mother because she was a virgin at the time, which was only a slight surprise. It made sense, when he thought about it, that Felix would choose a virgin. By a miracle, God had made her a virgin again, like Mary, Maggie said. It and other things proved her son was divine.

Sam tried to pay attention after that, but it was hard. The pictures in his mind were too enticing. Besides, now he had the information Brown instructed him to get. The clone was still alive.

Felix started talking about someone named Max and Bartolo seemed to agree he could be important. Bartolo said he'd had to conceal his trip here because, for ten years, the Vatican had monitored the travel of all priests and nuns who were there when Felix examined the Shroud. Apparently, someone in the Church wasn't sure the clone had died.

Half the time Maggie argued with Felix. The rest of the time she stared at Sam. Finally she said that God had brought Sam back from the grave to protect her son.

Sam was in. He had won her confidence.

They waited while he packed and checked out, then they all got in a taxi and headed for Porta Sousa, where Trenitalia had a direct departure to Arona at 5:22 p.m.

———

Maggie sat next to Sam on the train, silently praising God.

To have the man who loved her return was more than she could have dreamed. Her heart pounded. Her blood raced. Seeing his same old rascally smile, watching his Adam's apple move, seeing his fingers swipe carelessly into the side of his hair, was so overwhelming that every few minutes she feared she'd get sick or faint again.

She felt his hand close over hers and looked up at him, close to tears. He was much thinner, but she could still feel his strength. She clasped his hand in response.

She knew Sam didn't remember her. He didn't have the same sense of humor, didn't call her *Maggie my girl* like before, but their bond had survived. She could feel it in his touch. She could see it in his eyes.

"Where did we meet, Maggie?" he asked.

"I worked for Felix in New York. I was his maid. You were the doorman. I was Maggie Clarissa Johnson then. Here the townspeople call me Hetta Price."

His eyes didn't leave hers. "Hetta Price. I like Maggie better. How long did we know each other?"

"Five years."

"We were engaged all that time?"

The tears in Maggie's eyes spilled over. "No, we got engaged on the day you d—the day we thought you'd died."

"That was the day your son was born?"

"Yes."

"In Central Park?"

"Yes, Sam."

His expression changed and she knew he wasn't thinking of her.

"You want to know who shot you, don't you?" Maggie said.

"Damn straight."

"It was the people trying to kill me and Jess. He's my son."

"What people?""

"I don't know. I just know they worked for Mr. Brown. Did Felix tell you about him?" She felt Sam's grip loosen.

"Brown?"

"He lived in the penthouse where we worked. It turned out he was an evil, evil man. You did some personal work for him. Then you quit. You stayed with me and protected me. I was in labor when you were shot. I guess you don't remember."

Sam didn't reply. He gazed at the passing scenery and she wondered what he was thinking. He didn't speak until the lake and Arona were just coming into view: greenery, clouds, placid water, a charming lakefront.

"No, I don't remember," he said, looking deeply troubled. Absently he moved closer and stroked her hand, and Maggie was grateful for Antonella's cotton gloves and vaselina.

They caught a taxi from the train station in Arona and by the time it pulled onto via Sempione Maggie was jubilant. Here on this beautiful lake, shaped by the hand of heaven, she would live with Jess and Sam, wrapped in the love she'd never had. In all her days and all her nights, she would know love, see love, feel love, give love, receive love, be love. Through Sam and her son, joy would inhabit her.

Sam could take his time remembering. He could take his time recovering his full strength. If he never remembered it wouldn't matter because the love was still there. All the while they held hands, unperturbed by their pounding hearts.

Maggie wished he'd kiss her, but he just gazed into her eyes, squeezing her hand.

When the taxi stopped in front of the villa, she was surprised to see the gate open and a car parked half-on and half-off the road. The gate was never open.

She hurried in ahead of everyone calling, "Jess? Antonella?" but no one answered.

"They must be down at the lake," Felix called.

Bartolo sat on a garden bench as she hurried across the lawn, Sam and Felix behind her.

She reached the top of the stone steps framed by pink and purple hortensia and Maggie froze, stunned by what she saw. Antonella and Jess were on the porticiollo wall. She was in front and he was behind, clinging to her waist, hiding his eyes and weeping.

"Oh Madonna! Oh Dio!" Antonella cried, "Padre, Padre! Spirito Santo!"

Adamo Morelli's cheerful boat lay outside the porticiollo. He stood in it, wailing like a man insane, "Oh Madonna! Oh, Madonna!"

Then Maggie saw Carlo Morelli.

Instead of being at work in his restaurant or at the municipal center helping the town, he stood on the bank, his pregnant wife limp in his arms.

Carlo's insistent voice seemed to be asking for simple logic until she understood his words, *Fategli radunare i cigni!* "Tell him to call the swans." *Lasciate che il ragazzo la tocchi!* "Let the boy touch her." *Appena una volta! Appena una volta!* "Just once. Just once."

Maggie screamed, "What is he doing?" and headed down the stairs for Jess, but she felt her arm gripped by Sam.

"Don't go down there," Sam said. "It's not safe. Idiot thinks the kid's got some kind of magic power and can bring his dead wife back!"

"Oh, Sam!" Maggie cried, "Don't tell me she's dead!"

"As a doorknob, I'd say, from her color."

Felix said, "Fetch the boy, Sam; I'll get the priest."

"Oh, God! Get my son, Sam! Get my son!"

Sam stared an instant longer, his mission half accomplished. He could phone Brown and say he'd found the clone.

For now, he went down the stone steps and marched to the shore in unmasked disgust, passing Carlo Morelli. He didn't acknowledge the ridiculous man and his dead wife. He went to the porticiollo and plucked Jess from the wall. He came with no resistance, putting his arms tight around Sam's neck. He was light as a feather. Sam felt good as soon as the boy touched him until he remembered this was the kid he had to kill. He carried him across the bank, up the steps behind the hortensia, and placed him in his mother's arms.

Felix, the priest, and the woman named Antonella stayed at the shore with the man and his wife.

Sam followed Maggie and her boy into the garden, feeling unexpectedly jealous when the kid hung on her neck, still crying and shuddering like a little wimp.

The boy put his face on her breast, muttering about Krishna

not saving signora Morelli, whispering crap like, "Ti voglio bene Mamma."

Glumly Sam watched Maggie's soft hands stroke the boy's head and face, Sam longing to feel those hands on his body but knowing he had to wait. Still, he wished she were speaking to him instead of the kid as she murmured in a voice like an angel's, "Ti voglio bene. Ti voglio tanto bene, Jess. It's not your fault."

Chapter 19

Maggie heard footsteps outside Jess's bedroom window. She kissed her son's face and stood. He was sleeping. Felix had prescribed a mild sedative.

She looked out the window and saw the men coming. One carried the front, and one the back, of the stretcher on which signora Morelli lay, her stomach huge with the child who'd died with her. Behind them came Carlo like a man sleepwalking, then Dr. Cecagallina, Father Bartolo, Felix, and Adamo, softly wailing.

Antonella was down in the kitchen. She'd said she needed to cook so others would have the strength to weep.

Sam wasn't in the procession from the lake. He stood on the porch, guarding the front door. Maggie went downstairs and stood beside him. Out of respect, she felt she should be there when the signora's body passed.

"You should stay inside," Sam growled. "Who knows what these idiots will do?"

They did nothing but pass before the villa, not looking up as they carried signora Morelli to the waiting ambulance. They were displaying typically Italian self-containment about death. The woman was dead, now, so her body must be removed.

Maggie started inside, but Adamo suddenly left the small procession. He ran to the garden gate, shaking his fist up at the porch. "È un diavolo!" he screamed. "È un diavolo!" *He is a devil.*

"I'll take care of that creep," Sam said and started down the porch steps, but Maggie grabbed Sam's arm. "No, don't."

She slipped past him and went to Adamo Morelli.

"Oh, Hetta, Hetta!" he cried as she approached.

Maggie hugged Adamo. "Sono così spiacente." *I'm so sorry.*

Adamo clung to her, grieving because he'd loved signora Morelli too long and hopelessly to be properly reserved when she died.

When Adamo and the ambulance left, the house seemed to settle into an all-night pattern of despair, interrupted only by Antonella's mourning feast.

Jess woke and came to the table, not giving exuberant hugs to everyone as usual. He simply kissed his mother and sat down.

Felix never sat at the head of the table as if the villa were his, though he paid for every stitch of clothes on their backs, every morsel on their plates. He sat on Maggie's right, next to Jess. Maggie and Father Bartolo were at the ends.

Sam, risen from the grave, was squeezed in on her left, next to Antonella, who sat closest to the kitchen, ladling things onto plates. Signora Morelli's death had cast a somber pall over the yellow villa, just when Maggie yearned to be dizzily in love. Seeing the poor woman, her baby dead inside her stomach, had taken joy away.

It had launched hushed conversations in corners of the house, in the garden, at the lake. Maggie didn't care what was being said. For weeks she'd pondered what to do about Jess, about Felix. She'd come to a decision. The evening's events only hardened her resolve.

Meanwhile, half of everything Antonella cooked had been delivered to the Morelli's home—the lovers' feasts planned for Sam's return converted to funeral fare.

For antipasti, all kinds of marinated, sautéed, boiled, baked things, much of it tasting of delicious olive oil, *extra vergine*. Italians made a science of olive oil, equivalent to the science of wine. Maggie tasted the eggplant, mushrooms, artichokes, anchovy puffs, and calamari then gave up.

She noticed that Sam tried it all, often letting the first bite linger in his mouth, his eyes closed in ecstasy.

Antonella noticed, too, and kept filling Sam's plate, saying, "Buono?" and he would answer, "Non buono. Eccellente!" and she would say, "Mangi! Mangi!" urging him to eat. To Maggie it made sense that Sam had awakened with a hunger for the world.

After the antipasti came risotto, the buttery Italian rice dish. There was steak, fish, pasta marinara, fruit, a flavorful goat cheese.

For dessert they had *Dulcia Domestica*—dates stuffed with nuts and stewed in honey-sweetened wine—first made in ancient Rome, Antonella said. They emptied two bottles of *Barbaresco*, from the prestigious Nebbiolo grape grown on sunny Piedmont hills. Antonella had selected an aged *Marziano Abbona, Vigna Faset*, the signature humming bird poised on a branch beneath the name. Felix said it had finesse, intricate layering and a very long finish. Sam downed one nearly by himself as if it were soda pop. Maggie even let Jess drink some, watered down. For any stomach upsets her meal might cause, Antonella had a digestive liqueur from Abruzzo called *Centerbe di Tocco Casauria*.

Eventually, the melancholy silence was broken by the food, but the conversation went mostly over Maggie's head as Felix, Bartolo and even Jess discussed things she knew nothing about.

Then Felix paused and leaned forward, looking as if he were about to recite the Gettysburg Address.

"Jess," he said. "Will you excuse us for a while?"

"Yes, Uncle," Jess said.

Antonella rose and took Jess outside.

When they were gone, Felix said to her, "It's time we talked about moving you and Jess. Father Bartolo has kindly offered you both temporary shelter with the Poor Clare nuns until we can settle Jess—" He paused as if to gauge her reaction.

Maggie said, "Carlo Morelli is a Christian man, Felix. He'll be sensible. It's Adamo I'm really worried about. Antonella and I will help him with his grief."

Felix flushed. "But—"

Maggie rolled her eyes. "We're safe here, Felix. Just like we were on Cliffs Landing when I was pregnant."

Sam said, "Seems to me Maggie should have the final say in this. Besides, I can stick around."

Felix frowned at Sam. "I'm sure Maggie appreciates your taking her side, but you haven't been here, Sam. You can't judge. You don't know the complexities."

"I have an uncomplex way to protect them upstairs," Sam said.

"You mean a gun?" Felix asked in an even voice. "You haven't changed, Sam, have you? You need a handgun permit in this country. I know you don't have one. How did you sneak a gun past customs?"

Sam screwed up his mouth and didn't reply.

In all the months she carried Jess, Maggie had gotten used to knowing Sam was always armed. In principle she disapproved, but she spoke with more confidence.

"Jess and I aren't going to abandon the only home he's ever known. We're not going to a convent, Felix."

"A convent?" Sam said, frowning. "I don't see any reason for a convent."

"Neither do I," Maggie said.

She saw Sam arch an eyebrow in triumph.

Felix shot back a frosty glare as if their old rivalry would return—Felix wanting her to carry the clone and Sam not. There was no basis for it now.

Father Bartolo spoke with concern. "Italy is a very Christian country, Maggie, as I am sure you have seen. In any small Catholic town, it could be dangerous for our Jess to be thought to cast spells in the name of Krishna on behalf of someone who ultimately died, but especially in Arona which has the colossus of San Carlo beside La Rocca on the hill."

He was referring to the hundred-fifteen foot bronze and copper statue of the local saint looming down from atop La Rocca. Borromeo, a bishop, was born here at the castle, and he'd been a good man, but Maggie hadn't taken Jess to visit the statue. She wanted Jess to be awed by God, not by San Carlo Borromeo.

Bartolo continued, "If you stay in Arona, Jess must certainly become a Christian."

"I know," Maggie said.

When Antonella and Jess returned to the table, they all fell silent, exchanging glances.

Jess said, "Lo perdoni, per favore, Padre Bartolo." *Forgive me, Father Bartolo.* You are a Catholic priest. May we talk about religion? Signora Morelli's death is making me think about it."

"Si, of course," Bartolo replied.

Felix said, "Jess, I suppose the important thing about Christianity is Christ. It's Jesus' message itself."

"Yes," Bartolo said.

Jess asked, "You also believe Jesus' message is the true one, Uncle?"

"Some message," Sam said. "Look how he ended up. Nailed to a cross."

Felix spoke angrily. "That *was* the message, Sam. That he died to take away our sins. But in the end —and I hope you'll pardon me, Father Bartolo—how can we really be sure one religion is more right than the next?"

"I'm not following anybody who can't keep himself from being nailed to a cross," Sam said.

"Sam, that's not nice," Maggie interjected.

Felix ignored Sam. "Jess, unlike Hinduism, which has many Gods—"

"It does not!" Jess interrupted, in apparent distress. "Hinduism knows there is only a single God who takes many forms. To the Hindu, it does not matter whether God is worshipped as Krishna or Shiva or Jesus … or anyone else. Hinduism says all roads lead to God. It's just that some are faster."

"I think that's right," Felix said and Maggie knew what he was up to, now. He was trying to lead Jess away from Jesus.

Sam laughed. "All roads lead to God?"

"They do," Jess said and began to quote verses Maggie hadn't heard:

> Ah, my God, I see all gods within your body;
> Each in his degree, the multitude of creatures;
> See Lord Brahma throned upon the lotus;
> See all the sages, and the holy serpents.
>
> Universal Form, I see you without limit,
> Infinite of arms, eyes, mouths and bellies—
> See, and find no end, midst or beginning …

Birthless, deathless; yours the strength titanic,
Million-armed, the sun and moon your eyeballs,
` Fiery-faced, you blast the world to ashes …

Maggie said, "What in the world is that, Jess?"

"It is from the Theophany in the *Bhagavad-Gita*."

"But you promised me—"

"I didn't disobey you, Mamma. I had already learned it." He looked at Felix. "Because God is million-armed, Uncle Felix, you need not feel anguish over me." He stood and turned to Maggie. "Mamma, you must not be concerned. I cannot lose God, nor can you, nor can Uncle Felix nor Antonella nor can the Morellis," he turned to Sam and almost whispered, "Nor can anyone."

Maggie put her fork down. Felix stood.

Jess's eyes watered. "Krishna would not save signora Morelli because, because she is not lost—"

Maggie watched Felix reach out, but Jess backed away. "Mamma, Uncle Felix, there are voices in my mind. When I close my eyes I see people I have never met. Yet I am sure they know me and I know them. I saw Krishna save signora Morelli, then I saw her turn away and die for her own reasons."

Everyone stared at Jess.

"Who am I?" he said.

Antonella cried, "Misericordia! You are Jess Price!"

"Yes, Jess Price. An American name. Am I American?" he turned to Maggie, his voice anguished. "Are you … are you really my—"

"Jess!" Antonella said.

Maggie trembled and Jess went to her and hugged her. He was trembling, too. How long had he had this question on his mind?

"Other than our birthmarks, I do not look like you, Mamma. I do not look very much like Uncle Felix, really. Who am I?" His voice was full of dread.

It was true. Inexplicably, they both had crescent moon shaped birthmarks under their chins though Felix's DNA test proved they weren't genetically related. Jess otherwise looked like a beautiful young Arab.

With a father's instincts, Felix came around the table, lifted Jess and held him close. Maggie had the sense it was how he held Ariel, making a cradle of his arms so she could sit on them, her legs dangling down his body, her head on his shoulder, her arms around his neck.

Felix walked Jess back and forth across the floor while Antonella cleared the table and Maggie, praying for guidance, went upstairs to the salmon room and opened her armadio.

Tomorrow night at La Scala in Milan, the *St. Matthew Passion* by Bach was being performed. Maggie had read about it in one of Antonella's opera magazines. It said the Bach passion was so demanding it needed two choruses and two orchestras. It lasted almost three hours. Performances were rare and usually at Easter, but there was one tomorrow night.

Maggie searched for her long knit dress, hoping it was there, sure that the hand of God had guided her. She'd bought tickets, feeling certain the performance would stir Jess's soul and prepare him to hear who he was.

No matter what Felix, Bartolo or anyone else said, that's where they were going tomorrow night. It was the first step in her plan to tell Jess who he was.

She found the dress and, relieved, hung it on the armadio door.

Maggie knew you couldn't just walk up to a child and say, "By the way, I should have mentioned you might be a clone of the Son of God. If not, we don't know who your DNA belongs to. No idea. Maybe a guy named Max Segre but we can't find out for sure."

It was plainly urgent that Jess learn the circumstances of his birth.

She found a jacket to go with the dress and—her mind now clear—Maggie went downstairs.

Sam watched in admiration as Maggie took control of the villa. She kissed her son goodnight, said she'd be up soon then instructed Antonella to put Jess to bed.

Then Maggie turned to Felix and announced they were going out tomorrow night. To La Scala. He asked why. She said they were going, and that was that — she, Jess and Felix and whoever else wanted to come. She'd reserved a whole box so there was room. Would he please go into town tomorrow and buy Jess a new suit?

"What's playing at La Scala?" Felix asked.

"The *St. Matthew Passion*," she replied.

Felix turned purple and fumed at her.

Maggie calmly left and went upstairs.

Afterwards, Felix and Father Bartolo huddled across the room, ignoring Sam and talking to each other in lowered voices about Jess. At any other time it would have been rude as hell.

Sam didn't care. Let them talk. Let them go to operas. It wouldn't change anything. He'd already phoned the news about Jess to Brown.

For Sam, the bad part came when they went to their rooms. It turned out Antonella wasn't spending the night, which raised Sam's hopes that when Maggie eventually left the kid, she'd be in a room alone. He yearned to be with her, see Maggie's eyes blaze again like they had at first.

Those hopes were dashed when he learned Felix got to bunk in the room with Jess, leaving Sam to share a bed with Father Bartolo.

In the dark, Sam repeatedly tried to leave the room. He was unsuccessful. No matter how quiet he was, Bartolo sat up each time and, half asleep called Sam over to bless him.

Chapter 20

The next day Felix went obediently into town and bought Jess a
fine black suit, a pair of Raffaello shoes and a luxurious olive-
green shirt which just happened to match the long black knit
dress and embroidered jacket of olive, gold and rose that Maggie
had picked out to wear.

When she saw Jess in his suit, Maggie exclaimed that of all the
women in Milan, she would have the handsomest escort tonight.

She held his hand in the taxi they took to Milan, her purse
stuffed with tissues and his favorite candy. She walked beside him
when they emerged on Piazza della Scala, La Scala square, and
looked up at the statue of Leonardo da Vinci across from the
world's most famous opera house.

On all his visits, Dr. Cecagallina had talked of La Scala. "It was
insuperabile. No one had sung who hadn't sung there. La Scala *was
magnifica*."

Inside they climbed red-carpeted stairs to their box. Through
a door lined in rose-patterned red satin, they entered a booth with
gold-fringed red velvet drapes that hung above the red velvet
railing. The booth had rose-patterned satin walls. She and Jess sat
in front on the gilded velvet chairs. Felix, Father Bartolo and Sam
were on the rose-patterned sofa bench and velvet stools behind.
At first Sam lingered outside the booth as if its dark interior
frightened him. It was all those years in a coma, Maggie
concluded. Not Sam's fault. His jaw set, Sam eventually came in
and took a seat next to Bartolo.

Reluctantly, Felix cooperated. He handed programs to
everyone and when Maggie opened hers she sighed. On the left
were the German words Bach and his librettist wrote. On the
right, they were translated into Italian, which she couldn't read
very well. She would understand only parts of what was sung.

Jess was so excited he wouldn't sit properly in his chair. He leaned over the railing, gazing above and below at the four tiers. Atop them two galleries rimmed the horseshoe-shaped theater. Brilliant light fixtures adorned the gilded fronts of alternate boxes of the first three tiers. Above it all hung an enormous chandelier. Dr. Cecagallina had informed them La Scala was famous for its acoustics and for the great operas that had premiered here, such as *Turandot, Nabucco, La Gioconda* and, dearest to Maggie, Puccini's *Madama Butterfly*. It thrilled her to know Leontyne Price herself had sung here, where Jess would begin to learn the truth.

Rows of orchestra seats covered the floor. The stage and a huge orchestra pit were at the theater's open end.

Felix read from the brochure in his hand. "It opened in 1778. The boxes used to be privately owned and the interiors could be decorated as long as the external curtains and gilded pillars remained the same. Let's see, they have 365 lightbulbs in here. One for every day of the year. Many of the original crystal doorknobs and lamps were stolen by thieves, and—"

"How terrible," Maggie said.

Jess turned to her, "Oh, Mother. Isn't it grand? We're at La Scala! Can you believe it? Imagine who has been here since it was built in 1778! Perhaps Mahatma Gandhi!"

"And most of the world's crown heads since then, I'm sure," Felix said.

"As well as a great many popes," Bartolo said.

"And a great many little boys," Maggie added, drowning in pride and love at the sight of Jess in his elegant suit in the graceful chair.

Felix bent and said to Jess. "This will begin with a motet with a figured bass," and Jess nodded as if he understood.

Maggie heard applause as the house lights dimmed and the curtain rose. The stage was set with a giant abstract cross, dramatically lit and hanging in midair. In the background, simulated organ pipes reached in different directions like phalanxes of trumpets. Two orchestras faced each other and on tiers of steps behind them, two choruses were in place. With ropes for belts, they dressed in robes like Jesus might have worn. The conductor entered to polite applause, turned his back, tapped his podium and raised his arms.

When he lowered them, monumental music swirled into the air. Flutes. Violins joined by oboes and bassoons. Violas, violoncellos, a double organ. The sound was instantly engrossing, stunning, captivating. It froze the listener in mid-cough, mid-blink, hand halfway through the air. Then came soaring voices, each group distinct. One chorus sang a refrain to which the other replied. In the dim light, Maggie translated parts.

> Come; you daughters, help me lament ...
> Behold!
>   Whom?
>   The Bridegroom.
> Behold Him!
>   How?
>   ...Like a lamb.
> O guiltless Lamb of God
> Slaughtered on the tree of the Cross.

Sopranos in unison flung sorrow to the sky, basses sobbed, altos wept, whorling sounds of reckless beauty that shot tears down Maggie's face. No one but a genius could have written such a thing. Transfixed, Maggie listened, hearing children's voices chime, and then all voices in both choruses join in harmony. It was incredible. If time passed she didn't know it. When the prologue ended, there was no applause. The audience sat dazed.

They were no longer in an opera house in a city that had a name. They had bonded with the singers and the orchestras to live St. Matthew's depiction of the crucifixion of Christ.

During the prologue Jess had been perfectly still. Now he pulled his chair close to Maggie's, lay back, his eyes open, and put his head in her lap.

She stroked his forehead and whispered, "How do you like it, darling? How does it make you feel?"

"I don't know, Mamma."

When the music resumed, Maggie raised her eyes to the stage. There were soloists. Someone sang Jesus, another Judas, another Peter, another an Evangelist. Other unnamed soloists came forward in turn and Jess sat up when a particular tenor sang. He had an exceptionally beautiful voice.

The intermission came after Jesus was betrayed and taken from the Garden of Gethsemane. If parts of her hadn't been numb, Maggie wouldn't have realized she'd been sitting so long. The audience, who hadn't made a sound until now, rose to their feet in wild applause, shouting bravos. She heard some in nearby boxes weep from sheer emotional exhaustion.

The house lights came up and Maggie heard Sam let out his breath.

Maggie looked at Felix and knew they both had forgotten why they came.

Jess said lightly, "I need to visit *il gabinetto*."

Maggie started to accompany him but Felix whispered, "He's ten, not two," and Jess was gone.

In his absence, Maggie thought about Jess's reaction to the performance. To others the crucifixion was a remote event, a routine component of Christian belief. For Jess, it couldn't be. But he had to know it happened and feel it in his heart.

"I think coming here was a bad idea," Felix said.

Sam sat forward. "Excuse me for interrupting, Maggie, but even if the kid has Christ's genes, you don't seriously believe he's actually Christ? Hell, at most he'd be a twin, Felix, right?" Maggie heard bravado in his voice, as if Sam were still disturbed by the dark booth.

She thought of letting him sit in front, but knew he'd refuse. She turned around and studied the libretto. Felix sighed and tapped his foot while the audience milled about, waiting for the performance to resume.

"Oh, geez," Maggie heard Sam mutter.

When Jess returned, the curtain had just risen. The orchestras and choruses were back in place. Maggie asked, "Are you all right?

Do you want to hear the rest?"

"Oh, yes, Mamma! I want to stay. I didn't know the whole story. I am learning a lot. And the music! Oh, it is so beautiful. Johann Sebastian Bach must have really loved Jesus. The singers also love him. I hear it in their voices."

Maggie decided she'd done the right thing.

The music resumed with an alto aria that the second chorus joined. Over and over they sang, "Where has my Jesus gone?" Then the Evangelist described how the priests and elders sought false witness against Jesus as Peter silently watched.

Jess seemed more restless than before.

He put his head on the velvet railing, lay on Maggie's lap, and then leaned on Felix. He slid down to the floor and sat with his back against the front of the booth, his legs drawn up. He was just a little boy and the performance was long. The tenor Jess had been watching began to sing. She bent down to tell him, but he wasn't there. She looked around the booth and didn't see him. Where had he gone?

"He went back to the restroom," Felix whispered.

With organ chords accompanying him, the tenor sang,

> My Jesus holds his peace before false lies,
> So as to show us
> That his merciful will
> Is bent on suffering for our sake;

He was a thin young man, blond and too small for his suit. He seemed slight in comparison to his song. He sang about accusation as if he knew, first hand, what it was.

Maggie looked back to see if Jess had returned. He hadn't. As her eyes scanned the house, she wondered if she should search for him. Then she found him. Somehow he'd made his way behind the orchestra pit and was sitting on the stage before the tenor with the beautiful voice. If anyone else noticed Jess sitting there, they gave no sign.

Maggie rose. Was this the miracle she'd been hoping for? "Felix look," she whispered, but her purse dropped to the floor, and dozens of voices shushed her, including Felix who didn't seem to realize where Jess was. Slowly she sat down, watching Jess's head move as if he were singing, too. A bass viola accompanied the next solo and Jess lay at the musician's feet, his hands bouncing with the motions of the bow.

No one seemed disturbed or tried to make him leave.

Instead, people in rows further back were rising furtively from their seats to sit closer. Those in lower rows moved down to let them in until the front rows were packed.

In his brand new suit, Jess lay or kneeled here and there about the stage. Once he crouched at a violinist's feet and when she nodded he turned the page on her music stand. Maggie wondered if Italians were this tolerant of children or if something inexplicable was going on.

With a boy at their feet, the conductor and his two orchestras and two choruses continued until they reached *The Death of Jesus.*

Maggie thought they gathered courage to complete what they'd begun, like athletes nearing the end of a long race—knowing everyone was on Golgotha, preparing for Jesus to die.

Maggie was on Golgotha, too.

Such music.

She didn't consult the program, now. The Evangelist's recitative announced the ninth hour, then "My God, My God, why have you forsaken me?" Jesus cried.

Maggie kept her eye on Jess as he kneeled onstage, swaying to the music. "When I must die, O Lord, do not leave me," came the chorale. Then the earth quaked, the rocks rent, the graves opened and the soldiers and people sang, "Truly, this was the Son of God!"

Full of tragic beauty, the music swirled like wounded birds.

To Maggie everyone in their box, everyone she could see, were like wooden statues, like Lot's wife turned to pillars of salt, frozen by the final chorus as all the instruments played. The flute, the violoncellos, the bassoons, the violins. Soprano voices rose and fell, echoing the women on Golgotha: among them, Mary

Magdalene, the Virgin Mary and Zebedee's children's mother.

If you'd ever wished you'd been at Jesus' grave to mourn his death, this was the next best thing, Maggie thought. If the last sound you heard in life was Bach's closing chorus, your ears would rejoice.

There was tumultuous applause. Looking for Jess, Maggie rose and made her way down to the orchestra against the flow of people. She found him in an aisle seat beside the young tenor with the beautiful voice. People patted Jess's shoulder and ruffled Jess's hair as they passed. One woman who'd seen them together stopped and said to her in Italian, "You have a wonderful son."

Jess and the blond tenor were talking.

"Consider the lion," Jess said. "Must he overcome his roar, resist the females in his pride, must the lioness resist capturing prey in her claws? Consider the bear. Must he not hunger for salmon as they spawn? Must the bees denounce their sting or curb the sweetness of their honey?" Jess touched the tenor's arm. "You are as natural as they."

When he finished, Maggie tapped him on the shoulder, full of pride at his words, but wondering why he'd said them. "Come along, Jess. It's late. Felix is waiting. So are the rest. It's time we were getting home."

Jess rose and walked beside her.

"Why were you telling him that, honey?" she asked.

"He is upset because he is gay."

Where did Jess learn about that and why would it concern him? Then she remembered. Jesus had befriended those society rejected. It was just like Jesus to say something so brilliant, loving and scandalous.

Jess took her hand and whispered, "Mamma, do you think I will be crucified if I keep asking Krishna to make miracles?"

Maggie squatted in her finery and pulled him close. "No, darling, not while I'm around." She opened her purse and gave him a piece of candy.

He walked along beside her in his black suit and olive shirt, holding her hand and eating his candy.

Maggie knew he didn't realize the two choruses had been singing about him. As they reentered La Scala square, she decided that when Jess learned the poor, crucified body that hung on crosses the world over was once his, he'd need much more than Felix's science and Bartolo's religion.

She would tell him herself when they were alone and she could put him on her lap and hold him tight.

Chapter 21

Back at the villa, Maggie led Jess to her salmon room and when he'd done his ritual bounce on her mattress, finished fiddling with her things, she told him to open a dresser drawer. He knew it contained her Bible and when he withdrew it, Maggie said, "Take it, Jess. It's yours, now."

"Mother, it's your favorite book. Don't you want to read it anymore?"

She hugged him, whispering in his ear. "I know every word, darling. I hope it will be your favorite, too."

Jess took it to his room and as soon as she tucked him in, started reading. Maggie noticed he began with The New Testament and was relieved. It was only about as long as the average novel—which Jess could gallop through in an hour and a half. Soon he would know all there was to know about the man whose genes he carried.

Felix lingered in the hall as she put Jess to bed and when she emerged, Sam came out of the guest room.

"So, Maggie," Sam said. "I … uh … was wondering if you wanted to take a walk along the lake. Um, we could use a flashlight to find our way. It's a beautiful night, don't you think?"

Felix stepped between them and took Maggie's arm. "She and I need to discuss Jess, Sam. I'm sure you understand."

Sam's face went to war with itself: gazing at Maggie, scowling at Felix. She touched Sam's hand.

"Tomorrow, Sam, all right?"

"Yeah, right. Tomorrow. Sure, that's fine."

As they went downstairs, Maggie saw Sam give Felix the finger and she wanted to laugh. Neither time nor amnesia had cooled Sam's hot Irish blood. Her arms wanted to go around him and in her mind she promised, *Tomorrow, my other darling. Tomorrow, Sam.*

"Where would you like to go?" Felix asked.

Maggie looked to the front door. Without talking, they went out to the porch, through the garden and down to the deck over the lake. There she and Felix parted when they first came here ten years ago. It seemed good to plot the future here.

Maggie spread her hands on the railings and gazed toward the Gola. Though it was midnight, she could see the pre-Alpine hills by the strange, dim light that often lingered on the surface of the lake.

"I'm going to tell him, Felix, "she said. "Just me. No one else. He's my son."

"Exactly what is it that you plan to say?" Felix said. She knew he was trying to sound calm, but his voice strained with anger.

She turned around. "I'm going to tell him the story of his birth. Just the facts. I'll leave it up to him to decide what they mean."

"And there's nothing I can say to change your mind?"

"Felix, you didn't even notice he was onstage during the *St. Matthew Passion*. I did. You haven't been with him day and night. I have."

Felix paced the deck, and then returned to where she stood. "Maggie, I didn't want to bring this up, but you forget we have a contract. I have legal recourse. This has got to stop. Tomorrow morning I'm taking Jess away."

Maggie smiled gently at him. She had anticipated this in sleepless nights, wondering what she'd do.

"You don't have any legal recourse, Felix, unless you want to put Jess in danger. If you step in a court and make a claim on him, Theomund Brown will know we're alive. You might be killing Jess, and you know that."

This occurred to her when she saw Jess onstage at La Scala tonight. Unless he planned to kidnap Jess—which Sam would prevent—Felix had no power over them any more.

To her surprise, Felix came to the railing and stood beside her. Together they watched King Silent and two of his friends, asleep on the bank. "I guess there's no fooling you," he said.

Maggie smiled. He knew his contract was useless, too.

"All right, Maggie. On that I'll give in, but you must also give in. You and Jess have to leave here. Until I find another place, I'm taking you both to the convent of the Poor Clare nuns and I want no arguments on that. If necessary, I'll have Uncle Simone reclaim his villa. He will if I tell him why."

Maggie swallowed. It was just like Felix to overlook the obvious. Sam couldn't live in a convent. Felix was asking her to choose between her son and the man she loved. What hadn't occurred to Felix was that she and Jess could disappear.

At 2:00 am when she went to bed, Maggie looked in on Jess and found him rereading the New Testament, as if searching for what was crucial there. She told him it was time to sleep, now, took the book from his hands, kissed him and turned out the light.

In the night she dreamed of Sam.

She woke as the sun peeped from behind La Rocca Angera and turned the lake to shimmering jewels. Soon daylight would seep in around the window shutter. She wanted to feel the orange warmth on her shut eyes. Maggie lay there, thinking of Sam and waiting for sunrise.

Hearing a noise outside, she got up and opened the shutters. Jess was in the garden, crouched over something against the wall.

"What is it, Jess?" she called.

He didn't answer, but his demeanor sent her down the stairs and out onto the spiral-columned porch.

Jess rose, holding a dead bird in his hands. It was just one of the thousands of sparrows that lived here, probably fallen from a tree. Then Maggie saw a piece of paper attached to its leg by a string.

Jess held the bird and asked in a troubled voice, "Chi sono io? Chi sono io?" *Who am I.*

Under the bower of roses she took the bird from him and struggled to read the scrawled Italian words. *Riporta quest'uccello in vita. Hai bisogno di far pratica.*

It rudely suggested Jess use the bird to practice bringing dead things to life. Who had left it? Adamo? No, it had to be someone else. Felix was right. They'd have to go, and soon.

She kneeled and hugged Jess.

He whispered, "Please tell me, Mamma. I feel old enough to know the truth, no matter what it is. Sometimes I think I have always been old." He pulled back and stroked her cheek. "I think you are afraid that I won't love you. Is that it? Do not worry. Even if you are really not my mother, have no fear. When I think of love, I think of you. You are pure, so beautiful. I could hate the moon; I could loathe the stars before I stopped loving you. Ti voglio bene, Mamma. Always. Take me to the lake where it is peaceful and tell me there.'"

Anxiously, lovingly, Maggie translated their vow of parent-child love. "With all my heart, I wish you well, too, Jess. I desire good things for you."

It seemed that the sun delayed its rise; the birds withheld their morning songs. Even the mountains blocked the way of the clouds as Maggie prepared to tell Jess who he was. It was the time of the dogwoods, the tree that yielded wood for Jesus' cross. The lake house deck was covered in its white blossoms, thistled crowns at the centers, the edges spotted brown-red like blood.

They sat together on the deck where Jess first nursed and gained his foothold on life.

"Jess, darling, you've heard of the Shroud of Turin?"

He frowned in thought then said, "Yes. They say it is the burial cloth of Jesus."

"It is."

He looked surprised. "You are sure?"

"Absolutely sure. Scientists found type AB male blood on the Shroud."

"That is so interesting! But how do they know it is Jesus' blood?"

"Felix was sure at the time. So was I."

"That is exciting, Mamma! Did you know the Hindus recognize Jesus as another incarnation of Vishnu, just like Krishna is?"

Maggie sighed. "Is that right?"

"Yes, but go ahead with your story, Mamma."

She held out her arms. "Come to me, darling."

Jess came and stretched across her lap, his head in the crook of her arm, gazing at her, caressing her face. She ran her fingers through his sausage curls.

"Jess, Felix stole some of that blood from the Shroud. He brought it home and took out the DNA. He took one of my eggs, replaced my DNA with Shroud DNA. Then he put the egg back in me."

Jess grew still as all he'd known about himself tumbled down.

"Nine months later," Maggie closed her eyes. "You were born."

She heard Jess draw in his breath.

Maggie was so nervous she rambled on, explaining, but not looking at Jess. All about Felix's labs back in New York and Cliffs Landing, about Sam who'd saved their lives because he loved her.

As Maggie talked, the lake shimmered like diamonds. King Silent, the crippled swan, swam by without a mate, followed by what seemed the entire flock. The Weeping Willow dangled in the morning breeze. Jess played with the dogwood blossoms but didn't speak.

Maggie paused and studied him. He'd risen from her lap and seemed absorbed in watching the swans. His expression was blank. She couldn't guess his thoughts. Was he hiding disappointment at the loss of Krishna's million-armed God? Did he fear being the crucified Christ?

"Jess, darling?" she ventured. "Say something to your Mama before I go crazy."

The smile Jess turned on her began to dissolve Maggie's fears. He said, "It's just a story, Mamma. I heard every word, but it's only a story."

She hadn't expected him to dismiss it as a fairy tale. "It's true. Every bit of it."

Jess laughed. "Do you know the Irish myth about St. Patrick and the swans?"

"No, what is it?"

Jess returned to his lounge chair and gazed into the air. "Lir, a chief, married Eva and had four children. Eva died. When Lir remarried, Aoife, his new wife was jealous of the children because Lir loved them so. She cast a spell on them and turned them into swans. Nine hundred years passed. St. Patrick came to Ireland to bring the Christian faith. His children told him about the swans and when he prayed over them their feathers fell away revealing an old woman and three old men. When they died he buried them and as he prayed at their grave, St. Patrick saw four white swans wing their way to heaven."

Maggie didn't know what he was trying to say. Before her sat the Son of God, beautiful in his person and in his heart, at home in this country where after ten years she still couldn't read the language.

Jess rose to his feet and let a handful of dogwood blossoms float down to the lake. "Is my friend a swan or an enchanted child? How are we to know? To the Hindu, swanhood is the soul's destiny."

Concerned, Maggie said, "What do you believe, Jess?"

"Everything. If we must choose between believing and not believing, then believing is for me. It seems closer to the truth."

"Sweetie-pie, weren't you listening?" Maggie asked. "I just told you very very important things about yourself. Felix made you from DNA on the Shroud of Turin. She hung her head, and then raised it, knowing she must tell him everything. "Felix thinks the DNA actually came from a cut on the hand of one of his colleagues, a Jewish scientist named Max Segre. I believe the DNA belonged to Jesus."

Jess laughed again. "I am not Max Segre's clone, do not worry. And Felix didn't clone me from Jesus' DNA on the Shroud."

"Well, of course he did, sweetheart. I was there."

"Mamma, that's silly. That DNA would be much too old."

"Well, those are the only two choices."

Jess leaned his back on the railing and turned to her. "Thank you so much for giving me your Bible, Mamma. It explains things. In the night I woke and talked to God. Now with what you told me, I'm beginning to understand."

Then it seemed to Maggie that the morning was released from its spell. The sun rose behind La Rocca di Angera and bathed her boy in light.

His voice said, "So che sono, Mamma!" *I know who I am.*

"Oh Darling!'

"Mamma, it was your heart that made me. It was Felix's too. I came because you called me. I could come no other way. For you, I am he who died on the cross."

Jess was hidden in the light of the rising sun. All that was visible were the dogwood blossoms at his feet.

"Whatever do you mean, Jess?'

"Life is a story that we write with our beliefs." His next words seemed to come from the light around him. "Ask, and it will be given to you; seek, and you will find; knock, and it will be opened to you. For everyone who asks receives, and he who seeks finds, and to him who knocks it will be opened."

It was Matthew 7:7-8. Jess was quoting Christ. "What in the world are you trying to tell me?"

Jess said, "Once Jesus' disciples tried to cast out a demon and could not." He continued by quoting from the Bible. "Then the disciples came to Jesus privately and said, *Why could we not cast it out? So Jesus said to them, Because of your unbelief; for assuredly, I say to you, if you have faith as a mustard seed, you will say to this mountain, "Move from here to there,' and it will move; and nothing will be impossible for you."*

Maggie knew Christ had said all those things, but who took them literally today? No one except her Jess, at this moment, on this lake, and not for the world's ears but for hers alone. He couldn't possibly mean what he was saying. Anyone could create anything simply through faith? If it was true, such a message needed another Sermon on the Mount. It needed crowds of people to hear and scribes to record it. Then Maggie realized it had already occurred. Jess was repeating words sent down through the ages, but which no one in their right mind believed today—not literally. All her life she'd read her Bible, never once imagining Jesus could have meant exactly what he'd said. Was this the new message? That the old message was true?

Jess said, "Most assuredly, I say to you, he who believes in Me, the works that I do he will do also; and greater works than these he will do."

John 14:12. Maggie stared at her son.

"Jess, do you mean you remember now that you are Jesus? You remember saying these things?"

"No. I don't remember exactly. I have been shown who I am. I knew just a moment ago. I have Jesus' personality. I have a part of his soul. Hindus would say I was Jesus in a past life and now I am a reincarnation of him."

"Reincarnation?"

"Mamma, it does not matter what we call it. I am the mountain you have moved, as Christ promised. I am the greater work that you have done. You and Uncle Felix asked, you sought, you knocked, believing it possible to occur. You were answered, you found, it was opened. I have returned."

Maggie wanted to weep. How could he be saying this? She wasn't important. Everyone knew it, Maggie most of all. She had no power to accomplish such an awesome thing. "No, Jess. We were only instruments of God's will or he wouldn't have allowed it. You came to help the world. That's what God wants."

Jess quoted the Bible a final time, "Or what man is there among you who, if his son asks for bread, will give him a stone? Or if he asks for a fish, will he give him a serpent? You and Felix asked for me, Mamma, and I have come."

Maggie shook her head.

"Ask, seek, knock, and then believe. It is the secret Jesus gave us for daily life," Jess said. "On earth, God wants for us what we want for ourselves."

Maggie stood. "No, Jess! People get all kinds of evil wishes in their heads. That can't be right. That's, that's ... a misinterpretation. Besides, half the world's been praying to Jesus for two thousand years. What could possibly be so special about Felix and me that we somehow —"

He picked up dogwood blossoms, opened her hand and put

them in her palm. "The world did not seek my physical return," he said gently. "They did not believe they could open their eyes and see me in the flesh. You did, Mamma. You and Uncle Felix. It is for you that I have come."

The sun had risen.

Jess laughed, a little boy again. He hugged his speechless mother and scrambled from the deck as King Silent swam to greet him on the shore.

Chapter 22

Sam walked along via Sempione into town and on the Piazza del Popolo slipped into the Hotel Florida. The hotel was decorated like the private home of a frugal family. To save money, lights were out in the unused public rooms and the halls were dimly lit. He made sure no one was at the desk, took the old wooden stairs two at a time until he reached the third floor, went down the hall to a particular door and knocked. He heard shuffling. The door opened.

"So you came," Sam said.

As Sam entered, Dr. Lewiston yawned. "I'm here. Make yourself comfortable." He headed for the bathroom.

Sam walked past a double bed. It was covered in the kind of quilt somebody's grandmother would use. An unused single bed sat next to it. There was a table. He went to the window, opened the shutters and had to lean over the window box to see Lewiston's view of Lake Maggiore.

He heard the toilet flush then, "What's going on?" Lewiston shuffled out in his pajamas. "Why haven't you begun?"

Sam turned, withdrawing his gun from his jacket. Straight-armed he pointed it at Lewiston. He saw moisture promptly spread down the leg of Lewiston's pajamas as he raised his hands.

"I want answers!" Sam said

Lewiston trembled. "You're going to shoot me? In a room right on the square? With the window open?"

"No one saw me come in. I'll take my chances if I have to."

Sam almost felt sorry for Lewiston. He had the haggard, nervous, long-eyed look of a man who'd been stalked day and night and knew his strength was gone. Still Lewiston met Sam's gaze.

"What in the world do you think I could tell you? I don't know anything!"

"The last time I got stuck between Brown and these folks, I was shot and left for dead. Is that what Brown means to happen? Use me to kill this kid then you turn around and finish me off?"

Lewiston lowered his hands. "Of course not. I'm backup, like Brown said. Play sick; refuse local doctors; insist Felix call me in. I show up and if anything goes wrong I poison the boy. In either case, I pronounce the boy dead and try to make sure nothing goes wrong in the autopsy or with the coroner. Felix is going to be taken out of the way somehow."

"Why? Why would you do that?"

"I don't especially like having a sword of Damocles dangling over my family's head. To remove it, yes, I'll do whatever it takes."

"Yeah, well—" Sam believed Lewiston. He was too frightened to lie. Sam lowered the gun and turned back to the window.

"I just wish I knew what this boy could have ever done to Brown," Lewiston said.

"Seems to be enough that he's breathing."

"How will you do it?" Lewiston asked.

"Easy. Take him sailing. Up north past the Gola and out of sight. I could have done it already on my own, but squirrelly crap keeps happening. I think today is the day. Tomorrow at the latest. You don't need to come."

"What if something goes wrong because you didn't do what Brown told you?"

Sam eyed him. "Yeah, yeah."

"You don't even care. Why are you so willing to do this to an innocent little boy?"

Sam opened his wallet, pulled out a handful of bills and waved them, grinning. "I don't have a family," he said and headed for the door.

Lewiston called, "I'm sorry I ever saved your rotten …" His voice trailed off.

Sam didn't look back. He had a brilliant plan. It would get money out of Felix and rid him of Lewiston, too. Sam had no intention of letting Lewiston, a handsome black man, stay at the villa and hang around Maggie. Sam would do as Brown wanted, go back and drink the contents of Brown's first vial, meant to make him sick enough to warrant Felix summoning Lewiston, who'd been Sam's personal doctor all these years. Felix would never know Lewiston was already here. But when Lewiston showed up, Sam planned to convince Felix that he'd regained part of his memory and knew something crucial to Maggie and the kid.

However, Sam would say that if he spilled the beans it would force him into a lifetime of hiding and he was broke. Naturally, Felix would pony up a ton of money.

Then Sam would tell him Lewiston was there to kill the kid, which was true. Instead, Sam would turn the tables and kill that smartass Lewiston himself, assuming Felix didn't do it first. No more Lewiston. Sam would be a hero. Brown wasn't likely to give a damn as long as Sam followed through and killed the kid.

Sam concluded that's how he'd gotten shot before, not following Brown's instructions. He'd make the boy's death look like an accident as Brown wanted. Brown would shower Sam with money. Win. Win.

Lewiston's opinions didn't matter as long as he would show up at the villa when called and keep his hands off Maggie while he was at it.

She would need consoling soon and Sam couldn't wait. His two days at the villa had been pure torture. All he did was fantasize about her. Last night he'd slipped past Bartolo and listened outside her door. When he heard her breathing and knew she was asleep, he'd tiptoed in and pulled the covers back, feasting on the sight. She didn't sleep naked, but the nightgown she wore was thin enough. She was sweetly voluptuous, looked like honey, and she was untouched—had waited for only him. He'd managed to resist crawling in beside her, but just barely.

As he walked back to the house, Sam thought of her. He thought of the tears she would shed when Jess died. Too bad. Nice kid. Smart, too. But there was nothing Sam could do about it. Brown was a goal-oriented type. If Sam didn't deliver, Brown would just hire someone else.

When Sam reached the villa, Antonella stepped out on the porch. She was a small, keen-eyed woman, plump from the pasta she cooked, but not really overweight. He loved her souvenir aprons. Today it was Venice and the Bridge of Sighs.

"I wait for you, signor Duffy."

"Oh yeah? What is it, Antonella?"

In Italian she told him Bartolo had gone to Turin to make arrangements at the convent and Felix was inside on the phone, but he'd be leaving soon, too. Jess and Maggie were at the lake. Now that Sam was here, she was going home.

"Ciao, signor Duffy," she said.

Sam smiled. He liked her for some reason and she seemed to like him, too. Maybe it was all the great food. She loved to cook. He loved to eat.

"Ciao, Antonella."

After she left, Sam stood in the hall outside the living room door being careful not to disturb the doorbell pulley so Felix wouldn't know he was there.

He heard, "I miss you, too, sweetheart. I'll be home soon. I promise."

A pause.

"Don't cry, Ariel, don't cry Ari. It was just a bad dream. Daddy's fine. There are no goblins over here, no monsters and if I see one, I'll … I'll inject him with knockout drops and put him right to sleep. How's that?"

A pause.

"Of course I will. Yes, darling, I will. I love you, too. Think of me before you go to sleep and I'll think of you. Call Mommy to the phone, now. Bye, Ari. I love you."

Sam wished he hadn't heard this dumb conversation. He listened as Felix talked to his wife and gave advice about Ariel's nightmares. Then Sam stepped outside and walked in as if he'd just arrived.

He went into the living room, raising his eyebrows. As Felix hung up, Sam asked, "Everything fine?"

"Yes, fine."

He watched Felix pace, then stop and turn to him. "Listen, I need to make arrangements for Maggie and Jess. I need to—uh, let's see. By the way, Jess knows how he was born. Maggie told him. Funny thing what he said, though."

"What?" Sam asked, surprised to see Felix look insecure. He looked totally confused, in fact.

"Nothing, I guess. Nothing. I think it'll be easier, though, if I go into town and help make arrangements. The sooner they're settled, the better for everyone. Will you be here for a while?"

"You're thinking of taking them today?"

"No, tomorrow at the earliest, probably the day after. I have to get movers, make arrangements."

Sam nodded. "Go ahead. Anybody throws another dead bird over the wall, I'll just shoot them."

Felix looked aghast, and then he sighed and said, "That might not be a bad idea." He patted his pockets like he'd forgotten something, his *I'm-a-lord* look gone as if he wanted to vanish into his expensive suit.

Sam wondered what had happened to make the old cock-sure Felix disappear.

"All right. I'll walk into town. I could use the exercise. I'll probably be back in a couple of hours. Tell Maggie, would you?"

Definitely, Sam thought. As soon as Felix left, Sam raced up to his room and opened the shutters enough to see down to the lake.

Jess had on his trunks and was swimming in the porticiollo. Maggie had on a swimming suit, too, and a big scarf wrapped around her bottom like a skirt. Now and then the breeze lifted the edge of it and he could see her hips. Logically, nothing to shout about, but to him so nice.

Why did he want her so? Day and night he thought of nothing but her. His only fear about killing Jess was that she might find out and stay away from him.

Now was the perfect time since no one else was here. He could go out and take Jess sailing while she swam. But Brown said he should summon Lewiston first by playing sick. Sam decided to drink Brown's vial as soon as they started back to the house.

He watched her unwrap the scarf, dip her toes in the water, then bend over to dip her fingers in. Maggie had informed him the lake was often warmer than the air and even in the spring they swam sometimes.

The sight of her butt thrilled him, covered though she was. Slowly she waded in and slid down with her back against one wall, kicking her feet. Jess swam to and fro and Sam again felt jealous that he got to touch her, hug her, kiss her neck. He seemed to be consoling her, but, Sam reminded himself, not for long.

God, he wanted Maggie. He hated Brown for warning him off her and making him sit on his hands here for two whole days.

He looked down at his pecker, which was jutting out. He unzipped his pants and grabbed it, letting out a shuddering grunt. He watched Maggie sink lower in the water until it lapped into her cleavage, sloshing in and running out, and he grew dizzy with desire and breathed harder, groaning, glad no one was in the house. He imagined he was down there in the little harbor with her, running his pecker in and out of that cleavage, or finding her supposedly virgin cunt and banging it, banging it …No, he couldn't do that … but God, oh God, would it be good!—and then doing her underwater, holding her down, making her fuck him. It would be good, good, good.

Too quickly, he was hovering above the white-hot burning cliff, a beautiful devil calling his name. He heard her start singing as he hung blissfully there, but with no woman to hold onto he plunged swiftly over and down, down, down. He tried to keep his eyes on Maggie, far away in the porticiollo, but instead he dropped to his knees, saying, "Oh shit, not yet," and ejaculated in a pitiful spurt.

Frustrated, he looked out the window for renewed inspiration, but Maggie was on her way inside as if she knew he needed her. Again he grew aroused. The hell with Brown's instructions. He couldn't stand it anymore. She was coming to him at last. She would take him back to the white-hot burning cliff.

———

Maggie was trying to hold back tears as she approached the house. Jess had just announced his favorite song of the month was

"What a friend I have in Jesus." In his whole life he'd never heard it until this week. Maggie had sung it to him while he was growing in her belly but she'd stopped the night Sam died. Now that Sam was back—changed in mind and body, but not in soul—she'd started singing, "What a friend I have in Jesus," again.

It came out mournfully, though, not with joy, because Maggie was fighting a dawning depression and the same crushing uncertainty she saw in Felix's eyes when she told him what Jess said.

If Jess were really Max Segre's son, why would he talk like this? Saying they hadn't been chosen by God to restore his Son to the world? They'd brought Jesus Christ to life just to serve their own illusions, their own vanity. Jess had come just for the two of them? If so, what a terrible thing they'd done.

Now here was her boy, in this dark and troubled world, having to deal with dying pregnant women and dead birds. Who knew what else would come? And for what? For Felix whom she had always known was half mad and for Maggie, a plain and stupid, stupid woman. An unfulfilled woman, doing what unfulfilled women did. She felt if she went on a pilgrimage to the holiest place on earth, it wouldn't cleanse her erring soul.

This morning, when she confided in Felix, he had confided in her, too. Jess wanted to study in India. When she asked Jess, he said it was true. Yes, there were accounts that Jesus went there. But when she asked Jess again about saving the world, he said he couldn't because it wasn't lost. The many conflicting religions didn't disturb him, nor did the many wars. He said the world had a purpose that transcended present human understanding. A few sensed this, but most did not. To find a way through this troubled world, we must only be guided by love. When he returned from India, all he wanted was to live out his days with her, fulfilling the purpose of his reincarnation. Her happiness, Felix's happiness, were the sole missions of his life.

Maggie climbed to the spiraled porch, humming the spiritual though her stomach was tied in knots. The song seemed to mock her, given what Jess said. She'd tried to be cheerful for his sake, but all Maggie wanted was to run inside and hide herself.

She opened the front door and heard a strange cry as if someone was hurt. Not a cry, her name. "Maggie!"

It was Sam.

Fearfully she called, "Sam? What's the matter? Where are you?"

She found him by his voice. Maggie stopped when she saw him, questioning her eyes. He lay on her pristine bed, beneath Mary ascending, the salmon walls framing his nakedness. He was in a state she knew he wouldn't want anyone to see. He didn't act as if he noticed her at first.

"Oh, my lord, what's wrong? What's happened to you?" She grabbed a blanket from the closet shelf and rushed to drape it over him.

"Maggie, Maggie?"

Now he sounded like Jess did when he called, needing her. His body shook and his hands touched her face, finding her mouth and Maggie didn't stop him because she was struck through with pity and full of sorrow that her whole life was falling apart.

What was wrong with Sam? What had happened to this man she loved? Would he ever return to himself and gaze into her eyes, saying, *Maggie my girl* this and *Maggie my girl* that and whistling *Too-ra-loo-ra-loo-ral* to her when she was afraid, like she was now?

She let him open her mouth. Like a baby exploring, he stuck his fingers inside. Gently she tried to move his hand away, but he wouldn't let her. His fingers made suggestive movements in her mouth and in alarm she tried to push him away, but suddenly Sam threw his weight against her and she was lying on her back with him crawling on top of her. Now when he said, "Maggie!" his voice was no longer like a boy's.

Maggie was shocked to feel Sam's erection against her body, uninvited, see his eyes glaze over in lust and in the same moment feel his hand leave her mouth and pin her shoulder to the white coverlet and the other hand pull at the top of her swimsuit.

A memory flashed in her mind. Macon, Georgia where she was born. Three white men around her in the woods. What they'd tried to do before her father came.

She screamed, "Stop, Sam, stop!" but he reached inside the swimsuit to her breast.

She cried out, "No, no! Oh, please, don't!"

And at that moment, Jess was in the room, dripping water from the lake as if her cry had instantly transported him there. It tore her apart to see his face when he realized what was happening to his mother—here in the salmon room no male but him had entered until now.

Fearing his pain more than hers, Maggie shouted, "Go away, Jess!"

Instead he raced forward, holding himself straight like one of the knights on the walls of La Rocca di Angera. Like Arjuna in his chariot, he charged toward Sam and pulled his foot—just a little boy, after all, trying to get someone off his mother.

Sam stopped long enough to jerk his foot from Jess.

"Go away, Jess! Please, please go away!" Maggie cried.

Jess grabbed Sam's foot again. "Stop! You're hurting my mother!"

"I told you to go away!" Maggie cried. Then in a stern voice she shouted, "Go away!

Jess ran to the door. Sorrow on his face, he looked back and sobbed, "She is your beloved! Your beloved!" Then he slammed the door behind him and was gone.

"Interfering brat!" Sam said, but suddenly he let go of Maggie and rolled over to the other side of the bed.

Maggie lay still, breathing hard, unsure whether he'd lunge for her if she moved.

Sam was staring at her uncovered breast.

"What happened? " he said, looking confused. "Did anything happen?"

Slowly, Maggie pulled her bathing suit back in place.

"Did I do er … anything?" he asked. As he talked he handled his body shamelessly. "I mean … what happened?"

Maggie sat up, remembering her night at the shore waiting, waiting, waiting. She hadn't waited for this. Like Cio Cio San she was betrayed.

"I'm sorry," he insisted. "If anything *did* happen, I'm sorry. I respect you. I wouldn't do that. I mean I would do that. Believe me, I would, but only if it's okay."

As he talked, Maggie cautiously rose, watching his eyes grow frantic.

"Don't go. I … I'd like to touch you. I need to. Would you let me touch you? I … I said I'm sorry."

He was stumbling, mumbling.

"I'll keep still." He lay flat, as if to demonstrate. "I won't hurt you. I'll let you do what you want if you'll just touch me. Just a little bit."

"I can't," she whispered, wanting to pray to God for help—for herself as well as Sam—but the words wouldn't form on her lips. She was too full of shame and guilt over what she and Felix had done.

"Okay, then. That's okay. I understand. I mean I've got a slight problem down here as you can see and I do like you, Maggie."

Close to tears, Maggie hovered, afraid to move, thinking, *Sam? This isn't my Sam. It's somebody else.*

He gestured toward her. "You and I used to be together. They say I took care of you and your kid. We must have kissed, right? You must have at least let me kiss you, right? Didn't you ever want more? Didn't you ever want this, too?" He looked down, then back up at her. "It'll feel good. I promise. I'll keep my hands at my sides. I'll do exactly what you tell me. Nothing more. Nothing less. How's that sound?"

She backed up into her armless floral chair.

Sam, the man she loved, was finally in her bedroom by the beautiful lake. He was naked on her bed, as in so many of her dreams for ten long years. Only it wasn't Sam. It was a half-ruined shell of the man she'd known: his lusts doubled, his honor halved. She wanted to run, but her feet were blocks of stone.

"If you're really a virgin and that's the trouble, we don't have to go all the way. You could just …you could just use your hand if you want. I'll go down on you in exchange and make you feel good. I promise."

Now the tears Maggie had held back fell. This was like the nightmares she'd never shared with anyone. She'd had them off and on since the harrowing night of Jess's birth—terrifying visions of she and Felix stumbling into hell together, instead of the heaven-on-earth for which they'd reached. Her virginity would be mocked and stolen by faceless demons. Even asleep in this simple room, she'd had nightmares.

This was nothing like her dreams of love. They were similar to the beautiful *Song of Songs*, as Jess had said. Sam would kiss her with the kisses of his mouth, saying *Behold, thou art fair, my love, thou hast doves eyes, Open to me my love, my undefiled, Thy navel is like a round goblet and thy breasts are clusters of grapes. Come, my Beloved. You are mine.*

Sam rose from the white bed, still handling himself, then stopped as if he were afraid she'd run away. "Quit crying! I didn't mean it. Hell, yes I did, but it's not my fault. That God you keep talking about did this." He looked down at himself, then at Maggie's hips. "It was him that made a place for this to go, you know, not me." He clenched his fists. "How the hell am I supposed to ignore that when my mouth tastes like metal and I know I'm going to explode? I can't stop it. I wasn't meant to."

Maggie couldn't run. She was crying too hard. It felt like God was punishing her stupid, stupid designs—having the arrogance to sleep beneath the painting of blameless Mary, and imagine they were alike.

Sam seemed to grow desperate in response. "Shit! All right. I messed up. I knew I would. Don't cry. For God's sake, Maggie my girl, don't cry!"

What had he said? Maggie wiped her eyes. "What did you say?"

"What? Oh, that I'm sorry."

"No you didn't, you didn't, you said something else." Suddenly she felt insanely happy. He'd said, *Maggie, my girl.* How could he, unless he was starting to remember? Sam was here, if only in part. He was in this tormented body she'd longed for. Part of him knew who she was. The last time she turned from him, it was to carry out a plan for which the real God had punished her with ten years of loneliness and the guilt that was consuming her now.

All her fear disappeared. Maggie went to him. On tiptoe she reached up and hungrily, wildly kissed his mouth and his beard scraped her cheek like it had on that first night long ago. He'd climbed the garden wall in Cliffs Landing trying to rescue her from being Felix's guinea pig.

Maggie inhaled his smell like she had on that night, and Sam kept his promise. He didn't move toward her an inch, though she could tell he was fighting the frenzy he'd been in. She thought she could almost understand, if she tried. For ten years she'd lived with her unfulfilled desire for this man.

He moaned, "Maggie, Maggie, Maggie," and she backed away, breathing hard, her tears dry. She lowered the straps of her swimsuit, peeled it down, stepped out of it and stood before him, her mind made up to commit fornication. Why not? She wasn't Mary, chosen by God. Jess had made that crystal clear. She was a plain and stupid woman no man had ever desired except Sam. She wanted to reach under the pillow for her beautiful silken nightgown so she could give herself to him in the way she'd dreamed but it seemed a pointless thing to do.

"Oh, fuck!" he breathed.

"Don't hurt me, Sam. Keep your promise."

Shaking, he lay on his back, his hands beneath him, his eyes searching her body, every shadow and curve. "Touch me, Maggie, touch me any way you want."

And Maggie did.

She kissed him with the passionate kisses of her mouth and let him put his face betwixt her breasts; she put her tongue to his tongue, kissed his skin, put his penis to the part of her that had never known a man and gasped as he pushed and the blood ran down on her white bed. To her he was a roe or a young hart upon the mountains, just like in the *Song of Solomon*.

She clung to him as he took her to a place she'd never been, a white-hot blazing cliff where they heard angel voices. She knew he didn't want to leave and neither did she. Shivering they held each other over the fabulous, fiery cliff, and he taught her how to stay and hear the angels sing.

It lasted so long, Maggie thought her heart would burn entirely away, then he said, "Maggie, my girl, oh God!"

Maggie soared to the sky above, but found herself alone there. Sam wasn't with her. His frenzy had returned. He'd broken his promise and pinned her down. He was all over her body, gripping, kneading, slamming into her. The passion she'd felt changed to terror and searing pain.

What was he doing?

"Sam, stop."

He paid no attention.

She tried to scream but he clapped his hand over her mouth. Maggie fought.

Why wouldn't he stop?

But she was no match for Sam who was roughly using her body as he chose. This wasn't love. It was his body commanding hers.

She screamed against his hand until she thought she'd vomit or pass out. It lasted forever, her soul wanting to flee his invasion, taking her obscenely as if she wasn't even there, only her flesh, the openings of her body.

At length he rose atop her, his hips pounding hers, his gaze fixed on her weeping eyes, his breath shuddering in grunts. For the first time in her life, Maggie Johnson felt a man begin to ejaculate inside her. He didn't say words of devotion. Sam hung over her, and then his eyes rolled up, one hand tightened around her throat, the other convulsing on her breast, yelling," Fuuuuck meeee biiiitch!"

———

The sky was dark, the stars gone, the night empty except for a single sound. From a tape player came an aria from an opera. Its faint notes lofted into the still night sky over the lake, wailing beauty from the windowsill where Maggie leaned, the shutters open, her beautiful nightgown finally, futilely on. She'd never quite understood Cio Cio San's closing aria, but now she did. She knew why Leontyne Price sang like that. She was singing from a sorrow too deep for tears. It was music that would hush the night—make the swans stop swimming, the moon stop glowing. Each note fell so perfectly anyone would have to close their eyes, or lower their head, or sigh when it reached them.

Inside Sam snored, but only lightly, the elegant *Notre Dame de Rocamadour* on her bedside table, the black Madonna and child, turned to the wall as was Mary ascending. Whenever Maggie tried to leave, he awoke and prevented her, like she was carrion he hadn't finished feeding on. He didn't care what she felt, seemed to enjoy hurting her over and over.

Jess hadn't returned. Neither had Felix or Antonella, though Maggie realized they must have. They must have come back and heard or seen her with Sam, then left the house to keep from witnessing her sin.

In her shaking hand, Maggie clutched a carved jack knife—Jess's favorite—determined to prevent Sam from making her sin again.

The opera came to the chilling part where Cio Cio San's boy came in the room and she sang. *Tu? Tu? Tu? Tu? Tu?* "You? You? You? You? You? Little idol! My love, flower of the lily and the rose. This you must never know."

She looked down on the empty porticiollo, which had no Mirror Dinghy in it. Where was Jess? Where was her son? Her flower of the lily and the rose? How could she search for him, see him, lay a hand on his head, ruined as she was? How could she meet the village women's gaze in the market? Go to the Santa Marta church? Her decency and honor gone?

She listened to Madama Butterfly's lament of death—for a love once treasured more than life.

Maggie understood Cio Cio San.

She was in this death.

Chapter 23

The next morning Felix rose before Jess and Antonella. They had slept at her house, driven away from the yellow villa by Sam and Maggie. Felix had returned and found Jess crouched under Maggie's window, sobbing as he recited the *Song of Songs*, and praying for angels to come. Even when he saw Felix he kept praying and crying out that if he were really Jesus he would know how to help his mother.

Felix had stormed inside ready to cut Sam's throat. Then he heard the sounds from Maggie's room. He couldn't believe the woman who'd delivered Jess in a genuine virgin birth was squandering her purity this way. The sound of her passion repulsed him and turned him around. Outside he scooped Jess directly up and took him to Antonella's house.

Half the night Jess had cried.

Felix stayed awake trying to comfort him, but Jess wouldn't be consoled, convinced his mother was being hurt. Felix had never seen such anguish in a child. It made him so angry with Maggie he couldn't have slept anyway.

Now he was up with the dawn, determined to confront her. Sam had always been a low-life as far as Felix was concerned. Yes, for a while he'd been somewhat decent, but early on he'd tried to sleep with Maggie and when she refused he'd tried to bed Frances, his own sister, who hadn't exactly fought Sam off. True, when Maggie was pursued, Sam had rescued her, but that was his only saving grace. Sam's behavior was no real surprise.

Maggie's was.

She'd left Jess alone and frightened in order to satisfy her lust for Sam.

He tiptoed downstairs and out of the house and in five minutes was at the yellow villa's gate. He opened it and walked around the driveway in the morning mist, through the garden and into the house. He heard noises from the kitchen, went in that direction and was dumbfounded and outraged at what he saw. There they were against a wall, Maggie groaning with her eyes closed, Sam's motions as obsessive as a madman's.

Or was she sobbing?

Sam was naked, his back to Felix, but she had on street clothes as if she'd been trying to leave. One of Sam's hands held her wrists against the wall while the other moved on her body in frenzy.

A bloody jack knife lay open on the floor at their feet. Blood trickled from Sam's left shoulder.

Raggedly Maggie sobbed. She was sobbing as he pinned her against the wall.

Jess's innocent claim that the world didn't need saving flashed in Felix's mind. At the moment he fervently disagreed.

He saw a bottle of Antonella's prized Barbaresco wine, the Marziano Abbona, its signature humming bird poised on a branch beneath the name. It was left over from their dinner last night. Quietly he picked it up, wishing it were something cheap and putrid, and tiptoed closer as Sam ripped at Maggie's clothes and rutted against her, panting, "Come on, brown sugar. Let me in, damn it! Let me in!"

Felix lifted the bottle that housed the prestigious Nebbiolo grape and with satisfaction brought it down on Sam's bobbing skull.

Sam dropped and rolled to the side like a dead man. Felix ignored him. He bent over Maggie, who had slid to the floor, shuddering and trying to pull down her clothes. He wiped an ocean of tears from her face.

"Don't look at me, Felix," she gasped. "Take Jess and go away. Go away! I'm not fit to be around him anymore. If you've ever cared a thing about me, take him away!"

He noticed bruises on her neck, saw a scratch on her arm. Felix had done this. He had done it by allowing Sam free access to two of the most precious people he would ever know.

Felix swallowed and whispered, "Of course I'll look at you. I'll always look at you. And I certainly won't go away. I'm your friend and I love you. I'm going to help."

Sam moaned and Felix fought a passionate desire to repeatedly kick him, but Maggie fainted in his arms. Satisfied that Sam would stay put for now, Felix rose and carried her upstairs to her simple room, removed the stained white sheets and lay her down—the black Madonna, the Notre Dame de Rocamadour from 12th century France, turned to the wall on Maggie's bedside table.

"Maggie, wake up," he whispered, touching her cheek but she didn't stir. What had Sam done to her? Felix lost control, put his arms around Maggie and buried his face in her stomach in despair, crying out the "Salve Regina" as he had on the night of Jess's birth:

> Hail Holy Queen, Mother of Mercy, our life
> our sweetness and our hope. To thee do we cry, poor
> banished children of Eve;
> To thee do we send up our sighs, mourning and weeping in
> this valley of tears.

Maggie's eyes opened and drifted over his face. To no avail he tried to comfort her. She simply closed her eyes again, turned her face away, and almost visibly withdrew her spirit from the room. A cursory examination told him what Sam had done. Maggie's flesh was raw and bleeding. What guardian angel had prevented Sam from inflicting further injuries, he didn't know.

Even as Felix treated Maggie, it seemed impossible to believe anyone could have hurt her this way—second in his heart only to daughter, sister and wife. It made Felix feel ashamed of his gender, though there wasn't a man alive who didn't understand rape. It was the first thing soldiers did in war. He didn't ask Maggie to open her eyes because he wished he could close his own.

He put his face close to hers and stroked her hair. "I'll be back, Maggie. You lie still. You're safe, now. I'll be right back."

Felix went to Sam's room and found his gun. He took it downstairs and stood a long time over Sam, an angel and a demon wrestling for his soul at the sight of dried blood on Sam's scrotum and the fresh moisture that seeped onto his thigh. "Damn you to hell!" he shouted. Felix removed the safety and aimed at Sam's head, then his heart, then lower down, his hand violently shaking. "Damn you, damn you!" he cried, but he opened the chamber and removed the bullets, went outdoors and hid the gun in the garden compost heap.

He returned and looked down in rage on the naked Sam, still unconscious in the home of those who'd welcomed him, who would have loved him to the end of time. Felix wanted to take one of Antonella's knives and surgically prevent Sam from doing this ever again, but instead he dragged him out to the lake and, wanting to drown him, put him in the lake house. He came back and brought Sam's belongings and tossed them on the floor around him, wanting to set them afire and leave him to die there. Instead he did what doctors do and satisfied himself that Sam would live, then injected him with a sedative strong enough to keep him unconscious while Felix tried to ease the disasters Sam had caused.

By the time Sam awoke, Maggie and Jess would be in Turin at the convent of the Poor Clare Nuns—ideal for a world-ruined, heaven-cherished black Madonna and her son, his heart bleeding for the mother he adored.

Chapter 24

Dr. Chuck Lewiston was sick of waiting at the Hotel Florida. It had been well over twenty-four hours since Sam's visit and there had been no call. The delay made him uneasier. Lewiston was impatient to have this terrible business behind him.

From the lobby he gazed at the charming Piazza del Popolo where locals of this small town gathered under lanterns in the evening light. They were people leading simple lives—waiters, shop attendants, tour boat operators, fishermen. At first there'd been only two, then a passerby stopped to chat, then another and another. The women wore skirts and blouses, their hair short and simply curled, no makeup or jewelry except the beaded hoop or drop earrings worn in Italy since the Roman Empire. The men wore plain slacks with short-sleeved cotton shirts open at the neck. No Harvard medical degrees here, he imagined; no pools at villas in the hills. None under forty. They were surely the town stalwarts, their most valuable possessions the marvelous lake beyond the wall and their friendship with each other.

Soon they wandered off more or less together in the twilight as if to continue their conversation elsewhere. Lewiston, cell phone in hand, followed over the cobbled pavement, hoping they were headed for a local watering hole. It turned out that they were.

He entered a room with wooden tables and chairs, a white ceiling, and beige stucco walls with an unsigned mural of medieval Arona at one end. He took a table not far from them. With his high school Italian and quick refresher on the flight and at the hotel, he was picking up snatches of their talk.

Village gossip.

They kept saying *morta* and *morte* and *morire*—unexpected words. They were talking about someone's death.

He ordered a beer in his phrase book Italian, "Vorrei

una birra, per piacere."

When it came, he didn't notice because he was focusing on what the villagers said. Standing over him, the waiter cleared his throat. "Con permesso, Signore?" Lewiston took his arms off the small wooden table so the waiter could set down the glass.

"Scusi. Grazie," Lewiston said and sipped the beer, pretending he was looking out a window.

He heard, "La Madonna Nera." *The Black Madonna.*

He'd forgotten about Europe's mysterious black Madonna statues and hadn't realized there was one in the town. Lewiston thought of trying to find it, and then remembered he was an assassin, out to kill.

Suddenly the locals' conversation stopped. A man stood in the doorway, gazing vacantly around.

They greeted him with loud, cheerful calls of "Ciao, Carlo!" and one man patted an empty chair. The newcomer came and sat down. By their changed manner, Lewiston sensed they had great respect for Carlo, who was related to the deceased. They were acting like people did around the recently bereaved. A man said *morte* again and everyone nodded. They were offering condolences on the death of Carlo's wife.

The man thanked them, "Grazie, cari amici." *Thank you my dear friends.*

But he didn't look thankful. Carlo looked as if the only way he'd found this tavern was that he'd come here all his life, and that he knew the names of his friends only because he'd always said them. Someone offered to order him food, but the man looked confused, as if food could only come from the *morta* one—the wife, the signora, who'd no doubt fed him since they met.

He refused and seemed angered by a renewed offer.

Someone poured him a glass of wine and he put his head back and downed it. Then another man was at the door, but it was clear he didn't need a glass of wine.

"È Adamo!" someone said.

Carlo opened his arms and Adamo staggered into them. They cried unashamedly about the morta one. Then Adamo's fist smashed to the table.

"Eravamo errati! È un diavolo! È un diavolo!" Adamo slurred. *We were wrong. He is a devil.*

"Chi?" *Who?*

"Il ragazzo nella villa gialla vicino a La Rocca." *The boy in the yellow villa near La Rocca.*

Then the conversation became a verbal brawl. The child was a saint. The child was a devil. He was La Mamma Nera's son. Such love they had for each other, a kind not of this earth.

Adamo drunkenly declared God would punish the boy.

Lewiston paid his bill and left the man with the *morta* wife, sobbing in Adamo's arms.

Outside he hailed a taxi and asked the driver if he knew of a yellow villa near La Rocca where a black woman lived with her son.

An hour later, Lewiston stood beneath the cliff with the ruined castle on its top. The map he'd consulted said it was La Rocca di Arona. He'd had to consult a map because a taxi driver had first directed him to La Rocca di Angera. It was just an old castle on the other side of the lake. When Lewiston returned, having discovered La Rocca di Angera wasn't anywhere near via Sempione, he saw the same driver in the taxi queue. Lewiston complained to him and the man rudely drove off, providing no ride and no information. He said no black woman lived in Arona with her son and, if she ever had, she was gone now.

Lewiston suspected the townspeople in the tavern would have said the same if he'd asked, though he'd overheard their conversation. Prying strangers were not welcome. These people were loyal to each other.

Lewiston had come here on foot. Now he wound his way around La Rocca di Arona and onto via Sempione, looking for yellow walls.

He hesitated when he saw them, cars whizzing by as he stood against the little villa's gate. Did a woman like his wife live here with her child? A black woman?

Lewiston trembled, pressed against the gate, his mouth dry,

remembering the jade Porsche and the silver Aston Martin and the identical notes: *Don't drive off a cliff. Love, Chuck. Love, Dad.* Standing at the gate beneath the yellow walls, Lewiston yearned for his lost life: the security of home, pride in saving lives. He could take no pride in this.

He pushed open the unlocked gate and crept to the side of the driveway, wondering what had delayed Sam. Almost immediately he stumbled over a child's unpowered two-wheel scooter. They were just becoming popular ten years ago when Lewiston began caring for Handsome Jones. He remembered the fractures, the dislocated arms and knees that started pouring into the emergency room—the contusions, abrasions, strains and sprains. Lewiston found himself wondering if the boy he would help kill wore a helmet, elbow and kneepads when he rode.

He slumped onto the grass, raised his knees and dropped his head between them, trying to breathe.

""Chi è là fuori?" he heard in a stern male voice and snapped alert then to his feet. He tried not to tremble as he looked up at Felix Rossi, a man with whom he had so much in common, as their only meeting revealed—and so little. Rossi gazed down through the shutters he'd opened, his eyes wide with horror as if he'd witnessed the end of the world.

"Dr. Rossi, it's me," he said.

"Who is me?"

"Dr. Lewiston. Chuck Lewiston. I took care of Sam."

"You're here in Arona?" Rossi looked toward the road. "How? Why?"

Feeling sweat under his arms, Lewiston said, "Sam phoned and told me where he was—"

"He told you where he was? Incredible! But why am I not surprised?"

Lewiston wondered if Sam had already killed the boy. "Sam said he was feeling sick, like he might have seizures again and since I was planning to travel …"

"Seizures? My God, my God! I'll say he's had seizures, all right."

Had something happened to Sam? He said, "Is Sam all right?"

"Is he all right?" Rossi parroted, as if Sam's health was an absurd concern.

Lewiston concluded Sam was either dead or he'd done something dreadful. "Can I come in, Dr. Rossi?"

Rossi looked Lewiston up and down then nervously ran his fingers through his hair.

"Have you handled rape?"

Lewiston briefly closed his eyes. So that was it. Who had Sam raped this time? "Yes, I have."

"We could use your help up here," Rossi said and closed the shutters.

Lewiston's feet carried him up the driveway to the bower of roses. His eyes gazed on the fantastic lake. He entered the garden and climbed the steps to the porch with spiral columns, a Harvard MD, 1980, about to be gratefully welcomed by a Harvard MD-PhD, 1976.

———

In a cupboard beneath Antonella's staircase, in her house on the hills behind the plaza in Arona, Jess lay curled, nearly unconscious in the dark. He heard Antonella searching for him, calling him to dinner, but he couldn't rise.

He slipped from darkness into light and back again—the twin states that shape each other. He couldn't think. All he knew was this:

When he chose, he could feel the hearts of others—other people, the animals, the pulsing of the earth. Sometimes he'd think a thought, make a wish, and it would happen. One day he saw a baby bird fall from its nest and urgently wished it safety. He wished away its impending death, and with no feathers the baby bird flew.

Why he hadn't been able to help King Silent, his dearest friend, Jess didn't know. When they swam together, Jess caressing the crippled foot and weeping tears into the lake, King Silent only cavorted until Jess began to laugh. The swan's deformity had not changed. In prayer, Jess asked why. A voice from the darkness said he already knew.

To no avail he'd prayed for Sam to leave his mother alone.

In Antonella's cupboard, Jess hovered all alone between the manifest and the potential worlds. At length he rose and went into the kitchen with Antonella, but his heart remained in darkness with his mother and with Sam.

Chapter 25

There were waves in Sam's dream and it went on endlessly until it seemed only the swells of velvet terror in which he couldn't breathe were real, the ones of hollow loneliness, searing need. Whether each wave lasted five seconds or five centuries he couldn't tell. There was no time here.

Sometimes he heard or imagined voices that became part of the waves: *I'm my own woman, Sam, nobody owns me.*

Sometimes he heard a baby cry.

He was hearing it now. As it cried, stars were shooting from its mouth.

I'm my own woman, Sam, nobody owns me.

Now the wave formed kaleidoscopic scenes from his life. He was a seaman on a merchant ship, studying the world as he sailed it, reading the local papers, watching local TV, talking to cops in every port, becoming wise. He was a sailor who adored the ladies, especially whores, and who frequented sailors' bars to find them. They always loved to see Sam Duffy—free with his money, his wisecracks, his laughter. He could make up for the johns, make a working girl feel that someone cared for her that night. When sailors' brawls broke out, he waded in and rarely got the worst. He was a private eye, selling his knowledge of the world to the highest bidder. He could be counted on to deliver anything at all, unless hurting the defenseless was involved. He was balling a gorgeous babe named Coral, having the best sex of his life. He was watching over a woman he loved much more. Someone he'd die for.

He felt cold light.

Shivering, he raised his arm and was surprised to find that it moved. He gasped from what felt like real lungs.

The dream had changed.

Sam opened his eyes and thought his head would explode.

He was naked and the light was from the sun. A smell filled his nostrils and made him retch. He was lying in a pool of filth— apparently his own.

He heard barking. An animal was barking, though it sounded more like a puppy than a full-grown dog. Sam crawled out of the mess his body had made, then collapsed before wide doors that formed a wall. He pushed on the doors and saw a deck covered in dogwood blossoms. He glimpsed an unbelievable lake beyond and on the opposite shore cliffs and verdant hills.

His shoulder hurt, his head throbbed, he was disoriented and the light hurt his eyes, but Sam knew this definitely wasn't Central Park.

Where the hell was he?

He pulled himself to his feet, staggered onto the deck and when a new wave of nausea hit him, he slumped over the railing then tumbled hard onto the pebble-covered bank.

He lay where he landed, pain throbbing in his shoulder and behind his eyes, staring into the face of a swan.

It had a black and orange beak and an S-shaped neck and it looked so intelligent, Sam wouldn't have been surprised if it had started to speak. Instead it kept barking until other swans came. They proceeded to walk out of the lake and surround Sam where he lay.

He knew this wasn't normal swan behavior. They lived on both water and land. Sometimes they befriended people but they were often hostile, especially if they were nesting. Then they would aggressively attack intruders. They fed on underwater plants and weren't carnivorous, but Sam didn't like suddenly being surrounded by these birds. Some were nearly four feet high. Their wings could break bones.

Fighting nausea, he raised his head and rose to his knees. The swans lifted their necks and flapped their wings as if they'd all decided to stretch. He backed away from them, into the water, wondering what was going on. Not knowing made him feel dread.

One swan had stayed in the water. It backed up as Sam entered the lake. The other swans came in behind.

Sam took advantage of the chance to wash, not moving fast in case he got too dizzy. His upper arm was sore, as if he'd been stabbed. Semen was stuck to his skin and he wondered how he'd managed to not only crap and throw up on himself, but have an orgasm, too. As he washed he felt a thrill, a phantom passion he couldn't remember, and he yearned for the woman he'd been with, hoping she was real and not a figment of his dreams.

Soon he felt something brush against him and realized the first swan had tucked its head under his arm, nuzzling him like a pet.

That's when Sam noticed the black webbed foot growing on its back and realized the swan was deformed. It had stayed in the water because it couldn't walk. It was a big, noble and remarkably gentle animal and though it couldn't come ashore, it seemed to be the leader of the swans.

Sam stroked the bird's neck, wondering where he was and what had happened to bring him here. The other swans made figure eights nearby as if on guard. Were they watching over Sam and the cripple who was their king?

Perhaps he was in heaven.

He'd gone off, gun in hand, to protect a woman while she gave birth. Maggie, that's who. Perhaps he'd died defending Maggie and now was in heaven with these swans. It made sense. He was Irish. St. Patrick hung out with swans.

Or maybe he was in India's version of heaven. To the Hindu, those who realized truth, which they called Brahman, while still alive achieved swanhood, the highest state. All over India there were images of sacred swans.

The crippled bird particularly touched his heart. It was magnificent. Yet God, capricious as usual, had allowed it to be deformed.

In the cool water, under the cold sun, Sam reached out to the useless foot. He stroked it and the swan lowered its neck as if in shame. Sam felt sad for it, though he knew he shouldn't. After all this was heaven, glorious heaven on a lake full of splendor and radiance, where happiness reigned.

Tears pooled in Sam's eyes for no reason, as if this swan's deformity were the whole world's pain and Sam was somehow responsible for it. Tenderly he stroked the black webbed foot that had grown where it shouldn't and crippled a king.

In peace he floated in the water with the swan, his body's inner sickness easing. He began to hear other things, see things. Water lapping on the shore. Sea gulls cawing. Traffic.

He swam to shore and looked around, seeing the lake anew. There was a castle on the cliff on the opposite bank. He saw a hydrofoil in the water, churning toward the bank. He wished he had binoculars because he could have sworn it said, *Navigazione Lago Maggiore* on its side. Would heaven have Italian signs?

He went back into the little cottage and saw what he hadn't noticed before. A suitcase full of clothes. A wallet full of money. A drivers license, a passport. It had his photograph and the name Chuck O'Malley. It was the fake one he'd gotten so he could escape New York with Maggie and Felix, but the dates were wrong. What was happening?

Sam dried himself, trying to imagine the woman who had made him feel so good. He could tell he was going to long for her. If he hadn't needed to find out where he was and why, he would have lingered over this feeling. Instead he slipped on clean underwear and a pair of slacks, put on an ironed shirt, socks and shined shoes—all crisp and ready—as if he was meant to dress and get the hell out of here. He headed up stone stairs he discovered behind bushes overflowing with pink and purple flowers. At the top he turned to wave goodbye to the swans and saw only the leader.

Having drawn Sam into the water, it hadn't made another sound, though Sam had barked in imitation of its cry. In a low voice, he said, "Goodbye, King Silent" and watched it glide away. The name had come to him and seemed to fit.

————

Felix stood by as Dr. Lewiston bent over Maggie, his expression grave and unsurprised as if he'd seen this before. Both their medical bags sat open on her dresser. Lewiston had brought his because of Sam; Felix, as always, brought his.

Completing his examination, Lewiston took Maggie's hand, but she didn't acknowledge his presence. She kept her eyes closed. She hadn't responded all day.

Felix had tried to rouse her so they could leave for Turin and the convent of the Poor Clare nuns. He'd prayed beside her, talked to her, held her, but nothing worked. He'd tried wrapping Maggie in a blanket and bodily carrying her to a waiting cab. Out came her only words, "No, no!"

Felix couldn't ignore this, especially since her wishes had just been so brutally ignored.

Lewiston was gentle with her. He squeezed her hand and nodded for Felix to step outside. In the hall Lewiston passed his hand wearily over his eyes.

"She's suffering from a dissociative disorder, a defense mechanism precipitated by overwhelming stress and—" He paused.

Felix could have completed Lewiston's sentence: *Overwhelming sadness, due to a broken heart.*

"Right, no kidding?" Felix said. "Your patient, Sam Duffy, did that. You might have warned me."

"I wasn't sure then," Lewiston muttered.

"What does he have, some kind of paraphilias?"

"Yes, I think so. It's surely due to limbic system damage. He's probably having intense, repetitive fantasies," he glanced toward Maggie, "involving infliction of suffering on a non-consenting party."

Felix paced. "He wasn't like that before."

"No, I imagine not," Lewiston said. "I imagine someone would have killed him by now if he were." He looked toward Maggie on the bed, its stained white coverlet laundered by the housekeeper and replaced, the Virgin Mary ascending into heaven on the salmon wall above delicate swirls on the iron headboard. He seemed unable to picture her being savaged in this room.

"She was here, alone, with Duffy?"

Felix sighed. "Her son was here."

Lewiston blinked. "Too bad. He'll need attention, too. Where is he?"

Felix noticed Lewiston kept gazing at the black Madonna statue on Maggie's night table. Again its wise, serene face looked out on the room from beneath a jeweled crown. Felix wished he had moved it, but now it was too late. Lewiston had seen. Still, the chance of Lewiston attaching significance to it was remote.

"The boy's with friends," Felix said.

"Having the boy here might help her," Lewiston said. "People do die of broken hearts."

Felix wouldn't have called it that, but he'd certainly seen it—a patient starving the body to release the spirit, which wanted exit from the world.

"I'm not going to let that happen," Felix said and walked back to Maggie's bedside. He sat and stroked her forehead, hoping she didn't mind. She gave no sign, either way. The bruises on her throat had darkened and the sight of them filled Felix with rage. He pictured wrapping his hands around Sam's throat and squeezing until he was dead.

Felix took a deep breath.

Could this be God's punishment, like Maggie had mumbled in her sleep? Was Jess a mountain they had moved, the greater work they had done simply with their minds? Had they asked, sought, knocked and in answer God's son had really come?

Yesterday Felix asked Maggie to repeat what Jess had said. He'd been amazed at Jess's literal interpretation of Jesus' words. He doubted if anyone had viewed the gospel of Matthew in this way since it was written, some fifty years after Jesus' death. Jess not only thought he wasn't a clone of Max, he dismissed the importance of the Shroud DNA, and Felix's infamous contribution to genetics and cloning science. He thought that asking for something, then believing and expecting it would come, was enough—as if reality were entirely plastic and subject to change on a prayerful wish.

Yet Jess had wished for Maggie's safety, to no avail. Given this and Jess's Krishna obsession, it was very hard to believe Jess was

Jesus reborn. Still his interpretation of Matthew was stunning. In any case, Felix's sorrow about Maggie was complete.

"Medically, you've treated her as I would have," Lewiston said. "Now it's just a matter of time."

They heard a faint clanking sound and Felix rose from Maggie's bedside, knowing someone or something was outside. The front door bell had been jostled by a squirrel, a gust of wind, or a person lurking there.

"If it's Sam," Felix said, "I swear ... I swear I'll—" He went to Jess's empty room and grabbed a baseball bat that was leaning in a corner.

"Wait, Dr. Rossi!" Lewiston began.

Felix barely heard him. He scrambled down the stairs and yanked open the door, calling, "Chi è là?" *Who is it?* "Fatevi vedere!" *Show yourself!*

Lewiston came behind him and grabbed for the baseball bat but Felix jerked it away and stepped onto the spiraled porch, searching the stairs, the garden. He heard footsteps on gravel, saw a head peep around a corner of the villa. It was Sam.

"Felix Rossi?" Sam called. "Felix? Is that you? What in the world?" He gave a perfect imitation of innocent surprise, though Maggie lay upstairs, destroyed.

"Come here so I can kill you, Sam!" Felix shouted.

Sam's eyebrows flew up and he burst out laughing.

Enraged, Felix stormed wildly toward him, dragging the bat like a club, determined to drive it through his face.

Sam's smile disappeared. He backed up as Felix advanced.

"It's easy to bully a woman, isn't it? Face me, Sam! Face me!"

Again Sam smiled. "What the crap are you talking about?"

Felix swung and Sam feinted like a boxer. Laughing, Sam tried to grab Felix in a bear hug, but he lost his footing just as Felix gained his. Felix swung the bat and this time connected with Sam's hip. Sam yowled, got up, and scrambled away, shouting, "Are you crazy?"

Lewiston came, trying to grab the bat, but Felix swung it away.

"Sam, get out of here!" Lewiston called but Sam had gone to a tall tree on the property and was busy climbing it. When he got to a branch beyond Felix's reach, he paused and looked down as if he were about to laugh again.

Lewiston stood between Felix and the tree, trying to hold Felix back using his considerable strength from the long physical therapy of Sam.

Lewiston shouted, "Just get out of here, Sam!"

Rubbing his hip, Sam's smile disappeared. He shouted, "Who the hell are you?"

That's when they stopped.

Felix lowered the bat. Lewiston turned and faced the tree.

"Sam, it's Dr. Lewiston!"

"Dr. Lewiston who? Felix what the hell is the matter with you? Where are we? Is this Italy? How did we get here? Where's Maggie? What the damned hell is going on?"

Felix felt the wind pick up. Dogwood blossoms that had floated up from the lake house on the breeze sprinkled down on them where they stood.

Lewiston said to Felix, "If he remembers the past, then this near-term memory loss is hysterical. He's blocking out what he's done, and all that led to it."

They heard a muffled crash and Felix knew in his soul what it was. Something fragile breaking, like a glass, or a beautiful statue, or a woman's heart.

"Oh, Maggie!" Felix cried and ran for dear life back to the spiral-columned porch.

Chapter 26

Sam climbed down from the tree and ran behind Felix and Lewiston, his heart beating at what Felix had said. Maggie was here? His Maggie?

It seemed like only yesterday he was holding her in his arms, so in love he didn't care that she refused him until after her baby's birth. Him, Sam Duffy, who could have half the women in New York, went without sex for months for Maggie's sake.

It hadn't mattered because he adored her. In truth, he had loved Maggie the whole five years she'd worked for Felix, coming and going with dignity among the rich tenants, never letting anyone put her down, always kind. When he found out she'd gotten involved with Rossi's cloning scheme, Sam had disobeyed Brown to protect her.

When she and Felix lay hidden beneath Glen Span Arch, Maggie in the last moments of labor, he'd gone willingly after the gunmen who would have taken her life.

Sam's last memory was of her beautiful eyes, begging him to stay.

How could she suddenly be here?

He vaulted the steps to a porch with spiral columns and when Felix and Lewiston ran up a flight of blue tile stairs, he followed them, sensing their anxiety. He wondered what they thought was wrong but, if Maggie was here, everything would be fine. His eyes would drink her in like sunlight. He would kiss her forever and not let go. Tonight if she welcomed him to her bed, he'd open the window so he could see her in moonlight. He wanted the stars there when they made love.

He reached the second landing and saw Felix and Lewiston try the handle of a door. It was locked and as they banged on it, Sam grew afraid.

"Maggie! Open the door!" Felix called.

Sam's stomach knotted. He knew he had seen this door before. He felt dread so intense his pores opened and drenched his skin in sweat. He backed away as Felix put his shoulder to the door. If Maggie was there, why didn't she answer? Why had she locked herself in?

He heard wood splinter and saw the door give.

Felix shouted and so did Lewiston. All Sam's senses but one disappeared. He couldn't speak. He couldn't feel, hear, smell, or taste. He could only see one terrifying sight.

Maggie lay on the floor in a silken gown, empty bottles and vials scattered in the mess her body had made. Her torso writhed. Her chest pumped like a broken bellows trying to draw in air. Something vile drooled from her mouth. Her eyes were open but Sam knew they didn't see.

Outside her door, Sam dropped to his knees, the memory of a phantom thrill filling his mind with horror.

Someone had taken her by force. He had enjoyed her pain. Sam saw the bruises on her neck. He saw her terror and the climax it had induced in the man.

It wasn't him.

Please, God, it wasn't him.

All his life he'd been a rascal, just like Maggie always said. He'd loved the ladies, every one. He would have sooner turned down money than a roll in the hay, but this?

She lay on her back with one arm stretched in his direction across the floor. At her side, Felix and Lewiston were focused on her mouth, making her gulp something thick and black, which ran onto her cheek. Sam crept forward, stretched out his hand and touched three ragged nails at her fingertips. He'd never been particularly into God, but now his mind became a prayer.

Send her angels!

Jesus, Mary, God above!

Send angels!

In exchange, if I did this, drag my soul to hell where I belong.

———

As Lewiston forced an activated charcoal solution down Maggie's throat, Felix scrambled for the last of the empty bottles, yelling, "She's taken practically everything! God, she's taken it all!"

"That's the difference between a gesture and a suicide," Lewiston muttered.

When Felix shot a look at him, Lewiston added, "I did emergency for years, okay? Don't sit there like a statue, Rossi, get out a tube. I know you have one. We've got to do gastric lavage."

Felix scrambled up to Maggie's dresser where he and Lewiston's medical bags still sat, both open. Lewiston's was a small medbag, enough for seizure prophylaxis essentials; Felix's the ultimate.

"Just be glad you didn't have corrosives in that thing," Lewiston said, eyeing Felix's large bag with disgust.

"You're the big expert on rape," Felix retorted, before he realized they were both in distress. This was a physician's nightmare, to have contributed to a patient's harm, much less from within the life-giving doctor's bag. Doctors wanted to be Gods, realized they were not, but pretended anyway—until a moment like this.

As Felix turned to deliver the tube, his foot struck something beneath Maggie's flowered chair. Out rolled an empty bottle of her cuticle remover. He shouted, "Lewiston!"

"What?" He looked and his gaze fell on the bottle. "Damn! Oh, crap! Potassium hydroxide. A patient of mine killed herself with cuticle remover like that. How much was in there?"

"I don't know, for God's sake!"

"Oh, crap! It's eating her up inside. That's why she was writhing. It could kill her before the barbiturates even dissolve. If she wakes, the pain's going to be terrible. Do you have opiates? Morphine?"

"Yes! At least I did."

Lewiston stopped administering the charcoal. Together they got the tube down her throat, and then Felix ran to the phone and dialed 113 for an ambulance.

He had never treated a poisoning like this, but he feared Maggie would die. He saw the same fear in Lewiston's eyes, but emergency room doctors routinely pumped lifeless chests, reaching for the magic and pretending to be gods.

"We need milk!" Lewiston shouted. "Sam? Sam?"

Sam didn't respond. He held onto Maggie's hand like they were in another world. Silently his lips moved. Sam thought she was dying, too. Why hadn't his conversion occurred in time to do Maggie any good?

Felix bolted for the door and heard light footsteps on the stairs, then Lewison saying, "Maggie, no!" Turning, Felix saw Maggie's writhing suddenly stop. They watched worry and pain fall away from her face as her muscles relaxed, giving up her life. They heard Antonella scream, "Signora! Signora!"

"Milk!" Lewiston shouted, looking up. "Bring milk! Woman, move!"

As she ran downstairs, Felix dropped to his knees beside Maggie, calling, "Where is Jess, Antonella?"

"Non lo so, signor Felix. E' andato via."

"He ran away?"

Bright blood spilled from Maggie's lips.

"Get the milk!" Lewiston screamed, "Quick, people! We're losing her!"

Felix touched Lewiston's shoulder. She was already dead and Felix knew his life had fallen into ruins that would never be repaired.

"Mamma! Mamma!"

From nowhere Jess appeared and slipped into the room. Before anyone could stop him, he went to his mother, clasped his arms tight around her and laid his head on her still chest.

———

It was difficult being a little boy who heard voices. Until the other night, before they went to La Scala, Jess had kept it to himself because he couldn't have explained what they said.

One voice was like a song sung just for him. If he tried, he could see the sound vibrate the air and it felt like love. Another voice rolled like a drum beneath his ribs. He'd feel it surging as it was doing now and Jess breathed in time. It was the power of joy and he called it father because he had no other one.

With these two voices he was never alone. When he was sad, the song would help him cry. Sometimes it quivered until the air wept with him. When he was happy the drum rolled and filled his heart.

Together the song and the drum had often shown him people he didn't know. Twice they painted scenes from his real life. In the taxi on the way to Milan, they had shown him the stage at La Scala and the singer with the beautiful voice so he'd know what to do and say. They had shown him signora Morelli at the beach as she fell. They showed him Sam at the lake house. Jess sent the swans and appealed to God to heal Sam's mind.

Then as he sat down to his good dinner in Antonella's kitchen, the song and the drum had shown him this sight and warned him not to cry. He'd finished his pasta, drunk his limonata, and waited until Antonella picked up her copy of *Italy Italy* magazine that had arrived. It was for tourists, but Antonella said people who lived in a country never knew it and, besides, reading *Italy Italy* helped keep her English up.

When she dozed, the magazine in her lap, Jess had slipped outside into the night. It was easy to avoid others as he ran to the yellow villa, the song quivering, the drum pounding in his breast. He could see the light within the people in time to step aside into the dark.

As he lay on his mother's body her inner light did not shine. "Ti voglio bene, Mamma," he pleaded, knowing she didn't hear. She was too far away. He asked the song to sing, asked the drum to share its power of joy. He felt her heart beat, as he knew it would. He felt her breathe. Only then did he look up at those around him and see the colors of their sorrow, pity, anger and fear.

The dark stranger said, "Good God! She's sleeping! Peacefully sleeping. Unbelievable!"

Felix knelt and listened to her heart, checked her pulse. He threw his arm around Jess and kissed his head, crying, "I was wrong! You've saved her! My God, Jess, you've saved her!"

Jess shook his head, tears spilling down his cheeks, as he realized he was seeing what they did not—his mother's unwell spirit, all its power bent on her death. Like signora Morelli's soul it was sovereign over her life. She and her child had chosen death over future murder by her husband because she would fall in love with Adamo one day. Jess couldn't save his mother from rape because she believed she'd sinned and deserved bad things.

He could only delay, not alter, his mother's choice. Nor could Krishna, or Christ, or Buddha or Moses or any of the ones God had sent, though in his mind Jess was begging for their help.

They were not answering his cry and neither were the song and the drum. They were weeping like rain. They were throbbing like the thunder. They were saying she had asked, she had sought, she had knocked. In answer, heaven opened. Angels crowded his mother's room: on the ceiling, on the floor, beside her on the bed. At first they'd terrified him, but they were wonderful to see and they changed, as he desired: they had wings or they did not, they took the shape of people or glowed like candlelight.

Someone picked him up and Jess realized it was Uncle Felix. Jess laid his head on his uncle's shoulder and watched the angels who were waiting, waiting, waiting to take his mother home.

He half-heard the stranger say, "I just can't believe she's all right! But she seems to be. Here, let me take a look at the boy. After all this, he may need a sedative."

Jess didn't pay attention because in his mind he was arguing with the angels. *Yes, I know she will not really die if she dies, but I am very fond of the body she is in. I know I could not stop crying. This body I have delights in her voice. It is used to being hugged by her. I do not care about her life's higher purpose right now. I do not care what her suffering means, just end it! Please, make her as she was! If you take her, I will not stay here and you cannot make me!*

He stuck his tongue out at the biggest angel and let the stranger who was dark inside take him from his uncle's arms.

Chapter 27

Sam sat on the floor outside Maggie's open door, his back propped against the wall as he drifted in and out of sleep, thinking about the previous night. He had stayed at the door as they'd settled Maggie on the bed. Even when Antonella washed her, changed the sheets, scrubbed the floor, he stayed. Jess, his face on Felix's shoulder, had looked in the other direction until Antonella called, "Va bene. She is dressed." He and Jess spent the night there because Jess literally shrieked when they tried to take him from his mother's room.

Sam stayed because, for him, there was no other place. He had to see and try to remember. Was it him? Antonella grumbled, pushed him out the door and closed it, when she realized Sam was there and watching, but by then it didn't matter.

He knew the truth.

He wasn't sure why Felix and Lewiston hadn't thrown him out. Maybe because they were doctors and had medical terms for his behavior like amnesia, trauma-induced paraphilias, stem cell damage, instead of crime.

In the murky gray of early dawn, he heard tiptoed footsteps and opened his eyes. The door was ajar because through the night Felix and Lewiston took turns waking Maggie to check on her, giving her something called Naloxone, and calming Jess who woke when Maggie so much as stirred. Felix was out like a light in a stuffed chair by Maggie's bed, but Jess was creeping toward the hall.

As he approached, Sam flushed with shame. This was Maggie's child, whom Sam had saved—the one he'd planned to raise with her. Instead, Sam had nearly killed this boy's mother.

"Are you awake?" Jess whispered.

Sam whispered back. "Yeah, kid. Did you get some sleep?"

Jess looked away and rubbed his upper arm. "Dr. Lewiston

gave me something to help me sleep, but it didn't really work."

"Try to go to sleep, now. She's all right," Sam said.

Jess came closer. "Are you going to stay?"

Sam reached up to the boy's thick, dark curls and patted his head, feeling such guilt he would have cried if he'd been the crying type. He swallowed. "Listen, kid, you ought to go to bed, you hear? Your mother's fine now. She's made it through the night."

"She will get sick again!"

Sam smiled. "Don't worry. She's got two doctors who'll take care of her."

"No, Uncle Sam!" Jess sniffed back tears. "They did not help her last night. God did."

Sam sighed, thinking Felix and Maggie had done a real number on this kid. "You're a good boy. I don't doubt that's what your mother will believe."

"It's true!"

Sam clasped his hands, considering, then he said. "Jess, listen. The truth is that your mother ... accidentally swallowed some very bad things but, luckily, not what your Uncle Felix first thought. It still upset her stomach so her body, er ... got rid of it in every way it could. Your Uncle Felix and Dr. Lewiston put a tube down her throat and got a lot of it out. They neutralized the rest."

"No, she was d—dead. I begged God to save her and he did. Ask her for yourself. She will know because of who she is."

Sam reached out for Jess, who came and leaned into his side. "Is that right?" Sam said. "Well, well. All right, who is she?"

Quietly, Jess looked into Sam's eyes and said, "The Virgin Mary."

Sam flinched. There could be no worse rebuke, but he had a duty to Jess. Sighing, he held him at arms length. "Jess, you're a good kid. No, you're a great kid. I wish I'd been here to see you grow, but you've got to stop thinking things like that and especially don't tell them to other people, okay?"

Jess frowned at him. "I like you, too, Uncle Sam, but you do not understand things very well. Like Uncle Felix and Dr. Lewiston, you don't believe what you see."

Sam snorted. "You like me, do you?"

"I love you, Uncle, but I think you don't understand."

Sam hung his head. "You love me, eh? You're right, I don't understand." He looked up. "Okay, try me."

Jess knelt beside him and spoke expressively with his hands, like the Italians. "It is difficult to say in words, but I will try. The consciousness of Mary inhabits the earth. It seeks itself among itself." Jess looked at him expectantly.

Sam blew out breath. "Okie doke, and who do you think you are, Jess?"

"It is complicated, but the easiest way to say it is that most people would think I am a reincarnation."

"Of who? And don't tell me, 'Jesus'."

"Yes, in a way. Mamma told me and now I know it's true, but I have lived other lives too."

Sam caught Jess's effusively waving hands in his own. "Kid, listen, you can't go around saying or thinking that. You just can't."

"A part of you is just like me," Jess insisted. "I only seem different because I left the door open between heaven and earth when I was born. The consciousness of Jesus inhabits the earth. It seeks itself among itself."

Sam rose to his knees, pulled Jess to him in a hug and patted his back. "Okay. I heard you the first time."

As Jess wrapped his arms around Sam's neck, Sam looked in on Maggie. She was still sleeping peacefully as if she hadn't been torn apart. He knew without doubt who had hurt her. Against his will he'd felt it, even as he imagined her fear. Sam knew he was a dog. He'd always been a dog. He felt a great many men besides himself were, too. The decent ones controlled themselves. Around their own women, men became protectors to keep the other dogs away.

Sam glimpsed the black virgin statue on Maggie's bedside table, the Madonna ascending into heaven on the wall, and felt like he'd go mad. He'd heard Felix and Lewiston talk. Had she somehow really been virginal until night before last? He had no business hugging her son.

"You're a good kid," he said and took Jess's arms from around his neck. "I know you love your mother. God, I wish I'd been there for you all this time."

"You were! You were!" Jess exclaimed, "Don't you see? Your spirit inhabits my mother and me. The swans brought your spirit here."

Sam thought of the crippled swan, shook his head and stood.

"Okay, kid. That's enough. Go to bed, do you hear? You need some sleep."

Sam descended the stairs, went outside and through the garden down to the lake house. The sun was only now rising, but Antonella had been at work here, too. The mess was gone. His suitcase stood ready in a corner. Sam walked out to the deck, feeling an urge to swim with the swans again. For a minute he'd been happy there.

He looked in both directions along the shore of the lake. its mirrored surface just emerging from the drifting mists. King Silent wasn't there, nor were any of the swans. To Sam, it figured. Even among the animals, the word had spread about who he was. A villain.

He heard a child crying.

Sam looked up and there was Jess, staring woefully down at him from the branch of a dogwood tree he must have climbed.

Sam smiled. "Do I hear crying from up there? Jess, your mother's going to be all right. Really. I wouldn't lie to you."

When Jess didn't reply, Sam said. "Say, is that your Optimist and your Mirror Dinghy out there in the porticiollo? Do you sail?"

"Yes," Jess said.

"That's great. I sailed, myself, when I was young. How far have you taken the Mirror out?"

Jess raised his voice. "She will die without you!"

Sam's smile disappeared. He gave Jess a little salute. "Sorry, but you've got it backwards, son. I'm not exactly the best thing that ever happened to Maggie Clarissa Johnson, er, Price, that's for sure. Tell her … tell her goodbye for me. I've got to go."

Jess cried out, "Her soul is Mary's. She will forgive you!"

"Oh, holy freakin—" Sam whispered as he realized Jess knew what Sam had done and still was asking him to stay. Maggie's kid might not be Jesus but he was either addle-brained or close to being a saint. In comparison, Sam was a monster. He dripped with the blood of Maggie's heart. He hoped never to remember the rape in full. Then he'd go crazy for sure: in his mind seeing the suffering of the woman he loved, as his body remembered how good it probably felt.

"Some things a man can't ask a woman to forgive."

"She is your beloved," Jess said.

Sam went inside and grabbed his suitcase.

Quickly he left the lake house, left the deck, climbed the stairs behind the pink and purple hortensia blossoms and went along the driveway to via Sempione. He had no plan but to escape the yellow villa on Lake Maggiore's vast shore.

Chapter 28

Chuck Lewiston watched from a room in the villa as Jess climbed the tree and talked to Sam. He couldn't hear their conversation and wasn't really interested in what they said. Sam couldn't help anymore, but he wasn't a threat. He didn't remember Lewiston or his connection with Brown and probably wouldn't soon. If he did, he'd almost surely remember the rape and Sam's mind was protecting him from that. It was all up to Lewiston, now, which meant the boy wasn't long for this world.

Last night he had injected Jess with a special cocktail, the chief ingredient of which was an anticoagulant from an unknown plant he'd discovered himself in the African bush. It wouldn't show up on blood tests because there were no markers for it, and the abnormal platelets and such it produced would be non-specific. Conceivably, Jess could fall from the tree and bruise himself deeply enough that he'd bleed to death internally. More likely, it would take a few more doses. Then Lewiston need only trip Jess, see he fell down the stairs or cut himself on a broken glass. Meanwhile, the cocktail's other ingredients would keep his condition from becoming apparent to Felix Rossi, though Lewiston wasn't really worried about him. Rossi had primarily been a medical researcher. He was competent in clinical basics, but recognizing a sophisticated poison would be beyond him. That much was apparent from last night.

It was ridiculous for Rossi to believe that Maggie Johnson ingested a significant amount of potassium hydroxide and fell peacefully to sleep, where she still remained.

Rossi had seemed to believe the boy had healed her until Lewiston pointed out the obvious: the mother hadn't drunk her cuticle remover at all. It was just an empty bottle that had fallen to the floor. Her body, overwhelmed, had expelled most of the poison right away. They had helped her expel most of the rest.

Her writhing was hysteria. The blood came from biting her tongue. She had fainted, not died. In their panic they'd missed her weak pulse. A miracle hadn't, couldn't, have occurred right before their eyes on the bedroom floor.

Felix had seen the sense of this conclusion.

As Sam and his suitcase departed the villa, Lewiston felt unexpectedly alone. For ten years, he'd spent more time with Sam than anyone.

The kid climbed down from the tree, went out on the porticiollo and put his hand to his mouth, apparently calling. As Lewiston watched, swans came. The boy stripped and dived in with them though the water had to be cool this time of year. One swan let the boy put his hand on its back, and they floated along together like friends. If the swan bit him, Jess could die.

Watching the boy and the swans, the wall Lewiston had erected around his feelings began to shake. His own son had been gentle like that. How could he take this sweet boy's life? He wanted to run to the lake, call the boy, administer mephyton and a syringe full of Vitamin K. Jess would be fine in twenty-four hours.

Lewiston backed from the window and went out into the hall. He saw Rossi in Maggie Johnson's room. He stood at the door, watching Rossi take her blood pressure and pulse. Lewiston found himself wondering what Maggie was like. Did she speak with a perfect Rhode Island accent like his? Did she listen to Mozart and Brahms? They were both willing captives, in a way. He and his Mozart, she and her belief in a Christian God instead of Buku or Mawu-Lisa or Ngai. While he was studying Africa's tribal medicines, Lewiston studied tribal gods. He and Maggie Johnson couldn't recover what their ancestors lost so long ago. But he wondered if she missed it, like he did.

Pointless thoughts. Unrealistic. It didn't matter what Maggie Johnson was like. It didn't matter if she had a wonderful son. Lewiston would never sacrifice his wife for her, or exchange his son's life for Jess Johnson's. That's why Brown had sent the jade Porsche and silver Aston Martin. By trying to kill Sam in Brown's penthouse when the divorce papers came, Lewiston had shown

Brown that he would kill for his family.

The house phone rang.

He heard Antonella answer it from downstairs. She called out for Rossi to pick up the line in Maggie's room.

Rossi was taking Maggie's temperature with a digital ear thermometer. He looked up, asking with his eyes for Lewiston to take over, which he did.

Lewiston watched Rossi go to the phone and turn pale.

"My God! When?" Rossi said, sounding aghast.

Lewiston removed the thermometer, which registered normal, and Maggie Johnson opened her eyes. They were beautiful. Brown with green flecks. Looking into them, Lewiston saw she wanted to die.

"God! Oh, my God! Adeline, I'll be there! I'll take the first flight I can. Tell our lawyer to get on the phone and call the FBI, the damned mayor! Call the White House! Don't worry, we'll find her. I'll move heaven and hell. We'll find her!"

Lewiston bent to Maggie and whispered, "Hi, I'm Dr. Lewiston."

Rossi hung up, his eyes frantic until he saw Maggie. "You're awake. Thank God!" He sat on the bedside and anxiously stroked her hair. "How are you, Maggie?"

She nodded.

"Why in the world did you do that?" Felix continued. "Don't you know how completely we love you? Don't you know we need you? I need you. Jess needs you. How could he ever be happy with you gone? What Sam did doesn't reflect on you. You didn't do anything wrong!" He gazed in Maggie's dead eyes.

Lewiston doubted Felix recognized what he saw.

Maggie spoke kindly. "What's the matter, Felix? Who was on the phone?"

"No one. Nothing. Nothing to trouble yourself about, but—" He glanced up at Lewiston, then said to her, "Give us a minute, Maggie. We'll be right back."

They went out in the hall and closed Maggie's door.

Wringing his hands, Felix looked at Lewiston then back at

Maggie's door. At Lewiston. Back at the door.

"Any chance you could stay here? I've got a horrible emergency."

"What happened?"

"My daughter's been kidnapped!" Felix said, sounding terrified.

"Kidnapped?"

"She's only eight years old!"

"Good Lord," Lewiston said, uneasy. "Who would do such a thing?"

"The kidnapper left instructions for where to drop the ransom and closed with, *Don't drive off a cliff.* What does that mean? It said to publicize the note. Why?"

Lewiston's heart jumped. He could have told Felix no one would retrieve the ransom. It would lie, untouched, wherever Felix or a policeman left it. Lewiston thought of the phone number Sam probably hadn't called in over forty-eight hours because he was busy raping Maggie Johnson, then lying unconscious at the lake house: 1 888 Mr Brown.

Brown must have phoned the Hotel Florida and learned Lewiston hadn't spent the night. Hedging his bets that Lewiston was at the villa, Brown had in one stroke removed Rossi from the scene and sent a message for Lewiston to get on with it. That was Brown's style: unexpected and clever.

He had to let Brown know his message was received; otherwise it would be redelivered in different ways. Brown might send others to find and kill the clone and, in retribution, choose a wall, water beneath a Hudson River pier, or the foot of a chalky New Jersey cliff as the last resting place for a silver Aston Martin and jade Porsche.

In the hall, Felix heard Jess's footsteps coming up the stairs and realized his worst fear had come true. Without thought, Felix had chosen Ariel over Maggie and Jess. He'd planned to leave them in the hands of a stranger. Felix stooped to embrace the boy he'd made.

"How is my mother?" Jess asked.

Felix looked away. "Jess, I've got to go. I'll come back as soon as I can, but I need to take you and your mother to the convent in Turin. You'll stay with the Poor Clare nuns. Is Antonella here?"

"Not yet. Is my mother better?"

Felix managed a smile. "Yes, you can see her."

Lewiston whispered in Felix's ear, "Is that a good idea? She probably doesn't want him to see her injur—"

"Listen, I know her," Felix said. He nodded for Jess to open the door to Maggie's room. To Felix's chagrin, Maggie cried, "Don't! Jess, I love you! Ti voglio bene, but don't you come in!!"

"Ti voglio bene, Mamma. Ti voglio tanto bene," Jess said and quietly closed the door. He looked up at Dr. Lewiston with sad, brown eyes, and then he said to Felix, "We don't want to go to the convent. Dr. Lewiston—" Tears rolled down Jess's face. "Dr. Lewiston, will you take care of me if my Mamma dies?"

"Oh, Jess!" Felix said. "Your mother won't die, but I can't leave the two of you alone with … well, with a stranger."

Jess took Dr. Lewiston's hand and stood beside him. "We are never alone. We are always with God."

Felix took Jess's hand from Lewiston's. They went downstairs and out into the garden. Beneath the roses he picked Jess up, patting his back. The morning sky was gray, making the villa's scenic vista surreal. A light wind swept across the lake, churning up whitecaps and ruffling their hair. Felix pressed his face into Jess's shoulder and held back sobs.

"Don't cry, Uncle," Jess said and hugged his neck. "You must trust. You must trust God, even now. If you must choose, always pick what your heart treasures. When you do, you are picking heaven because God is love. I am not more important than Ariel. She is not more important than me."

"How did you know about Ariel?" Felix whispered.

"I—I had a feeling," Jess said.

Felix put Jess down and kneeled before him. "Now is the time to tell me, Jess, really tell me. Are you saying that if I leave you'll be all right because you are absolutely sure of who you are?"

Jess looked down and didn't answer. He turned and ran inside into the living room. Felix found him with the telephone in his hand, asking for a taxi, "La destinazione è la stazione," he said. Felix didn't interrupt.

Jess hung up. "Your taxi is coming. I will be all right, Uncle Felix. So will my mother, even if we walk through the valley of the shadow of death, remember?" He looked toward the stairs. "Though I am so fond of the form my mother is in and of this pretty place."

"Oh, Jess; there's no need to think like that," Felix said. "If you insist on staying, Father Bartolo will be back tomorrow. Antonella is here. I'll phone Uncle Simone and tell him to come."

They heard the doorbell clank and Antonella came in, newly arrived from church where she'd gone early to pray for Maggie.

"Where your treasure is, there your heart is also," Jess said, braving a smile. "You feet must be, too." Then he ran and hid his face in Antonella's apron.

Felix left the room. Gripping the wrought-iron railing, he took the blue tile stairs two at a time to pack.

Chapter 29

Lewiston hung back so Jess and Antonella could say their goodbyes to Rossi as he got in the taxi.

"Take good care of them," Rossi said, looking as conflicted as a man could. He nodded to the driver.

The taxi entered via Sempione and disappeared in the direction of town. Lewiston was the one who closed the gate.

Back at the house, Antonella went to take a tray upstairs, while Jess and Lewiston ate the lunch she had prepared. Melon. Osso Buco. Limonata for Jess. A ruby red wine for Lewiston.

"How did you sleep last night?" Lewiston asked, hurriedly eating. He had to leave and talk with Brown without rousing their suspicions then get back before this Simone person arrived tonight. Someone named Father Bartolo would come tomorrow, but there'd be no convent, now. Maggie would no doubt continue to resist being moved. If not, Lewiston would say she was too ill.

Jess mumbled. "Not too well. The medicine you gave me didn't work."

Lewiston had the med case in his jacket pocket. "Maybe if I give you more you'll sleep better tonight."

Jess stood without urging and came to him. "All right."

Lewiston took out the case, installed a needle in the syringe, unwrapped the needle and inserted it into the vial.

He swabbed Jess's arm, pinched his flesh and put the needle in. Jess looked at Lewiston as he emptied the syringe. If the boy really were Jesus, he'd know what was going on. Obviously he didn't.

"You're a good boy," Lewiston said when he finished.

"Yes, everyone says I am," Jess replied and returned to his chair, picking up his glass and downing all his limonata to quench what Lewiston knew was a sudden thirst.

Lewiston knew he'd go to hell for this, but his wife and son would survive. He put his napkin on the table and said, "Tell

Antonella I'll be right back. I have to walk into town."

Jess rose and followed him to the gate. Was he curious about Lewiston's destination? Would he voice suspicions to anyone?

He looked so cute, standing there, a slight, long-legged boy whom everyone picked up and hugged, who constantly threw his arms around people, saying he loved them. Lewiston saw a taxi whizzing down the road and flagged it, knowing every step he'd ever take, every breath he'd ever breathe, would take him closer to perdition.

He looked up to say goodbye to Jess.

The sun was glinting off the boy's skin somehow; it was beaming its reflection in his eyes. Jess smiled as if Lewiston were his best friend on earth.

"I didn't ask where you are going because I know," Jess said.

"How could you know?"

"All roads lead to God eventually."

Lewiston turned away and gave the taxi driver a different destination. Not to God, but to the devil who, according to plan, was temporarily ensconced in a palatial villa in the hills above the posh town of Stresa, just sixteen miles north of here—waiting to hear this boy was dead.

———

Maggie sensed the house was virtually empty. She hadn't heard whispered conversations drifting in through the shutters or through the keyhole for a while, hadn't heard feet scuffling back and forth in the hall.

She pulled the covers back to look at her flannel nightshirt. Long and buttoned up the front, it had a Peter Pan collar and long sleeves. This one was white with dainty forget-me-nots. She had a pink one with baby's breath and one with sky blue plaid. Now it seemed outlandish to her that she, a woman forty-five years old, had taken it into her head to wear such childish gowns.

Underneath, she had on her usual white cotton panties. They came up to the waist.

Maggie knew she should be dead. About twenty times over, she should be dead.

Before becoming Felix's maid in her former life, she'd worked in hospitals and labs. Then Felix had paid for her to take a nursing assistant course. When she opened Felix's bag, Maggie had known not to take only a handful of barbiturates like most attempted suicides did. Methodically cramming pills into her mouth she'd swallowed handfuls, drunk vials of medicine, liberally washing it all down with water from the pitcher Antonella kept in her room. Still she'd feared it wouldn't take effect before Felix and Dr. Lewiston got back. So she'd picked up her cuticle remover. Potassium hydroxide.

Maggie had opened her mouth wide, thrown back her head and opened her throat. She'd done her best to pour the whole bottle straight down, avoiding her lips and tongue because the pain might cause her to hesitate.

Still it had taken all her will power not to stop in agony. She knew she'd fallen to the floor but, after that, Maggie didn't remember anything.

Why her throat hadn't collapsed, why her stomach hadn't burned away, she didn't know.

She thought some of the drugs must still be in her system because last night and this morning Maggie had been seeing things.

The salmon walls swirled whenever she looked at them, and mocking faces appeared. They came out this morning. Lewd ones were there last night, their tongues lolling and lapping—from the ceilings, from the walls, trying to glimpse what no one should have seen except her beloved, if she'd had one.

For the dozenth time, her eye fell on the arched feet of the oval mirror Felix had bought her ten years ago.

She took a deep breath, said, "One, two, three," meaning to get up, strip off her gown and look at her body. The bruises ached. She could feel a scab forming on the long scratch on her arm.

For the dozenth time, Maggie didn't rise. It was so hard to breathe, she felt as if she'd faint if she tried to stand. She had to drag in air in loud, throaty gasps and was glad no one could hear.

Her hand mirror was on the dresser. If she crawled to the edge of the bed, ignoring the mocking faces, she could get it. She could open the drawer to her nightstand and take out the flashlight she kept there. She could slip down under the white embroidered covers in the dark, slip her panties off, say, "One, two, three," then with the flashlight and the mirror see why she hurt so much down there.

It would help remind her why she needed to die.

If only she could breathe.

She wondered if God had anticipated rape when he made the average man bigger and stronger than the average woman, gave men all that testosterone? If rape was natural, why didn't all men do it, though? They obviously could. Why were some women spared such a thing, but not her?

She decided it would probably take a theologian to explain how dreadfully she had offended God: comparing herself to The Virgin Mary, wanting to lure the Holy Ghost, trying to be a second Madonna.

To Maggie her punishment was fair and it fit the crime.

All day she'd fantasized about her next suicide attempt, knowing her soul was already damned. From her hospital work, she knew rape victims usually wanted to die at first. When a woman couldn't control what happened to her body, it was like she didn't exist. Might as well make it official.

The difference between them and Maggie was that she wasn't faint-hearted. She intended to persevere.

She imagined for the dozenth time waiting until tonight when it was dark. She would sneak out to the porticiollo with her tape of Cio Cio San. She'd get in Jess's little Optimist and point it north toward the Gola. No, she'd slip into a neighbor's rowboat. She was sure she could get to the deep part of the lake, too far out to swim back to shore. While she was still in the boat, she'd turn the tape on low because sounds traveled on the lake at night and she couldn't risk waking up the whole South Basin. She'd listen to Leontyne Price sing Cio Cio San's last words: *Tu? Tu? Tu? Tu? Tu?*

"You? You? You? You? You?" *Little idol! My love, flower of the lily and the rose. This you must never know, not for your pure eyes is Butterfly's death … Farewell, my love. My little love, farewell!*

Or was it the mocking faces making her think this way? In fact, it crossed her mind that Sam might not have really raped her. After all, she'd taken her own swimsuit off. How would that sound in a court of law? Shamefully, she'd enjoyed the sex at first, though it was plain from the start that the Sam Duffy she loved wasn't the same man lying naked on her bed. He'd undergone some sort of Jekyll/Hyde change. Maggie had voluntarily stripped for Mr. Hyde based only on one phrase: *Maggie, my girl.* Any court would say she'd asked for it.

She just hadn't known she could be so hurt. She hadn't known he'd deliberately degrade her, take pleasure in her terror and her pain. She didn't know she would feel so unclean, so dirty, so polluted.

She glimpsed a mocking face in the salmon wall and heard it say, *Maggie Clarissa Johnson, virgin mother of Jesus? Ha-ha-ha!* Maggie didn't mind it as much as the lewd faces with lolling tongues she'd see tonight.

She couldn't inflict them on Jess, on good-hearted Antonella, and certainly not on a convent full of nuns who were pure and didn't blaspheme in their devotion to God.

Jess should be with them.

That settled, she went back to fantasizing about the deep part of the lake.

Chapter 30

Sam sat by the open window on the train that would leave for Milan, getting his last glimpse of Arona. It was market day and he could hear crowds at the stalls lined up near the tour boat docks and stretching along the rim of the lake's south basin. Images of what had happened at the yellow villa drifted through Sam's mind and most were painful.

He smiled when he thought of Antonella, though, and especially when he thought of Jess. He pictured him in the hall this morning, trying to convince Sam his spirit had been here all these years through the swans. Yes, Sam had been crippled in body and mind and Jess had made friends with a crippled swan. It was a stretch to even consider it a coincidence. Suddenly it struck Sam what else Jess had said: *Dr. Lewiston gave me something to help me sleep, but it didn't really work.* He'd rubbed his upper arm.

Strange.

The memory made Sam feel cold, sitting on the train. He was no doctor, but if sleeping pills made you sleep, Sam figured a shot in the arm should make you pass right out. Why hadn't Jess slept?

He watched conductors usher the last passengers on, helping them with their suitcases. Sam couldn't shake the cold feeling. He grabbed his suitcase and hustled off the train before it left.

Then he felt silly, standing there on the platform alone.

Jess had twenty-four hour care from two Harvard-trained physicians, as Sam found out from listening to them last night. Why should Sam, who wouldn't know a sleeping pill from an aspirin, worry about Jess's shot?

Sam sat down and waited ten minutes for the next train to Milan, boarded and, once again, got off.

Instinct.

It came from having seen the world, having been a private eye, and from what he'd done for Brown in the eleven years he'd worked for him. Sam knew half the time when things didn't add up, it was just because. It was the other half you had to worry about. He needed to satisfy himself Jess was all right.

Apparently, Chuck Lewiston knew all about the past ten years of Sam's life. On the train Sam realized he knew nothing about good ole Chuck. How had they run into each other? Where had they run into each other? Why had Chuck taken an interest in him for ten long years, enough to come to Italy? He hadn't liked the way Chuck peered at him, as if he were a freak or a mental patient. Sam didn't remember phoning him to say he was sick, but then he didn't remember anything clearly between Central Park ten years ago and waking up in Maggie's lake house yesterday.

There'd been no time to catch up. No sooner had Felix appeared with his bat and chased Sam up a tree, than Maggie was found writhing on the floor. He, Felix and Lewiston had exchanged hurried facts in angry or impatient snatches as they tried to save Maggie and watch over her through the night. That's all.

This morning Sam left without learning the full story of what had happened at the yellow villa.

He looked up at the schedule posted on the brick wall. The next train would be here in twenty minutes. He sat down on a bench, sure he was being paranoid, and then decided he didn't care. He picked up his suitcase, left the platform, went outside and caught a taxi.

As it drove toward via Sempione, Sam decided to talk to Felix about Jess's shot—make sure everything checked out. Then he could stop worrying and leave for Milan. He would fly back to the States with only Maggie on his conscience, instead of Jess as well. His wallet was still full of the money he got from Felix ten years ago. Enough to start a new life. Actually, he didn't recognize the wallet, though it had to be his. It had his drivers license. He'd found it with the rest of his things.

The taxi stopped and Sam got out, went through the gate and down the driveway. He stood in the garden and looked up at the window he knew belonged to Maggie.

Sam's feet wouldn't go into Maggie's house.

Instinct?

No, he didn't want to risk having Maggie see him. She shouldn't have to. He would satisfy his curiosity without disturbing her.

He headed for the lake, where Jess apparently spent most of his time. He would be there now or he'd come soon. Sam would ask him to get Felix. They'd talk at the lake house. Maggie would never know Sam was here.

He paused atop the stone stairs behind the hortensia bushes to look down, and then he saw them. Jess had lured Antonella into his eleven-foot Mirror Dinghy or was it Antonella who had taken him there to cheer him up? Still wearing her souvenir apron, she perched beneath the red sails, looking uncomfortable, ducking and pulling the jib sheets when she was told. Jess handled the little boat like he was an Olympic medal winner, sitting out on his toe-straps, his bottom barely clearing the small chop on the water's surface. Sam could hear them laughing. What a good woman Antonella was.

He went down the steps and out into one of the porticiollo's crows' nests. He waved to them. Soon Jess dropped his mainsail and brought the boat in under jib alone. As it passed through the opening between the crows' nests, Jess threw a line to Sam who walked forward with the rope while Jess jumped out and guided the boat the last bit to the beach, dragging it up on shore with Sam's help. While Jess secured the sails, Sam steadied the boat so Antonella could step ashore. Today, Florence and the Campanile di Giotto were on her apron.

He didn't realize she had a three-foot paddle in her hand until it smashed onto his shoulder.

"Criminale!" she said in a low cry, as if she meant to curse him and beat his brains out without waking Maggie up. "Come osi mostrare ancora la tua faccia?" How dare you show your face here again?

The paddle landed on his other shoulder as she continued in Italian, "Filth!"

Sam glimpsed Jess watching with innocent eyes, as if he'd known this would occur.

"Son of Satan!" He turned away and the paddle caught his upper back.

Sam didn't try to take the paddle and he certainly wasn't going to fight. Antonella might win, in her present state of mind.

"Go away!"

He ran back to the bank and scooted across the shore to the lake house, but she jumped from the boat, waded into the water, and followed him, catching him on the arm.

"What right do you have to speak to this sainted boy? How dare you come near his guiltless mother? Go away before I kill you!"

"Antonella—," he pleaded.

"You are garbage oozing from a drain"—a very ladylike way of saying he was shit. Sam agreed.

It was Jess who stopped her, throwing his arms around her waist and crying, "Ferma! Ferma! l'amica del cuore di mia madre" *Stop! Stop! friend of my mother's heart.*

Sam couldn't take much more of this. He already felt lower than crud.

"Antonella, Jess!" he said. "Devo parlare con Felix, quindi devo andare." *I must speak to Felix; then I'll leave.*

Antonella stopped and glared at him. "Signor Felix is gone."

"When will he return?"

"Non presto." *Not soon.*

"You mean not today, but tomorrow?" Sam said, speaking English.

"Not tomorrow or the next tomorrow," Antonella said, grudgingly. "We do not know when signor Felix returns. Signor Simone does not come until tonight. Padre Bartolo comes tomorrow." She tapped the paddle against her upper arm as if she also considered this fact upsetting.

Sam went to Jess and knelt in front of him. "How are you feeling?"

Jess looked toward the lake. "Sometimes I feel sick to my stomach."

"Since when?"

"Last night."

Antonella stroked Jess's hair and looked accusingly at Sam. "He worries about his mother, of course."

Sam nodded and looked away. What did it mean that Felix was gone?

Jess said, "Uncle Felix's daughter, Ariel, has been kidnapped."

"Kidnapped?"

Sam looked up toward the villa, all his instincts screaming, *Get them out of here!*

"Antonella," Sam said. "In spite of everything, I have to ask you to trust me. Do you have a car we can borrow?"

Jess jumped up and down in sudden excitement. "See, Antonella? I told you he would come back for us. You must help him. Sam will save my mother and me!"

She put her hands to her face, looked up to the villa, then back at Sam, saying, "Misericordia!"

"Please help us, Antonella," Jess said. "Please, please!"

Cautiously her eyes lit up. "You take them away?"

"Yes, I think so," Sam said.

She glared fiercely at him. "You do no more—" She looked at Jess, stretched up to whisper in Sam's ear, "no more rape?"

That's when Sam lost it. His eyes filled with tears as he looked up to Maggie's window. "You could beat me to death with your paddle if it would erase that, Antonella."

"See? I told you!" Jess said to her in glee. "God took pity and made a miracle. Sam is her beloved now."

"Sia lode al Signore!" Antonella exclaimed. *Praise God.*

"You have a car?" Sam repeated.

"I have a car."

"Where is Dr. Lewiston?" Sam said, scanning the house.

Antonella shrugged and said, "I do not like this Lewiston," but Jess replied, "He left in a taxi and went north. Uncle Sam, it is possible that we should rush."

And rush they did.

Antonella left and returned in ten minutes with her little Fiat Punto. She packed a bag for Jess and one for Maggie without waking her and put them in the trunk along with Sam's suitcase.

Sam said, "Antonella do you know what Felix did with my gun?"

She and Jess looked at each other and disappeared, she into the house, Jess into the garden. Jess returned and handed Sam his gun, only slightly soiled by the compost heap. "I do not like violence but this belongs to you."

Antonella returned with the bullets Felix had hidden.

There was only one thing left.

Waking Maggie and persuading her to get in the car with her son and the man who'd hurt her.

Chapter 31

Like a condemned man taking pleasure in a final wish, when Lewiston first arrived in Italy, he'd spent an afternoon touring the local area before going to the Hotel Florida.

Now his taxi wound through tiny streets in lush hills above the upscale town of Stresa. He could see the Borromeo Islands on the azure lake below: *Isola Bella*, "beautiful island;" *Isola Madre*, "mother island;" *Isola Pescatori*, "fishermen's island." They were the biggest tourist draw on this part of the lake, given Isola Bella's perfectly preserved 17th-century palace, its famed terraced gardens where white peacocks lived. It was one of the great palaces that had once served as hotels for traveling royalty. Napoleon and Josephine had stayed there. Their rooms were said by the palace steward to smell bad when they left.

The taxi slowed before a gated villa, its impressive sun-bleached walls barely visible through the trees of the five-acre park over which it presided. It was probably the poshest villa in Stresa with botanical gardens of its own. Brown had bought or rented it. He and Sam were told to report here if things didn't go to plan.

Lewiston got out and walked across the lawn, gazing at the white peacocks, the pheasants and other birds. Brown wouldn't be outdone by Isola Bella. He reached the villa's wide pebbled terrace and walked along the side of the building to the back. On the lawn below was a swimming pool fit for a Roman emperor. Seeing no one, Lewiston entered the villa through a door in the glass wall that looked out on the three islands.

"Hello, Lewiston," a voice said from somewhere in the spacious room.

On a chaise beside a floor-to-ceiling canvas, Theomund Brown put down his book. Lewiston recognized that the painting was by the Columbian artist, Botero, whose work hung in prestigious galleries. It showed a grotesquely fat man sitting at a table with his equally obese daughter. On plates in front of them lay tiny diapered baby dolls. The man and the girl held forks and, between them, a bottle of sauce stood erect. Lewiston wondered if Brown realized or cared it was social commentary.

"Sam's memory came back," Lewiston said, knowing Brown liked his information straight.

Brown curtly motioned to a nearby glass cart. "Pour yourself something and tell me about it."

As Lewiston did, he heard high heels on the tile floor and looked up. Coral appeared, dressed for a swim in a gold thong bikini, dragging a dazzling gauzy wrap along the floor behind her, chestnut hair spilling in waves onto her back.

Brown turned and gazed. She passed without acknowledging either of them. She was beyond stunning, but the playfulness he'd witnessed when they first met seemed gone.

Staring at her backside as it bounced magnificently out the door, Brown said in appraisal, "The goddess of love."

Lewiston poured a glass of wine, sat on a cantaloupe colored couch and didn't speak until spoken to.

"What does Sam remember?"

"Everything except me and his ten years with you. He raped the boy's mother. She tried to kill herself."

Brown sat up, looking angry. "What an imbecile! You've done your part?"

"Yes, and it's untraceable. A few more shots and they'll think he's become a hemophiliac. If he gets a bad bruise or cut, it'll be over. Can I ask a question?"

Brown looked irritated, but said, "Go ahead."

"Why didn't you just send professionals to wipe out everyone in the villa? Why this?"

Brown sniffed. "You shouldn't watch TV, Chuck. The meritorious minimal isn't depicted there. Did Rossi leave?"

"Yes, he did."

"Who's at the house now?"

"The housekeeper, the mother and the boy. Sam took off in

disgrace for parts unknown. The uncle from Turin isn't coming until tonight and a priest tomorrow. For now, Maggie and Jess are in my care."

Brown laughed aloud. "Kidnap his daughter and the hell with the Lamb of God!"

"The boy really is strange. He persuaded Rossi to leave them with me. He talks like Jesus."

Brown turned pale in a way Lewiston had never seen him do. He stood and walked to the glass window, watching Coral swim. "If you miss your wife, Chuck, the goddess of love will oblige."

Brown turned, his gaze incredible. Lewiston saw the same terrifyingly cold purpose, but something else was there—a hint of fear?—in his eyes. Could that be? Brown was afraid of a simple boy? Did he know something Lewiston didn't? He couldn't possibly think Jess was really Jesus. Lewiston thought of the black Madonna statue on Maggie Johnson's bedside table.

He dismissed the thought. It was inconceivable.

"For now, let's join Coral, shall we?" Brown said. "Then I may have something to show you before you leave."

Lewiston glanced out at Coral, whose swimming decorated the pool. He'd never been unfaithful to his wife, not once in twenty-two years of marriage. Of course he'd fantasized. What man didn't? He should have immediately said *no* to Brown's offer of Coral because he didn't intend to be unfaithful now, but then he also hadn't planned to murder a ten-year old child.

Brown flicked a switch and Mozart filled the air. It was Lewiston's favorite aria: "Se Mai Senti Spirarti Sul Volto." *If you ever feel my dying breath on your face.* He often played it while caring for Sam. Lewiston forced himself not to bitterly laugh. Brown had planned this. In the opera *La clemenza di Tito*, Sesto is seduced by the princess Vitellia into plotting to kill the emperor so she can gain power. Deeply torn, but compelled by love, Sesto is embroiled in her schemes and finally exposed. He sings a last tragic love song, saying he won't betray her, before going to the Senate to be condemned to death.

That was Lewiston. Willing to kill. Willing to corrupt his soul.

In the opera it all worked out. Lewiston knew it wouldn't for him.

Brown opened the glass door and the music followed them outside on speakers artfully hidden among exotic bushes and trees. Sesto's wail of grief was so gentle, so absent of reproof. A woman always sang it in a trouser role. As they approached the Roman pool where the splendid Coral floated on her back, watching as they came, Lewiston recognized Cecilia Bartoli's voice over Mozart's violins: *If you ever feel my dying breath on your face.* They reached the pool. Lewiston thought of the little boy who would bleed to death from a cut. It was too soon to relax, assuming he ever could. He waved to the alluring Coral and said to Brown, "I have a feeling I should return."

"By all means go, then," Brown said. "But if anything else goes wrong, come back. No phones anymore."

Lewiston nodded and walked away.

———

As Maggie slept she thought she heard the words, "Magnificat anima mea, Dominum." The Magnificat. It was the "Song of Mary" from Luke 1:46-55. In Latin its first words translated to: "My soul magnifies the Lord."

Maggie thought it was a woman's voice saying the Magnificat. She opened her eyes.

Antonella stood at her bed, wiping tears away. It hadn't occurred to Maggie that someone might cry over her.

"Antonella—," Maggie began, but her throat was sore, either from Sam, from all her gasping, or from what she'd drunk. She sat up and found Antonella's arms suddenly around her. Without meaning to, Maggie shuddered and pulled back. Her body didn't want to be touched.

"Mi spiace, signora," Antonella said, in apology.

Then Antonella set her jaw as if she didn't intend to apologize further. She pulled the pristine covers off Maggie and started talking non-stop. Signora had to get up. Jess was upset. He knew she wanted to send him to a convent. He would go, if she insisted, but only if signora got up and first went on a pilgrimage with him. A real pilgrimage. If signora would go on a pilgrimage just this once, Jess would agree to live in a convent or a boarding school until he was grown.

Maggie lay there, trying to pull her flannel nightgown all the way down in case faces were staring from the salmon walls. She couldn't think. She wondered how Jess knew her decision. Then she thought, *Oh, that's right. The Son of God would know.*

But a pilgrimage? A real one? A journey for the faithful and the sick? It was something she'd always dreamed of, but Jess would see her. He would see the bruises and the scab. She couldn't go.

Antonella went into Maggie's bathroom and returned with a basin of warm water. She dipped one of Maggie's terry cloth washcloths in and, careful of the bruises, quickly began scrubbing Maggie's face, ears and throat.

"Stop, Antonella," Maggie complained.

Antonella didn't stop. She grabbed the hem of Maggie's flannel gown covered with forget-me-nots and, to Maggie's horror, hitched it up and pulled it over her head. She started scrubbing Maggie's underarm as Maggie tried to cover herself with her other hand.

"Stop, Antonella!"

"No, signora. Mi spiaci, signora."

Now she was scrubbing her stomach, then very gently over the scab on her arm, then her legs and feet as Maggie shivered and tried to cover herself with her hands.

Antonella rinsed the washcloth and put it in Maggie's hand. She pointed to her hips and said, "Now you!" and turned her back.

Maggie shivered.

Antonella repeated, "Now you!"

Looking anxiously for the faces on the wall, Maggie ducked under the covers and did as she was told as best she could because it hurt.

"Finita? Finita?" Antonella kept asking.

"Okay, finita," Maggie finally said, coming out from under the cover and feeling abused.

Then Antonella patted her dry with a towel. She brought clean underwear and told Maggie to put them on.

She brought one of the dresses Felix had sent over the years— a simple design by Mondi, a pair of Gucci slip-ons, and Maggie's favorite peach hat. She didn't ask permission, but put them on Maggie like she was dressing a doll. She pulled Maggie to her feet and walked her out to the hall and down the stone stairs, her purse in hand. Antonella ignored it when Maggie began to gasp, began to hang on to the railings, making Antonella have to pull her hands away.

"Take me back!" Maggie whispered when they reached the door. "Tell Jess we'll go tomorrow, Antonella!"

Relentlessly, Antonella cajoled, pushed and pulled until Maggie was on the spiral-columned porch, then down the porch steps, into the garden, then beneath the roses in front of the driveway.

Only there did Antonella pause and say, "Signora, coraggio. *Be brave*. Pray. Say The Magnificat of the Madonna."

Maggie sensed people in the driveway beyond the roses. If Jess was there he would see her throat. He would cry. He would see the faces with the lolling tongues and be afraid. To delay, she recited The Magnificat from her new King James Bible:

> My soul magnifies the Lord,
> And my spirit has rejoiced in God my Savior.
> For He has regarded the lowly state of His maidservant;

She stopped, unable to continue with Mary's words.

Antonella finished it in Italian, "For behold, henceforth all generations will call me blessed. For He who is mighty has done great things for me, And holy is His name—"

Maggie looked at thin clouds in the pale blue sky. "Nobody's going to call me blessed, Antonella, but I thank you for being my friend."

When Antonella hugged her, she tried not to pull away.

"Va," said Antonella. *Go.*

Maggie stepped into the driveway and saw Antonella's Fiat Punto. She looked around and, seeing no one else, went to the open front passenger door and sat inside, closing the door.

"I am here behind you, Mamma," she heard from the back seat.

Maggie raised her hand to cover her neck and looked up at the lost safety of her bedroom window. "Sweetheart, what is this pilgrimage?"

"It is the most important pilgrimage, the one you take to yourself."

"Yes, yes." She couldn't think. "Where are we going?"

"This is a pilgrimage to you. Mamma, did you fasten your seatbelt yet?"

Maggie fastened her belt and reached back for Jess to clasp her hand. She had no idea what he meant but she trusted him.

Jess said, "Here is our driver."

———

When Sam went to the car he didn't pause. He opened the driver's door, got in and started the little Punto, not looking at Maggie or Jess. He just wanted to get moving and let whatever happened, happen on the road. He heard the sharp breath Maggie drew when she saw him. Quickly he put the car in gear. He knew she shifted toward the door, reached for the handle. He grabbed the wheel with one hand and with the other reached over and kept her from opening the door. He heard her trying to drag in air as Jess soothed her, "Ti voglio bene, Mamma. It is all right, it is all right."

In the rearview mirror, he saw Jess wave to Antonella. As the car pulled onto via Sempione, they almost hit a man standing on the road by the gate. He saw them and waved urgently as if to make them stop. He looked like a local man.

"That's Adamo Morelli," Jess said. "Can we go back and talk to him?"

"Not now, Jess, not now."

They headed south away from the lake, toward their two perfect destinations. Jess had found them. The first was Crea and the second was Oropa, far up a mystic mountain. They were sanctuaries to which, according to tradition, Christians had come in pilgrimage for nearly two thousand years. They housed two of the three Black Madonnas St. Eusebio was said to have brought from the far east in 350 A.D. The third was in Sardinia, an island two hundred miles south. Too far to visit.

Sam had learned all this from Jess, who in the past two days had found black Madonnas all over Europe on the Internet. At one time, four hundred fifty had been counted, two hundred seventy-two of them in France. They were fast disappearing or being altered, but here in Italy twenty-seven remained in twenty-one different towns. To Sam, they certainly made sense. The likelihood that the real Mary, an early Semite, had blue eyes and white skin under the Middle Eastern sun was pretty ridiculous.

Jess was taking his mother on a pilgrimage to the black Madonnas.

That was fine with Sam. Oropa had seven hundred rooms for pilgrims. They could stay there until Sam decided what to do. Most of all, he had to make sure Lewiston didn't give anything else to Jess.

Sam told Antonella to say Jess went to see Dr. Cecagallina who persuaded Maggie to go away for a few days to improve her state of mind. Lewiston could stay at the house until they returned. That should put Lewiston off guard and keep him from trying to follow right away.

As they passed La Rocca, heading for the highway, Sam risked a glimpse at Maggie. She was pressed against the door, her eyes fixed on an unmoving point ahead, her breathing quiet. She hadn't responded even to Jess since Sam got in the car. He wanted to pat her hand, but it was better this way. He knew Maggie wasn't here, in her mind.

When Jess fidgeted in the back, Sam felt sorry for him. Jess's whole world had changed in just days. No one had thought to pack anything to entertain him on the trip. Sam took out the penknife he'd had for over twenty years. It was the only personal possession in his suitcase. He'd bought it on a merchant voyage to Alaska. Its grip was made of whale ivory and had scrimshaw on it.

"Do you have a penny, Jess?" Sam said.

"Yes, Uncle Sam, I do." He handed it to Sam. "Why do you need it?"

"Just an old superstition. If I give you this as a gift, it severs friendship. You have to buy it. Here, son. This is yours."

Sam tossed the knife in the back.

Chapter 32

Sam reached Serralunda di Crea in just over an hour by way of Borgomanero, Vercelli and Casale Monferrato, which were more or less on a direct southwest line to Turin in Italy's Piedmont. As they drove, the Alpine foothills disappeared and they passed scattered towns and fields of rice for risotto. Sam didn't have to worry about what to say to Maggie because she'd fallen deeply asleep.

On the way, Jess laughed with him about Antonella's onboard navigation computer, which ran by satellite link. Antonella said she only bought it because, when she ventured to market towns outside of Arona, she kept getting lost. Sam had plugged in their destination and their starting point. The computer's female voice spoke to him in Italian, saying, "per piacere," *please*, when instructing him to make a turn. If Sam didn't, the computer became testy, repeating the directions for the turn. Miss it a third time and it questioned his intelligence.

Jess laughed his head off at that, rolling around and holding his stomach in the back of the car. Sam deliberately missed a turn to make him laugh more.

It was comforting to hear, because Sam realized the full gravity of Maggie's frame of mind. She'd retreated far into herself and had no intention of ever coming out. If it weren't for Antonella and Jess, she wouldn't be here. She'd be making a new plan to take her life.

That's why Crea was a disappointment.

He found the sanctuary at the top of a green hill. Both priests and kings strove to be closer to God than the average rabble. He decided to leave Jess and Maggie in the car and check Crea out. No chance they'd be bothered because they'd told no one where they were headed, including Antonella. He went inside the church but found no black Madonna and child. A woman at the gift shop gave him a brochure. It read:

The statue venerated at Crea was experimented on during the restoration period in 1981 by Prof. Gian Luigi Nicola and consequently, as described in the verses of the song of songs, lost its poetic and famous image as the <<brown Madonna>> This famous canticle quotes <<I am the brown Madonna and in all her loveliness>>

The restoration produced a white Madonna, creamy beige at best. Sam felt angry with the people of Crea, before realizing he was really upset with himself. They'd just painted a statue. He'd done worse. Etched in Latin on the original marble where the Madonna stood were: *Nigra sum sed phormosa.* "I am black but comely."

Yeah, right.

He went through a door with a sign that read: *Ex-Voto corrido. The exit is at the end.*

It was a long room lined with votive offerings—framed depictions of near-fatal accidents, car crashes, people crushed by carts or barrels or falling crates; people shot, thrown off horses, children sick in their beds or run over by automobiles. In each, the Crea Madonna, always black or brown, hovered above in the sky. The homemade art thanked her for the miracle that saved their lives. Professor Nicola hadn't experimented on them.

Still Sam didn't see the point of bringing Maggie in here. If the color of your Madonna was important, Crea could complicate things.

He returned to the car and told Jess what he'd found.

They drove north, Sam debating whether to question Jess about the next location, but he didn't.

They were quiet. Jess didn't laugh at the navigation computer anymore.

Sam retraced their route back to Casale Monferrato and Vercelli, then left the highway and went west on a smaller road. In a tiny town called Cavaglia, Jess cried, "Stop! Stop!" as they whizzed down a street.

When Sam backed up, the navigational computer insulting

him, Jess jumped out and opened Maggie's door. "Mamma! Wake up, Mamma!"

Maggie opened her eyes and followed as Jess pulled her across the street and pointed through a blue chain-link fence at a Madonna and child. They stood in a niche in the building's wall and she wore a gold crown, a gold robe beneath a blue cloak. She had gold hair, as did the son perched in her hand. Their skins were very dark brown. Her expression was serene. Jess had found a black Madonna for his mother.

Sam went over and read the building's sign. It was a *scuola materna*, an elementary school.

Maggie said, "It's very pretty, Jess," but that was all.

Back in the car, Maggie resumed staring at a point in space. Whatever Jess had intended, it hadn't worked. They headed for Oropa as the navigation system told Sam to turn into a street that didn't exist, then berated him when he didn't.

The drive took an hour and a half, not counting a stop in Cavaglia and one for drinks and *panini* along the road. Maggie found a scarf in the glove compartment and wrapped it around her throat. She never looked at Sam or said a word to him. He never said a word to her.

But when they reached the Sanctuary and Sacred Mountain of Our Lady of Oropa, 1159 meters above the sea, as the sign said, Sam knew Jess's pilgrimage had been a good idea.

If there was a God, he was here.

He was behind the huge square pillars that supported the iron gates; he was through the wide opening and in the four massive courtyards formed by rows of colonnaded buildings. He was on the flower-laden lawns, up the great flight of steps that led to a regal gate in the cloistered walls. He was on the looming mountain, shrouded in smoky clouds, as if pilgrims went up the stairs and entered heaven. God was here. All the pilgrims through all the centuries had found a part of him and left a trace of God in the air.

Jesus Christ was on the entrance lawn, hanging on a wooden cross, and Sam thought some of Maggie's old self emerged. As they passed, she positioned herself between Jess and the body on the cross.

The first courtyard's ground level housed shops and a pharmacy. Above were the pilgrim's rooms. Slowly they ascended the great staircase, went through the royal gate called the porta regia and to the upper courtyards. A fountain was in the center. In Oropa's peculiar quiet, you could hear the water run.

Jess seemed to be expanding into Oropa, as if gravity was releasing its hold on his bones. His arms twirled, his feet skipped so fluidly they almost danced. He ran ahead to the fountain, took one of the long-handled ladles hanging from chains and drank Oropa's water. He dug up pebbles from the grass with Sam's scrimshaw knife and skipped them along the walk. Effortlessly, he returned a soccer ball that had been kicked in his path.

Sam went back to the visitor's center and checked them into two cheerful, spare, clean rooms. They had pale walls with small crosses and an occasional religious print, wooden floors and chairs, wrought iron or wooden beds, blue or yellow spreads. No phones, TV or radio. He got a twin suite for Maggie and Jess and a junior suite for himself, paying with the money in his wallet. If it was really Felix's money from long ago, why had Lewiston considered Sam a charity case? If it wasn't Felix's money then Lewiston's story was equally fishy. How had Sam obtained thousands of dollars at EverCare?

For now it was enough that Maggie and Jess were safe, and that she had time to think before she went and killed herself. No risk of that around Jess.

For three days they slept at Oropa, ate at Oropa, hiked Oropa's trails, never glancing at a newspaper. They took the ski lift up the mountain, bought a camera and took photographs, visited the library, the two ex-voto galleries, visited the Sacro Monte with its twelve chapel shrines celebrating Mary's immaculate conception, her coronation, the nativity and so on.

All the while, Maggie avoided looking at Sam. She wouldn't go to see the black Madonna and neither did Jess.

It seemed to happen by accident. On the fourth day Jess

wandered into the large church with the massive dome and Maggie followed, looking for him. Sam lagged behind, staying out of the way as he'd done for four days.

Inside, it struck Sam for the first time that Oropa was a monument to femininity. The predominant marbles used in the church were rose and cream and gold. Coral flowers with green leaves were inlaid in the marble floor beneath their feet. Religious scenes along the walls were done in pastel colors, especially sky blue. Yes, a small crucifix was tucked away in the lobby, but there was no stern-faced white-haired God, no disciples. He'd seen few male saints at Oropa. Those in paintings were in the background.

This was the Virgin's shrine, made clear by a monumental painting of the black Madonna, which dominated the church behind the altar. It resembled the Madonna at the elementary school, her skin black but her visage and clothes distinctly oriental. At the base of the massive ceiling dome, large letters were inscribed. Part of the text was from the Magnificat he'd heard Antonella recite to Maggie. Jess translated from the Latin.

> ...henceforth all generations shall call me blessed/he has regarded the humble state of his servant/divine mother of the immaculate conception of the house of david/perpetual virgin/co-redemptrix/mother mediatrix.

They walked along the left aisle, under the huge painting's gaze, and at the first shrine saw a statue of The Lady of Oropa, a basket overflowing with red roses at her feet. Votive candles blazed around the ebony mother and child.

Maggie seemed interested in the pews, the pillars, the marble beneath their feet, anything but the statue, much less the massive painting behind the altar. And they hadn't even reached the real Madonna yet. The one St. Eusebius brought here in 350 A.D. was in its original location: the old Sacellum he and his disciples built into the rocks. The wooden statue hadn't deteriorated in its 1600 years here, it was said.

Sam wondered how he'd get Maggie to the real shrine if she was having trouble with this.

It was Jess who intervened.

He took Maggie's hand, led her to the statue, kneeled down and kept pulling on her hand until she kneeled, too. But she didn't look up; she didn't pray.

For Sam it was a bitter sight: a real black Madonna kneeling with her real child, but too ashamed or hurt to look at a piece of gilded wood.

Sam went and stood close behind them.

Instinct.

No one else was around. He tapped Jess's shoulder as if he were cutting in for a dance.

Jess looked petulantly up.

"She's not a goddess, she's a woman," Sam said.

He could see Maggie grip Jess's hand, but Jess peered at Sam, then whispered, "Ti voglio bene, Mamma," and slipped his hand away. Using the back of benches for propulsion, Jess hopped in his loose-limbed way to the other side of the church.

Sam kneeled next to Maggie. He avoided touching her.

He cleared his throat, wondering what to say. He remembered the Act of Confiteor from his Sunday school days, and said,

"Oh, my God, I am heartily sorry for having offended thee.

I detest all my sins because I dread the loss of heaven and the pains of hell.

But most of all, because of thee my God, who art all-good and deserving of ... of ... all my prayers."

Or something like that, anyway.

Maggie turned and looked at him for the first time in four days. She didn't have to speak. Her beautiful eyes said, *Why did you betray me?*"

He answered, "Maggie, it wasn't me! I swear to God it wasn't me. I didn't know what I was doing!"

She looked unmoved.

"I didn't, I didn't. How could I? I swear I didn't. I swear to God, I swear to God!"

Still she didn't speak.

"I had amnesia. I didn't know you at all. I didn't even know myself. Something was wrong with me, but I still wanted you, I guess. You must have stuck in my mind but my dumb-assed mind must have been stuck on sex! It wasn't me, it wasn't me, it wasn't me! I didn't come to my senses until Felix hit me over the head. Or maybe it was the swans or ... I don't know. Maggie, it wasn't me!"

He looked up at the black Madonna statue, smelled the perfume from the roses, saw the candles shining.

Sam looked back and he knew. Maggie had crept to her threshold and was trying to decide: stay in here or come out and be embarrassed, hurt, ashamed. He declared, "Maggie Clarissa Johnson, I love you with all my heart! I've always loved you, Maggie! Sweetheart! Darling! I love you, I need you, I'll never hurt you again. Here's my hand to the Mother of God, to the Son of God, to God himself, and to you."

He saw a slight alteration in her forsaken gaze. "What are you apologizing for," she said, "if you don't even remember what happened, Sam?"

Then he did.

All of it.

It came shrieking into his mind like a nightmare, choking his breath, appalling his eyes, stopping the beating of his heart. He bent to the cold marble railing as the frightful scenes tore through his mind. He whispered, "Maggie, my girl. Oh God, Maggie, my girl."

He took his real black Madonna by the hand.

Her mouth opened in horror but he stood and took her other hand, pulling her to her feet, knowing what to do. "Come with me, Maggie. You've got to. Please trust me. Please!"

Jess came running from across the church. "Sam, where are you taking my mother?" he demanded. He looked like he'd pull Sam's foot.

Sam could hardly talk for what he was remembering. "She's a woman, Jess, and I'm a man. Go back to your room. It'll be okay."

He took Maggie out of the church, the clouds massive and gray and ominous on the mountain. He took her down the long boulevard in front, down through the porta regia, down the great stairs and toward his pilgrim's room, Maggie resisting only a little as if she didn't want it known she was being abducted in public. But when they approached his door she planted her feet and wouldn't let him move her.

"Maggie, I won't hurt you," he said and quickly picked her up as she beat him in the face, opening a cut.

Inside, Sam deposited her on his yellow couch and himself in a wooden chair halfway across the room. As she trembled in fear and rage, he phoned down to the office and asked if one of the nuns could see to Jess for a while. Then he recited to Maggie what he'd done, every dreadful thing—as delicately as he could, but honestly. He described her cries, how he'd hurt her, how it had felt, and the terrible thoughts he'd been thinking. But he spoke from the perspective of a man who was now sane and who loved her and who was wretched with regret.

She trembled less. He sensed she was peeping out.

Then he went to his bed.

"Maggie, when you're ready and only if you're ready I want you to come to me. Come to me and let me try to hold you! Let me undo what I did."

She looked as if she'd kill him.

An hour ticked away in silence.

Maggie stayed on the yellow couch, knees together, arms wrapped in fury around her shaking chest, her gaze fixed on the wooden floor in Sam's room. She thought if she looked there and nowhere else, this would stop happening to her—alone again in a bedroom with the man who'd treated her like less than a whore. At least, she supposed men asked a whore's permission before doing the things Sam had. Maggie didn't think women should be called whores, but for this situation she needed the word.

Sam's description of his attack on her was laughable—as if mere sentences could compare to the act itself—as if his experience of forcing a woman was the same as being forced. She didn't need his validation that she'd been raped. She was there. She had endured every moment.

Briefly she lifted her gaze. At least there were no faces on the walls in Oropa, which is why she'd stayed without complaint. She'd seen no lolling tongues. She could sleep. And, until now, Sam had kept away from her.

This was infuriating, though. Who did Sam think he was, implying his body could erase his body's crime? Fight fire with fire, was that it? Did he think he was God, that his hands were magic wands? He was offensive beyond Maggie's ability to describe. If she could only think a little clearer, she'd be planning how to cut his throat.

She glanced over at the bed and saw he lay on his back, staring at the ceiling, hands folded on his chest, ankles crossed. Arrogant.

"Would you like a glass of water?" he asked.

Angrily, Maggie set her jaw and resumed staring at the floor.

"Would you like something else to drink?"

She didn't reply.

Sam rose. He said, "I'll get you something. I'll check on Jess," and left the room.

Maggie sighed in relief and uncrossed her arms. She looked out the window at the mountain. Then she fell asleep on the yellow couch.

When she opened her eyes it was late afternoon. She could tell by the angle of the sun. A pillow was under her head, a blanket over her body. She smelled pizza.

Sam's voice said, "I'm glad you didn't leave while I was gone. I wouldn't have blamed you if you did."

Why hadn't she? Maggie couldn't remember.

"I found Jess. He was happily reading a book in his room. *Pilgrim's Progress*, he called it. The nuns got him some food. He ate in the courtyard. He's fine."

Maggie heard children's voices outside the window. She got up, keeping the blanket around her, and looked out. Jess was playing soccer in the courtyard. It was the first time she'd seen him play a game with other boys. He ran about shouting and the other boys shouted, too, their faces full of happiness.

"I brought wine," Sam said. "A Chianti. Not as good as Antonella's, probably, but it says *classico*."

Maggie returned to the couch. She ate the pizza and ignored the wine.

Then it was early night and Sam opened the shutters to the stars. As the moonlight poured in he whispered, "Maggie, it was dumb of me to make you come here against your will. It's all right. I'll take you back to your room. I know now that you can't forgive me and you shouldn't."

Maggie would never tell Sam she forgave the unforgivable, but something happened when he said those words. She looked at the plain door and imagined herself outside it. Instead of feeling safe, like she expected, Maggie suddenly knew she'd feel worse than alone. She'd feel stricken, as if she'd lost something vital. On this long day in his room, Maggie had changed. She wasn't sure she wanted to leave anymore. To her, that alone was shameful. Somehow her feelings were betraying her, like Sam had betrayed her. They were letting down her guard. She should leave.

She looked toward the door, trying to decide. When she left, she knew it would be forever. She began to fear this unknown ending that lay beyond the room's plain pilgrim's door. It was taking Sam's place as the enemy.

Sam said, "I just wish I could undo it. I wish I could give you the amnesia I had. Then you wouldn't have to remember. I'd give anything if you didn't have to remember!"

In front of the open window, he began to sob. His face in his hands, he sank down, crying. Maggie had never seen him really cry—his big shoulders shaking, all six foot two of him collapsed in woe like a little boy. It was a curious sight that she watched because of its strangeness. What did the tears of her violator mean? He cried as if the stars had disappeared, as if the sun would never rise above the mountain, as if time had ended, but Maggie could see that the moon was still in the sky and that the night was still night.

"Sam?"

He didn't seem to hear her.

"Sam?"

He stood, his chest heaving, tears dripping from his chin.

Maggie turned and looked at her enemy—the plain pilgrim's door. She trembled, gathered courage, and in a steady voice said, "If you want to, you could stop that and come over here, Sam."

And he did.

At first he sat next to her, sniffing and wiping his face. A long while later he touched her hand then put his arm across her shoulder—two compatriots who'd crossed a battlefield together. Her knees together, her arms pulled tight against her chest, she leaned cautiously against his side. She slept.

Late in the night she awoke to feel his kiss on her fingertips. She let him hold her in both his arms, not moving, not caressing, just whispering how he loved her, how he'd make it all right.

When the last star was fading from the sky, Maggie touched his face where she'd opened up the cut and told him he'd made his point. Maybe a good thing could help dilute a bad thing.

Sam asked if she was sure. She said she was. He was so gentle it made her weep.

They were like newlyweds. Sam was sure they rocked the ghosts of the pilgrims. Maggie was sure they didn't disturb them at all. He held her. He sang the Irish reel, "Sleepy Maggie" that they'd danced to long ago. He whistled *Too-ra-loo-ra-loo-ral* like he had while she carried Jess. They kissed for hours. He stroked her, caressed her, their clothes on.

All that day they stayed in bed and Jess had to knock on the door to find out if they were dead.

When Maggie finally visited the real black Madonna in the Basilica, Jess, in the courtyard—seeing his mother's serene face—knew her heart had found the bliss beyond happiness or sadness. *Ti voglio bene, Mamma*, he whispered. He watched her cross the courtyard, her spirit well, her inner light returned.

Chapter 33

After four days of waiting, Lewiston reported back to Brown for further instructions. He was told to return to Maggie's and wait some more. Brown said he would use other resources to locate the clone, if they didn't come back.

Brown smiled at Lewiston and renewed his offer: Coral would oblige if he missed his wife.

Lewiston smiled back, wondering if this was another setup. "Why?" he said, "Do you want photos to blackmail me into another project?"

Brown turned to him, an oddly normal look in his eyes. "Coral's the best thing here and you've earned her, Chuck. There are no projects after this. I give you my word this time. I hadn't before."

"Don't you want me to get back to the villa?" Lewiston said, almost believing him.

"An hour won't matter."

"But suppose—" Lewiston paused, thinking. "Oh. You have the villa under surveillance, now, don't you?"

"For four days," Brown replied.

Again Lewiston found himself standing next to Brown at the Roman pool, embarrassed, the same music drifting on the garden air: *If you ever feel my dying breath on your face.*

Coral had swum to the edge of the pool when she saw them. Now she kicked away on her back, froglike—open close, open close. She and Brown must be able to read each other's minds.

Brown pointed to the bathhouse, shaped like a Roman temple.

"There are trunks and towels in there," he said, "unless you'd rather do without. You're doing a good job, Chuck. Enjoy yourself before you go."

Coral reached for a gold spaghetti strap as if to take it down.

"No." Lewiston coughed. "That's all right.

She stopped and smiled, closed her eyes and put her head back, floating, sun glinting on the tiny gold triangles that covered so little, though they made up the top of her swimsuit.

Brown took a last gulp of the probably vintage wine he'd been drinking and tossed the remainder on the grass. He set the glass on a nearby table and wandered off toward two streams that fell over the hillside into waterfalls. A multi-colored parrot took off from its perch and flew behind him.

How could he be so casual while holding people's lives in his hands?

Lewiston sat on a lounge chair in his jacket and tie, watching Coral. In his years of hospital work he'd seen hundreds of female bodies, many of them beautiful. It was hard to impress him on that score, but Coral did.

She swam up, reached out of the water and tugged at his pant leg like a little girl, then blinked cutely.

"Would you like some company?" she said. She smiled, but not with her eyes.

Lewiston sighed. "I'm not sure."

"Take your time, I'm here," she said. She turned and did a lap of the pool. From the other side she called, "I've been with black men before."

Lewiston chuckled. Why did she think that mattered? "Have you? Who?"

"A basketball player. Can't name him, but you know him. Mostly African diplomats though."

"Did you have fun?" he asked.

A pause. "I sure did."

He listened to Mozart's *If you ever feel my dying breath on your face*. Brown was playing it again. No other music stirred him like this. Brown had learned that from eavesdropping on Sam's room. It was as if Lewiston were an actor starring in a movie of his own life and this was the theme music.

"Coral when you keep men company, do you feel lonely?"

The question made her look away. "I think my line is: I'm a big girl."

It was getting hot. He took off his jacket and tie and gazed at her. "You're magical, you know."

Coral laughed. "Maybe I used to be magical. Now I'm just the woman they saw in half to please the crowd. Come in," she said and swam to the edge again.

He stood. "Maybe I will."

"Don't put anything on, Doc, okay?" Her voice was kind.

Lewiston stripped naked under the Italian sun but he didn't go in the water right away. Instead he stepped back from the end of the pool and let his feet feel the grass, remembering when he'd last done this in Africa. He'd been visiting a Maasai tribe's medicine man. For a week he'd lived there while the strong young men— dressed in red garments and beads, with their spears and walking sticks and red braids flying—taught him how to jump in the grass. He couldn't believe how high they jumped, their arms often rigid at their sides. Soon he had, too.

Lewiston wriggled his toes in the grass, remembering how he'd tried to harden his feet like the Maasai men. Theirs were so incredibly calloused, they could walk barefoot in the bush. He took off at a full trot and launched himself far down the length of the pool. When he surfaced, he heard Coral applaud. By the time he shook the water from his face, her bikini was floating.

She swam toward him and they looked at each other.

Lewiston ran the side of his thumb gently down her cheek. "I don't want to make you feel lonely."

Coral smiled with her eyes this time, like the Maasai women did. "You couldn't, honey. Sam beat you to that."

Lewiston raised a cautioning finger. Had she forgotten Brown bugged everything?

"We can talk," Coral said, grinning wickedly and pointing up. "The music?"

Lewiston laughed. Brown had meant to taunt him by putting the Mozart aria on repeat, but it also masked their conversation. Over and over they heard the impeccable violins and Cecilia Bartoli's beautiful voice sing, *If you ever feel my dying breath on your face.*

He said, "I'm sorry about what Sam did to you."

"Yeah, I know. It wasn't the first time, though, just the worst. Thanks for taking care of me."

"No problem."

"What I hated more," she said, "was that Brown sent me back to Sam's bed."

For a while they floated, listening to the violins.

"Let's swim," Lewiston said.

Side by side under the sun they did laps, trying not to choke on the water they took in and laughing when they failed. Coral showed him her underwater ballet. Lewiston demonstrated his backstroke and how he could stand on his head in the water. They had to stop swimming because they were laughing so hard.

They held onto the side.

Lewiston looked at Coral's face, bright with something close to joy. If a lovelier woman existed on earth, Lewiston couldn't imagine her. Her beauty arose from a womanliness that transcended race. It felt like tragedy that she was here with Brown, sleeping with whomever he fed her to. It felt like an aria should be sung about Coral, about what Handsome Jones did to her and what Brown repeated daily in his way.

Lewiston wasn't different from her, though. He performed at Brown's bidding, too. It tormented Lewiston not knowing why Brown wanted the cloned boy dead. If Lewiston had to kill him, surely he had a right to know.

"What in the hell is Brown afraid of?" he said aloud.

Coral lay back in the water, looking up at the sun, her sinuous movements accompanying the music. Lewiston walked beside her, tenderness for Coral and hatred for Brown, warring in him.

"How can he do this to people? Why does he do it?"

Coral's hands went to her breasts, squeezing, and Lewiston responded against his will. She turned in the water and caressed him, made him groan, but he stopped her and backed away.

"I won't let Brown use me to hurt you," he insisted.

They treaded water, gazing at each other, until their breathing calmed.

"I just wish I knew what in the world he's afraid of!"

If you ever feel my dying breath on your face.

Coral moved slightly away, regarding him. "You really want to know?" She had whispered, but to him her words roared.

Lewiston froze. "Yes." Then in anguish he sighed, "No."

"Suit yourself."

"Coral, for God's sake, he might do something awful to you if he learns you told me."

She raised her face to the Italian sun. "He's already done something awful to me. I owe him."

Lewiston's heart sped up.

"I think part of it has to do with the Catholic Church. He's always talking to this Cardinal. But I think the real reason might be something else. There's a leather bound book. He keeps it in his desk. It has gold lettering on the front that reads: *DeathScopes.* The astrologer who did them for Brown's father invented the name."

"You're kidding."

"Nope, I'm not. The DeathScope said his father would drown in a foreign country."

"Did he?"

"Sure did. His father's yacht was struck by lightning and floundered off the coast of Malta in a storm. That's when Brown took the DeathScopes seriously."

"My God."

"The astrologer did one for Brown. He's supposed to be assassinated."

"Wow."

"Get this. It's got something to do with the Star of Bethlehem. The astrologer said it's some kind of configuration that happens every twenty years and it's in Brown's house of death or something like that. I don't understand astrology."

"Are you saying—?"

"Sure am. He'd totally freaked out about that Jesus clone. He tries to hide it, but I know."

If you ever feel my dying breath on your face.

Lewiston gazed at the woman who'd just risked her life for

him. They hardly knew each other, but they understood each other perfectly.

She blew him a kiss, got out of the pool, a smile of satisfaction on her lips. She put her high heels on and, buck naked, dragged another dazzling wrap behind her on the walkway toward the villa's sun-bleached walls. The goddess of love.

Lewiston climbed out when she disappeared. He dried himself with the intention of putting his clothes on, but it was good to feel the grass under his feet, the sun and air on his skin. He squinted, picturing flat-topped acacia trees, their large thorns used for protective boma around Maasai huts. He imagined the incredible smells of the grass after a rain, as if everything were awakening—a combination of smell and celebration of life.

He wandered through the park among the pheasants and the white peacocks, feeling peaceful in spite of what he'd done and still would do.

There was Brown.

He stood near, looking down on the terraced gardens of Isola Bella far below, his platinum hair ruffled by the breeze. His head was so large he looked like an idol. His prominently jointed thumbs had a powerful grasp. It struck Lewiston that, on earth, Brown wanted to be the only God.

He cleared his throat.

Brown turned and said, "I see you dispensed with swimming trunks."

Lewiston felt himself flush. He'd forgotten he wore no clothes. "Yes, uh, sorry."

Brown smiled. "I saw it in you. It's why I chose you. Did you find Coral as delightful as prime ministers do?"

"Yes," Lewiston said.

"Excellent. Good." Brown's penetrating eyes searched his. "I take it there's something on your mind."

"It's about the boy—"

"Yes?"

"He's just a kid. He's no threat to anyone."

Brown regarded him coolly a long time, and then he said,

"What have you been thinking, Chuck?"

Lewiston held his gaze. "You want to be the only God."

Brown burst out laughing. "I love educated men with dramatic minds. Chuck, I'm going to tell you something. Do you believe in astrology?"

Brown hadn't heard what Coral told him. "Of course not."

"Sensible. Neither did I. The wise men were astrologers, Lewiston. They were following a conjunction of Jupiter and Saturn, which periodically reoccurs. In my horoscope it rules my death. The Jesus clone may be the trigger. Can't have that."

"And there's no other reason?"

Brown sniffed. "If there were I wouldn't tell you."

"Listen, you can't really think—"

Again Brown laughed in macabre delight. "Go back to Coral, Lewiston, unless you're finished with her. Do your part and leave mine to me."

"But he's just a kid."

Brown stopped smiling. "I'd hoped this wouldn't be necessary." He held out a photo.

Lewiston took it. It was his wife. It was snapped in the labor room as she gave birth to their son. How had Brown gotten it? How dare he carry it around? Lewiston's eyes filled with angry tears.

"You're … you're loathsome!"

"I don't want to harm them. Chuck you've done as I asked. Keep at it another few days and you'll be free. On my honor. You'll never hear from me again." Brown held out his hand and looked at him with near fondness. "That's the truth."

Numbly, Lewiston shook Theomund Brown's hand.

Brown turned back to his commanding view of Lake Maggiore, the three Borromeo islands shimmering like emeralds below—big tour boats, ferries, sailboats, yachts, moored nearby or carrying visitors to and fro.

A few more days.

Lewiston started back to the villa.

On a balustrade, hiding in the reeds, he saw a white peacock hen grooming her chick. On her head was a white crown. The chick's had yet to grow.

Lewiston paused and watched them, feeling the grass beneath his feet, thinking of Maggie, the secret Madonna, hidden away with her child.

He thought of what Sam had done to her and he found himself jumping in the grass. Jumping like the Maasai as Mozart played. Jumping high.

"Lewiston!" he heard suddenly and stopped.

Brown was staring in amusement at him.

If you ever feel my dying breath on your face.

Brown chuckled and returned to parading before his incomparable view. He stopped by a stream where it became a waterfall and swept over the emerald green hillside.

Civilization had encroached upon the Maasai, prohibiting lion hunting as a manhood rite, but they could still kill lions that stalked their cattle. Lewiston walked toward Brown, his feet quiet on the grass, like a lion—like the Maasai who hunted them, swift and beautiful as nature impelled. He crept close, his gaze intent. With arms strong from ten years of physical therapy on Handsome Jones, Lewiston shoved at Brown's forbidding back.

The idol head turned, Brown's eyes opening in stunned comprehension and contempt—asserting, even now, he was still the only God.

Brown gasped, "You!"

He lunged away from the hillside and into Lewiston's startled arms.

Lewiston's powerful right hand quickly reached for Brown's sternocleidomastoid muscle and the carotid artery beneath, his thumb finding the lethal spot. He'd have to maintain pressure for two whole minutes, a long time when a man is trying to scream bloody murder, fighting for his life, making choking sounds, his heels gouging out clumps of grass and leaving evidence.

With his left hand, Lewiston tried to push Brown forward once again, but he no longer had the advantage of surprise. Brown resisted with all his strength, pushing back hard enough to topple Lewiston from his feet.

Lewiston couldn't squeeze tighter and leave a telltale bruise. Straining, Chuck Lewiston, MD closed his eyes and thought of Brown having the photo of his wife in labor, thought of the dead senator's wife, thought of Brown sending Coral back to Sam, thought of Maggie Johnson's gentle son and her beautiful dead eyes.

Lewiston struggled to his feet, bringing Brown with him. He had to risk letting go of Brown's neck. He released his grip. He shoved at Brown, almost losing his own balance.

Brown gasped. He lurched. Suddenly his heels gave way. He tumbled over the hill, colliding with tree limbs in slow motion, bouncing off boulders and breaking like a mannequin instead of a man. He fell with a thud beside the waterfall.

Lewiston looked down on Theomund Brown's still form and saw blood pooling.

He held his arms rigid at his sides and like the Maasai jumped high.

He saw an uprooted clump of grass, bent and patted it in place. Then he ran like hell back to the swimming pool and dived in.

It didn't take long.

In the distance a woman screamed.

As Lewiston did laps in the pool, a horde of politzia invaded the grounds, trampling any footprints he might have left in the grass.

There were no scandalized looks when he emerged in the raw and had to get into his clothes. In Italy, swimming naked in a completely private pool was virtually required.

Coral emerged and looked over the hill. Did he see a Maasai woman's pride in her eyes?

Ignoring Lewiston, she expressed dumbfoundment, turning heads, glazing eyes. Lewiston carefully let it drop that he was a doctor and that Brown had been drinking. The politzia noted there were no fences where the park swooped over a hill. Lewiston, grave in feigned shock, hid what he was thinking: *don't drive off a cliff.*

Chapter 34

Jess cut his finger on the way to Turin airport.

Sam was planning to put them all on a plane and go to a country other than the U.S.A. He'd told Antonella to pack Maggie's Hetta Price passport. She'd packed the Jess Price passport, too.

Sam was pretty sure he remembered everything now: Brown, the penthouse, Lewiston, the money, Coral, and that Lewiston would kill Jess. He just didn't know how.

Ten minutes away from Turin and their escape, playing with Sam's scrimshaw knife in the back seat, Jess nicked his finger and said, "Ouch!"

Maggie and Sam had been holding hands. He was driving with his left as her right hand smoothed the leather on the Punto's armrest. She turned around and saw a small stream of blood run down Jess's hand. She reached in her purse for a tissue, told him to hold it over the cut, then fished out a piece of his favorite candy left over from La Scala for him to pop in his mouth.

They were about to take the exit for the airport when Jess said, "It's still bleeding."

Maggie turned, her eyes focused on his finger as if nothing else existed. "Are you sure you're holding it tight?"

"Yes."

"Let me see."

Jess held his hand up and they saw the tissue was almost completely red. She lifted it and the tiny stream fell in drops into her palm. Not a lot, just steadily.

She smiled at Jess and said, "Well, we'd better get that stopped or the flight attendant won't like what the upholstery on your seat looks like."

Jess laughed.

Sam was already pulling over. He knew not to believe Maggie's smile. She put her hand up so Jess couldn't see her mouthe *doctor,* *hospital* to him. He stopped the car long enough for Maggie to get out and climb in the back seat. As Sam took off in the opposite direction, he saw her press a clean tissue to Jess's finger and rest Jess's head against her body.

Sam didn't know where a hospital was. He drove along, looking for a policeman or cab driver to ask, feeling panicked and getting angry that Felix wasn't here to take care of Jess, the clone he'd made, feeling angry that Lewiston, a fine doctor, was on Brown's side.

He pulled up to the first rest stop, saw the fear in Maggie's eyes and turned around to Jess. "How's it now, son?"

"It's still bleeding. Not a lot, but ..." He could tell Jess was scared.

Sam went inside the rest stop, asking each person as he went, "Dove è l' ospedale?"

"Non so."

"Dove è l' ospedale?"

"Non so."

They didn't know because they were passing through, like him. He approached the cashier, but she chose that moment to disappear into the back. Sam paced, waiting for her to return, rifling through the on sale newspapers for an American one. He found *USA Today,* and saw the stories: *American billionaire dead in Italy. Eccentric scientist's kidnapped daughter found.*

Sam ran back to the car, handed the papers to Maggie, and then examined Jess's finger.

Looking at the papers, Maggie said, "I think we can go back home, Sam. Brown's men won't still be looking for us, will they?"

Sam thought Jess looked pale. He shook his head. He was sure nobody cared about Brown's personal agendas but Brown. Then he remembered Antonella's navigation computer. It could find him a hospital.

Maggie whispered, "Dr. Cecagallina's there and Antonella. Jess will be taken care of and it's not bleeding so fast we can't make it and be safe. It's better if we go home."

"But—"

"Please, Uncle Sam. I'd like to see Antonella and Uncle Simone again."

"Jess, I just want to be sure you get to a doctor."

"Uncle Sam, I think it's all right. There is a song. There is a drum."

"You thought signora Morelli would be all right, too, Jess, remember? I can't risk—"

Suddenly Maggie, the love of his life, was irate. She snatched off her peach hat and said, "Get in this car and drive, Sam Duffy. Stop wasting time. Jess said it's all right, so it is."

"But—"

"Get in! Drive, drive! God in heaven, stop standing there wasting time. Just drive! Merciful heaven—"

Sam got in the Punto. With Brown dead, Lewiston was probably on a plane back to his own life. If not, if Lewiston was still at the villa, he'd take out his gun and shoot good ole Chuck between the eyes.

———

When the Fiat Punto pulled through the yellow villa's gate, Jess, who usually moved like a human bird, fell getting out of the car and scraped his knee. He pulled his pants leg up and the blood ran down.

Cool as ice, Maggie said, "I'll call Dr. Cecagallina."

Sam picked Jess up and followed as she ran up to the porch, her keys in hand.

Someone opened the door. Sam couldn't see who because the person moved away.

Sam said, "Wait, let me go in first." He gave Jess to Maggie, who whispered Dr. Cecagallina's number as Sam pulled his gun.

Sam stepped into Maggie's living room. Chuck Lewiston sat there on Maggie's floral couch, his legs crossed, wearing a linen suit and flipping through the pages of a magazine. He looked up and asked, "Where's the boy?"

"Why do you want to know, Chuck?" Sam said. He went and pushed Lewiston in the chest then, keeping his eyes on him, walked toward the phone. "Give him a little more something in that shot, huh? Is that what you have in mind? I remember everything now, Chuck. What was in the shot?"

Lewiston sat up, adjusting his suit, and Sam realized Lewiston hadn't shaved. He looked like he hadn't eaten in days. Something was wrong.

Lewiston said, "I killed Brown."

Sam hung up the phone.

"Let me treat the boy. He's very sick. I can save him."

"You killed Brown?" Sam wanted to believe him. Lewiston was a good doctor. He was right here. "Why did you kill Brown?"

Lewiston said, "It was the peacocks, the smell of the grass."

Sam picked up the phone and dialed Dr. Cecagallina. As he waited for his call to be answered he eyed Lewiston, the picture of calm intellect in his summer suit. *Peacocks and grass*, Sam thought. *Yeah right.*

When he hung up, the doctor was on the way. Sam cut some of Antonella's clothesline and tied Lewiston and his suit to the chair.

Sam brought Jess and Maggie inside and Maggie phoned Antonella. She arrived, out of breath, and told them Lewiston had gone away and returned last night, roaming around and asking for the boy. He'd hardly eaten since they went on their pilgrimage. Today, when Lewiston kept changing into different suits, she left.

Fifteen minutes later, when Dr. Cecagallina hadn't arrived and Jess's sheets were stained with blood, Sam took out his gun and herded Lewiston up to Jess's room. He cocked the gun, held it to Lewiston's head and said. "If he's not better in an hour, Chuck, you die."

Lewiston said he was administering a massive dose of Vitamin K and also mephyton and that Jess had to stay on absolute bed rest for forty-eight hours. Dr. Cecagallina came and when he heard Jess had received anticoagulant by mistake, he concurred in the treatment, adding a saline solution to increase blood volume.

Together, Maggie and Antonella forced Lewiston to eat, shave and rest. They didn't have to cook for him.

News of Jess's recovery from a brush with death had spread in the village, causing a stream of grilled, baked, boiled, steamed and marinated dishes to arrive, most of them bathed in delicious olive oil. Even Carlo Morelli came to offer good wishes on behalf of the town. He looked tired, but he seemed compelled. He said that because Maggie and Antonella had tried, if unsuccessfully, to help his wife, it was his honor to respond in kind. He said he was putting his brother, Adamo, into a treatment center for alcohol addiction—something he should have done years before.

Carlo insisted on visiting Jess. Sam went with him, gun in hand. Though he'd promised to be quiet, Carlo Morelli fell to his knees at Jess's bedside and sobbed. Maggie and Antonella had to ease him out of the room so Jess wouldn't wake.

That night, Maggie and Sam slept on the floor in Jess's room, holding each other, Maggie thanking God and repeatedly getting up to watch over Jess, while a crescent moon poured its light in through the shutters and the sky filled with stars.

———

Within an hour of Lewiston's treatment, Jess's bleeding slowed. By the next morning it had stopped. Forty-eight hours later Jess was well.

Lewiston, recovered too, walked next to Sam by the lake, morning mists floating on the water. Sam understood Lewiston now. Sam had been to hell and back, himself.

It was a cool morning and Sam wondered where King Silent, and the other swans had gone. They were usually around, waiting for Jess, but not in the past two days. He glanced sideways at Lewiston, who looked human again, "You know I had amnesia, Chuck. Chances are I won't remember what you told me about Brown, if it ever comes up."

Lewiston smiled. "Thanks, Handsome Jones."

"Who's that?"

"Nothing. Inside joke. I'm a doctor, though. I killed. I'm supposed to save people."

"In my book, you did. You saved Jess, probably Ariel, Felix's daughter. No telling who else. You sure as hell saved Maggie." Sam looked up to her window. "She couldn't survive without that kid." Lewiston nodded. "I might turn myself in."

Sam didn't try to dissuade him. A conscience was a personal thing. Instead he wrote down a name and address, and handed it to Lewiston.

"If you do, call this guy. Ten years ago he was at this address and I'm betting he still is. If not, let me know. He's a lawyer and a friend. Tell him I sent you. Tell him what happened. Have him contact me. I know things about Brown that he can use in court and get you off with a light sentence, if you decide to confess, that is."

"Yes, if. Thanks," Lewiston said.

"Just one favor?"

"Name it."

Sam looked up at the house. "Coral. Do you know where she is? How she is?"

"Yeah. I think she went back to New York."

"I told Maggie what I did to Coral when I was—you know— messed up and she's insisting I go back and make amends."

"She knows how Coral feels."

———

Two days more and Maggie and Jess stood at the gate, waving goodbye to Dr. Lewiston and Sam. They were taking a taxi to catch the train and a flight back to New York.

Maggie and Sam had spent a passionate night saying goodbye. He promised to be faithful while he made amends to Coral. He said he'd visit Felix to give the exhaustive details Felix begged for over the phone. In a week Sam would be back.

In his absence, the days grew warmer.

Life at the yellow villa returned to what it had been in all the years Maggie, Jess and Antonella lived there alone. They took pilgrimages in the village and surrounding countryside, even visited the colossal statue of San Carlo Borromeo up on the hill. During the visit, Maggie learned something that took her breath away. When Borromeo was Bishop of Milan back in the late 1500s, there'd been a plague. He'd prayed for it to end, tirelessly visited and helped the sick, and promised God to make a pilgrimage on foot to Jesus' Holy Shroud if Milan was saved. The plague did end quickly and Borromeo began his journey. At the time the Shroud was in France. Duke Emanuel Philibert, hearing of Borromeo's vow, ordered the Shroud brought to Turin to save the saintly bishop from the rigors of the Alps.

Jess had grown up in the birthplace of the man for whom the Shroud was brought to Turin. This convinced Maggie their presence here was part of God's plan.

During these happy days, Jess's reading increased. His mind seemed to be taking in all the learning of the world. Maggie listened as he recited to her from the *Bible*, the *Bhagavad-Gita*, the *Upanishads*, the *Torah*, the *Tao Te Ching*, the *Qu'ran* and told her about the eight-fold path of Buddha.

She didn't try to correct him, but treasured each day as Jess talked, read, swam, sailed the lake that seemed to belong to them alone, and played with King Silent, the crippled swan.

On the morning of Sam's return she and Jess had breakfast out on the lake house deck. Maggie laughed at Jess, who was toying with astrology again and trying to cast her chart. She was Pisces, it seemed. He was Virgo with a Pisces Moon. True, Maggie was compassionate and Jess fed on information like it was food, but according to sun sign astrology they didn't get along and Jess was at war with himself.

In jubilation he climbed up into the dogwood tree, calling to her. "I am Virgo, the studious virgin. You, Madre dear, are Pisces the sympathetic fish. Perhaps there is a little something to astrology." He paraphrased from the *Bhagavad-Gita*, "You burn with the bliss and suffer every sorrow of every creature within your own heart, Mamma. Krishna holds you in the highest."

Maggie laughed and closed her eyes, thinking she heard music floating toward her on the breeze: a song and a drum. The sound felt vaguely familiar, yet she knew she hadn't heard it before. The song seemed to vibrate the air with love. The drum beat a rhythm of joy within her. It was as if they were trying to comfort her.

Then Maggie heard a terrifying voice. It cried, "Astrologia? Krishna? Si, si, Adamo! È un diavolo! È un diavolo!"

Carlo Morelli appeared below on the lake's pebbled bank as if he'd been hiding all along beneath their deck. Where had he come from? How long had he been there? Maggie glimpsed red and green at the corner of the porticiollo. Adamo's boat. Even from here she could tell he was in a drunken stupor.

No doubt for the first time in his life, Maggie realized, signor Carlo Morelli was drunk, too.

"What do you want?" she screamed to Carlo.

He swayed on his feet then in wild fury reached down, picked up large stones from the shore, and hurled them one by one toward Jess in the tree.

Maggie's beating heart followed the stones. She saw the vibrating air through which they flew. The drum pounded, the song wept.

Jess looked at signor Morelli and said, "Father forgive him." Then he gazed at his mother and her alone, love in his eyes, burning her with tenderness.

She saw each stone strike. His face. His neck.

She saw Jess let go of the dogwood tree.

For a moment Maggie thought he would fly.

Then she saw him drop. She saw him fall. A wounded swan.

Her world exploded.

Carlo Morelli gazed at Jess in shock, his mouth open, and ran away.

Crying, Maggie dropped to the deck and pulled Jess into her lap. He lay on her body like a feather. She could barely feel his weight. His throat rattled with each breath. His chest rose, but she could tell his lungs barely filled. He was leaving—this earth, this lake, this life. The song and the drum told her so. How could he leave her? Her very flesh gave him birth. She had nursed him with her milk, fed him with her hands, and with her lips kissed his childhood wounds, dried his tears.

His eyes opened. "You are crying."

"Oh, that terrible, terrible man!"

"No, Mamma," Jess whispered. "My death will teach signor Morelli to love."

Violently she shook her head and raised him to her, put his head softly on her shoulder and rocked him like she'd done all through his growing years.

She heard barking and looked up. All the swans had come.

"No, no, no!" she cried as King Silent took position just below the deck and swam in regal figure eights as if on watch.

Maggie looked down on Jess. "Don't! Don't! Please, my sweet darling. Make one more miracle for your poor Mama. Stay here with me!"

When she laid him on her lap again, he closed his eyes.

Maggie looked up and prayed, "Oh, Father! I still need him. Don't take him back! Don't! Please don't!"

She felt Jess touch her face. When she looked down, his eyes shone like the dawn.

"Mother, I am your sorrow and your laughter. I am the tears you shed. You will not be alone. I am with you always. I am the father, I am the mother, I am the child."

"No, no!"

He touched her stomach. "Another one will come."

"Oh, Jess!" she cried. "You are my only one!"

"Lay me down."

She didn't move.

He whispered, "Please."

She slid him gently from her lap and held his hand, hanging on each labored breath he took.

He whispered, "Ti voglio bene. Ti voglio tanto tanto bene. Ti voglio proprio bene."

Maggie kissed his hand and cried, "Ti voglio tanto tanto bene. TI voglio bene!"

He smiled. "Turn away from me now."

"No, no, no!"

"Turn away. TI voglio bene, bene."

Maggie moved from her son and looked away. As she did, she grew quiet and a hush filled the air as if there were no world, no creation, no sky to hold the stars, no earth beneath her, no villa on a glorious lake stretching to the horizon. In a vision she saw her darling Jess, million-faced and million-armed like the God of Krishna. Jess was a bearded man in sandals, people following for his love; a naked Hindu bathing in the sacred Ganges; he was a priest in robes saying mass before an altar and a cross; he was a feathered shaman in holy trance; he was a rabbi reading from the Torah then multi-armed Shiva, doing a dance of death; he was a monk in orange robes; a Bible-thumping Baptist preacher in his dusty southern tent; a Muslim performing As-salat on his musalla. He was all the names she'd ever heard whispered in her sleep. He was the Ancient One, the Anointed One. He resided in all hearts. Still he was her son.

Maggie wailed out sobs as if their source were the womb that bore him. Again she heard the song and the drum.

Without cause she felt intensely happy, as if each cell in her body had chosen to rejoice. She thought time stopped. The world stopped. Then a swan rose from the water. The others spread their wings behind him and took majestic flight toward the sun. In the silence, Maggie turned. The deck was empty as was the shore. Jess Johnson, savior of the world, was gone.

No one saw King Silent after that. Another male with two strong limbs came and mated with a female who was alone. He became the leader of the swans.

— THE END —

About the Author

J R Lankford is the author of the scientific-religious thriller *The Jesus Thief*, which BOOKLIST called "great stuff" in a starred review. Published in 2003, it was nominated for awards, translated into multiple languages, optioned for film, and used in college courses such as "Genetics in Literature" at Copenhagen University. She lives with her husband in Texas where she is at work on the next novel in this series.

In 2001 I returned to northern Italy by way of Paris with my grandson, Devar. He lived in Michigan at the time and I'm in Texas. We met at O'Hare airport in Chicago and flew to Paris, then took the bullet train south to Torino, Italy (Turin) where we stayed for a few days, filming the locations I would feature in *The Secret Madonna*, sightseeing, and eating the delicious food. After a week we went east by train across Italy's Piedmont to beautiful Arona, nestled against the southern bank of Lake Maggiore near the border between the Italian and Swiss alps. Maggie's yellow villa is located there, and it's where much of the book takes place.

In those magical days with Devar, it was easy to imagine the bond between Maggie and her son, Jess. It was easy to picture Jess feeding the swans at the lake, like Devar did, or being handsome in his suit, though restless in his seat like Devar was at La Scala, the opera in Milan. It was easy to imagine, "the carefree movements" Maggie came to know as Jess's physical grace.

Three characters in the novel are named after friends Devar and I made in Italy: Piero Giachino, our driver and translator, his wife, Antonella, and Andrew Cecagallina at La Scala in Milan. Piero and Antonella took us on the wonderful trip to Oropa and he was a constant source of jokes. Andrew provided behind-the-scenes facts. Both Piero and Andrew helped with the Italian in the novel. Any mistakes that remain are entirely mine.

Thanks also to my my sister Julie Lee who, along with my husband, was my first reader during the writing. Thanks to my brother, John Rhines, who spied grammar gaffes in an early draft. Special appreciation goes to the incomparable members of NovelPro, the online workshop I founded. Critques from these talented authors always improve my work.

I would not be a writer were it not for my late parents -- poet Julia Watson Rhines Barbour and Jacinto Aneille Rhines, who filled our home with books, my mind with ideas, and my heart with love.

My husband, Frank Lankford, picked up where they left off, supporting me with the latest computers and supplies, with research trips abroad and reference materials, long before I'd published a single line.

JRL/2008